PRANAS T. NAUJOKAITIS • MAURIZIA RUBINO

RUGRATS™

THE LAST TOKEN

RUGRATS: The Last Token, November 2019. Published by
KaBOOM!, a division of Boom Entertainment, Inc., 5670 Wilshire
Boulevard, Suite 400, Los Angeles, CA 90036-5679. © 2019 Viacom
International Inc. All Rights Reserved. Nickelodeon, Rugrats and
all related titles, logos, and characters are trademarks of Viacom
International Inc. Created by Klasky Csupo, and Germain. KaBOOM!™
and the KaBOOM! logo are trademarks of Boom Entertainment, Inc.,
registered in various countries and categories. All characters, events,
and institutions depicted herein are fictional. Any similarity between
any of the names, characters, persons, events, and/or institutions in
this publication to actual names, characters, and persons, whether
living or dead, events, and/or institutions is unintended and
purely coincidental. KaBOOM! does not read or accept unsolicited
submissions of ideas, stories, or artwork.

BOOM! Studios, 5670 Wilshire Boulevard, Suite 400, Los Angeles, CA
90036-5679. Printed in China. First Printing.

ISBN: 978-1-68415-462-3, eISBN: 978-1-64144-579-5

Rugrats™

THE LAST TOKEN

WRITTEN BY
PRANAS T. NAUJOKAITIS

ILLUSTRATED BY
MAURIZIA RUBINO

LETTERED BY
MIKE FIORENTINO

COVER BY
CHRYSTIN GARLAND

DESIGNER
MARIE KRUPINA

EDITOR
MATTHEW LEVINE

SPECIAL THANKS TO
JOAN HILTY, LINDA LEE, JAMES SALERNO,
ALEXANDRA MAURER AND THE
WONDERFUL TEAM AT NICKELODEON.

★ ★ ★

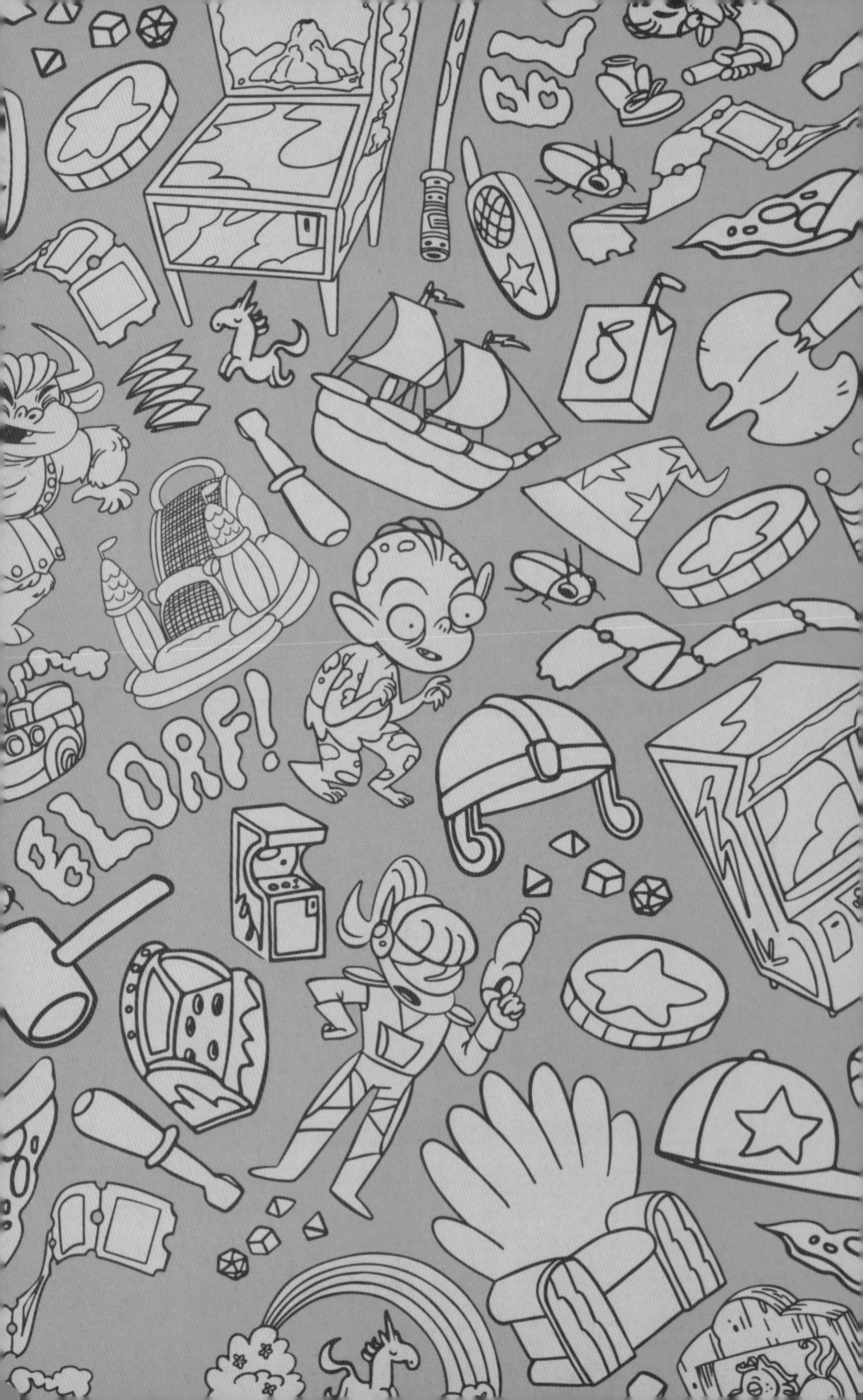
BLORF!

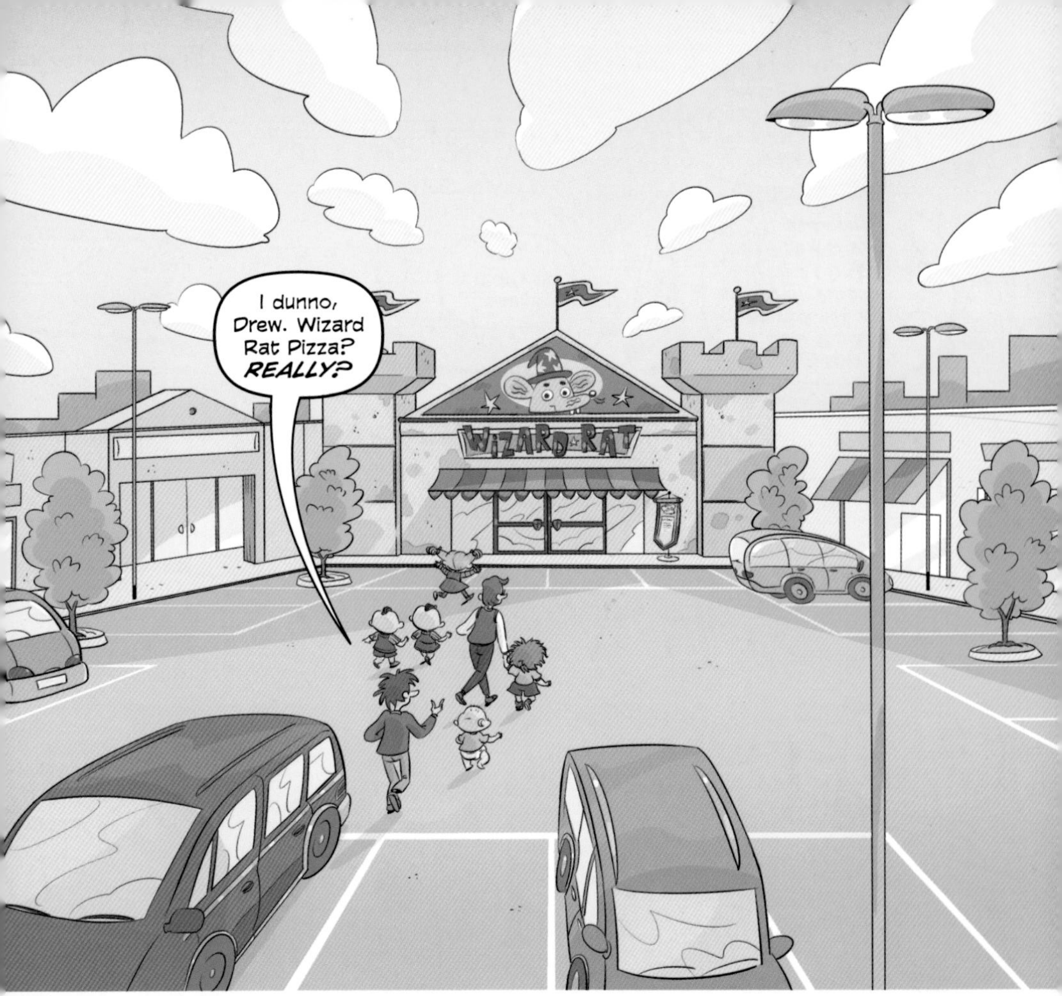
I dunno, Drew. Wizard Rat Pizza? REALLY?
WIZARD RAT

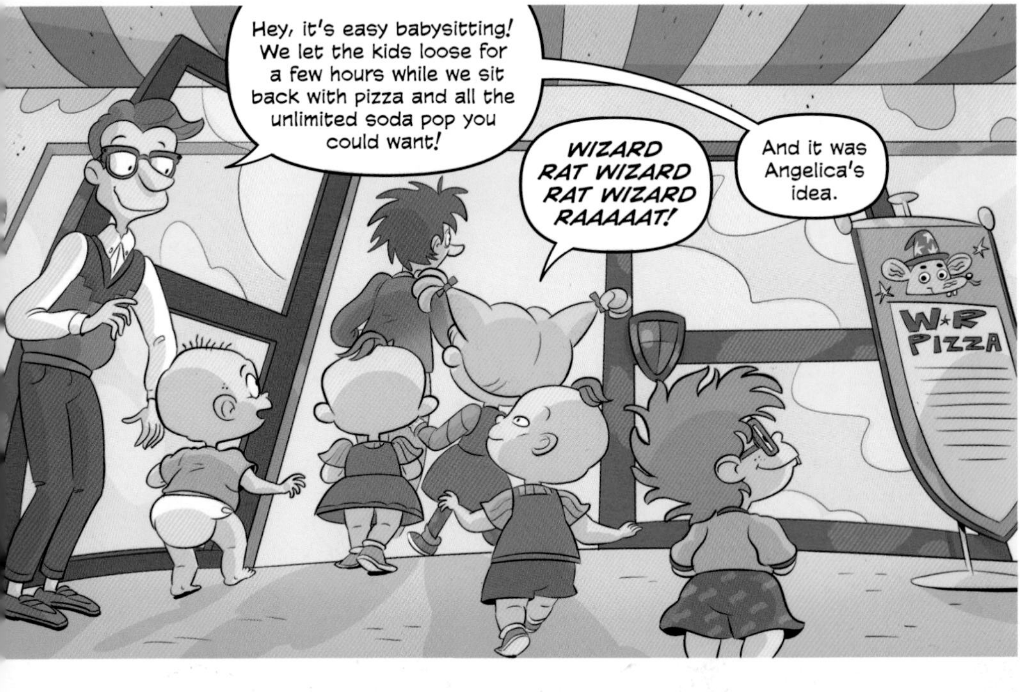
Hey, it's easy babysitting! We let the kids loose for a few hours while we sit back with pizza and all the unlimited soda pop you could want!
And it was Angelica's idea.
WIZARD RAT WIZARD RAT WIZARD RAAAAAT!
W★R PIZZA

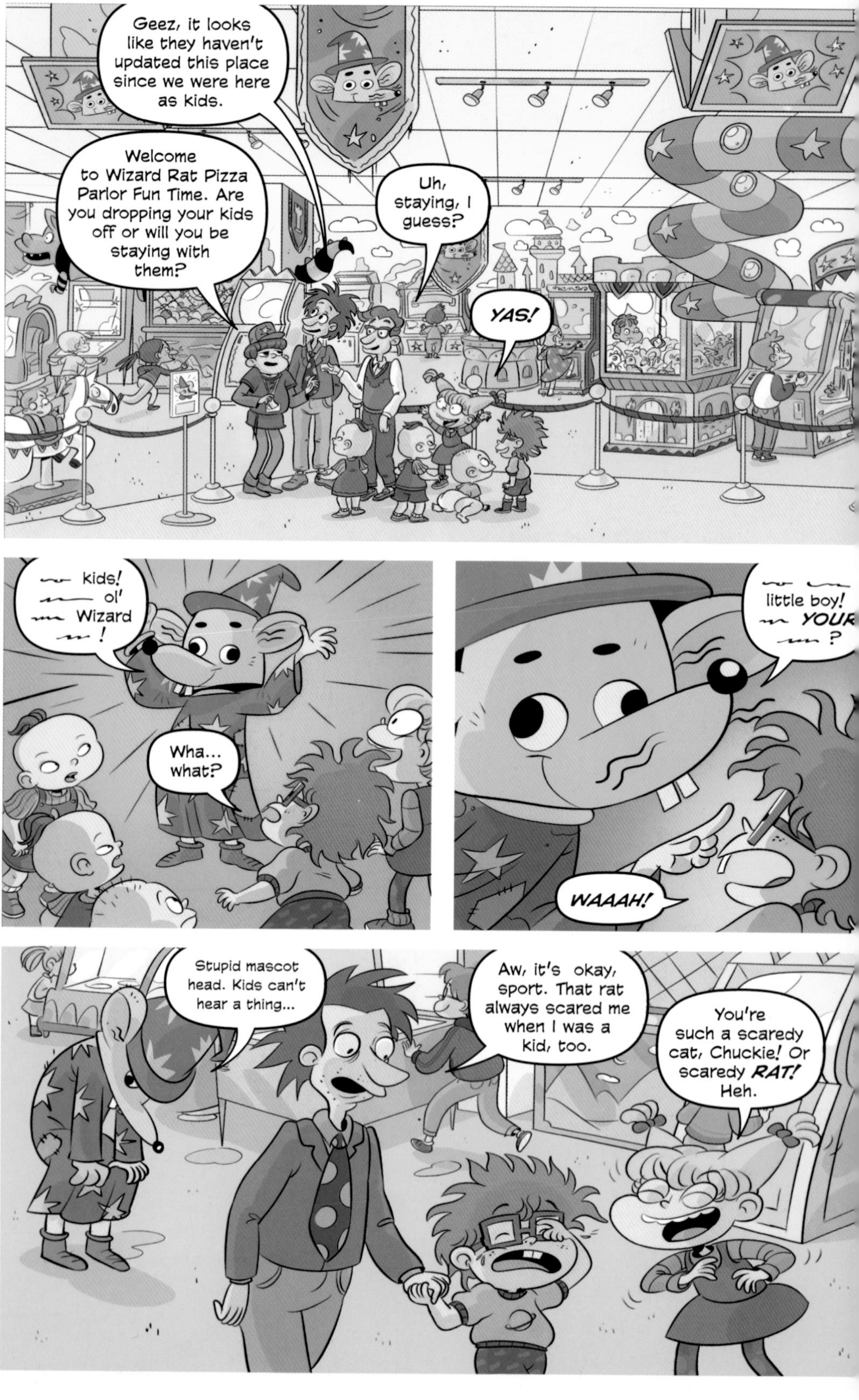
Geez, it looks like they haven't updated this place since we were here as kids.
Welcome to Wizard Rat Pizza Parlor Fun Time. Are you dropping your kids off or will you be staying with them?
Uh, staying, I guess?
YAS!
kids! ol' Wizard !
Wha... what?
little boy! YOU ?
WAAAH!
Stupid mascot head. Kids can't hear a thing...
Aw, it's okay, sport. That rat always scared me when I was a kid, too.
You're such a scaredy cat, Chuckie! Or scaredy RAT! Heh.

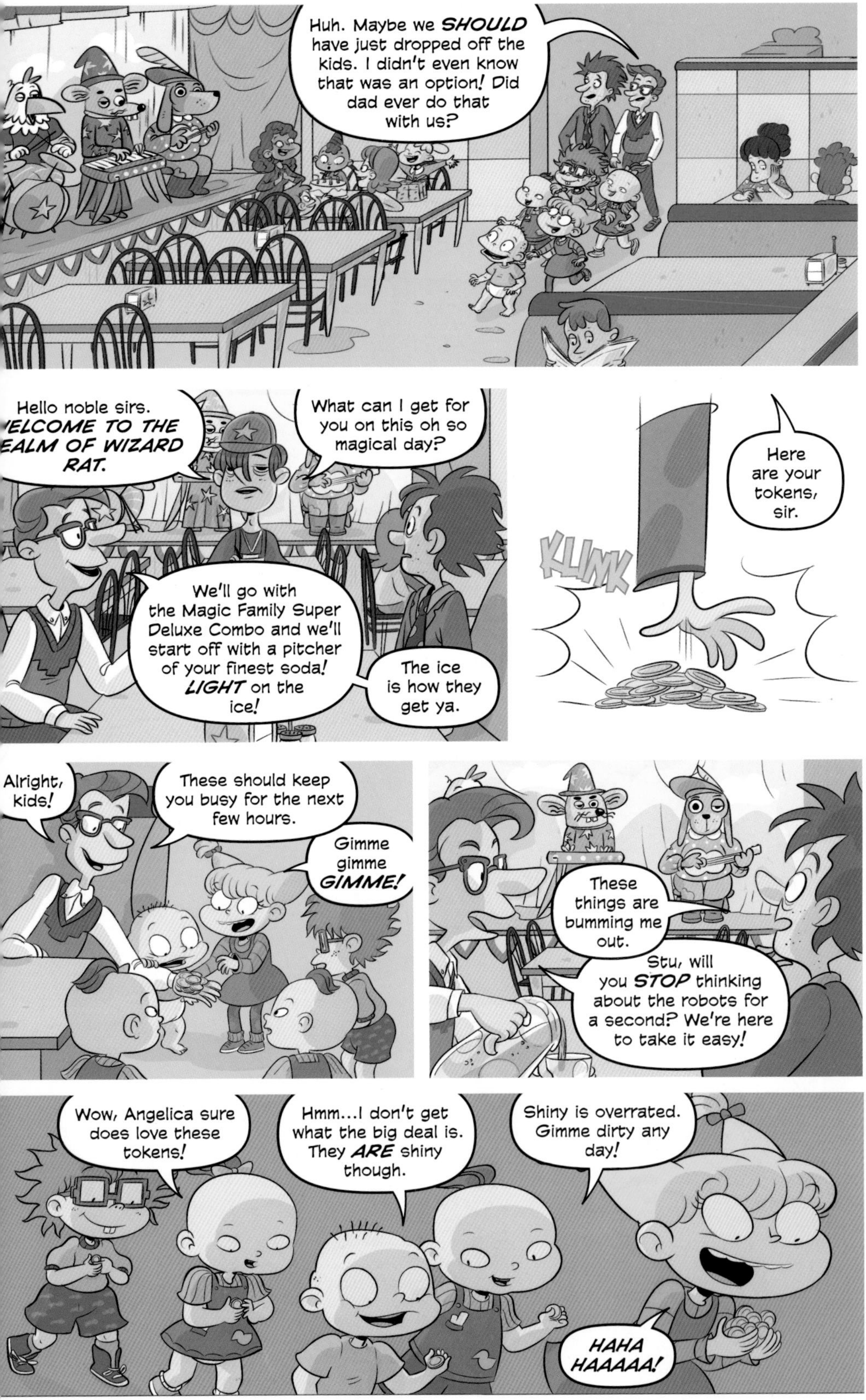
Huh. Maybe we SHOULD have just dropped off the kids. I didn't even know that was an option! Did dad ever do that with us?
Hello noble sirs. WELCOME TO THE REALM OF WIZARD RAT.
What can I get for you on this oh so magical day?
We'll go with the Magic Family Super Deluxe Combo and we'll start off with a pitcher of your finest soda! LIGHT on the ice!
The ice is how they get ya.
Here are your tokens, sir.
KLINK
Alright, kids!
These should keep you busy for the next few hours.
Gimme gimme GIMME!
These things are bumming me out.
Stu, will you STOP thinking about the robots for a second? We're here to take it easy!
Wow, Angelica sure does love these tokens!
Hmm...I don't get what the big deal is. They ARE shiny though.
Shiny is overrated. Gimme dirty any day!
HAHA HAAAAA!

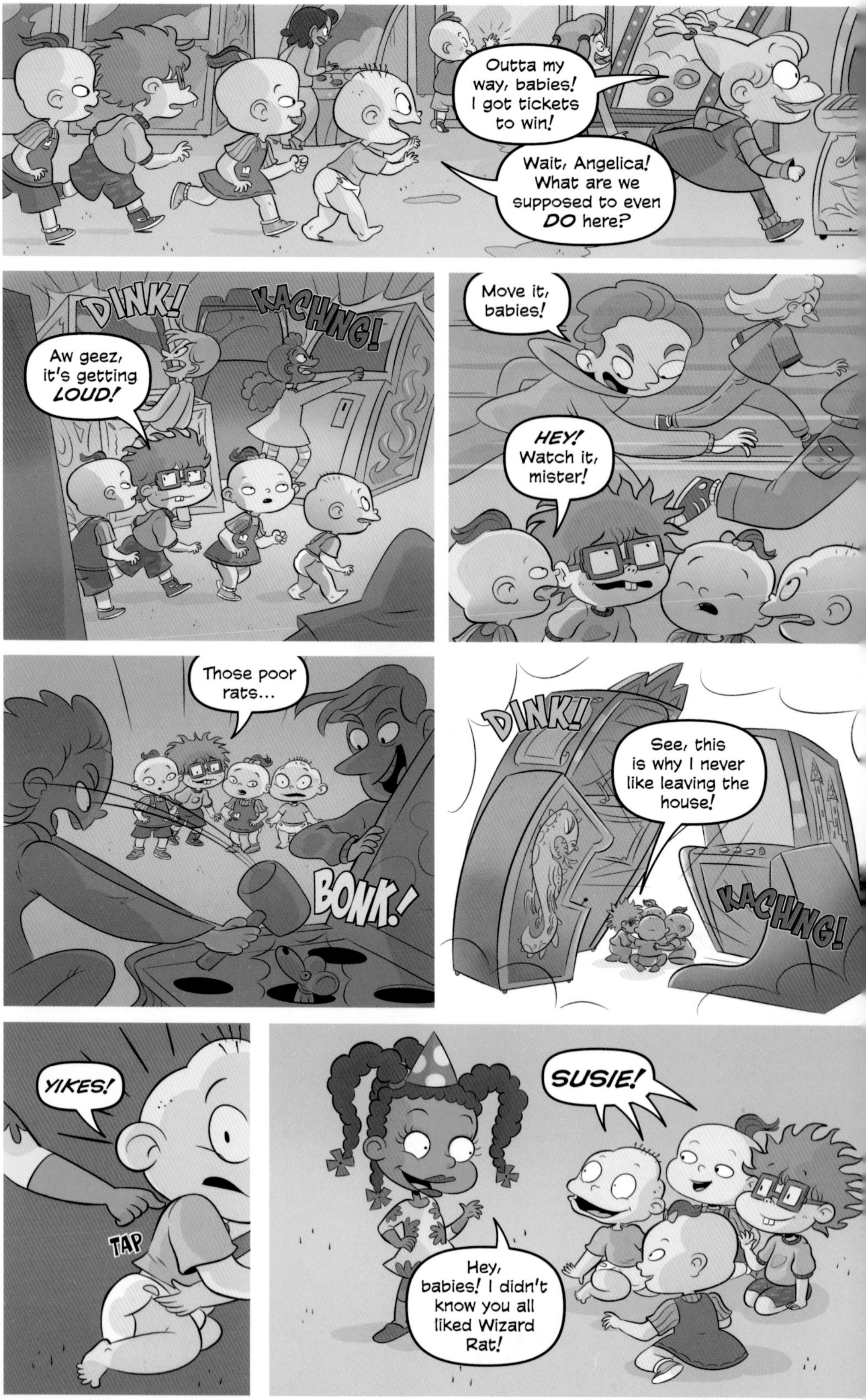
Outta my way, babies! I got tickets to win!
Wait, Angelica! What are we supposed to even DO here?
DINK!
KACHING!
Aw geez, it's getting LOUD!
Move it, babies!
HEY! Watch it, mister!
Those poor rats...
BONK!
DINK!
See, this is why I never like leaving the house!
KACHING!
YIKES!
TAP
SUSIE!
Hey, babies! I didn't know you all liked Wizard Rat!

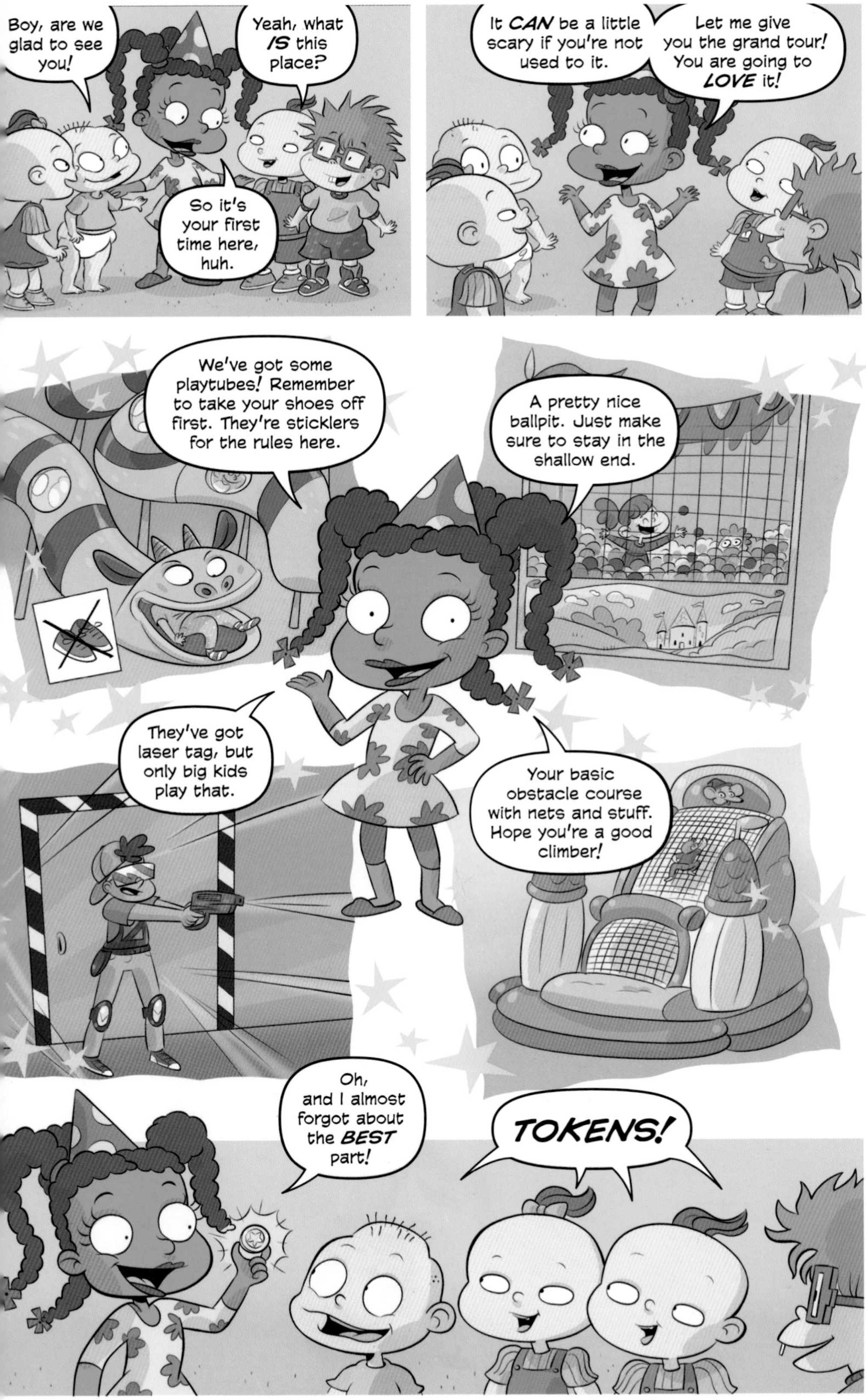
Boy, are we glad to see you!
Yeah, what IS this place?
So it's your first time here, huh.
It CAN be a little scary if you're not used to it.
Let me give you the grand tour! You are going to LOVE it!
We've got some playtubes! Remember to take your shoes off first. They're sticklers for the rules here.
A pretty nice ballpit. Just make sure to stay in the shallow end.
They've got laser tag, but only big kids play that.
Your basic obstacle course with nets and stuff. Hope you're a good climber!
Oh, and I almost forgot about the BEST part!
TOKENS!

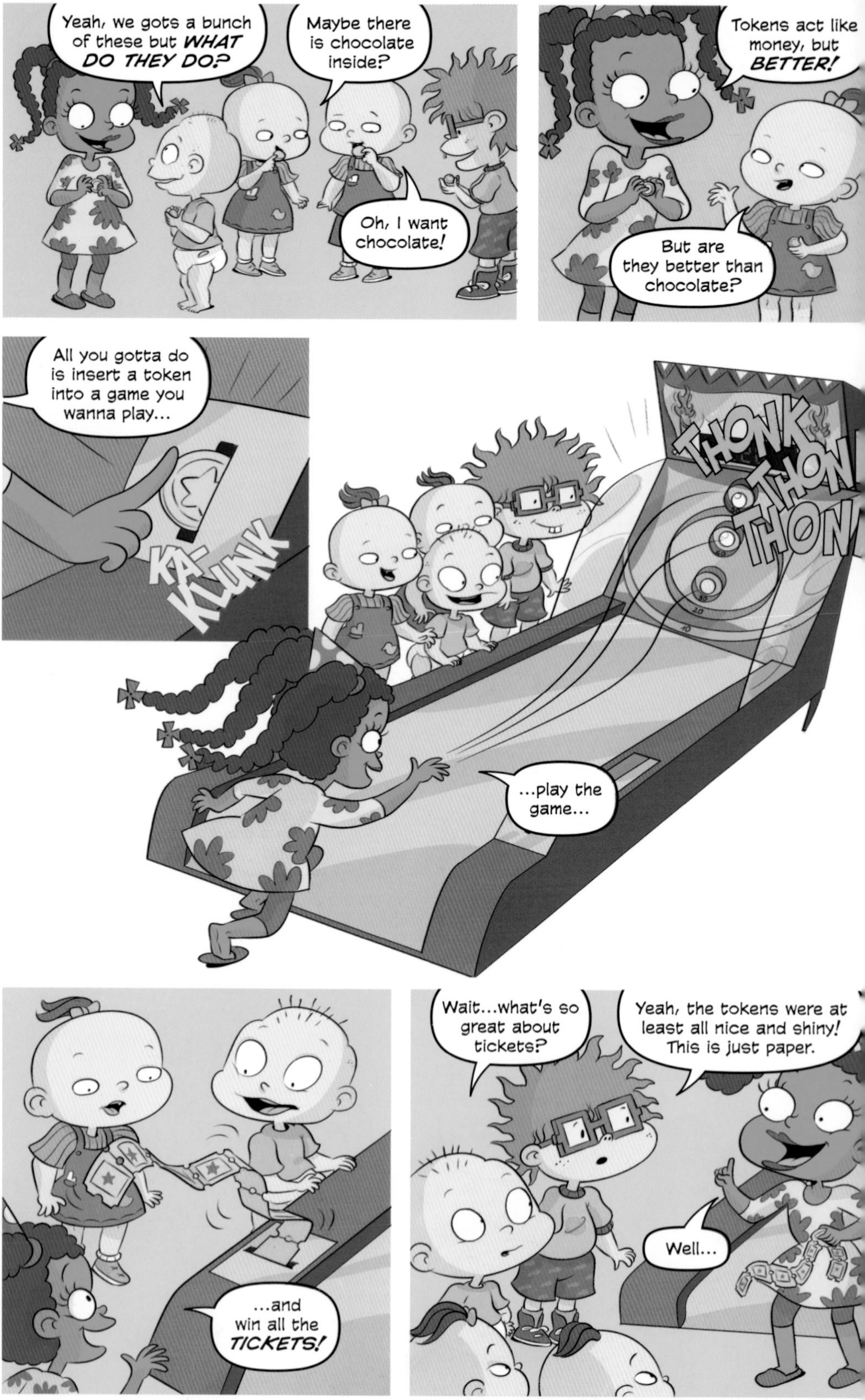
Yeah, we gots a bunch of these but WHAT DO THEY DO?
Maybe there is chocolate inside?
Oh, I want chocolate!
Tokens act like money, but BETTER!
But are they better than chocolate?
All you gotta do is insert a token into a game you wanna play...
KA-KLUNK
THONK THON THON
...play the game...
...and win all the TICKETS!
Wait...what's so great about tickets?
Yeah, the tokens were at least all nice and shiny! This is just paper.
Well...

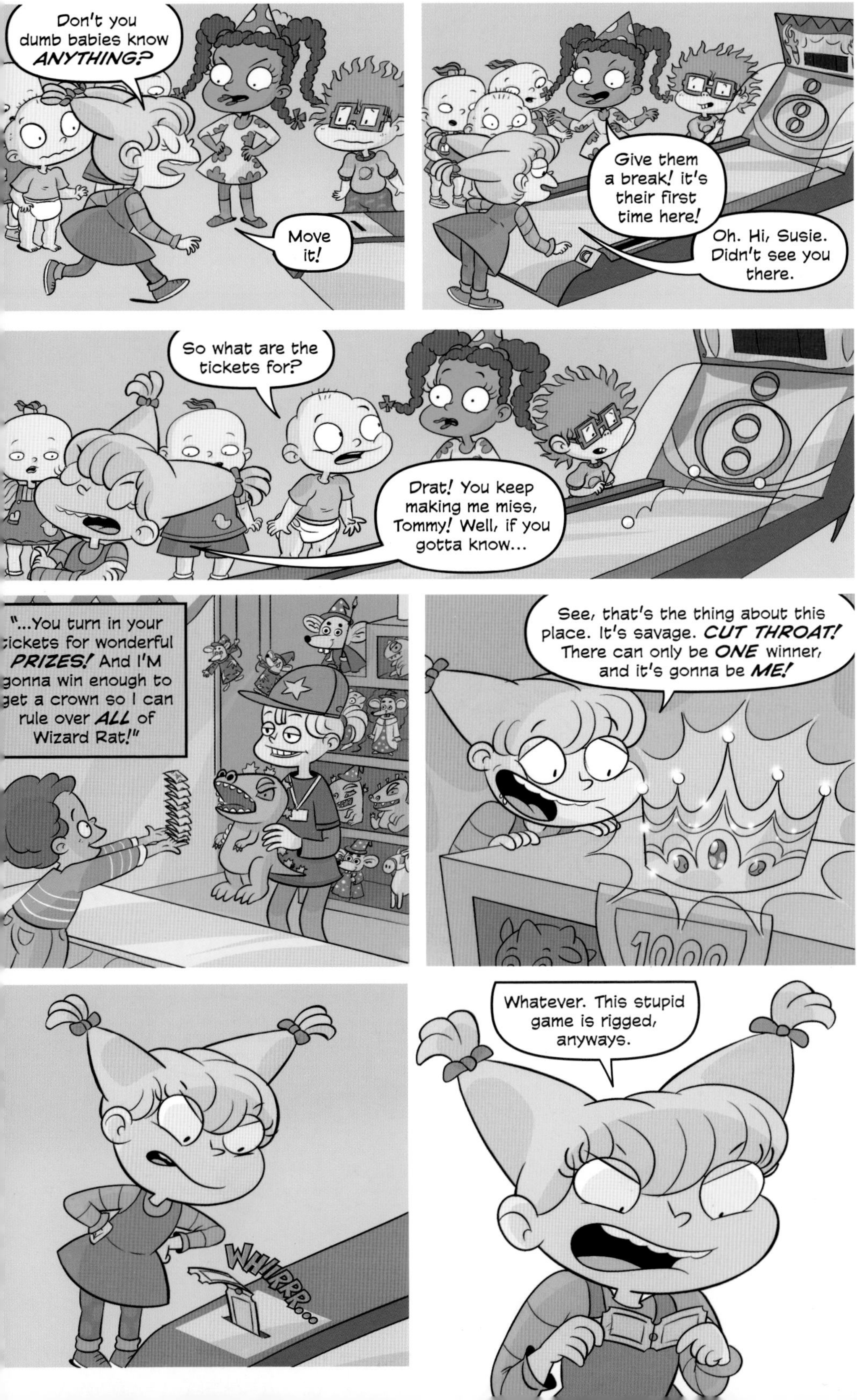
Don't you dumb babies know ANYTHING?
Move it!
Give them a break! it's their first time here!
Oh. Hi, Susie. Didn't see you there.
So what are the tickets for?
Drat! You keep making me miss, Tommy! Well, if you gotta know...
"...You turn in your tickets for wonderful PRIZES! And I'M gonna win enough to get a crown so I can rule over ALL of Wizard Rat!"
See, that's the thing about this place. It's savage. CUT THROAT! There can only be ONE winner, and it's gonna be ME!
WHIRRR...
Whatever. This stupid game is rigged, anyways.

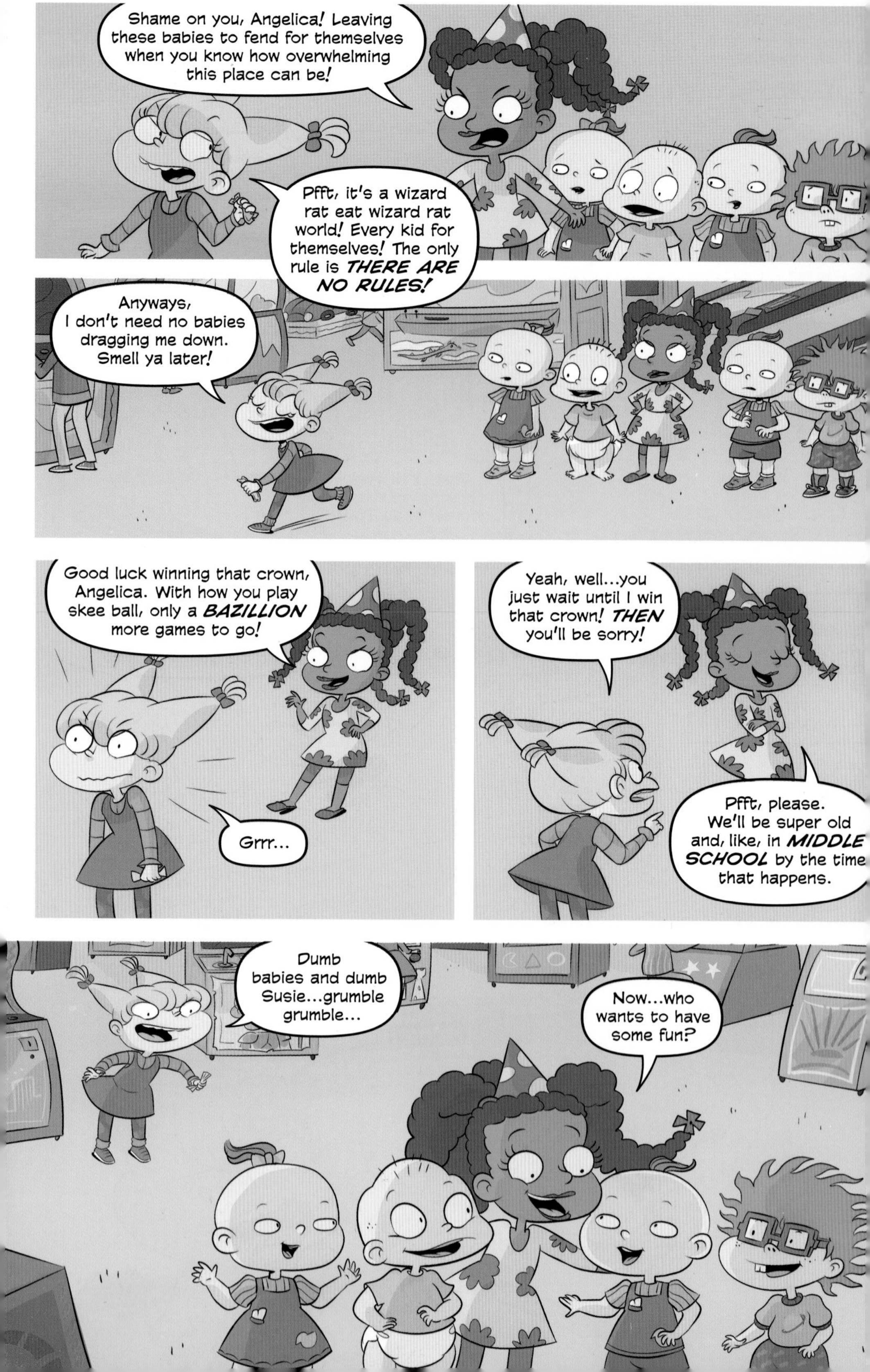
Shame on you, Angelica! Leaving these babies to fend for themselves when you know how overwhelming this place can be!
Pfft, it's a wizard rat eat wizard rat world! Every kid for themselves! The only rule is THERE ARE NO RULES!
Anyways, I don't need no babies dragging me down. Smell ya later!
Good luck winning that crown, Angelica. With how you play skee ball, only a BAZILLION more games to go!
Grrr...
Yeah, well...you just wait until I win that crown! THEN you'll be sorry!
Pfft, please. We'll be super old and, like, in MIDDLE SCHOOL by the time that happens.
Dumb babies and dumb Susie...grumble grumble...
Now...who wants to have some fun?

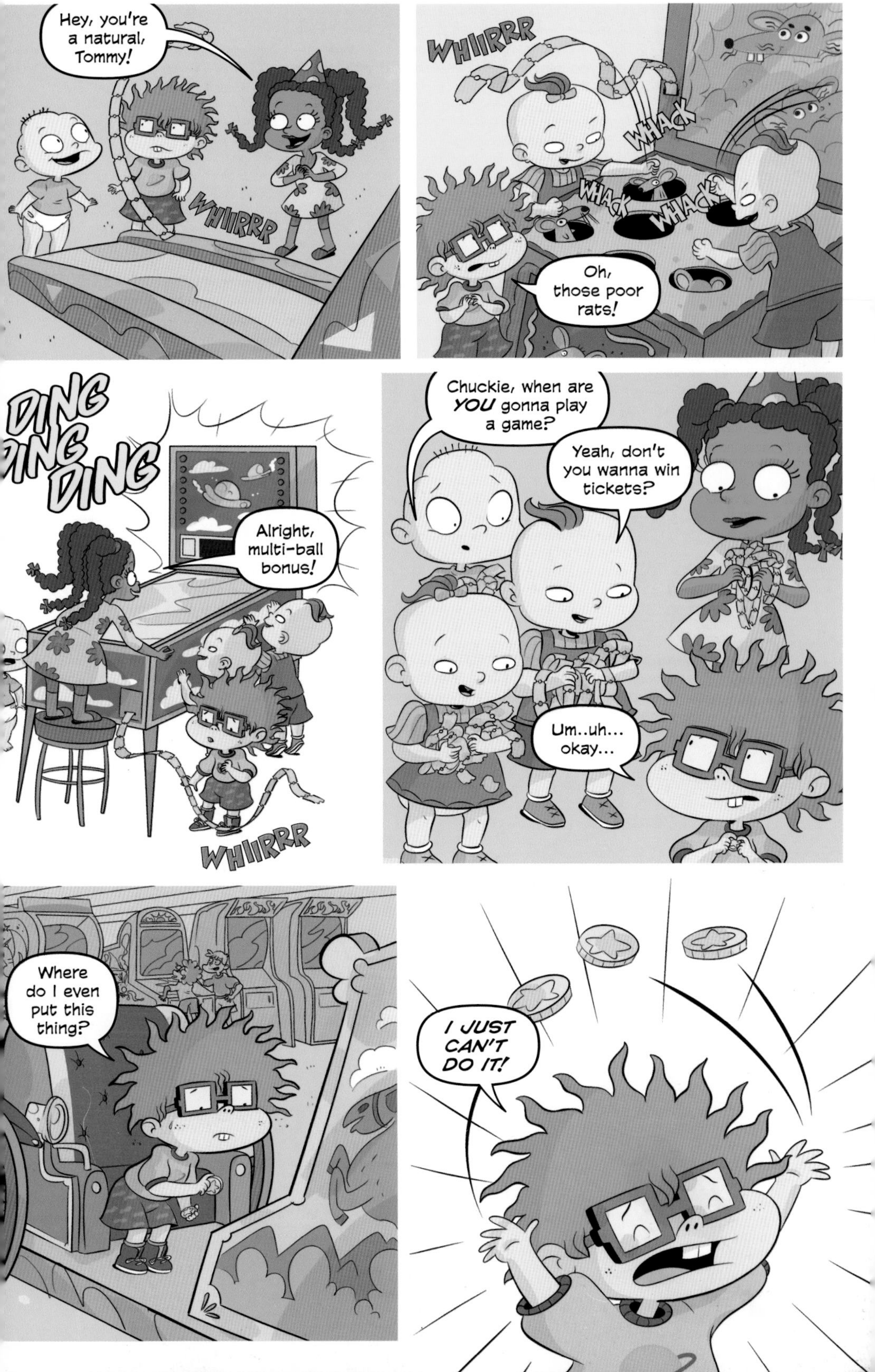

Hey, you're a natural, Tommy!
WHIIRRR
WHIIRRR
WHACK
WHACK
WHACK
Oh, those poor rats!
DING DING DING
Alright, multi-ball bonus!
WHIIRRR
Chuckie, when are YOU gonna play a game?
Yeah, don't you wanna win tickets?
Um..uh... okay...
Where do I even put this thing?
I JUST CAN'T DO IT!

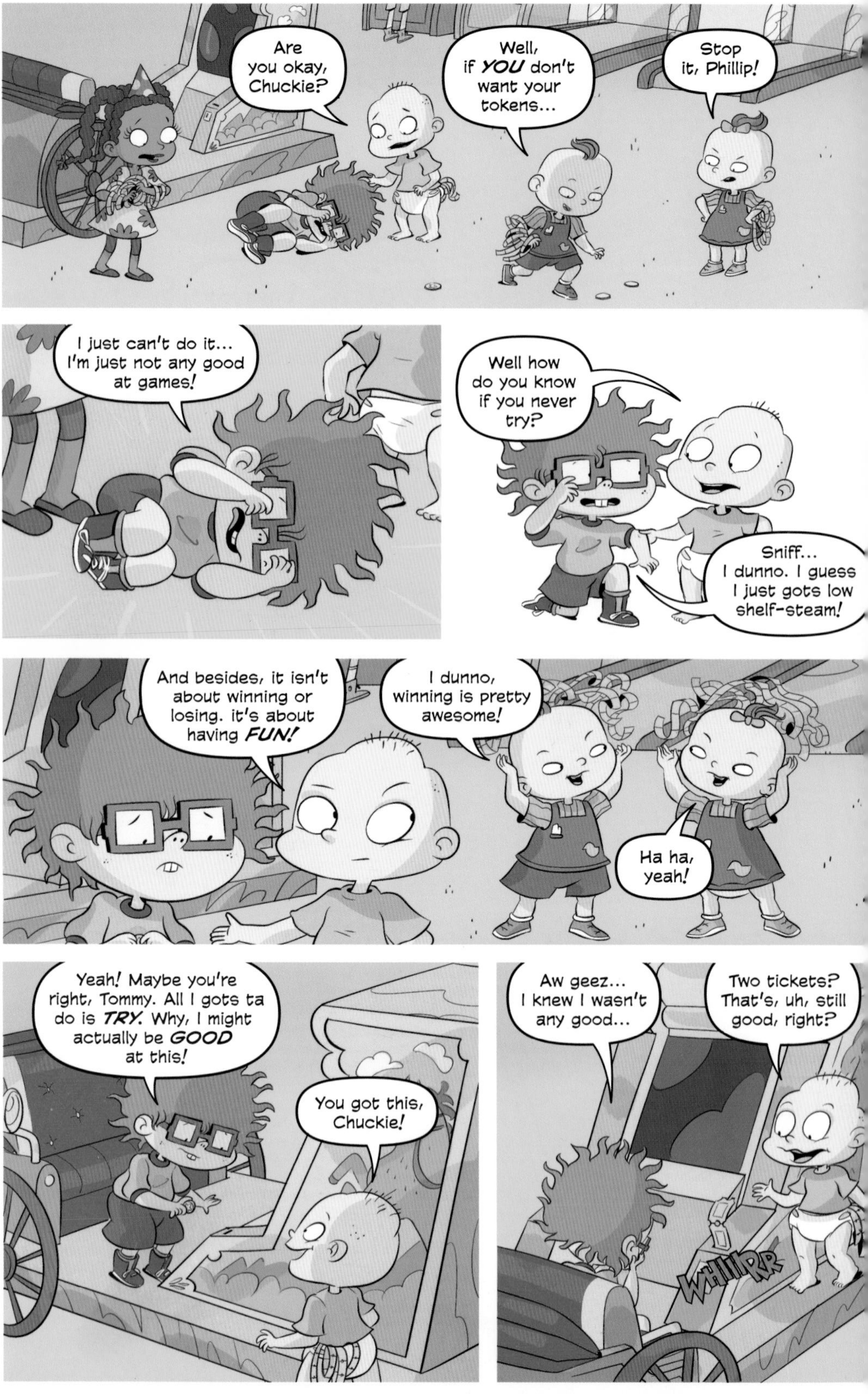
Are you okay, Chuckie?
Well, if YOU don't want your tokens...
Stop it, Phillip!
I just can't do it... I'm just not any good at games!
Well how do you know if you never try?
Sniff... I dunno. I guess I just gots low shelf-steam!
And besides, it isn't about winning or losing. it's about having FUN!
I dunno, winning is pretty awesome!
Ha ha, yeah!
Yeah! Maybe you're right, Tommy. All I gots ta do is TRY. Why, I might actually be GOOD at this!
You got this, Chuckie!
Aw geez... I knew I wasn't any good...
Two tickets? That's, uh, still good, right?
WHIIIRR

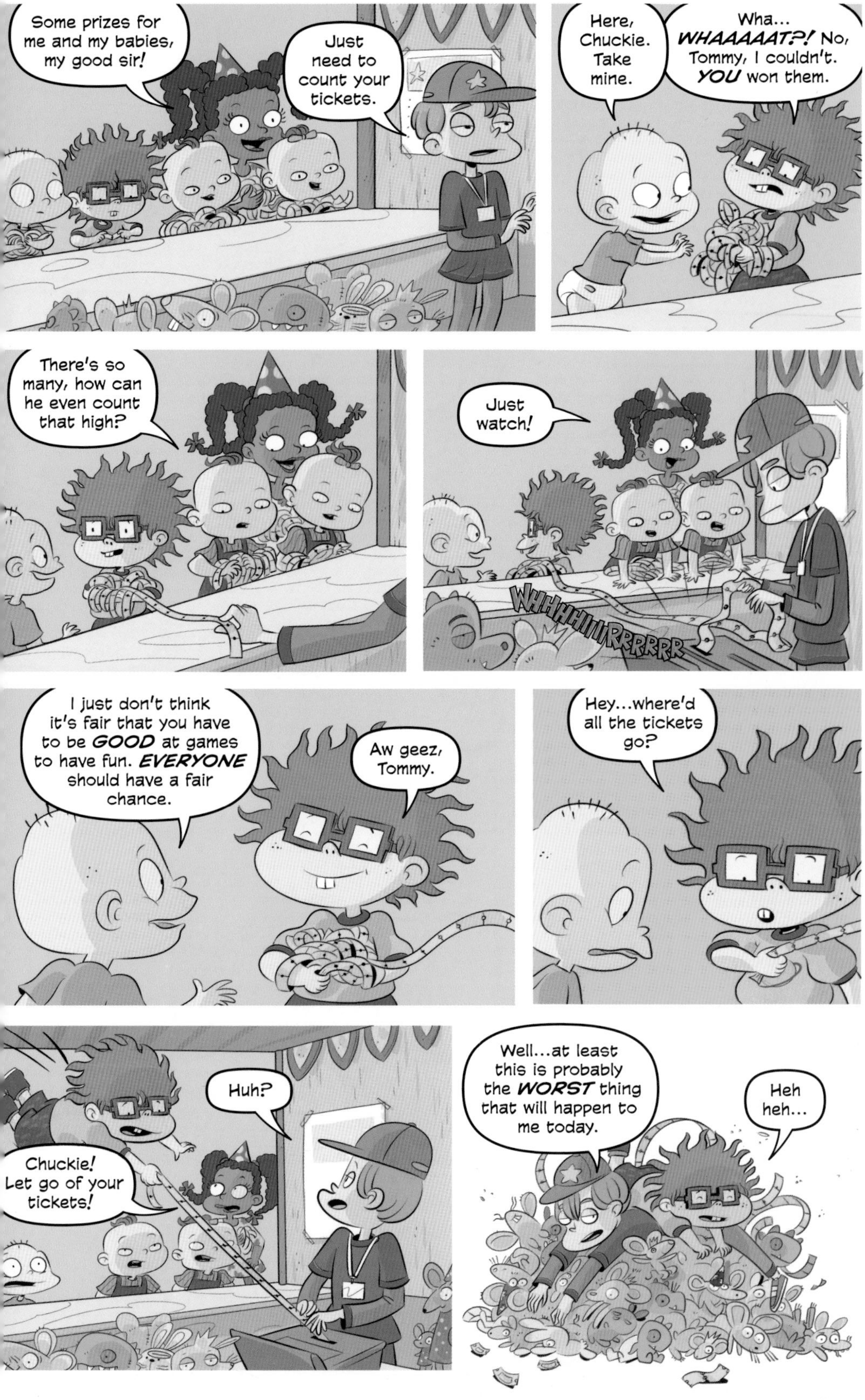
Some prizes for me and my babies, my good sir!
Just need to count your tickets.
Here, Chuckie. Take mine.
Wha... WHAAAAAT?! No, Tommy, I couldn't. YOU won them.
There's so many, how can he even count that high?
Just watch!
WHHHHIIIRRRRRR
I just don't think it's fair that you have to be GOOD at games to have fun. EVERYONE should have a fair chance.
Aw geez, Tommy.
Hey...where'd all the tickets go?
Chuckie! Let go of your tickets!
Huh?
Well...at least this is probably the WORST thing that will happen to me today.
Heh heh...

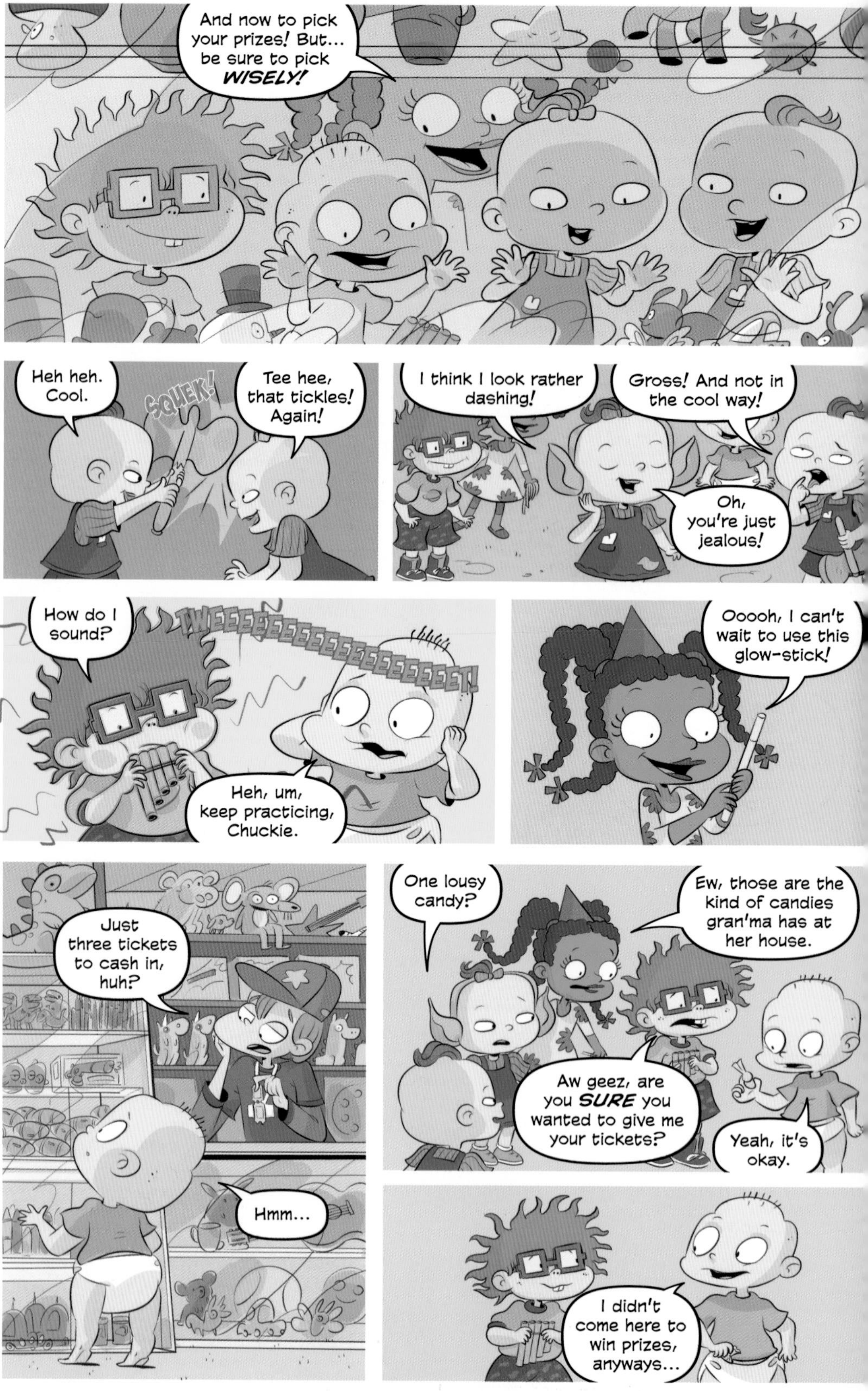

And now to pick your prizes! But... be sure to pick *WISELY!*
Heh heh. Cool.
SQUEK!
Tee hee, that tickles! Again!
I think I look rather dashing!
Gross! And not in the cool way!
Oh, you're just jealous!
How do I sound?
Heh, um, keep practicing, Chuckie.
Ooooh, I can't wait to use this glow-stick!
Just three tickets to cash in, huh?
Hmm...
One lousy candy?
Ew, those are the kind of candies gran'ma has at her house.
Aw geez, are you *SURE* you wanted to give me your tickets?
Yeah, it's okay.
I didn't come here to win prizes, anyways...

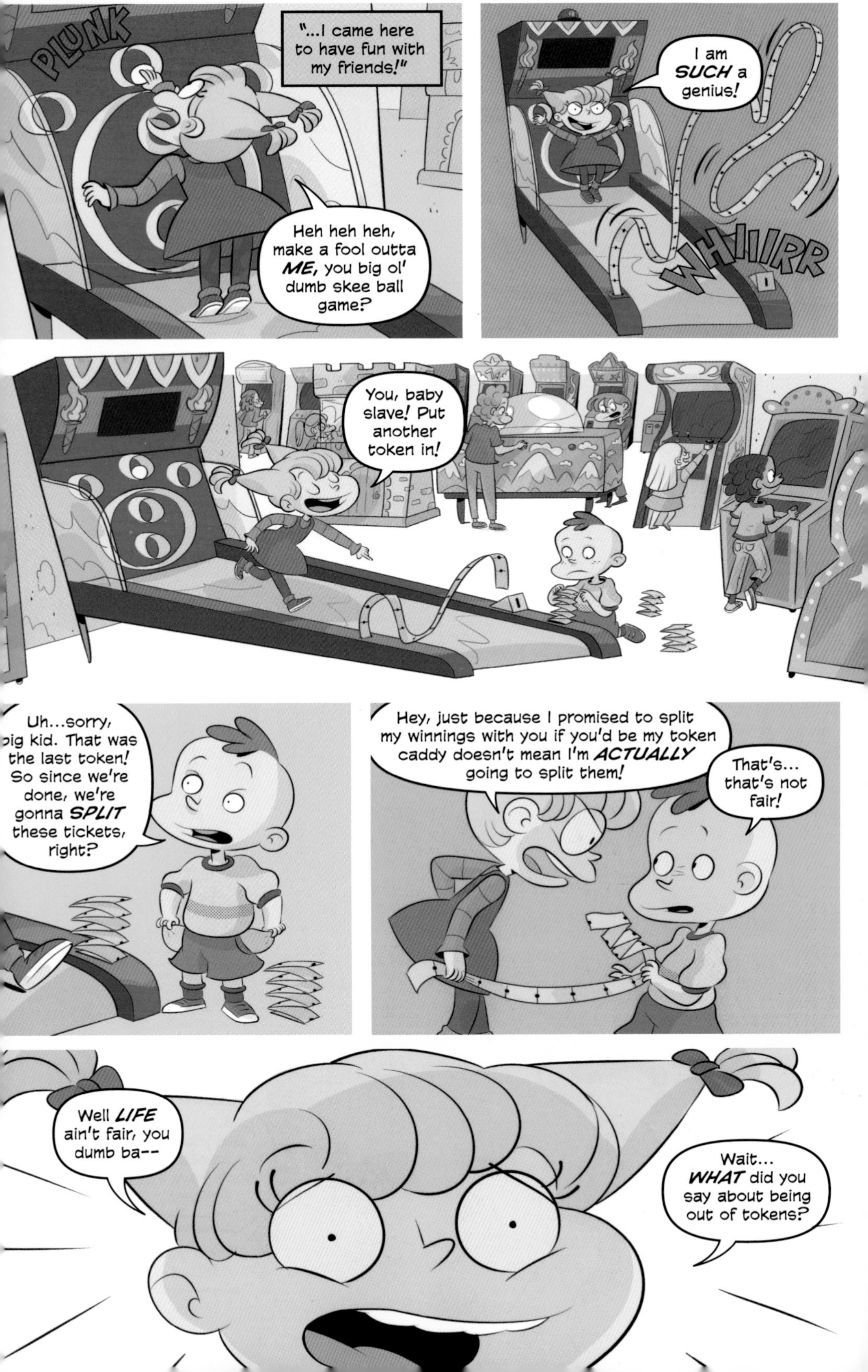
PLUNK
"...I came here to have fun with my friends!"
Heh heh heh, make a fool outta ME, you big ol' dumb skee ball game?
I am SUCH a genius!
WHIIIRR
You, baby slave! Put another token in!
Uh...sorry, big kid. That was the last token! So since we're done, we're gonna SPLIT these tickets, right?
Hey, just because I promised to split my winnings with you if you'd be my token caddy doesn't mean I'm ACTUALLY going to split them!
That's... that's not fair!
Well LIFE ain't fair, you dumb ba--
Wait... WHAT did you say about being out of tokens?

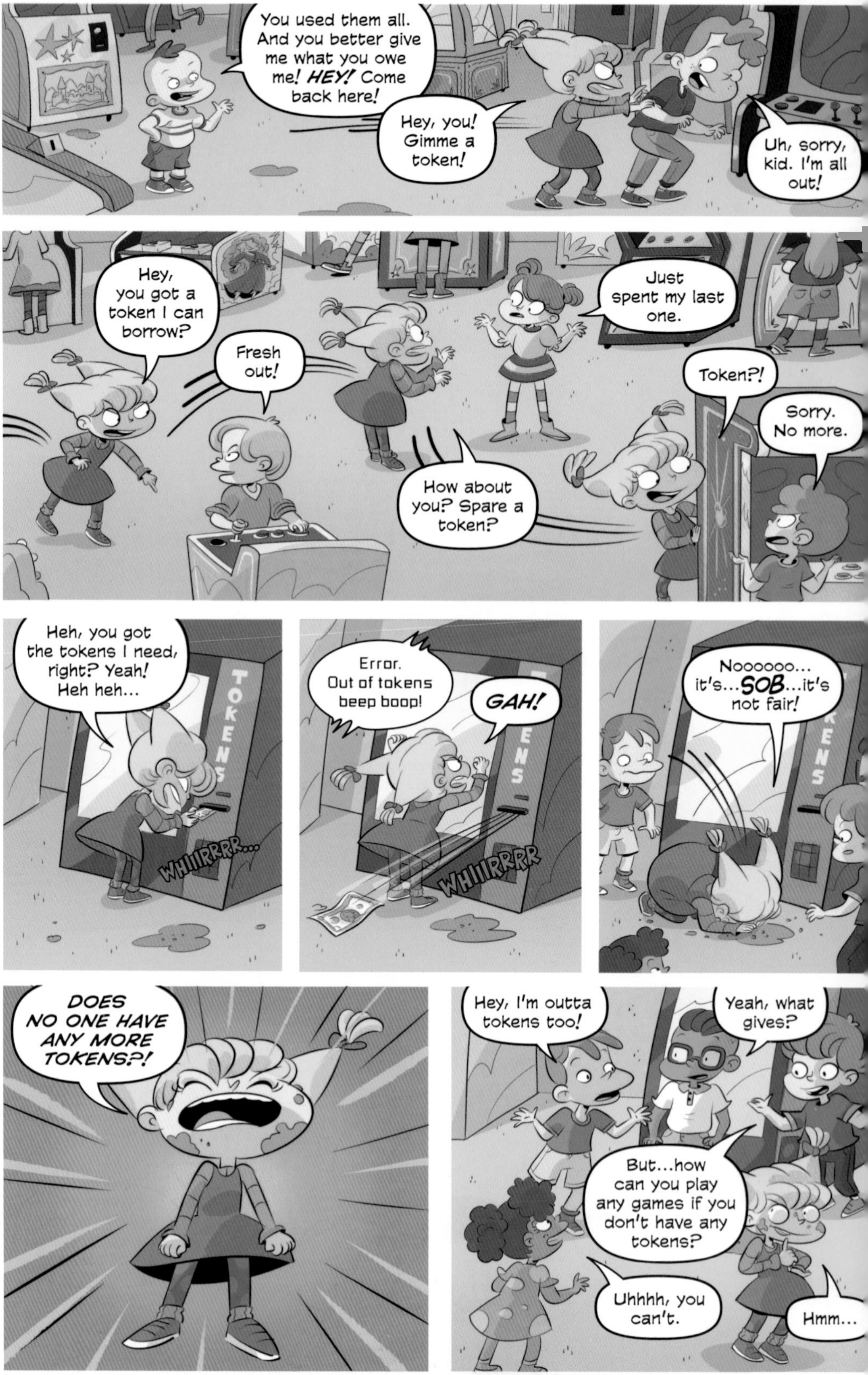

You used them all. And you better give me what you owe me! HEY! Come back here!
Hey, you! Gimme a token!
Uh, sorry, kid. I'm all out!
Hey, you got a token I can borrow?
Fresh out!
Just spent my last one.
How about you? Spare a token?
Token?!
Sorry. No more.
Heh, you got the tokens I need, right? Yeah! Heh heh...
TOKENS
WHIIIRRRR...
Error. Out of tokens beep boop!
GAH!
WHIIIRRRR
Noooooo... it's...SOB...it's not fair!
DOES NO ONE HAVE ANY MORE TOKENS?!
Hey, I'm outta tokens too!
Yeah, what gives?
But...how can you play any games if you don't have any tokens?
Uhhhh, you can't.
Hmm...

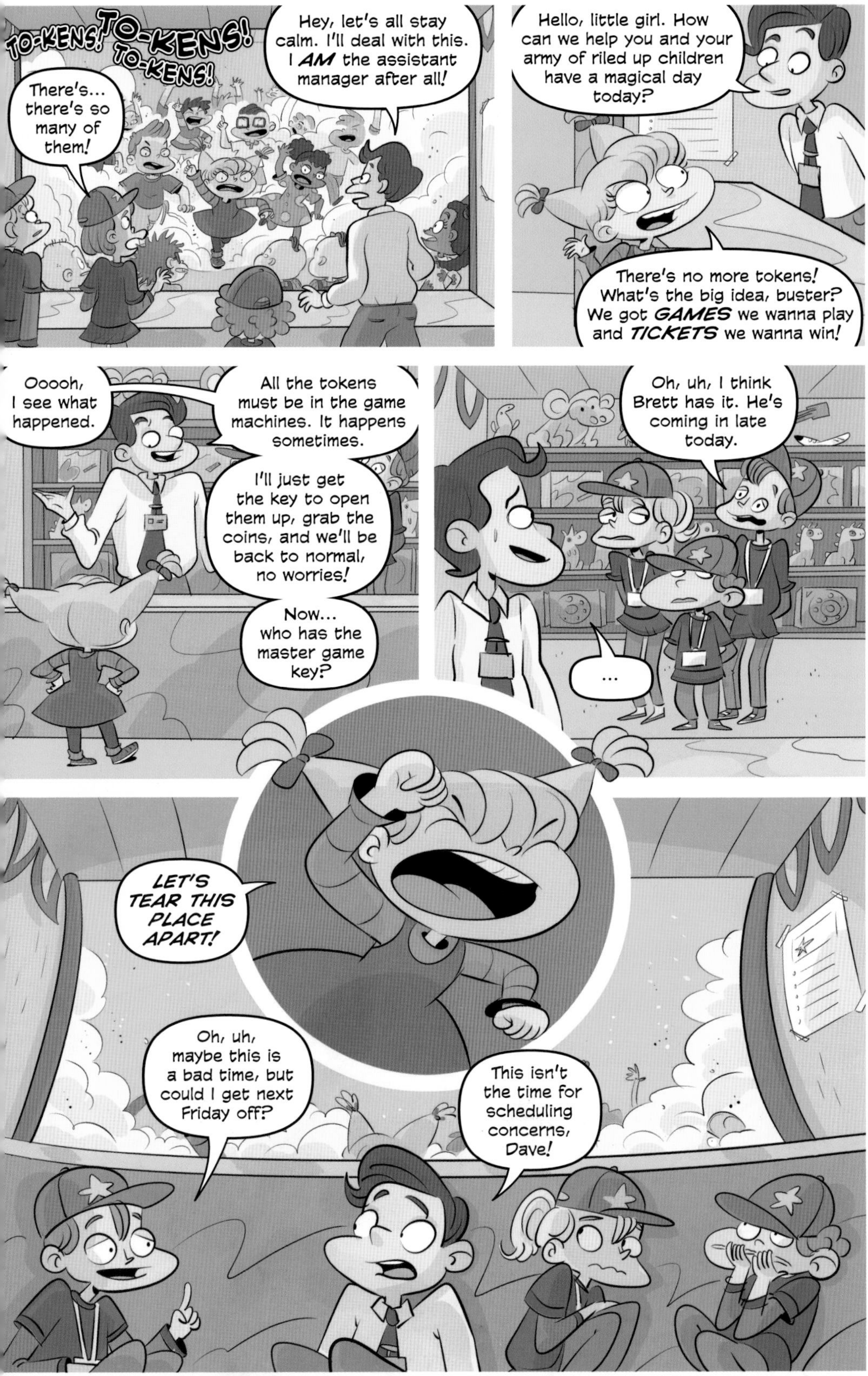
TO-KENS! TO-KENS! TO-KENS!
Hey, let's all stay calm. I'll deal with this. I AM the assistant manager after all!
There's... there's so many of them!
Hello, little girl. How can we help you and your army of riled up children have a magical day today?
There's no more tokens! What's the big idea, buster? We got GAMES we wanna play and TICKETS we wanna win!
Ooooh, I see what happened.
All the tokens must be in the game machines. It happens sometimes.
I'll just get the key to open them up, grab the coins, and we'll be back to normal, no worries!
Now... who has the master game key?
Oh, uh, I think Brett has it. He's coming in late today.
...
LET'S TEAR THIS PLACE APART!
Oh, uh, maybe this is a bad time, but could I get next Friday off?
This isn't the time for scheduling concerns, Dave!

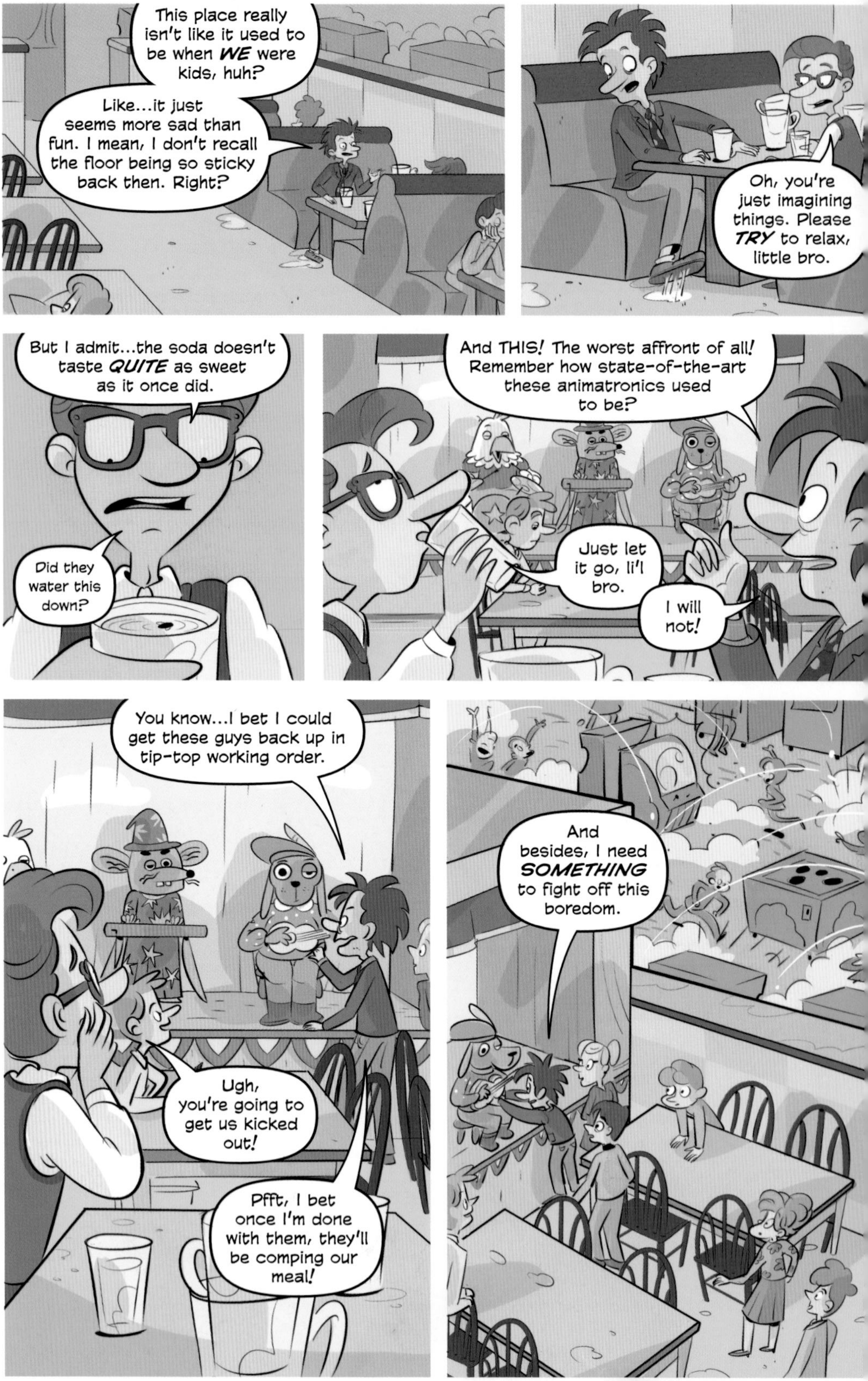
This place really isn't like it used to be when *WE* were kids, huh?
Like...it just seems more sad than fun. I mean, I don't recall the floor being so sticky back then. Right?
Oh, you're just imagining things. Please *TRY* to relax, little bro.
But I admit...the soda doesn't taste *QUITE* as sweet as it once did.
Did they water this down?
And THIS! The worst affront of all! Remember how state-of-the-art these animatronics used to be?
Just let it go, li'l bro.
I will not!
You know...I bet I could get these guys back up in tip-top working order.
Ugh, you're going to get us kicked out!
Pfft, I bet once I'm done with them, they'll be comping our meal!
And besides, I need *SOMETHING* to fight off this boredom.

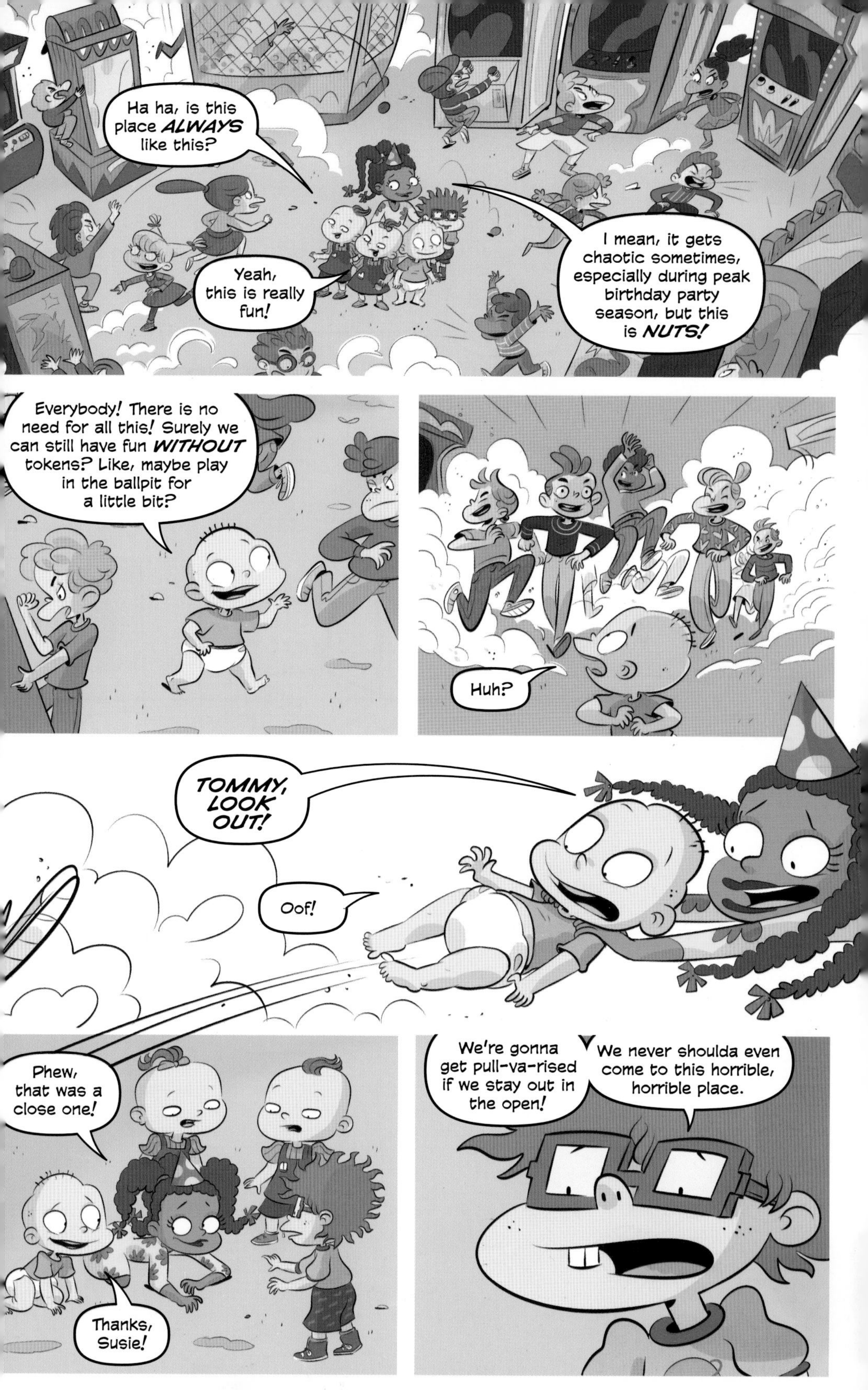
Ha ha, is this place ALWAYS like this?
Yeah, this is really fun!
I mean, it gets chaotic sometimes, especially during peak birthday party season, but this is NUTS!
Everybody! There is no need for all this! Surely we can still have fun WITHOUT tokens? Like, maybe play in the ballpit for a little bit?
Huh?
TOMMY, LOOK OUT!
Oof!
Phew, that was a close one!
Thanks, Susie!
We're gonna get pull-va-rised if we stay out in the open!
We never shoulda even come to this horrible, horrible place.

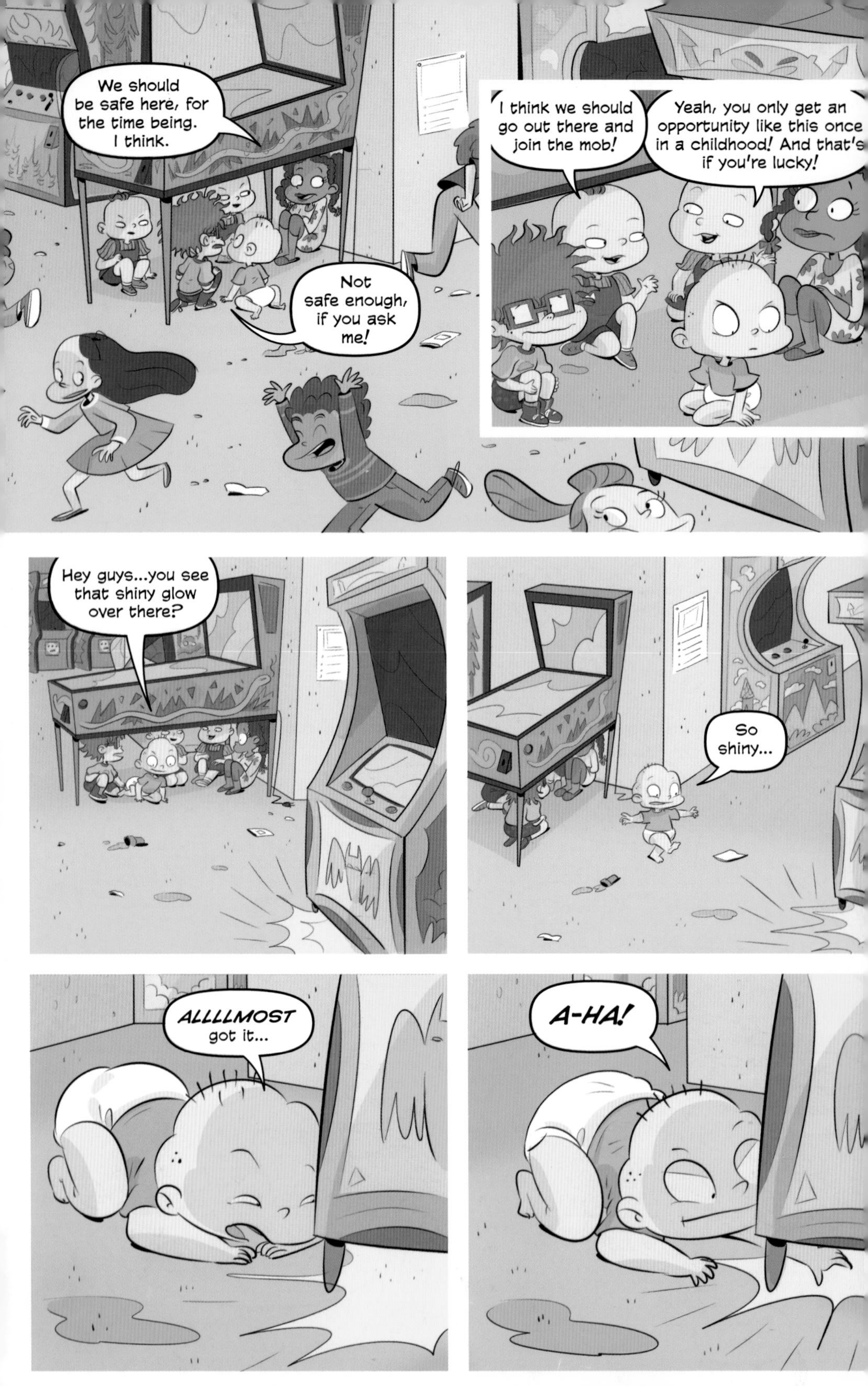

We should be safe here, for the time being. I think.
Not safe enough, if you ask me!
I think we should go out there and join the mob!
Yeah, you only get an opportunity like this once in a childhood! And that's if you're lucky!
Hey guys...you see that shiny glow over there?
So shiny...
ALLLLMOST got it...
A-HA!

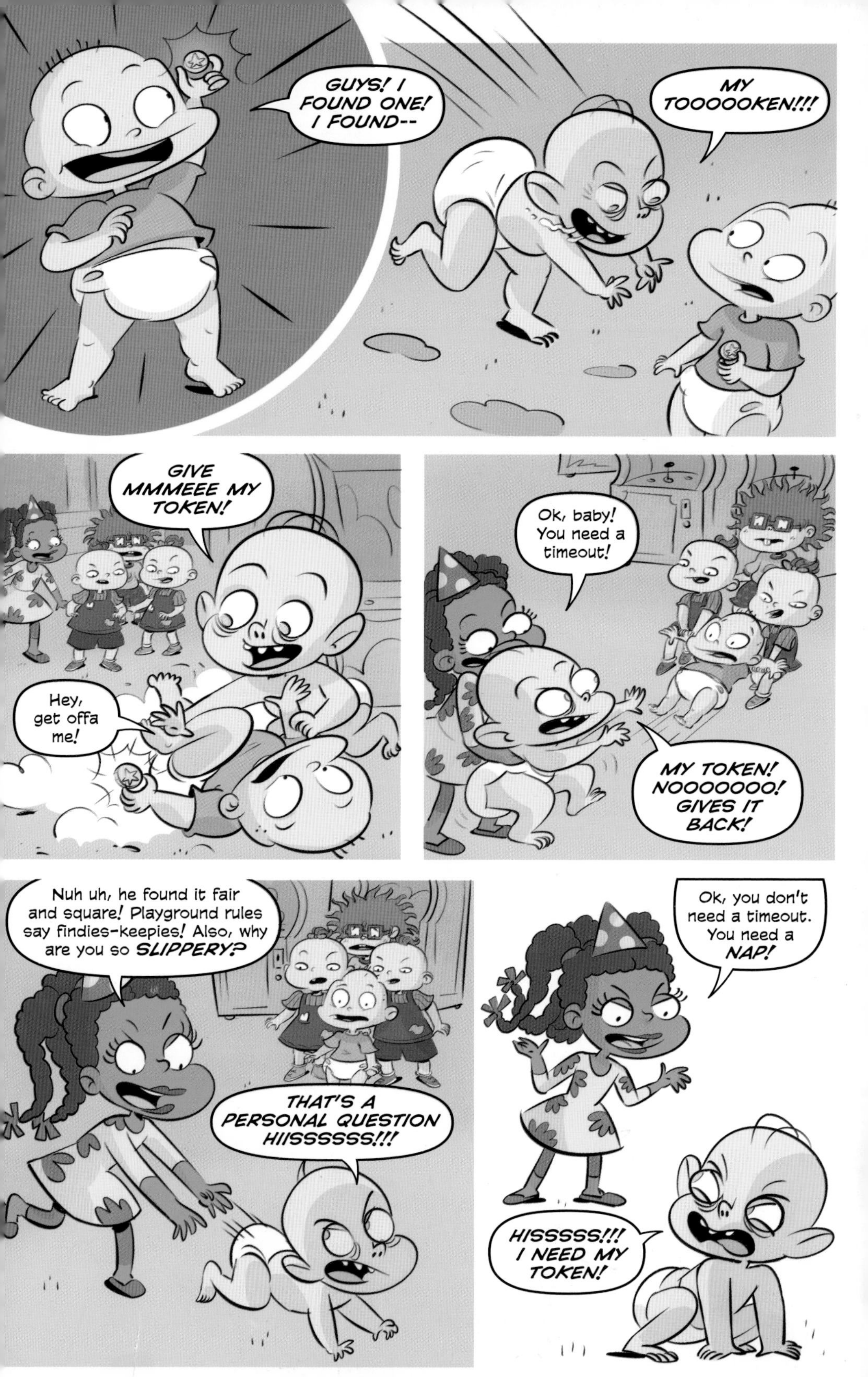
GUYS! I FOUND ONE! I FOUND--
MY TOOOOOKEN!!!
GIVE MMMEEE MY TOKEN!
Hey, get offa me!
Ok, baby! You need a timeout!
MY TOKEN! NOOOOOOO! GIVES IT BACK!
Nuh uh, he found it fair and square! Playground rules say findies-keepies! Also, why are you so SLIPPERY?
THAT'S A PERSONAL QUESTION HIISSSSSS!!!
Ok, you don't need a timeout. You need a NAP!
HISSSSS!!! I NEED MY TOKEN!

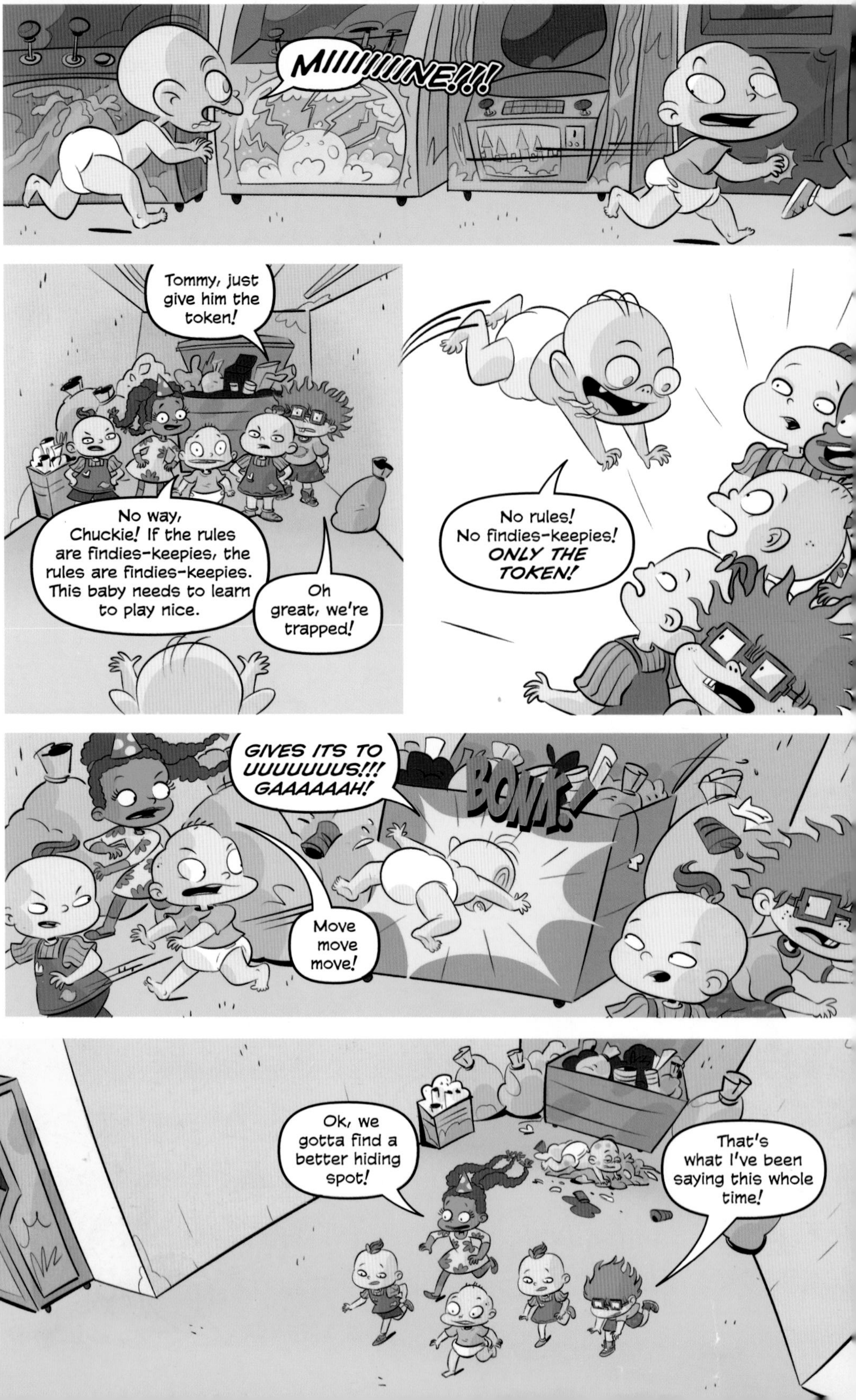
MIIIIIIIINE!!!
Tommy, just give him the token!
No way, Chuckie! If the rules are findies-keepies, the rules are findies-keepies. This baby needs to learn to play nice.
Oh great, we're trapped!
No rules! No findies-keepies! ONLY THE TOKEN!
GIVES ITS TO UUUUUUUS!!! GAAAAAAH!
BONK!
Move move move!
Ok, we gotta find a better hiding spot!
That's what I've been saying this whole time!

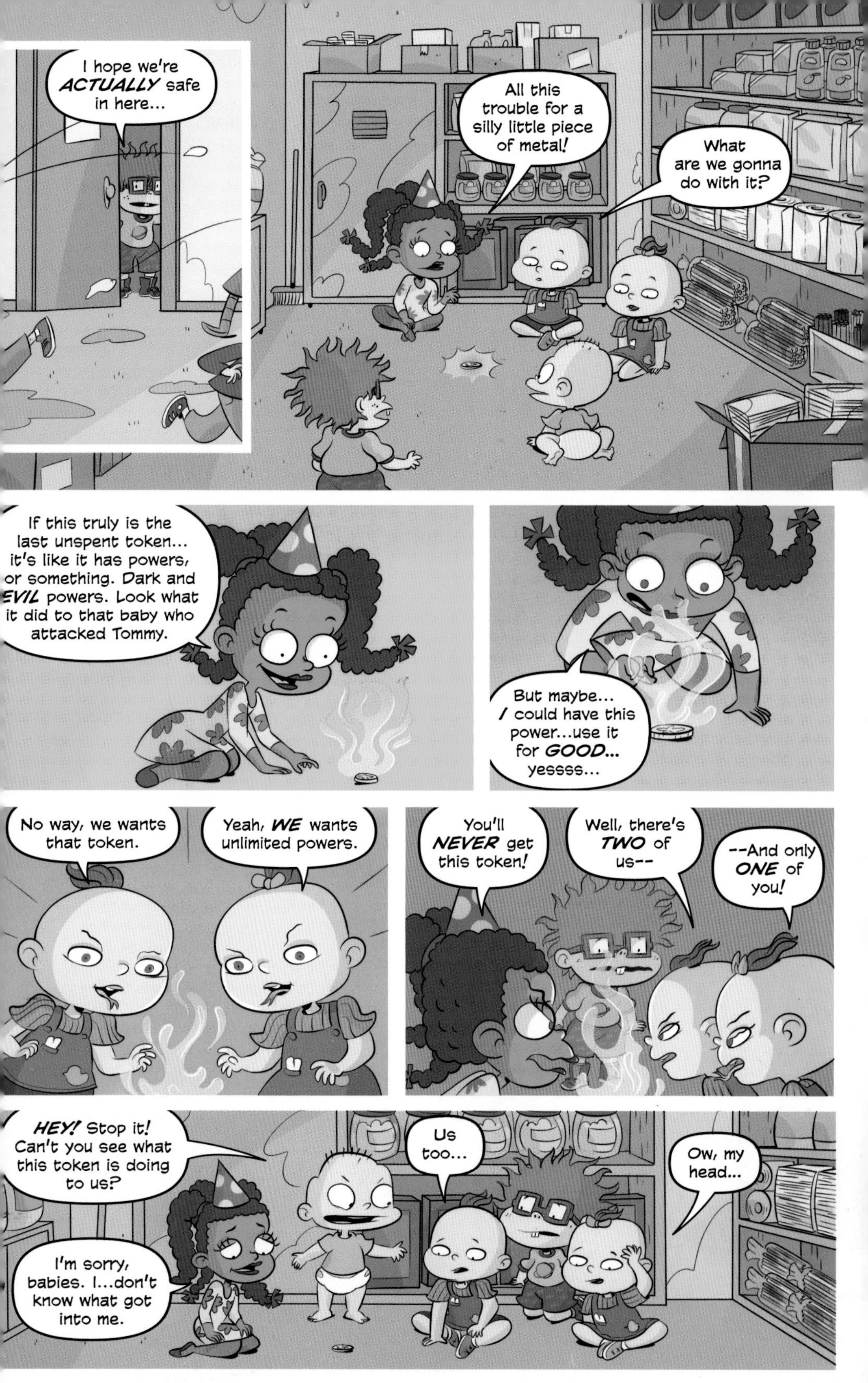
I hope we're ACTUALLY safe in here...
All this trouble for a silly little piece of metal!
What are we gonna do with it?
If this truly is the last unspent token... it's like it has powers, or something. Dark and EVIL powers. Look what it did to that baby who attacked Tommy.
But maybe... I could have this power...use it for GOOD... yessss...
No way, we wants that token.
Yeah, WE wants unlimited powers.
You'll NEVER get this token!
Well, there's TWO of us--
--And only ONE of you!
HEY! Stop it! Can't you see what this token is doing to us?
I'm sorry, babies. I...don't know what got into me.
Us too...
Ow, my head...

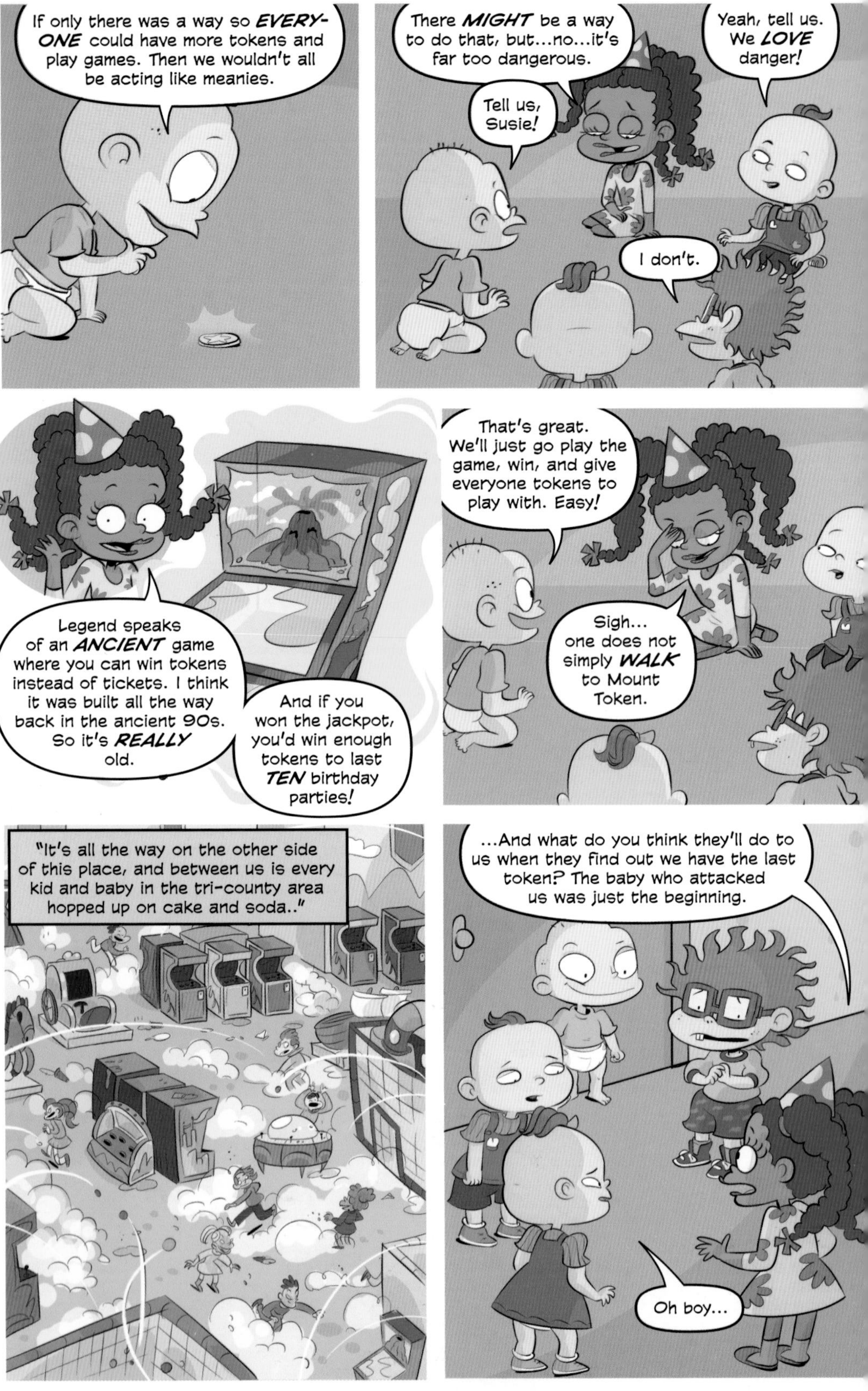
If only there was a way so EVERY-ONE could have more tokens and play games. Then we wouldn't all be acting like meanies.
There MIGHT be a way to do that, but...no...it's far too dangerous.
Tell us, Susie!
Yeah, tell us. We LOVE danger!
I don't.
Legend speaks of an ANCIENT game where you can win tokens instead of tickets. I think it was built all the way back in the ancient 90s. So it's REALLY old.
And if you won the jackpot, you'd win enough tokens to last TEN birthday parties!
That's great. We'll just go play the game, win, and give everyone tokens to play with. Easy!
Sigh... one does not simply WALK to Mount Token.
"It's all the way on the other side of this place, and between us is every kid and baby in the tri-county area hopped up on cake and soda.."
...And what do you think they'll do to us when they find out we have the last token? The baby who attacked us was just the beginning.
Oh boy...

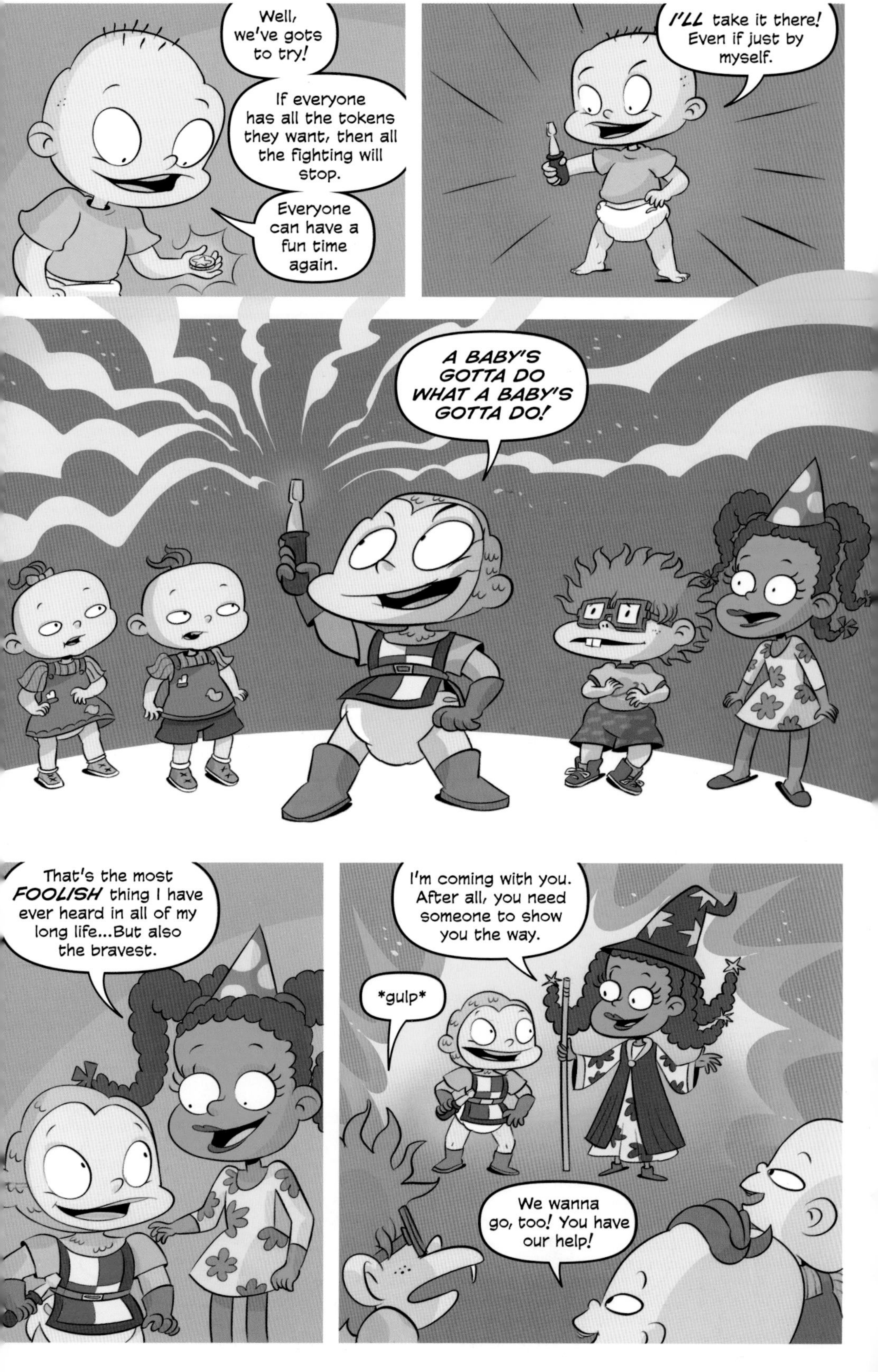
Well, we've gots to try!
If everyone has all the tokens they want, then all the fighting will stop.
Everyone can have a fun time again.
I'LL take it there! Even if just by myself.
A BABY'S GOTTA DO WHAT A BABY'S GOTTA DO!
That's the most FOOLISH thing I have ever heard in all of my long life...But also the bravest.
I'm coming with you. After all, you need someone to show you the way.
gulp
We wanna go, too! You have our help!

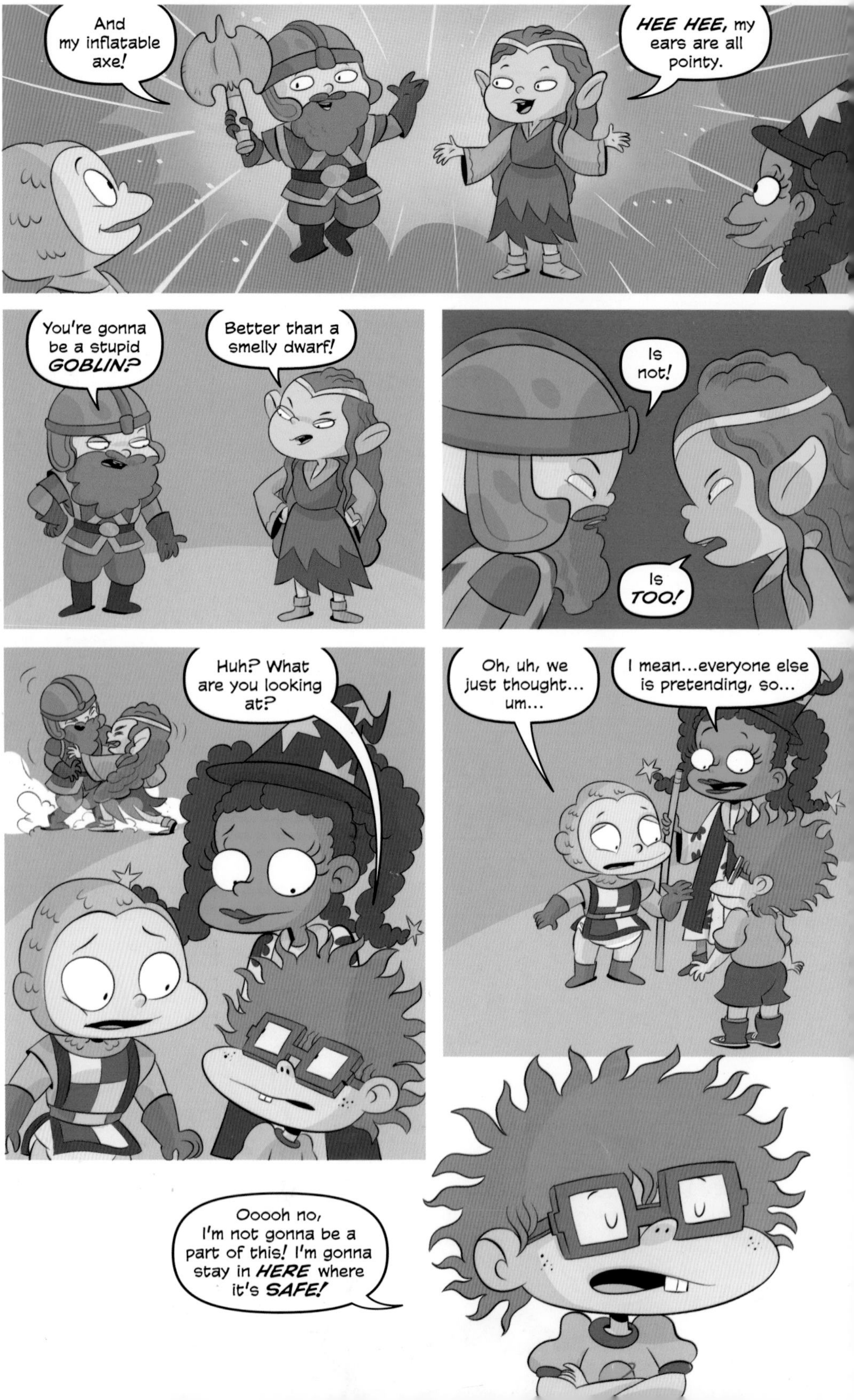
And my inflatable axe!
HEE HEE, my ears are all pointy.
You're gonna be a stupid GOBLIN?
Better than a smelly dwarf!
Is not!
Is TOO!
Huh? What are you looking at?
Oh, uh, we just thought... um...
I mean...everyone else is pretending, so...
Ooooh no, I'm not gonna be a part of this! I'm gonna stay in HERE where it's SAFE!

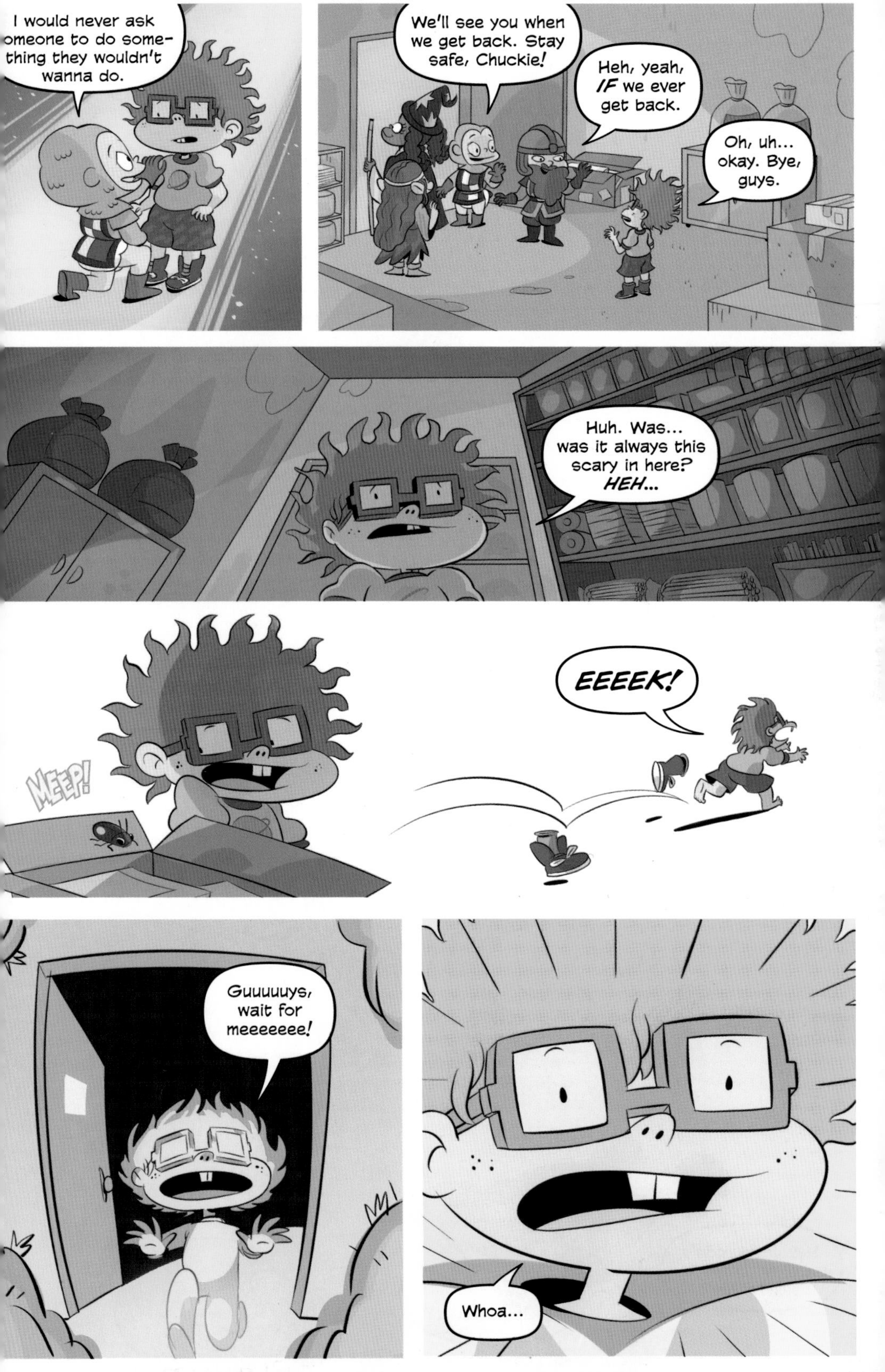
I would never ask
omeone to do some-
thing they wouldn't
wanna do.
We'll see you when
we get back. Stay
safe, Chuckie!
Heh, yeah,
IF we ever
get back.
Oh, uh...
okay. Bye,
guys.
Huh. Was...
was it always this
scary in here?
HEH...
MEEP!
EEEEK!
Guuuuuys,
wait for
meeeeeee!
Whoa...

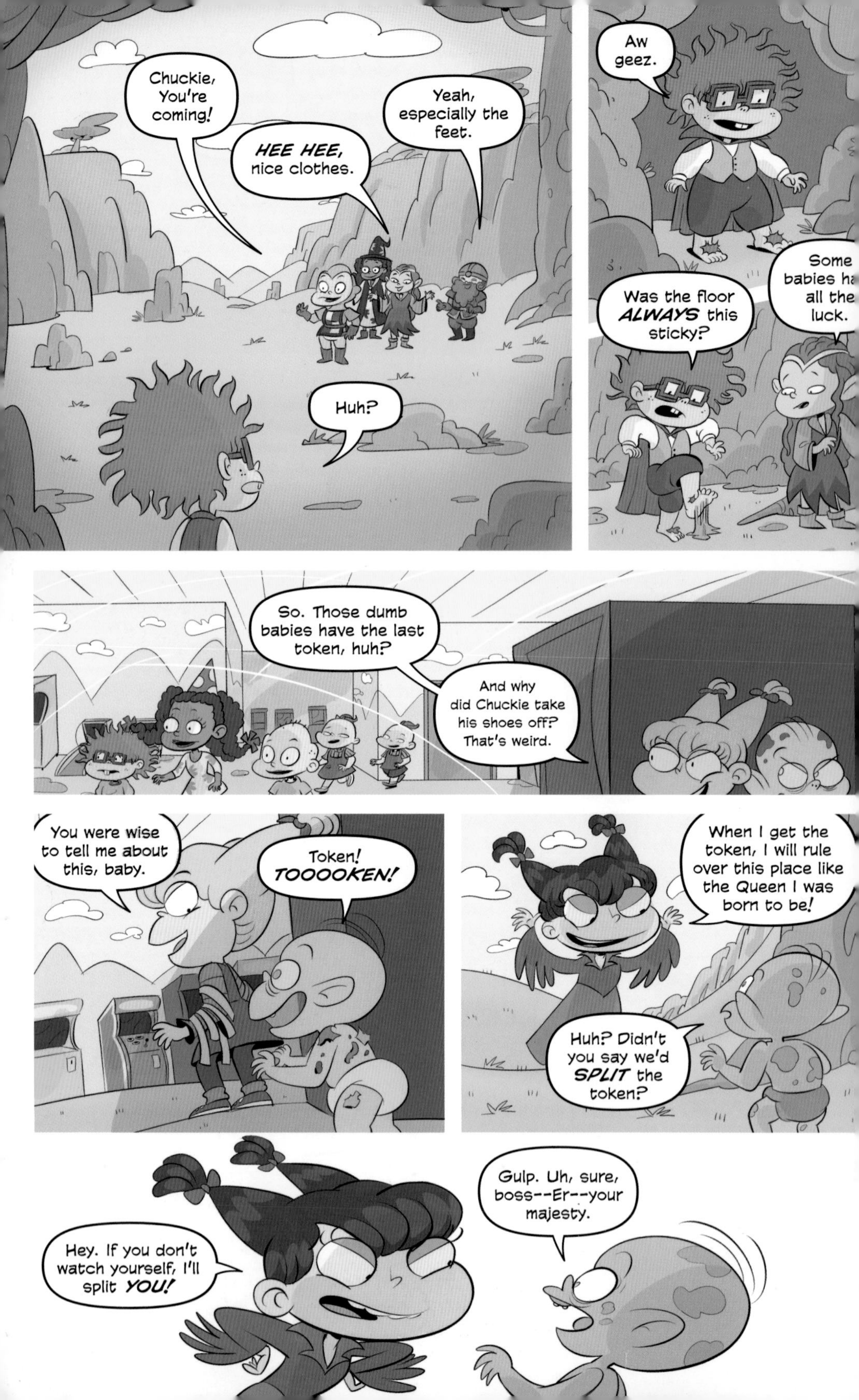
Chuckie, You're coming!
HEE HEE, nice clothes.
Yeah, especially the feet.
Huh?
Aw geez.
Was the floor ALWAYS this sticky?
Some babies ha all the luck.
So. Those dumb babies have the last token, huh?
And why did Chuckie take his shoes off? That's weird.
You were wise to tell me about this, baby.
Token! TOOOOKEN!
When I get the token, I will rule over this place like the Queen I was born to be!
Huh? Didn't you say we'd SPLIT the token?
Hey. If you don't watch yourself, I'll split YOU!
Gulp. Uh, sure, boss--Er--your majesty.

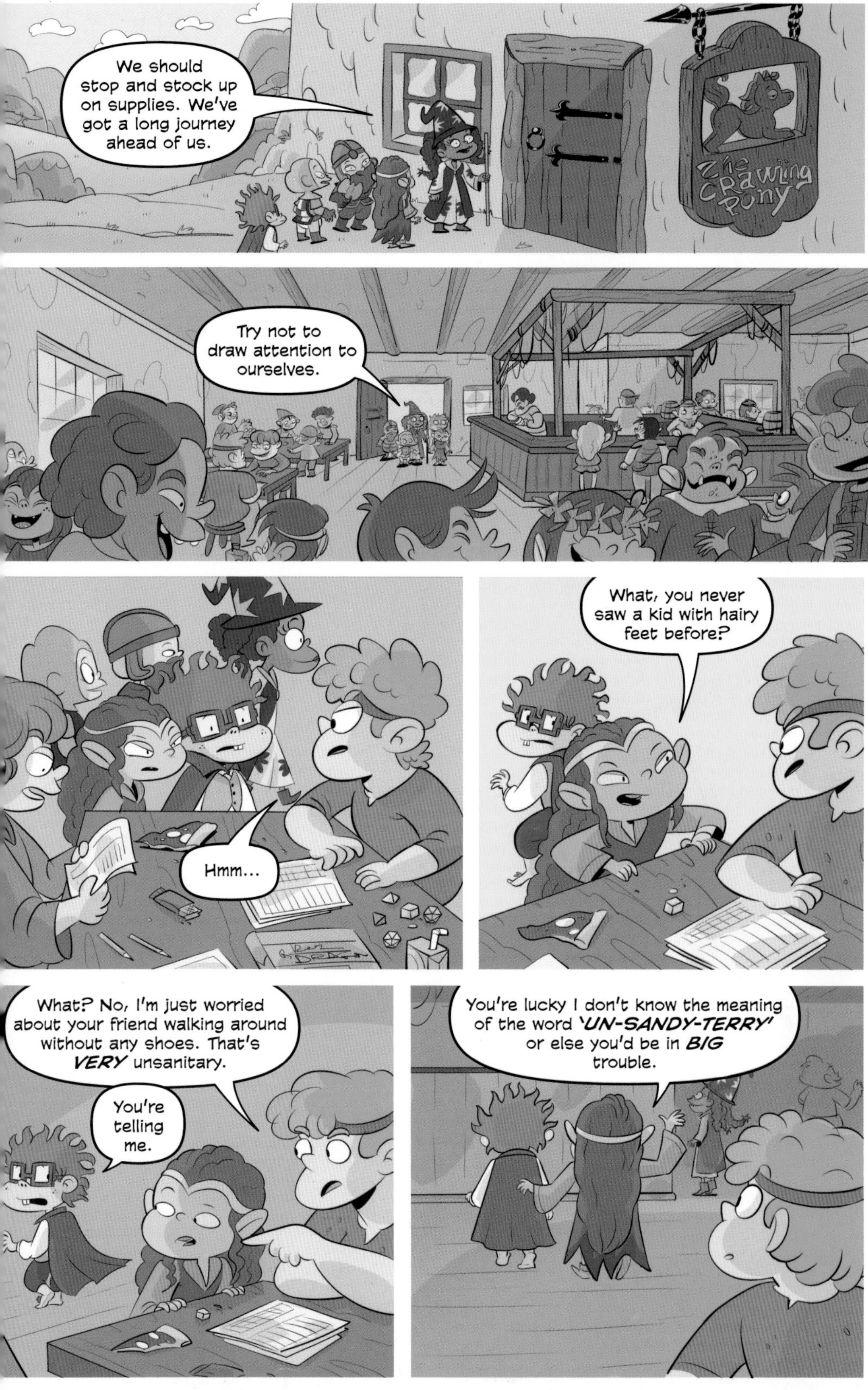
We should stop and stock up on supplies. We've got a long journey ahead of us.
The Crawling Pony
Try not to draw attention to ourselves.
Hmm...
What, you never saw a kid with hairy feet before?
What? No, I'm just worried about your friend walking around without any shoes. That's *VERY* unsanitary.
You're telling me.
You're lucky I don't know the meaning of the word *'UN-SANDY-TERRY'* or else you'd be in *BIG* trouble.

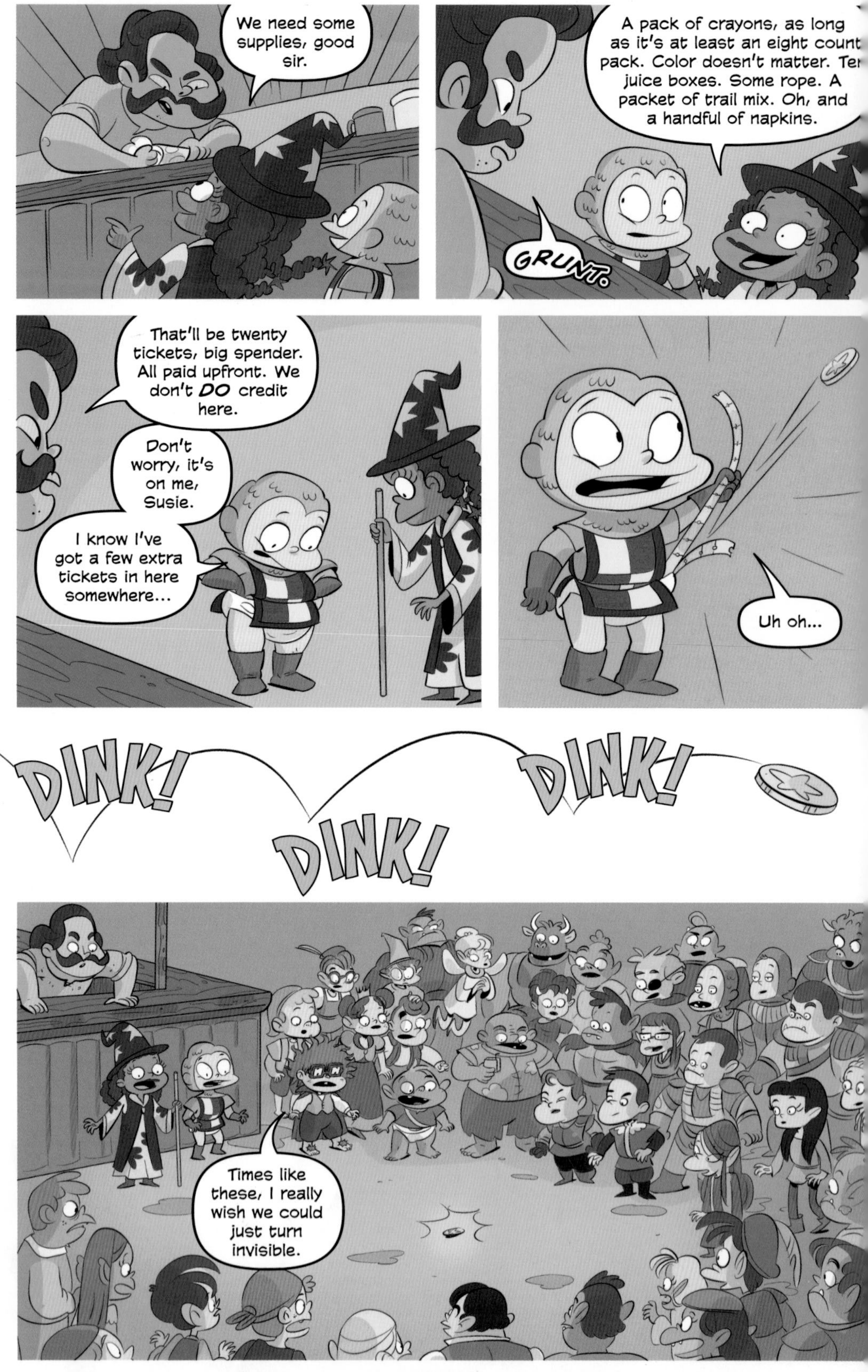
We need some supplies, good sir.
A pack of crayons, as long as it's at least an eight count pack. Color doesn't matter. Ten juice boxes. Some rope. A packet of trail mix. Oh, and a handful of napkins.
GRUNT.
That'll be twenty tickets, big spender. All paid upfront. We don't DO credit here.
Don't worry, it's on me, Susie.
I know I've got a few extra tickets in here somewhere...
Uh oh...
DINK!
DINK!
DINK!
Times like these, I really wish we could just turn invisible.

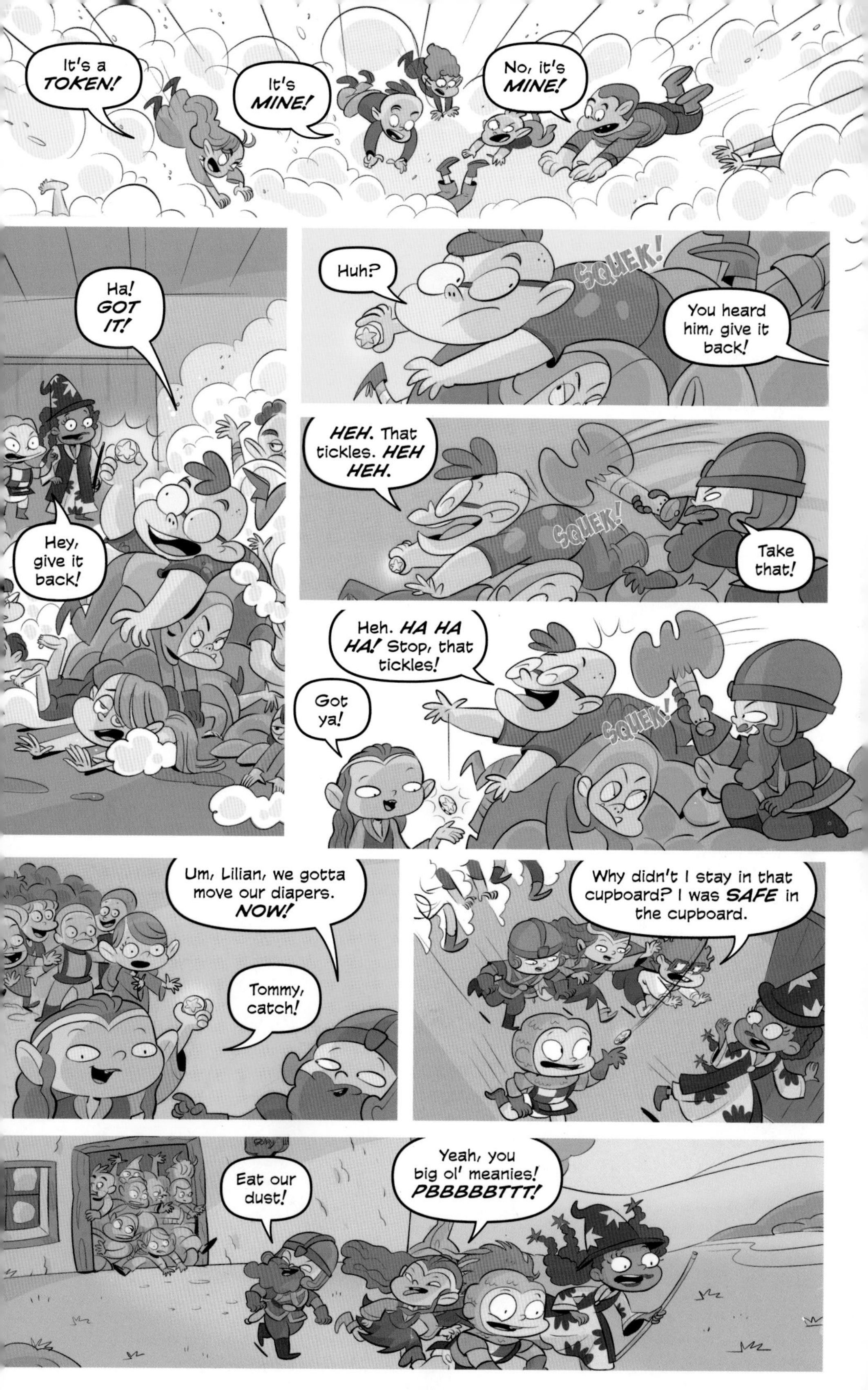
It's a TOKEN!
It's MINE!
No, it's MINE!
Ha! GOT IT!
Hey, give it back!
Huh?
SQUEK!
You heard him, give it back!
HEH. That tickles. HEH HEH.
SQUEK!
Take that!
Heh. HA HA HA! Stop, that tickles!
Got ya!
SQUEK!
Um, Lilian, we gotta move our diapers. NOW!
Tommy, catch!
Why didn't I stay in that cupboard? I was SAFE in the cupboard.
Eat our dust!
Yeah, you big ol' meanies! PBBBBBTTT!

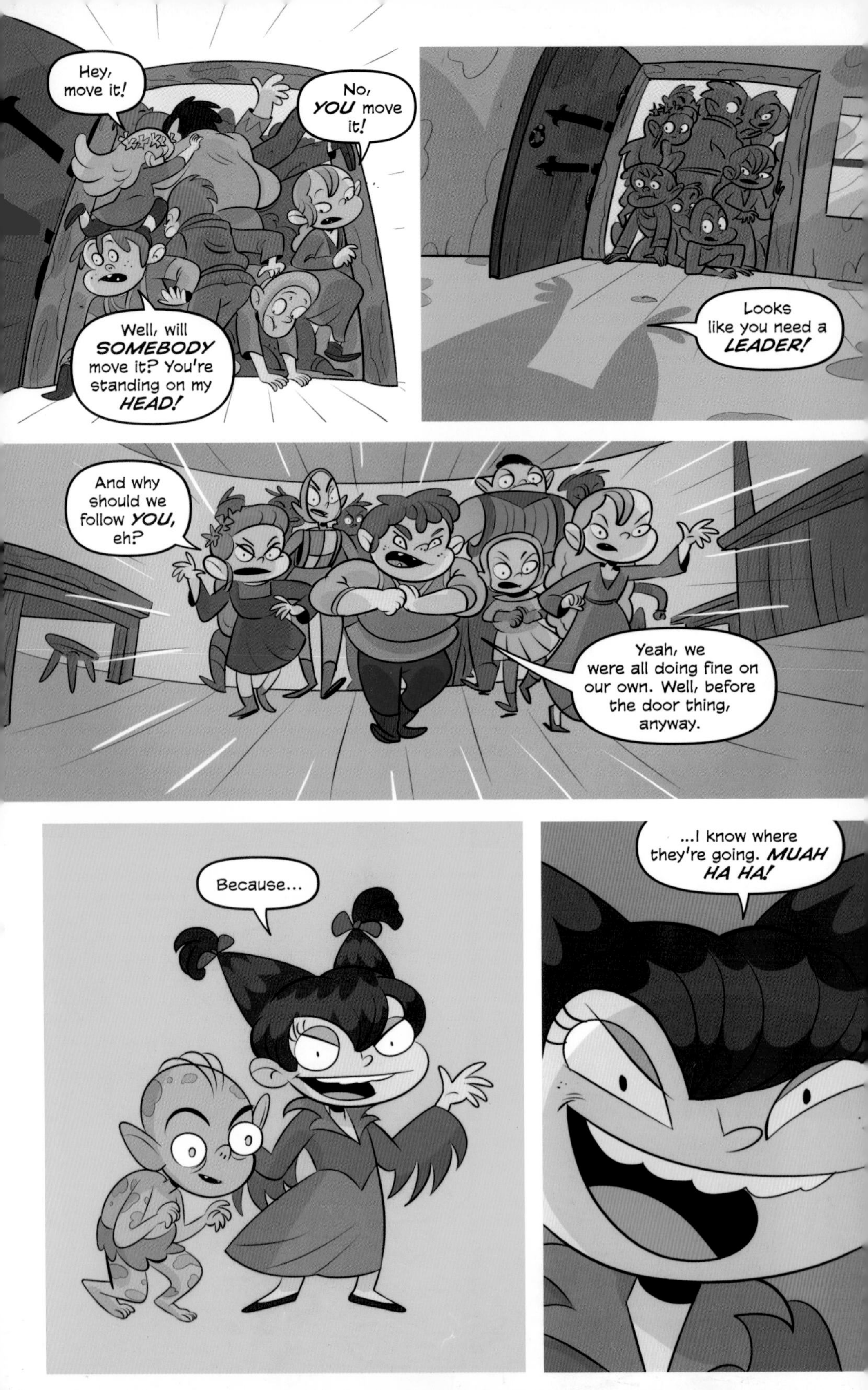
Hey, move it!
No, YOU move it!
Well, will SOMEBODY move it? You're standing on my HEAD!
Looks like you need a LEADER!
And why should we follow YOU, eh?
Yeah, we were all doing fine on our own. Well, before the door thing, anyway.
Because...
...I know where they're going. MUAH HA HA!

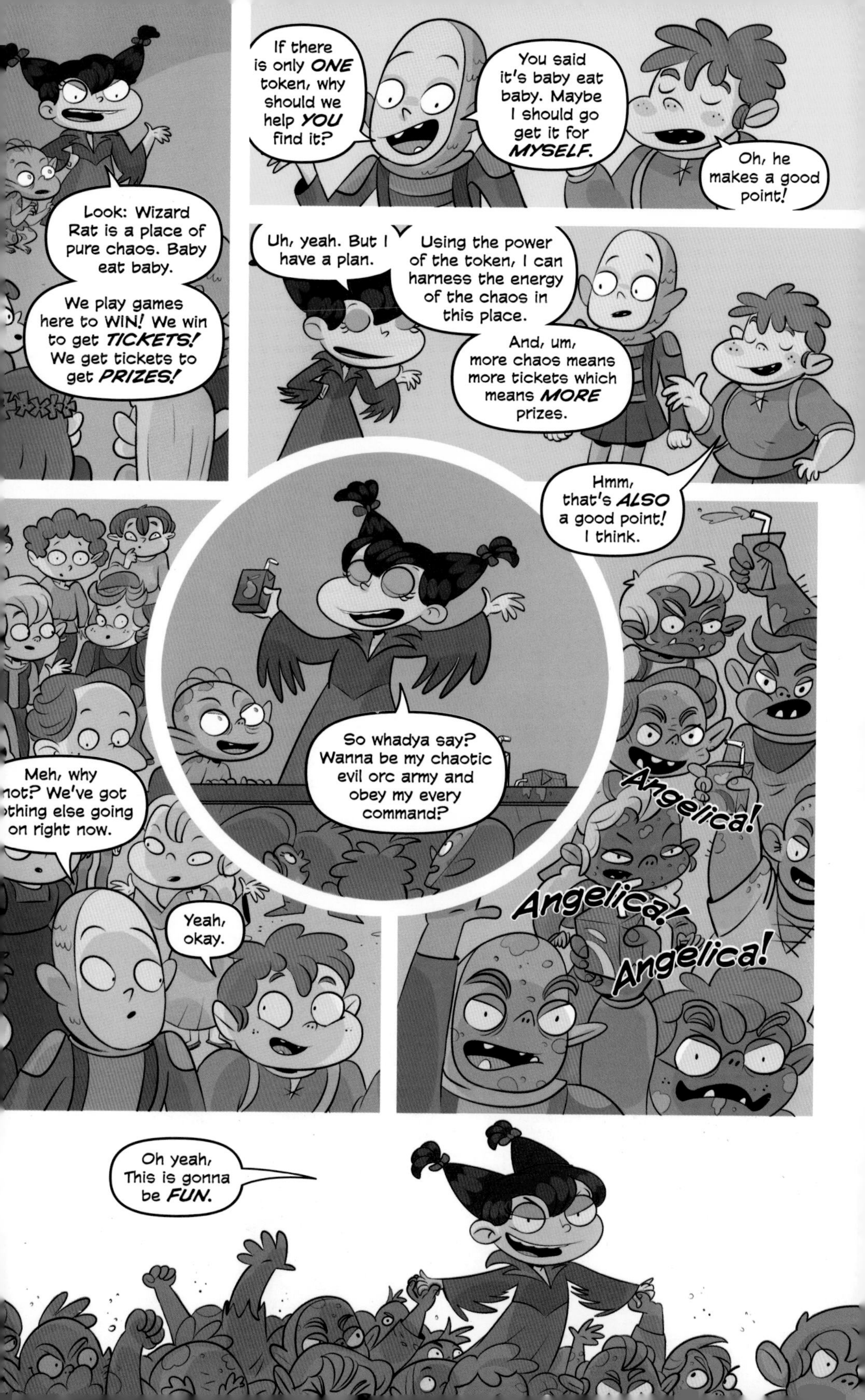

Look: Wizard Rat is a place of pure chaos. Baby eat baby.
We play games here to WIN! We win to get TICKETS! We get tickets to get PRIZES!
If there is only ONE token, why should we help YOU find it?
You said it's baby eat baby. Maybe I should go get it for MYSELF.
Oh, he makes a good point!
Uh, yeah. But I have a plan.
Using the power of the token, I can harness the energy of the chaos in this place.
And, um, more chaos means more tickets which means MORE prizes.
Hmm, that's ALSO a good point! I think.
So whadya say? Wanna be my chaotic evil orc army and obey my every command?
Meh, why not? We've got nothing else going on right now.
Yeah, okay.
Angelica!
Angelica!
Angelica!
Oh yeah, This is gonna be FUN.

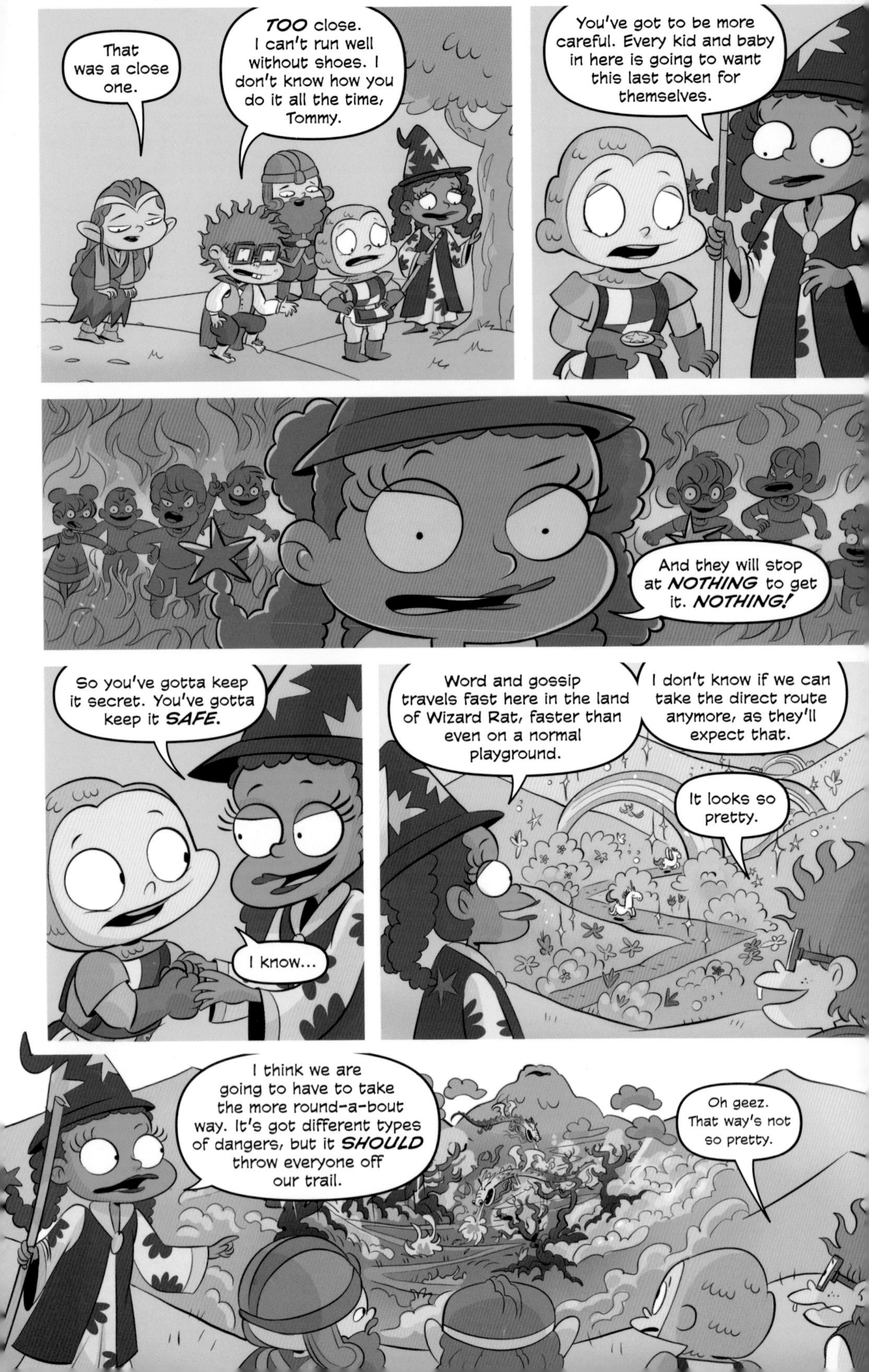
That was a close one.
TOO close. I can't run well without shoes. I don't know how you do it all the time, Tommy.
You've got to be more careful. Every kid and baby in here is going to want this last token for themselves.
And they will stop at NOTHING to get it. NOTHING!
So you've gotta keep it secret. You've gotta keep it SAFE.
I know...
Word and gossip travels fast here in the land of Wizard Rat, faster than even on a normal playground.
I don't know if we can take the direct route anymore, as they'll expect that.
It looks so pretty.
I think we are going to have to take the more round-a-bout way. It's got different types of dangers, but it SHOULD throw everyone off our trail.
Oh geez. That way's not so pretty.

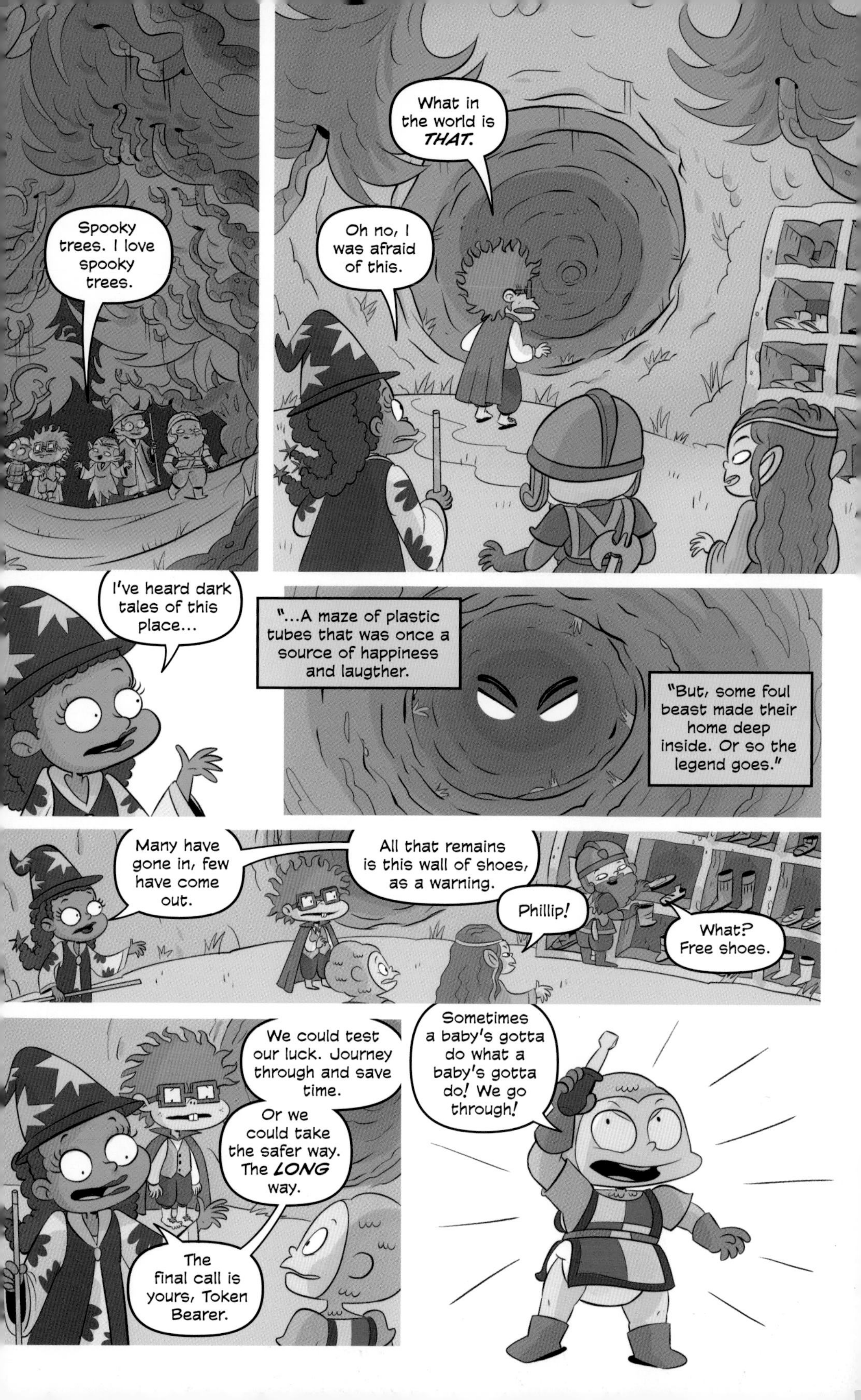
Spooky trees. I love spooky trees.
What in the world is THAT.
Oh no, I was afraid of this.
I've heard dark tales of this place...
"...A maze of plastic tubes that was once a source of happiness and laugther.
"But, some foul beast made their home deep inside. Or so the legend goes."
Many have gone in, few have come out.
All that remains is this wall of shoes, as a warning.
Phillip!
What? Free shoes.
We could test our luck. Journey through and save time.
Or we could take the safer way. The LONG way.
The final call is yours, Token Bearer.
Sometimes a baby's gotta do what a baby's gotta do! We go through!

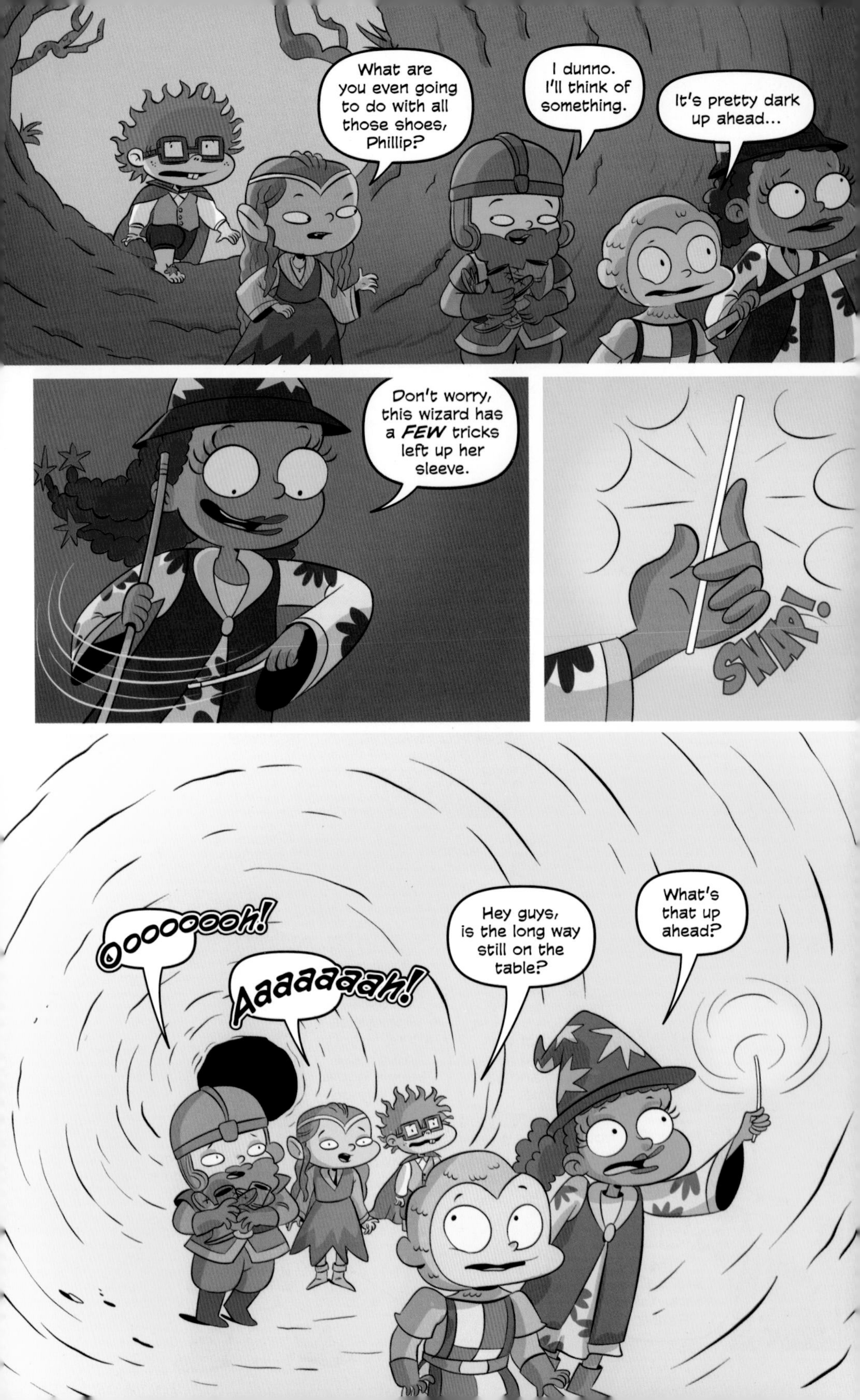
What are you even going to do with all those shoes, Phillip?
I dunno. I'll think of something.
It's pretty dark up ahead...
Don't worry, this wizard has a FEW tricks left up her sleeve.
SNAP!
Oooooooh!
Aaaaaaaah!
Hey guys, is the long way still on the table?
What's that up ahead?

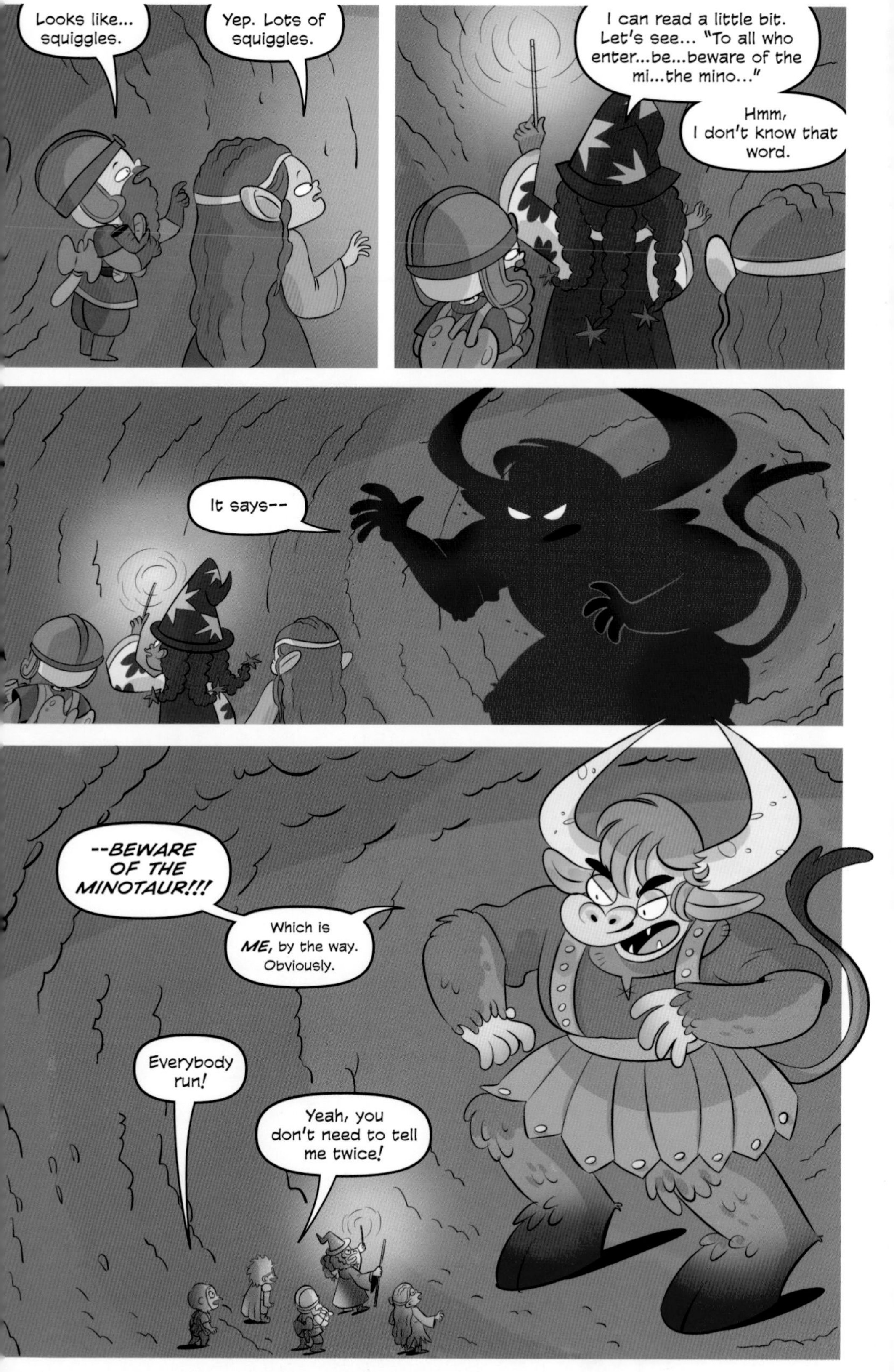
Looks like... squiggles.
Yep. Lots of squiggles.
I can read a little bit. Let's see... "To all who enter...be...beware of the mi...the mino..."
Hmm, I don't know that word.
It says--
--BEWARE OF THE MINOTAUR!!!
Which is ME, by the way. Obviously.
Everybody run!
Yeah, you don't need to tell me twice!

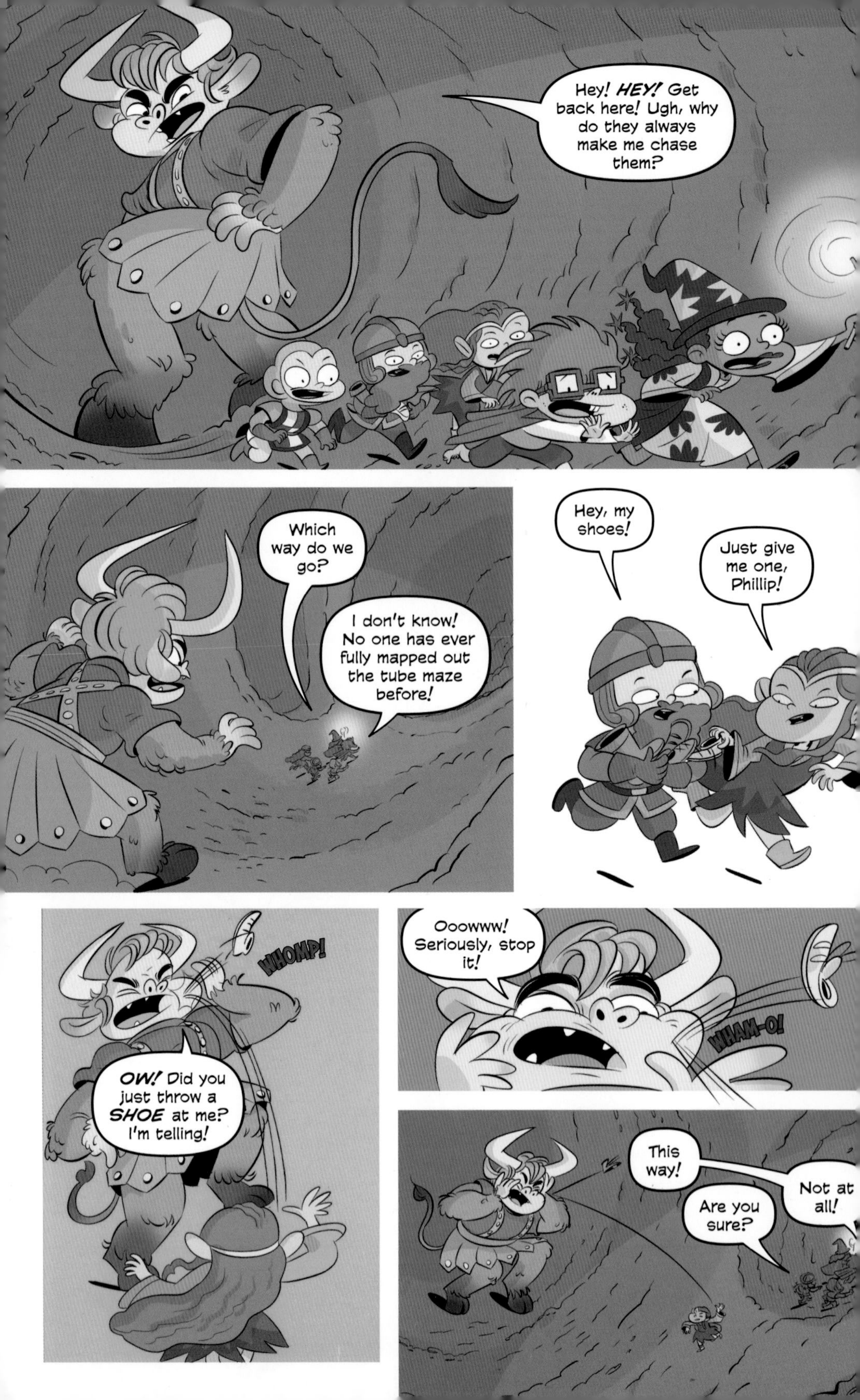

Hey! HEY! Get back here! Ugh, why do they always make me chase them?
Which way do we go?
I don't know! No one has ever fully mapped out the tube maze before!
Hey, my shoes!
Just give me one, Phillip!
WHOMP!
OW! Did you just throw a SHOE at me? I'm telling!
Ooowww! Seriously, stop it!
WHAM-O!
This way!
Are you sure?
Not at all!

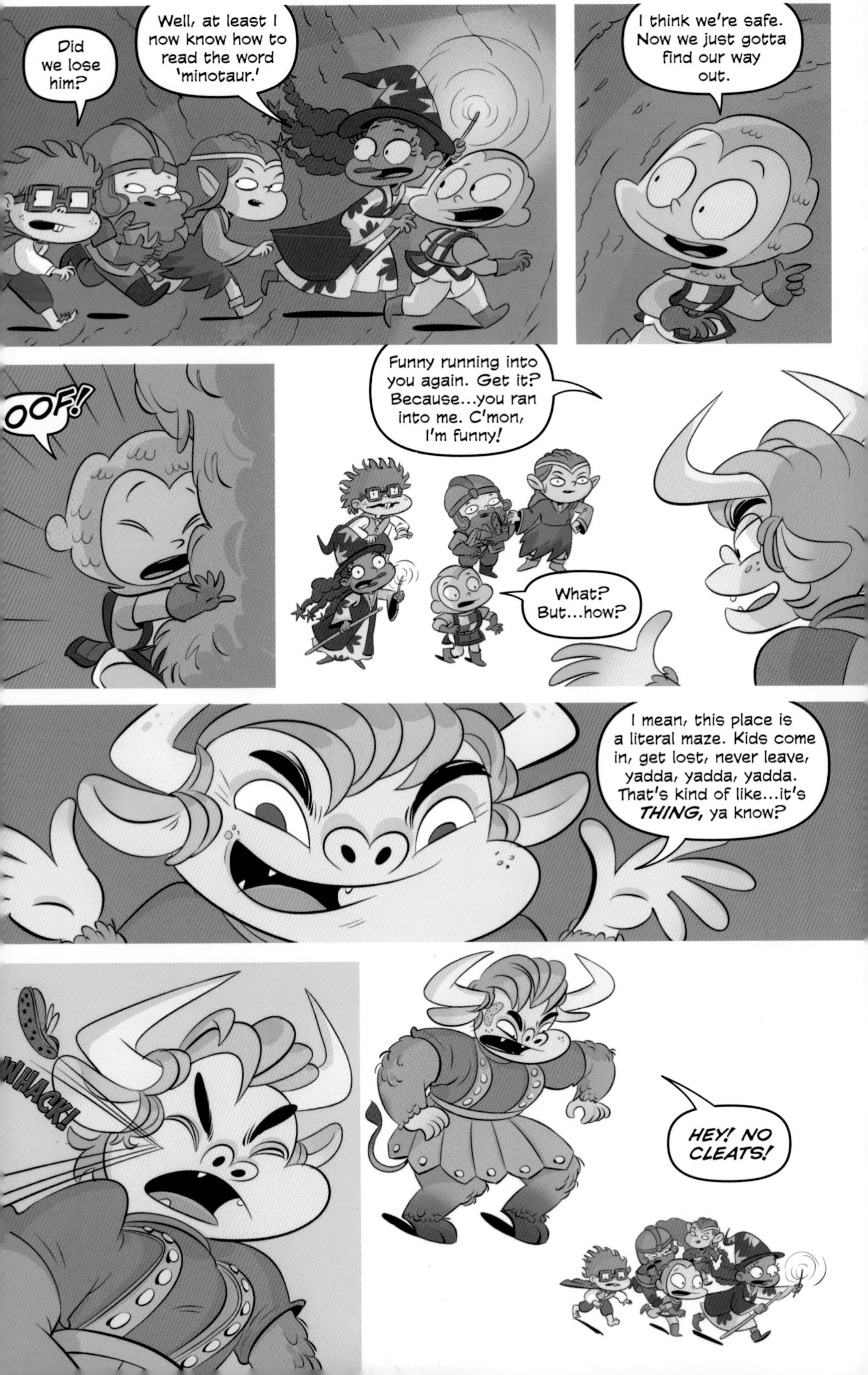
Did we lose him?
Well, at least I now know how to read the word 'minotaur.'
I think we're safe. Now we just gotta find our way out.
OOF!
Funny running into you again. Get it? Because...you ran into me. C'mon, I'm funny!
What? But...how?
I mean, this place is a literal maze. Kids come in, get lost, never leave, yadda, yadda, yadda. That's kind of like...it's THING, ya know?
WHACK!
HEY! NO CLEATS!

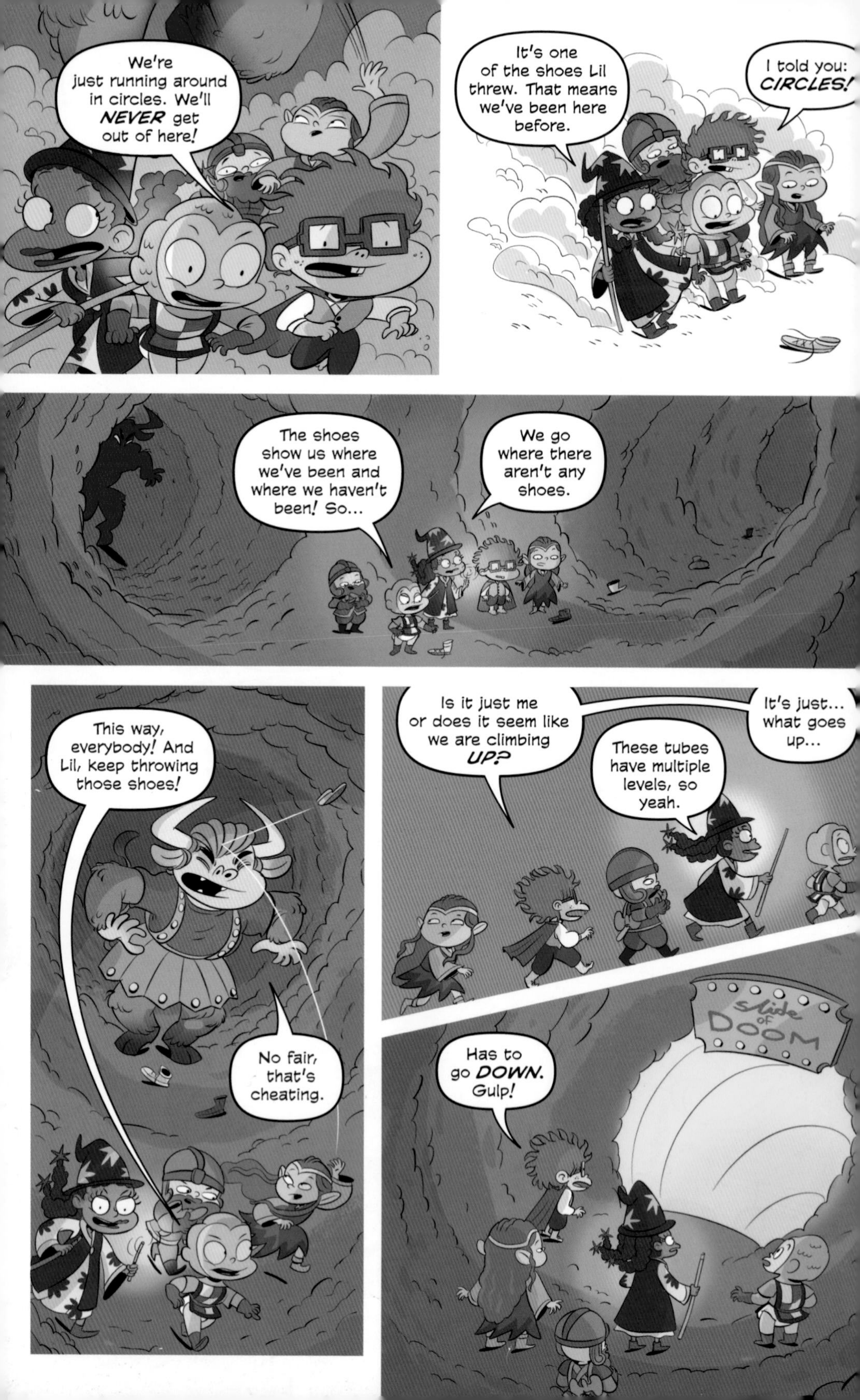

We're just running around in circles. We'll **NEVER** get out of here!
It's one of the shoes Lil threw. That means we've been here before.
I told you: ***CIRCLES!***
The shoes show us where we've been and where we haven't been! So...
We go where there aren't any shoes.
This way, everybody! And Lil, keep throwing those shoes!
No fair, that's cheating.
Is it just me or does it seem like we are climbing ***UP?***
It's just... what goes up...
These tubes have multiple levels, so yeah.
Slide OF DOOM
Has to go ***DOWN.*** Gulp!

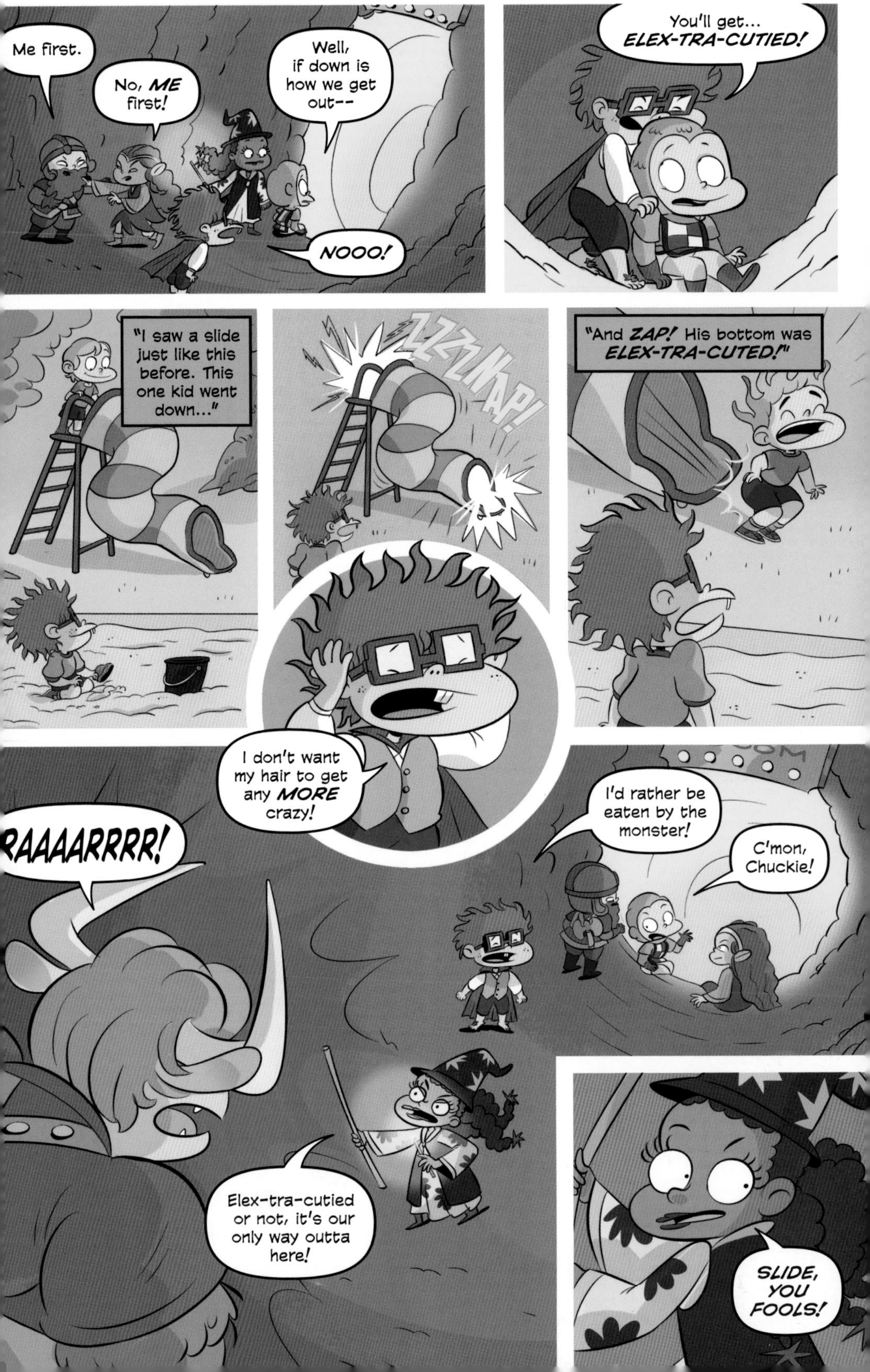

Me first.
No, ME first!
Well, if down is how we get out--
NOOO!
You'll get... ELEX-TRA-CUTIED!
"I saw a slide just like this before. This one kid went down..."
ZZZZZAP!
"And ZAP! His bottom was ELEX-TRA-CUTED!"
I don't want my hair to get any MORE crazy!
I'd rather be eaten by the monster!
C'mon, Chuckie!
RAAAARRRR!
Elex-tra-cutied or not, it's our only way outta here!
SLIDE, YOU FOOLS!

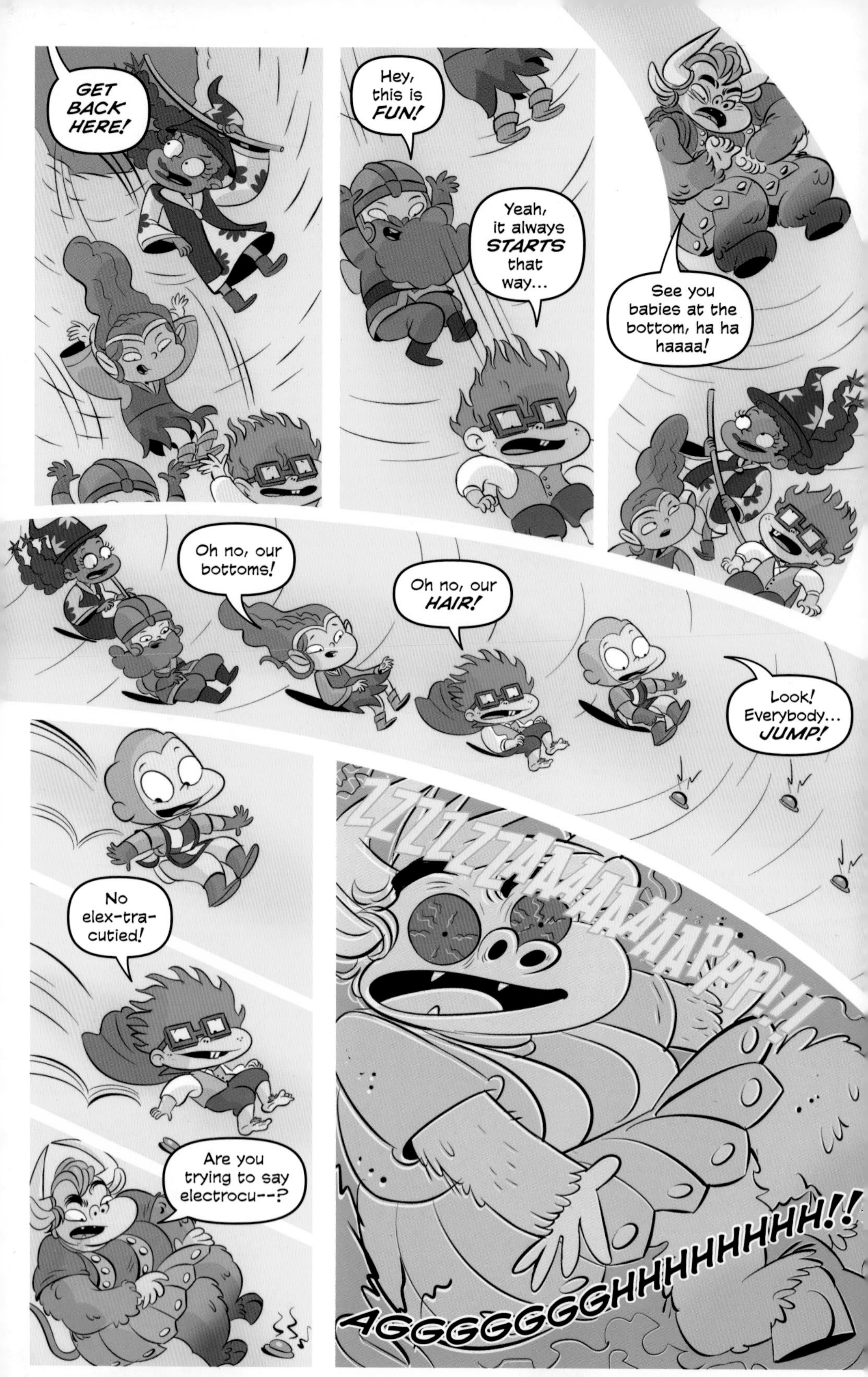
GET BACK HERE!
Hey, this is FUN!
Yeah, it always STARTS that way...
See you babies at the bottom, ha ha haaaa!
Oh no, our bottoms!
Oh no, our HAIR!
Look! Everybody... JUMP!
No elex-tra-cutied!
Are you trying to say electrocu--?
ZZZZZZAAAAAAAAAPPP!!!
AGGGGGGGHHHHHHHH!!

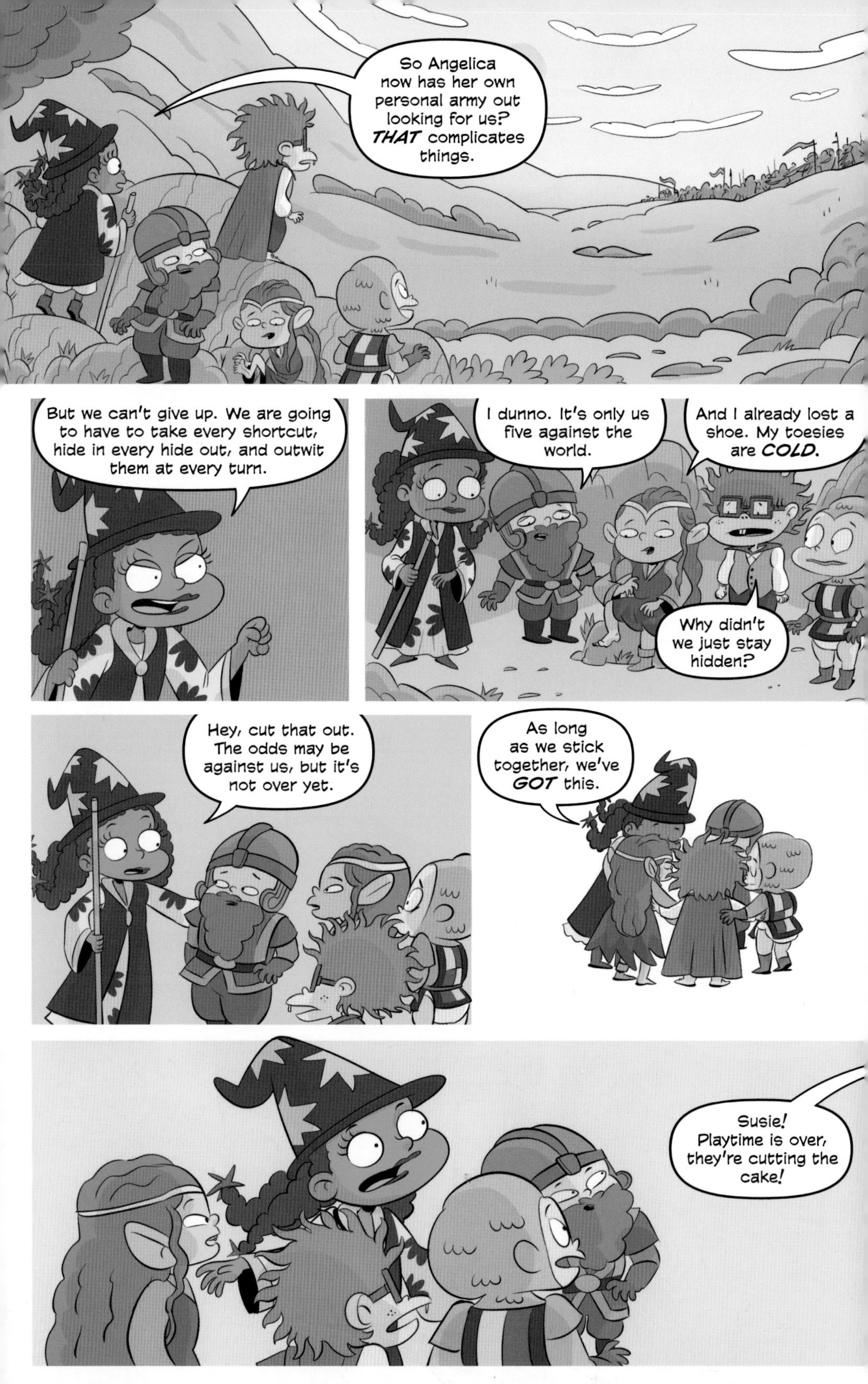
So Angelica now has her own personal army out looking for us? THAT complicates things.
But we can't give up. We are going to have to take every shortcut, hide in every hide out, and outwit them at every turn.
I dunno. It's only us five against the world.
And I already lost a shoe. My toesies are COLD.
Why didn't we just stay hidden?
Hey, cut that out. The odds may be against us, but it's not over yet.
As long as we stick together, we've GOT this.
Susie! Playtime is over, they're cutting the cake!

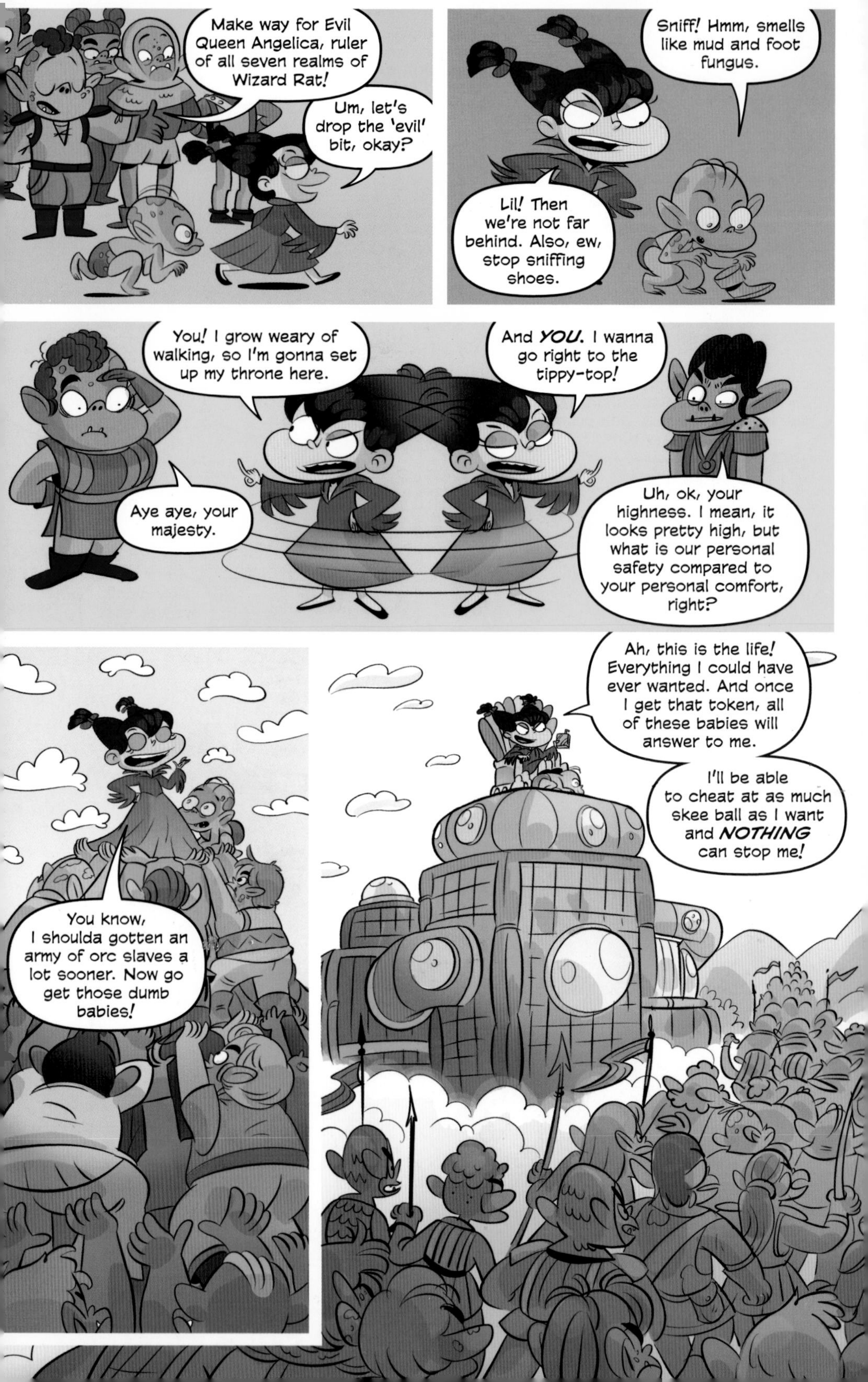
Make way for Evil Queen Angelica, ruler of all seven realms of Wizard Rat!
Um, let's drop the 'evil' bit, okay?
Sniff! Hmm, smells like mud and foot fungus.
Lil! Then we're not far behind. Also, ew, stop sniffing shoes.
You! I grow weary of walking, so I'm gonna set up my throne here.
And YOU. I wanna go right to the tippy-top!
Aye aye, your majesty.
Uh, ok, your highness. I mean, it looks pretty high, but what is our personal safety compared to your personal comfort, right?
You know, I shoulda gotten an army of orc slaves a lot sooner. Now go get those dumb babies!
Ah, this is the life! Everything I could have ever wanted. And once I get that token, all of these babies will answer to me.
I'll be able to cheat at as much skee ball as I want and NOTHING can stop me!

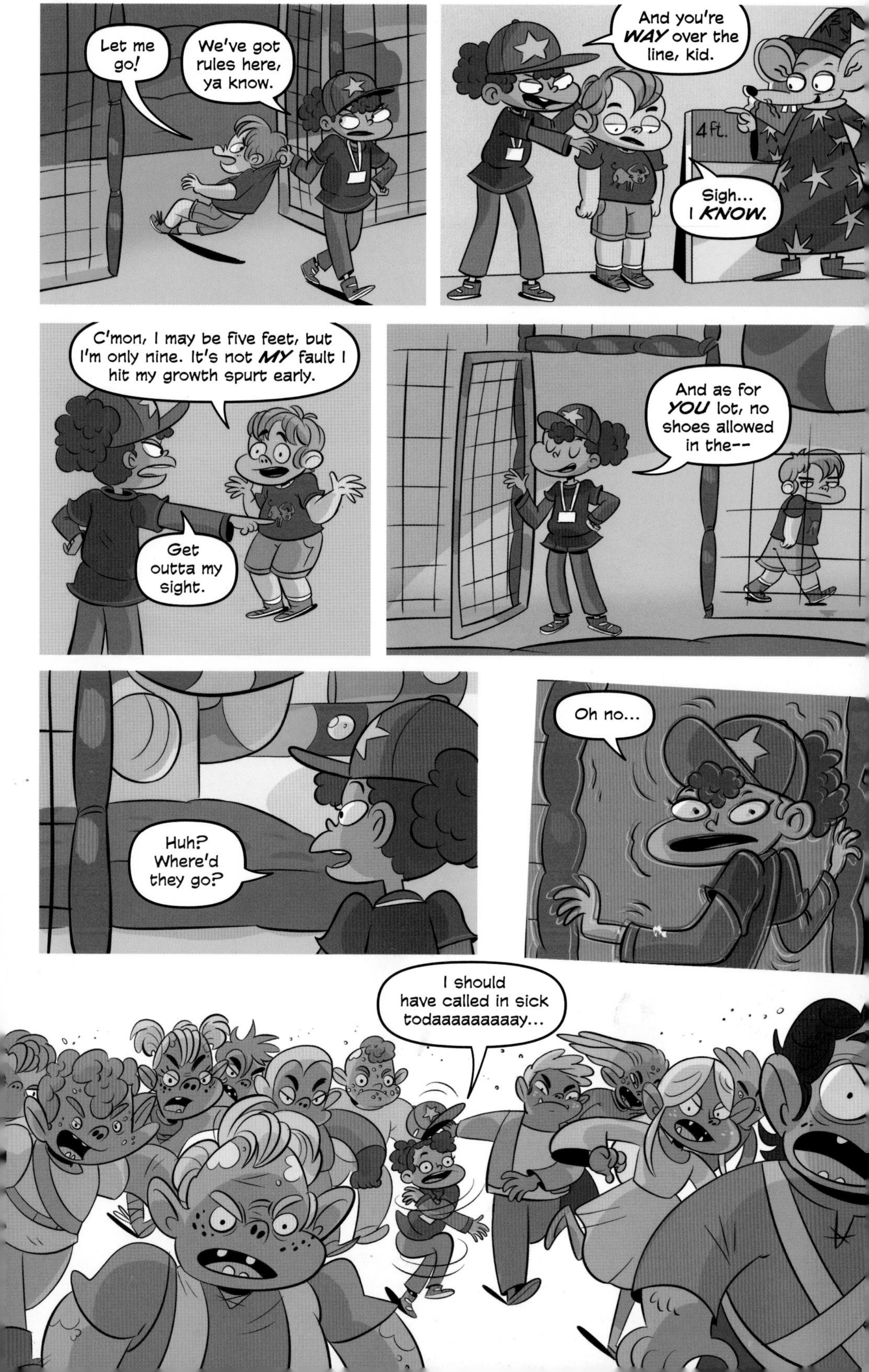
Let me go!
We've got rules here, ya know.
And you're WAY over the line, kid.
4ft.
Sigh... I KNOW.
C'mon, I may be five feet, but I'm only nine. It's not MY fault I hit my growth spurt early.
Get outta my sight.
And as for YOU lot, no shoes allowed in the--
Huh? Where'd they go?
Oh no...
I should have called in sick todaaaaaaaaay...

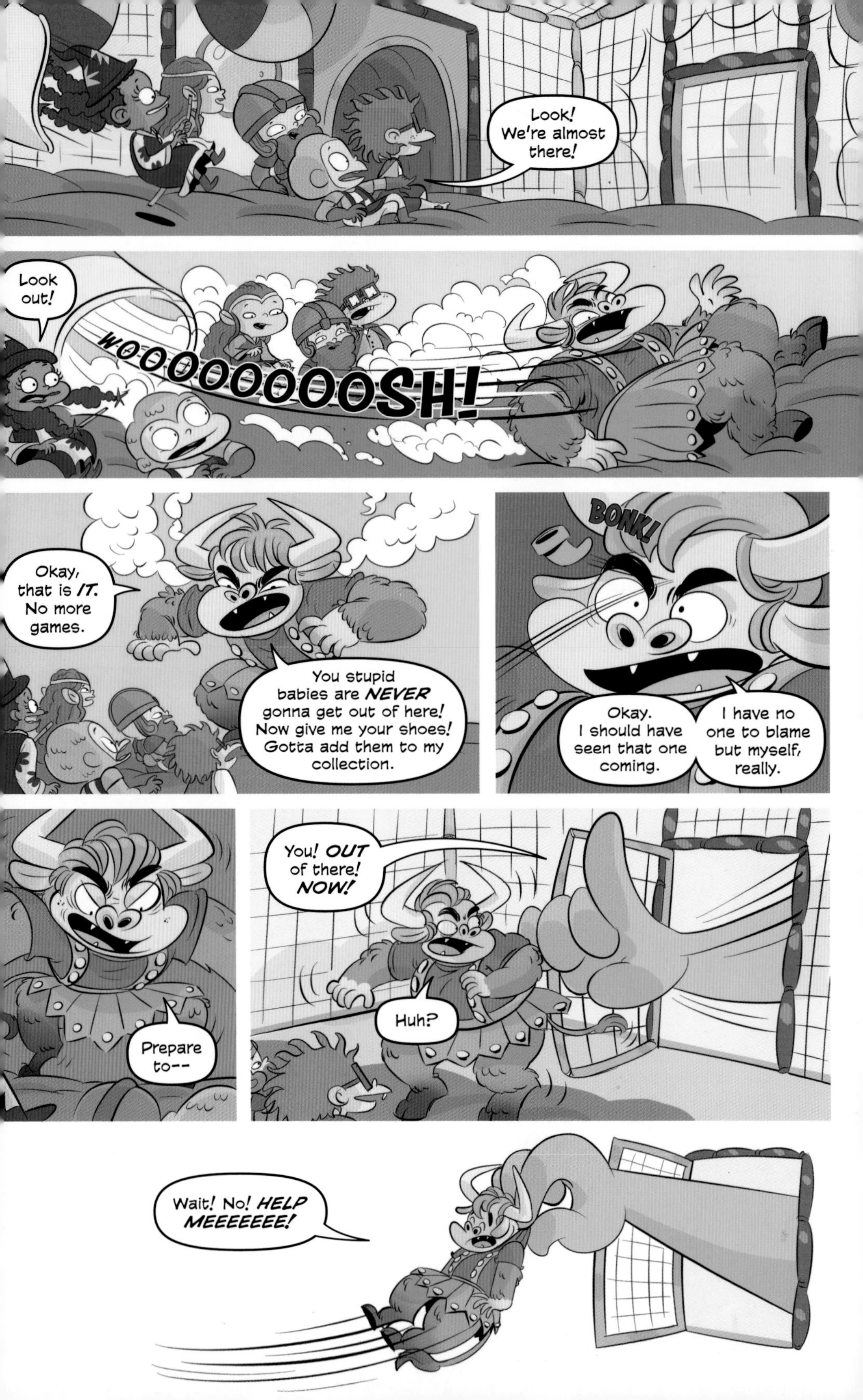
Look! We're almost there!
Look out!
WOOOOOOOOOSH!
Okay, that is IT. No more games.
You stupid babies are NEVER gonna get out of here! Now give me your shoes! Gotta add them to my collection.
BONK!
Okay. I should have seen that one coming.
I have no one to blame but myself, really.
Prepare to--
You! OUT of there! NOW!
Huh?
Wait! No! HELP MEEEEEEE!

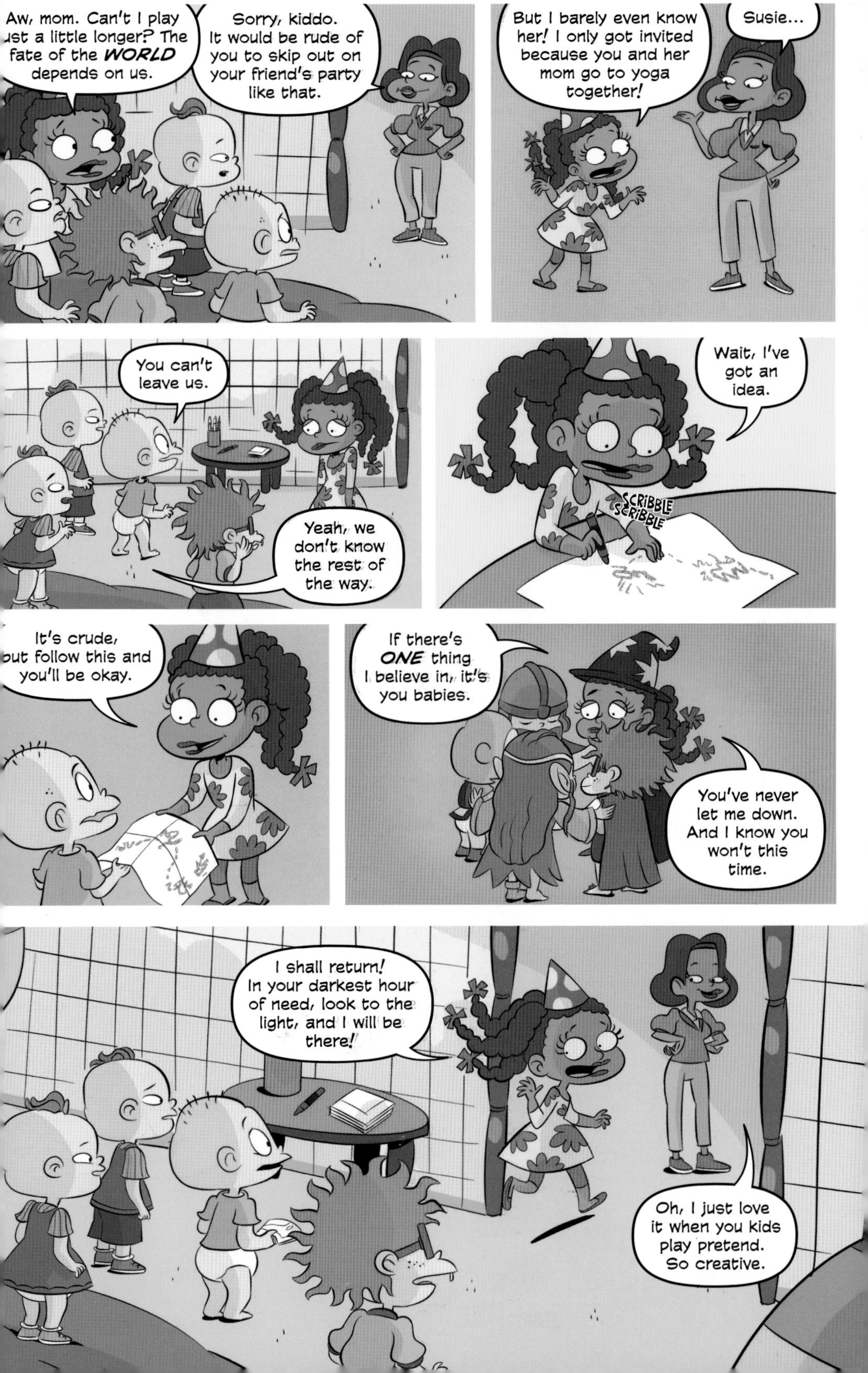

Aw, mom. Can't I play just a little longer? The fate of the WORLD depends on us.
Sorry, kiddo. It would be rude of you to skip out on your friend's party like that.
But I barely even know her! I only got invited because you and her mom go to yoga together!
Susie...
You can't leave us.
Yeah, we don't know the rest of the way.
Wait, I've got an idea.
SCRIBBLE SCRIBBLE
It's crude, but follow this and you'll be okay.
If there's ONE thing I believe in, it's you babies.
You've never let me down. And I know you won't this time.
I shall return! In your darkest hour of need, look to the light, and I will be there!
Oh, I just love it when you kids play pretend. So creative.

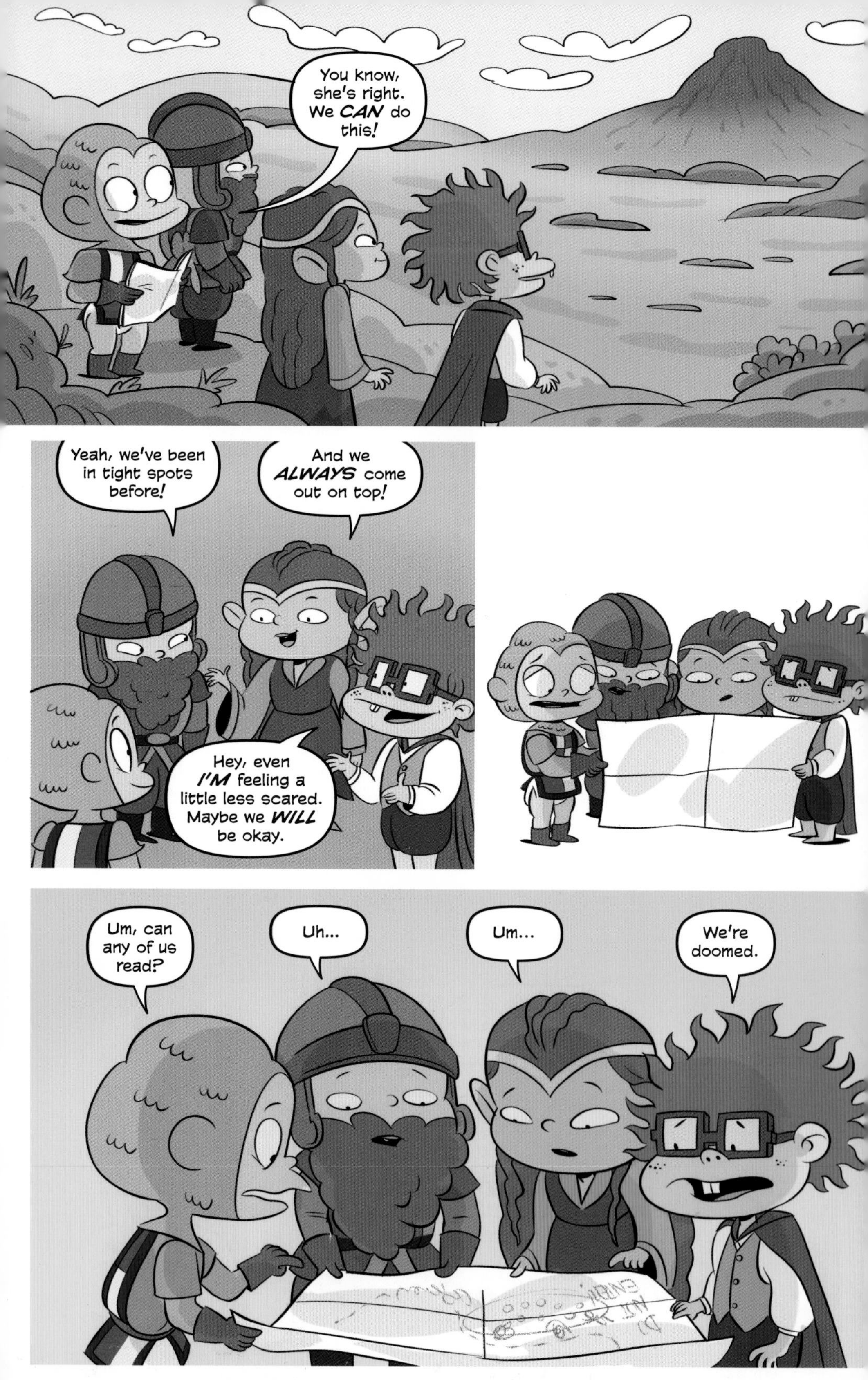
You know, she's right. We CAN do this!
Yeah, we've been in tight spots before!
And we ALWAYS come out on top!
Hey, even I'M feeling a little less scared. Maybe we WILL be okay.
Um, can any of us read?
Uh...
Um...
We're doomed.

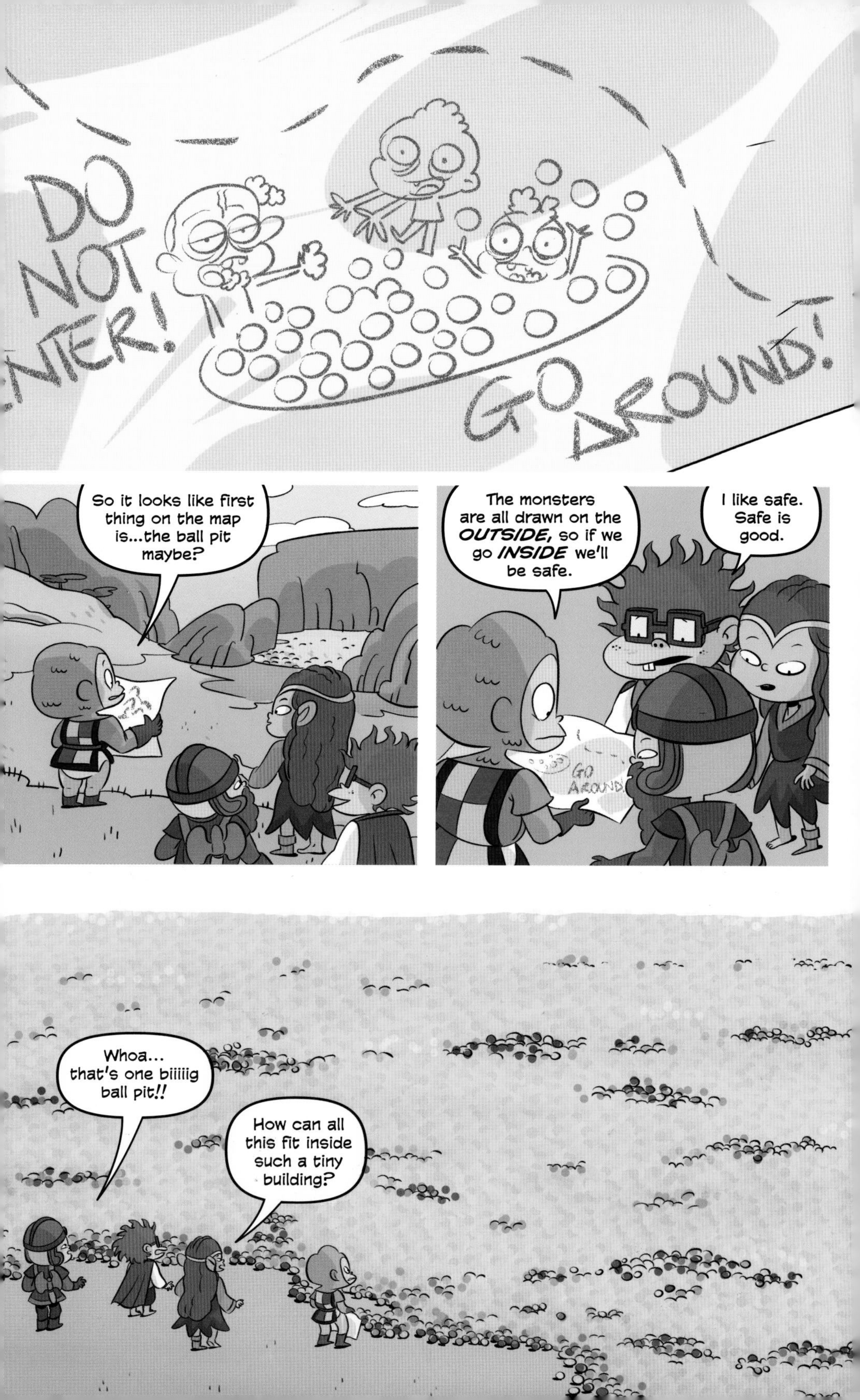
DO NOT ENTER!
GO AROUND!
So it looks like first thing on the map is...the ball pit maybe?
The monsters are all drawn on the OUTSIDE, so if we go INSIDE we'll be safe.
I like safe. Safe is good.
GO AROUND!
Whoa... that's one biiiiig ball pit!!
How can all this fit inside such a tiny building?

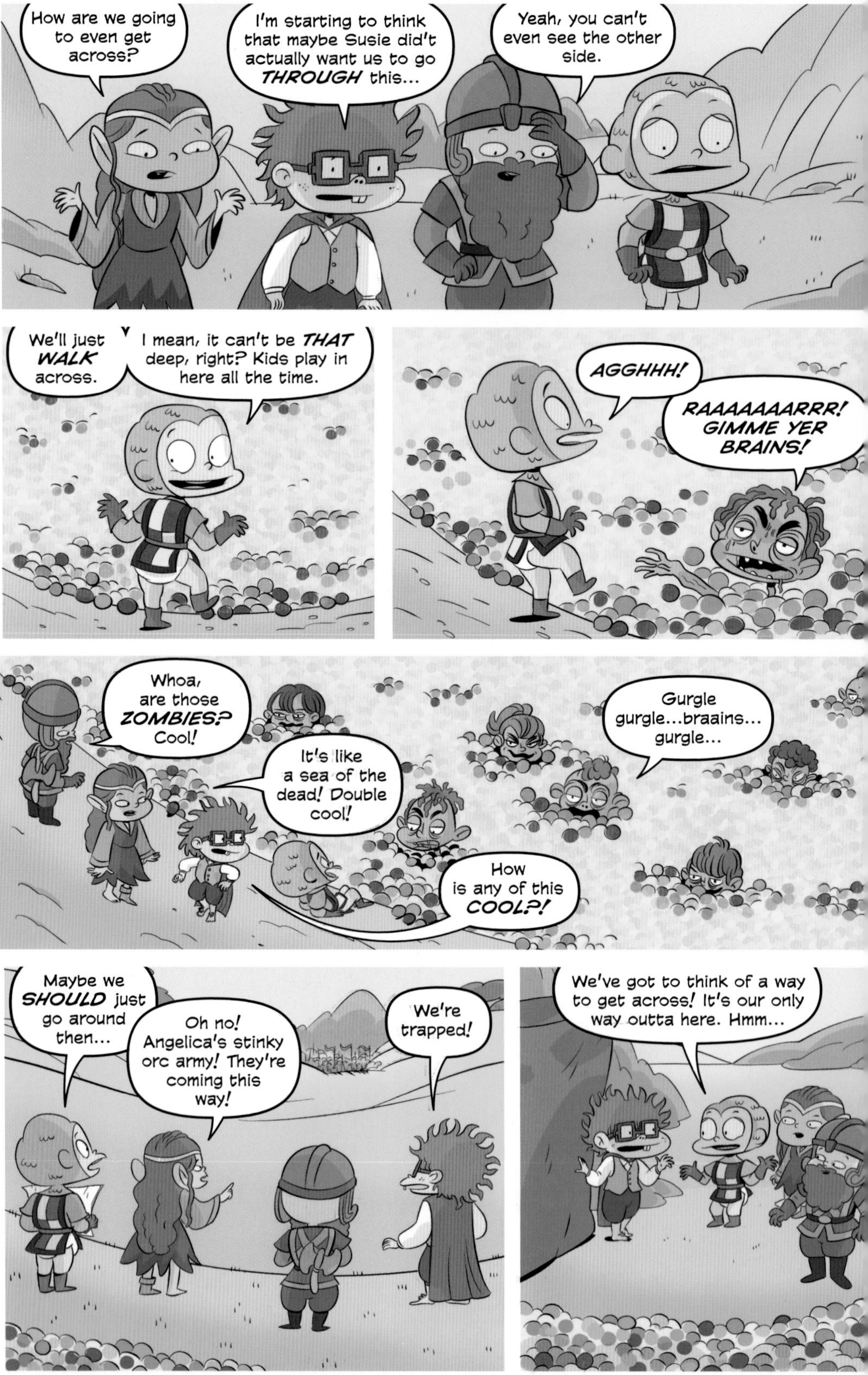
How are we going to even get across?
I'm starting to think that maybe Susie did't actually want us to go THROUGH this...
Yeah, you can't even see the other side.
We'll just WALK across.
I mean, it can't be THAT deep, right? Kids play in here all the time.
AGGHHH!
RAAAAAAARRR! GIMME YER BRAINS!
Whoa, are those ZOMBIES? Cool!
It's like a sea of the dead! Double cool!
Gurgle gurgle...braains... gurgle...
How is any of this COOL?!
Maybe we SHOULD just go around then...
Oh no! Angelica's stinky orc army! They're coming this way!
We're trapped!
We've got to think of a way to get across! It's our only way outta here. Hmm...

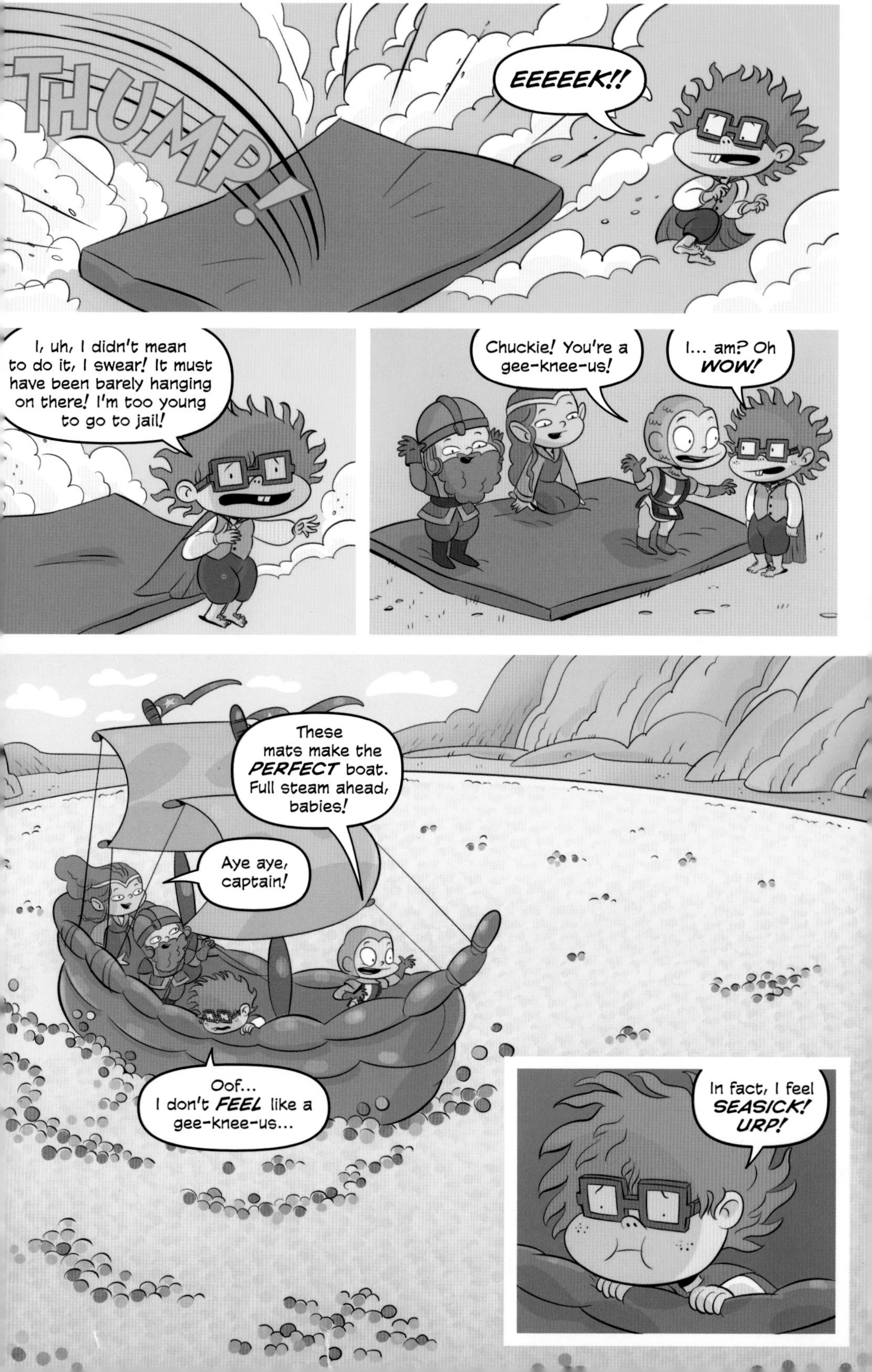
THUMP!
EEEEEK!!
I, uh, I didn't mean to do it, I swear! It must have been barely hanging on there! I'm too young to go to jail!
Chuckie! You're a gee-knee-us!
I... am? Oh WOW!
These mats make the PERFECT boat. Full steam ahead, babies!
Aye aye, captain!
Oof... I don't FEEL like a gee-knee-us...
In fact, I feel SEASICK! URP!

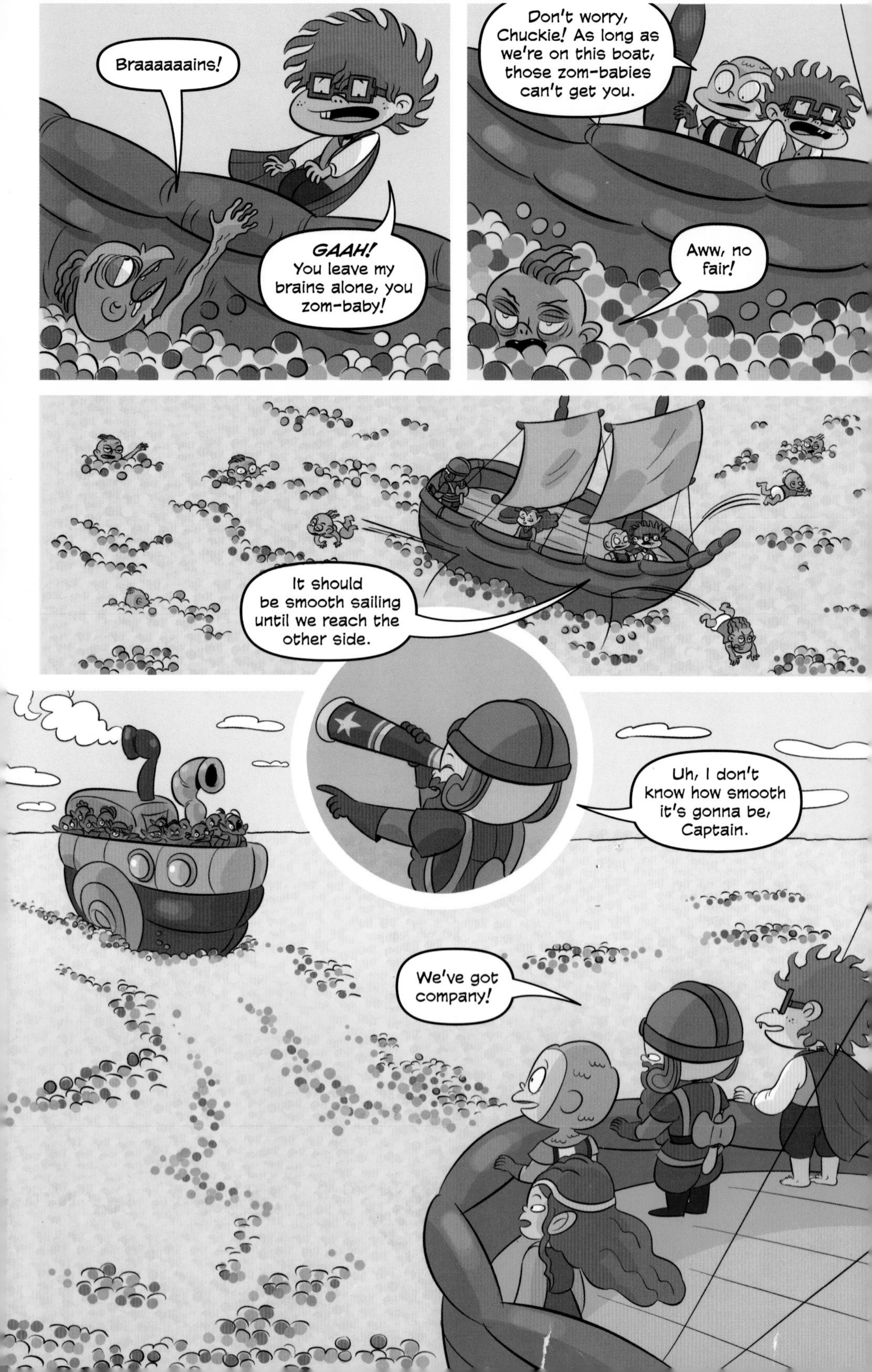
Braaaaaaains!
GAAH! You leave my brains alone, you zom-baby!
Don't worry, Chuckie! As long as we're on this boat, those zom-babies can't get you.
Aww, no fair!
It should be smooth sailing until we reach the other side.
Uh, I don't know how smooth it's gonna be, Captain.
We've got company!

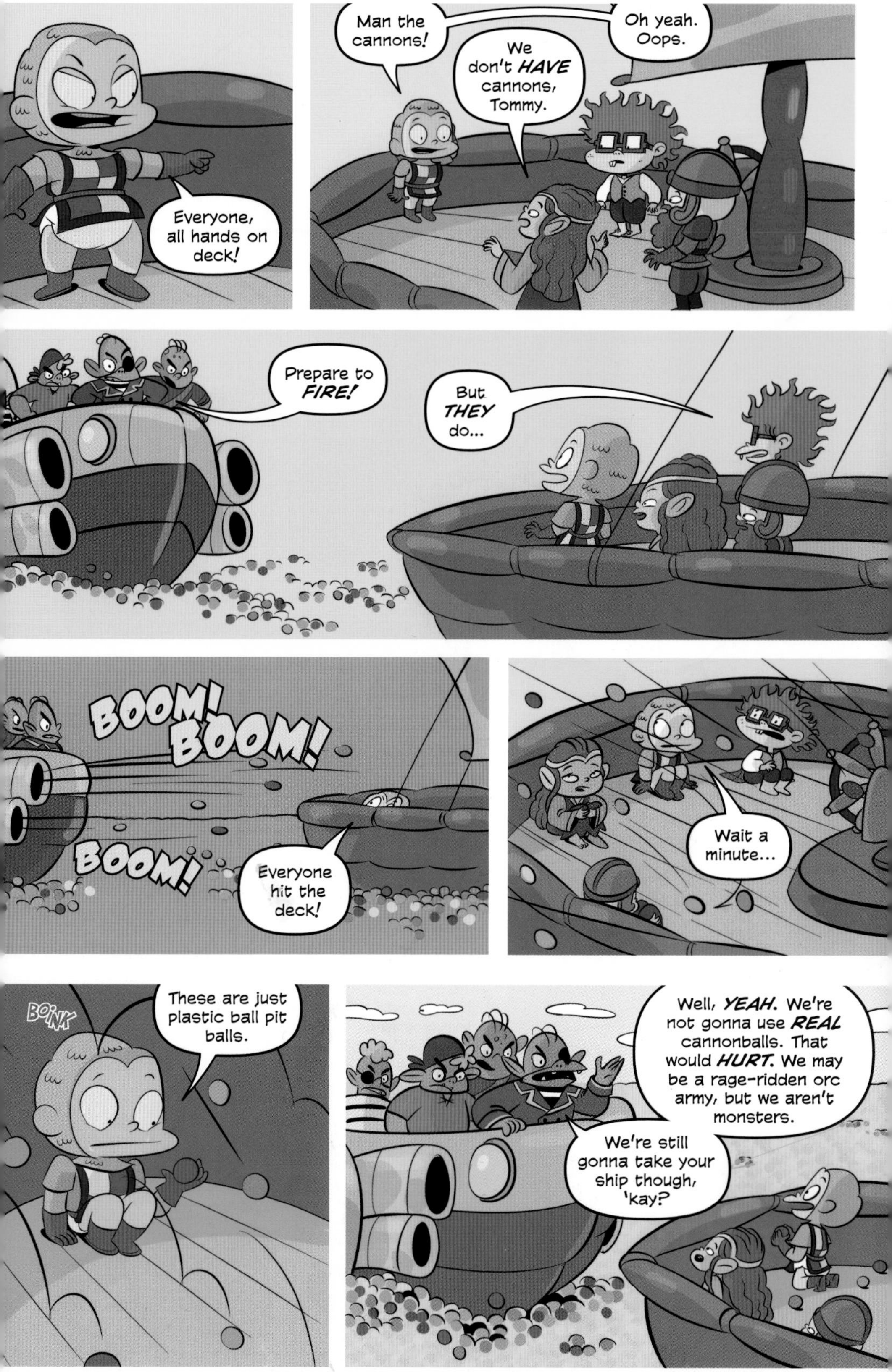
Everyone, all hands on deck!
Man the cannons!
We don't HAVE cannons, Tommy.
Oh yeah. Oops.
Prepare to FIRE!
But THEY do...
BOOM! BOOM!
BOOM!
Everyone hit the deck!
Wait a minute...
BOINK
These are just plastic ball pit balls.
Well, YEAH. We're not gonna use REAL cannonballs. That would HURT. We may be a rage-ridden orc army, but we aren't monsters.
We're still gonna take your ship though, 'kay?

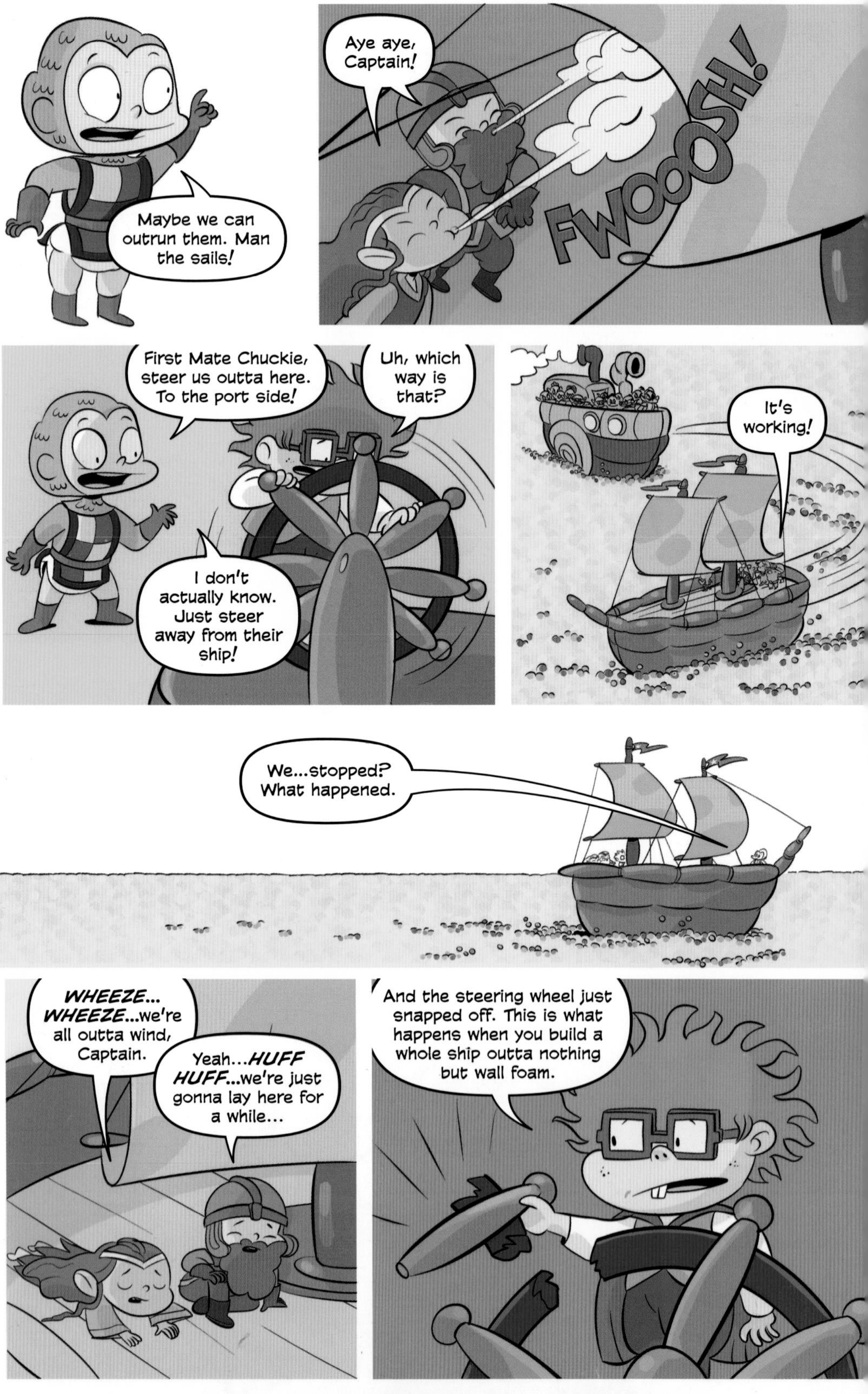
Maybe we can outrun them. Man the sails!
Aye aye, Captain!
FWOOOSH!
First Mate Chuckie, steer us outta here. To the port side!
Uh, which way is that?
I don't actually know. Just steer away from their ship!
It's working!
We...stopped? What happened.
WHEEZE... WHEEZE...we're all outta wind, Captain.
Yeah...HUFF HUFF...we're just gonna lay here for a while...
And the steering wheel just snapped off. This is what happens when you build a whole ship outta nothing but wall foam.

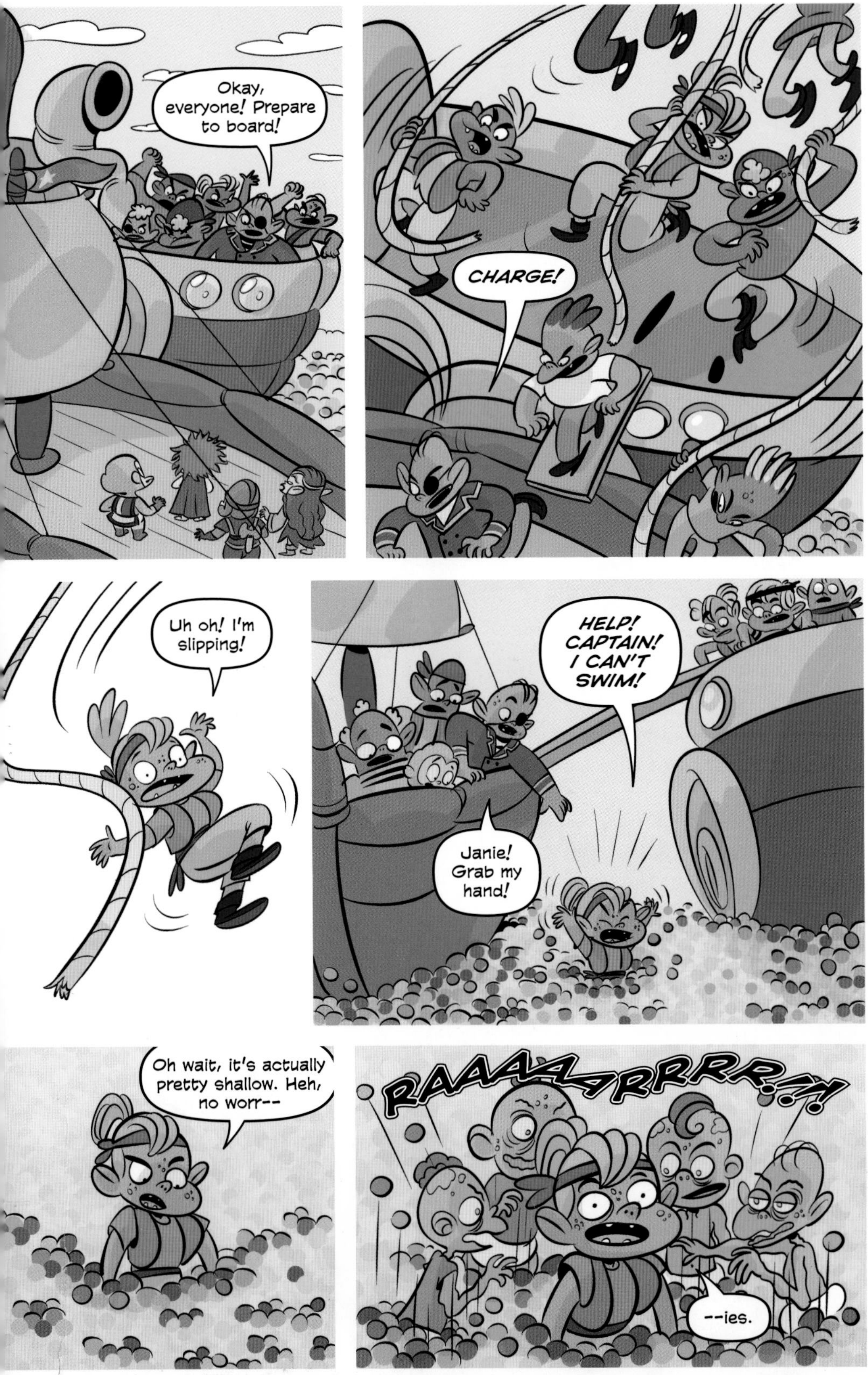

Okay, everyone! Prepare to board!
CHARGE!
Uh oh! I'm slipping!
HELP! CAPTAIN! I CAN'T SWIM!
Janie! Grab my hand!
Oh wait, it's actually pretty shallow. Heh, no worr--
RAAAAARRRR!!!
--ies.

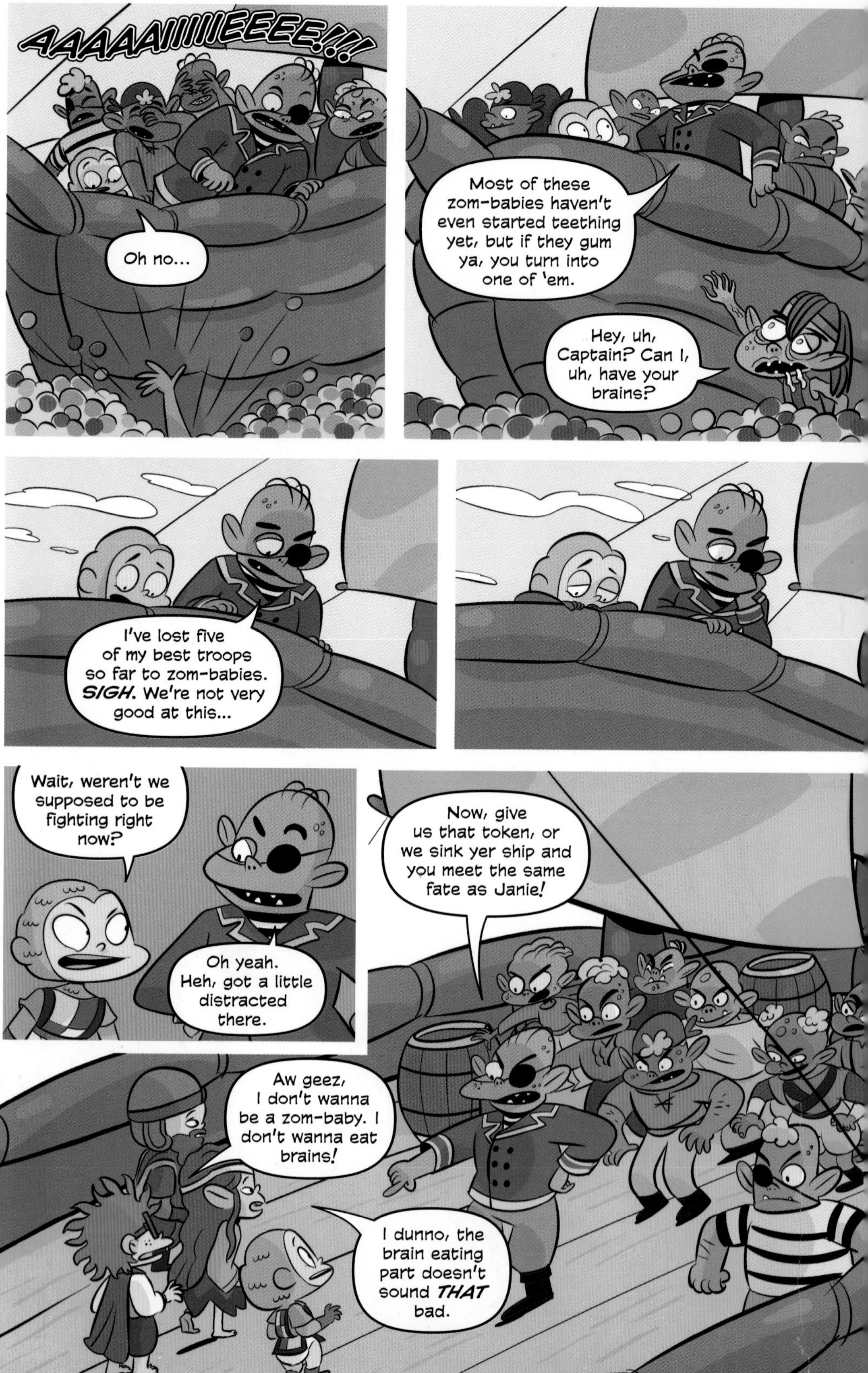
AAAAAIIIIIEEEEE!!!!
Oh no...
Most of these zom-babies haven't even started teething yet, but if they gum ya, you turn into one of 'em.
Hey, uh, Captain? Can I, uh, have your brains?
I've lost five of my best troops so far to zom-babies. SIGH. We're not very good at this...
Wait, weren't we supposed to be fighting right now?
Oh yeah. Heh, got a little distracted there.
Now, give us that token, or we sink yer ship and you meet the same fate as Janie!
Aw geez, I don't wanna be a zom-baby. I don't wanna eat brains!
I dunno, the brain eating part doesn't sound THAT bad.

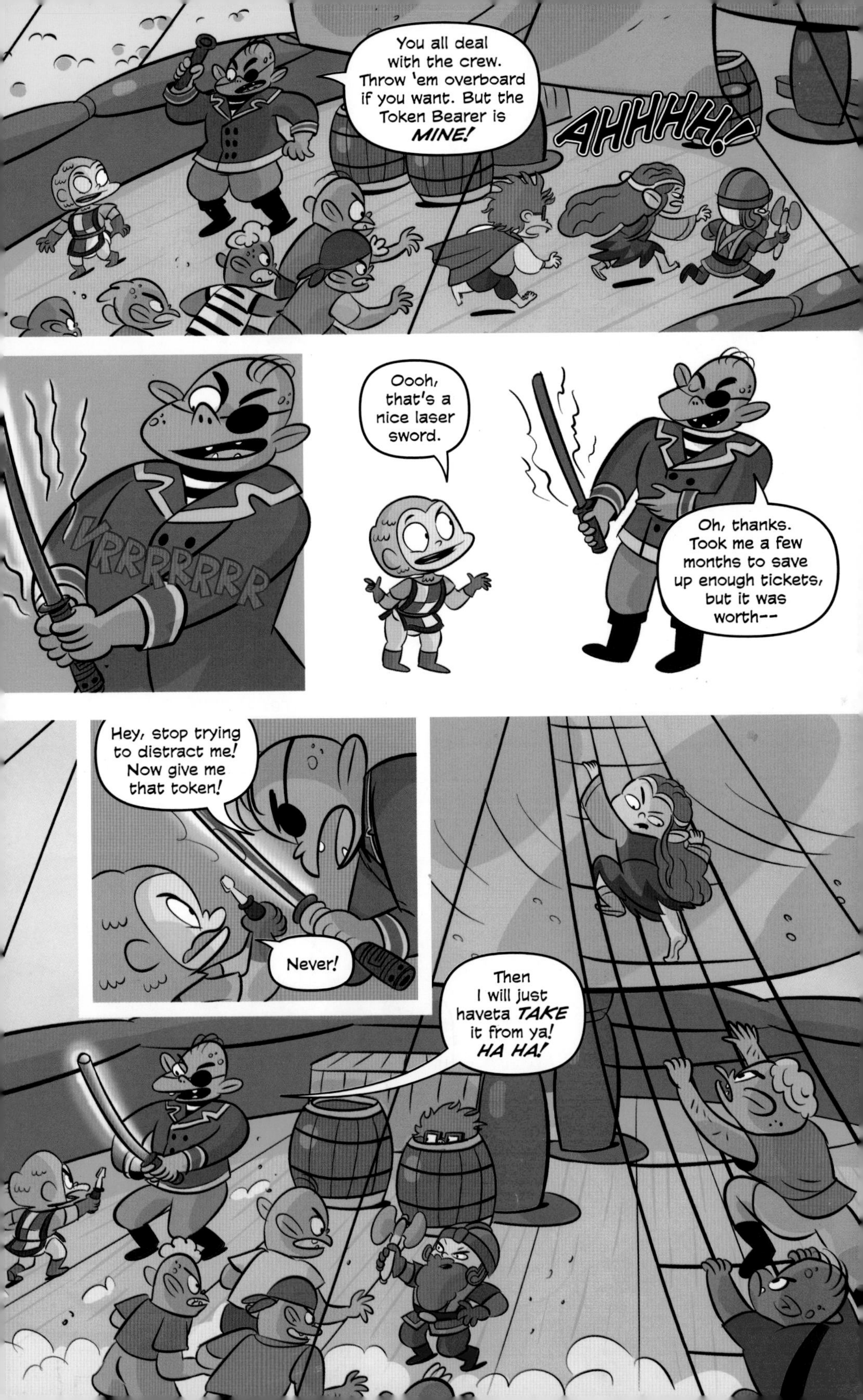
You all deal with the crew. Throw 'em overboard if you want. But the Token Bearer is *MINE!*
AHHHH!
VRRRRRRR
Oooh, that's a nice laser sword.
Oh, thanks. Took me a few months to save up enough tickets, but it was worth--
Hey, stop trying to distract me! Now give me that token!
Never!
Then I will just haveta *TAKE* it from ya! *HA HA!*

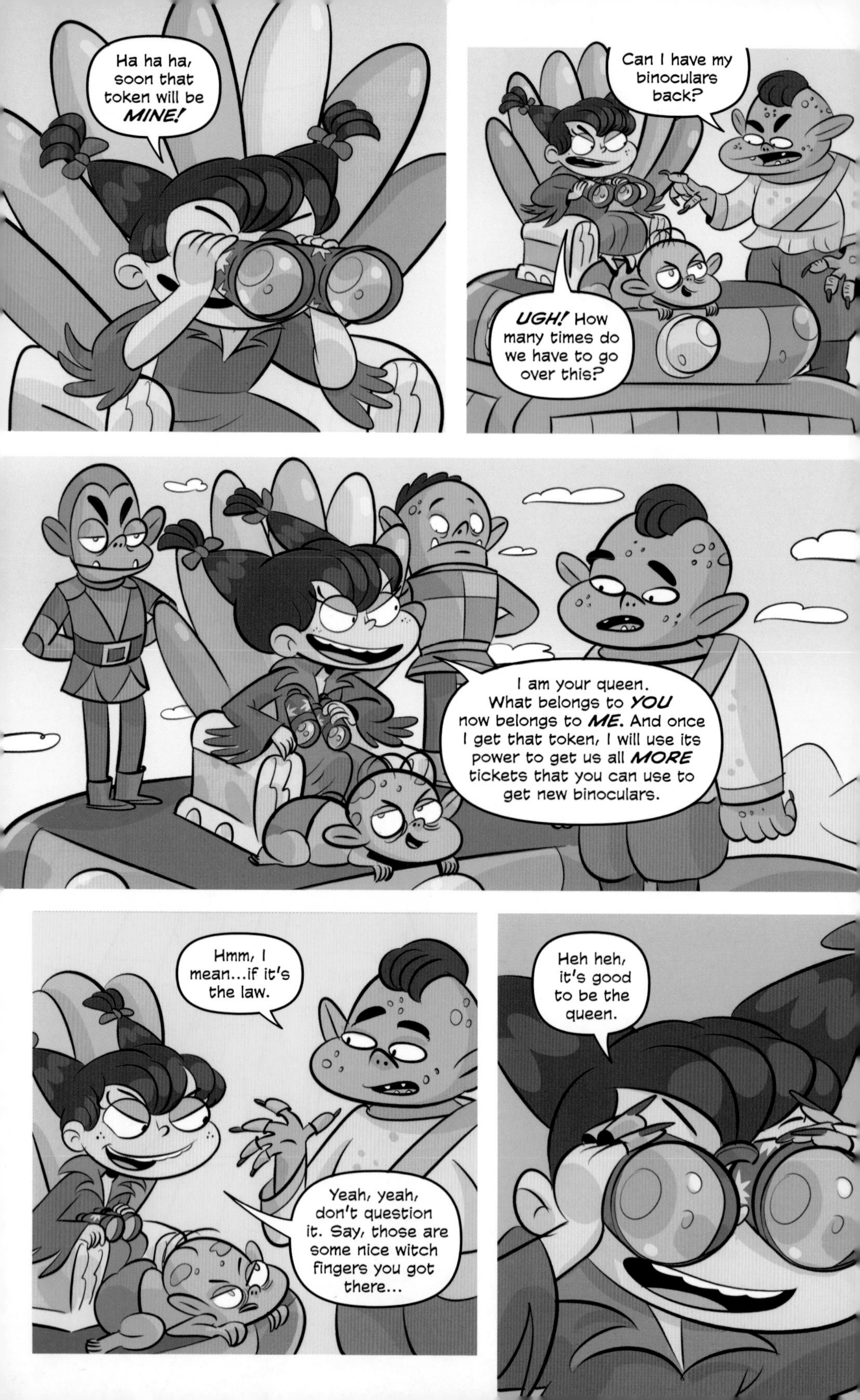
Ha ha ha, soon that token will be *MINE!*
Can I have my binoculars back?
UGH! How many times do we have to go over this?
I am your queen. What belongs to *YOU* now belongs to *ME*. And once I get that token, I will use its power to get us all *MORE* tickets that you can use to get new binoculars.
Hmm, I mean...if it's the law.
Yeah, yeah, don't question it. Say, those are some nice witch fingers you got there...
Heh heh, it's good to be the queen.

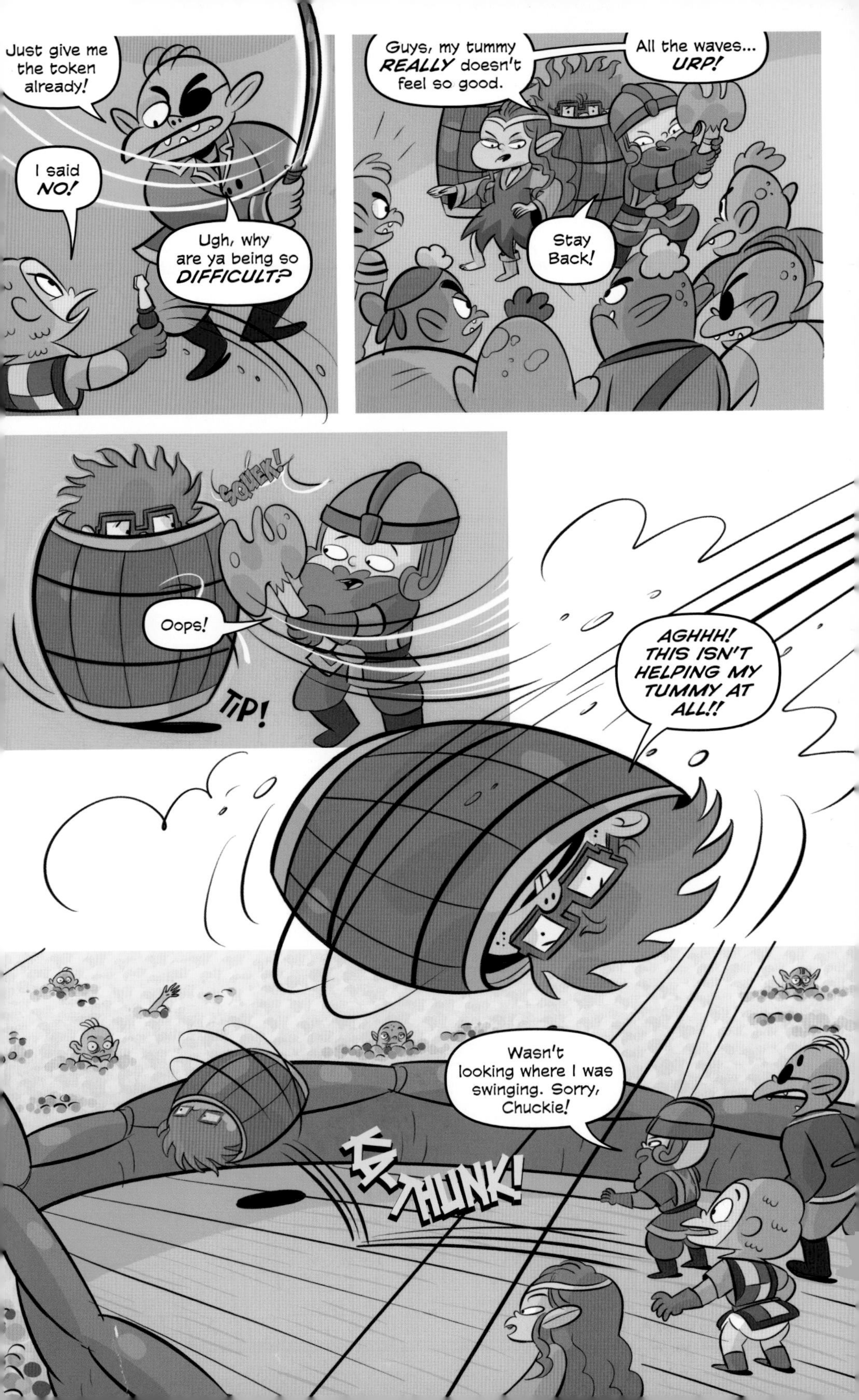
Just give me the token already!
I said NO!
Ugh, why are ya being so DIFFICULT?
Guys, my tummy REALLY doesn't feel so good.
All the waves... URP!
Stay Back!
SQUEEK!
Oops!
TIP!
AGHHH! THIS ISN'T HELPING MY TUMMY AT ALL!!
Wasn't looking where I was swinging. Sorry, Chuckie!
KA-THUNK!

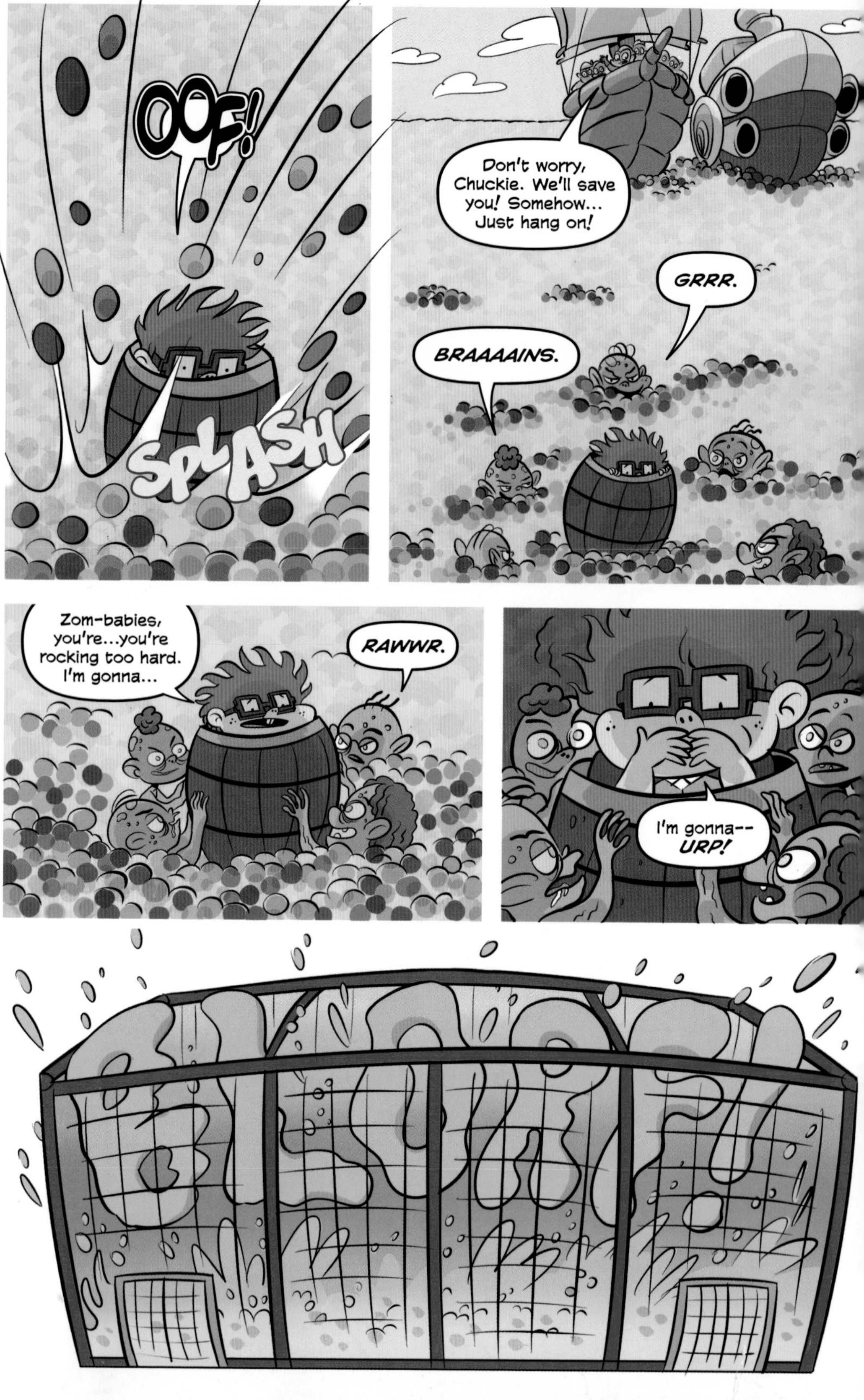
OOF!
SPLASH
Don't worry, Chuckie. We'll save you! Somehow... Just hang on!
GRRR.
BRAAAAINS.
Zom-babies, you're...you're rocking too hard. I'm gonna...
RAWWR.
I'm gonna-- URP!

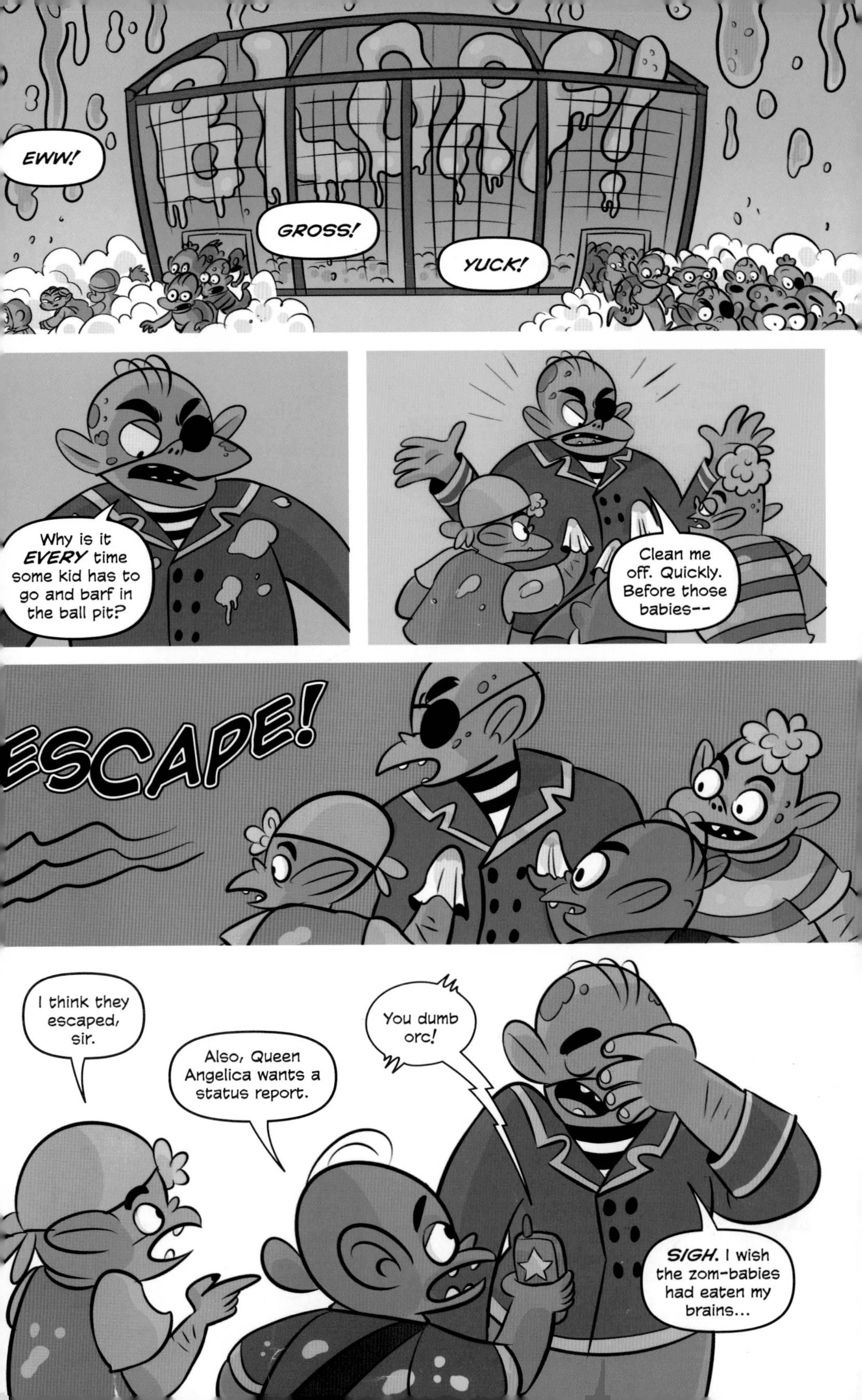
EWW!
GROSS!
YUCK!
Why is it EVERY time some kid has to go and barf in the ball pit?
Clean me off. Quickly. Before those babies--
ESCAPE!
I think they escaped, sir.
Also, Queen Angelica wants a status report.
You dumb orc!
SIGH. I wish the zom-babies had eaten my brains...

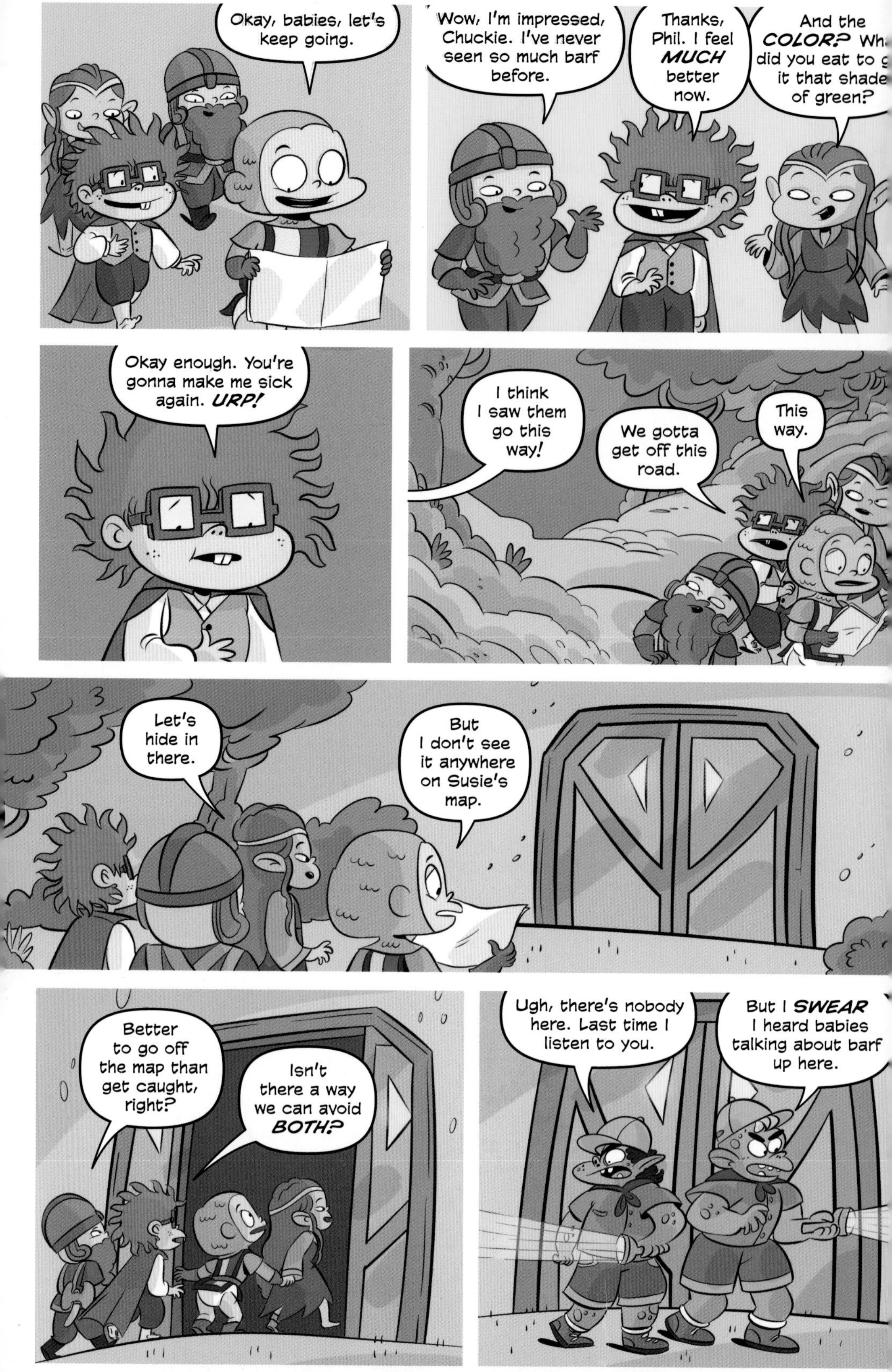

Okay, babies, let's keep going.
Wow, I'm impressed, Chuckie. I've never seen so much barf before.
Thanks, Phil. I feel MUCH better now.
And the COLOR? Wh did you eat to g it that shade of green?
Okay enough. You're gonna make me sick again. URP!
I think I saw them go this way!
We gotta get off this road.
This way.
Let's hide in there.
But I don't see it anywhere on Susie's map.
Better to go off the map than get caught, right?
Isn't there a way we can avoid BOTH?
Ugh, there's nobody here. Last time I listen to you.
But I SWEAR I heard babies talking about barf up here.

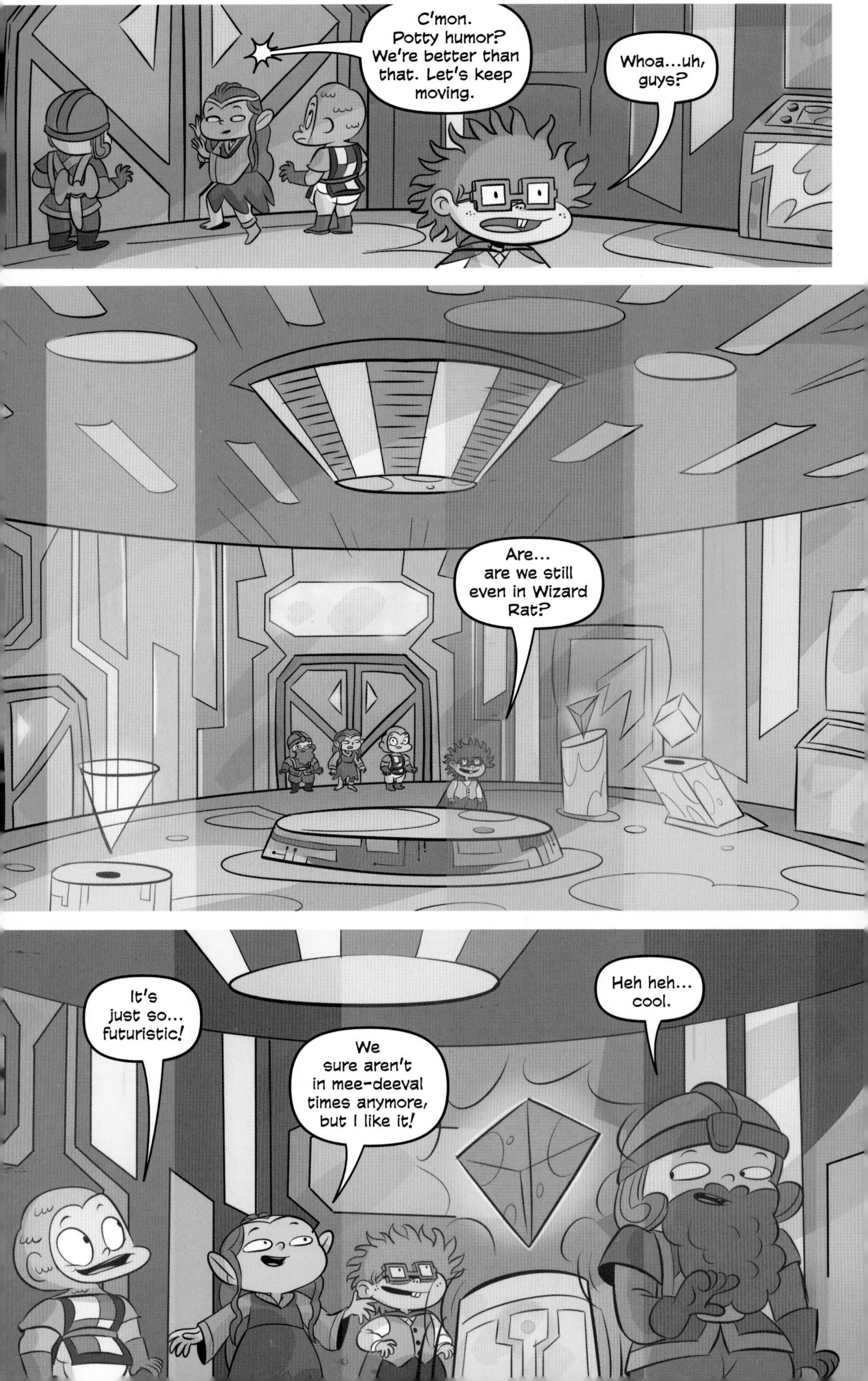
C'mon. Potty humor? We're better than that. Let's keep moving.
Whoa...uh, guys?
Are... are we still even in Wizard Rat?
It's just so... futuristic!
We sure aren't in mee-deeval times anymore, but I like it!
Heh heh... cool.

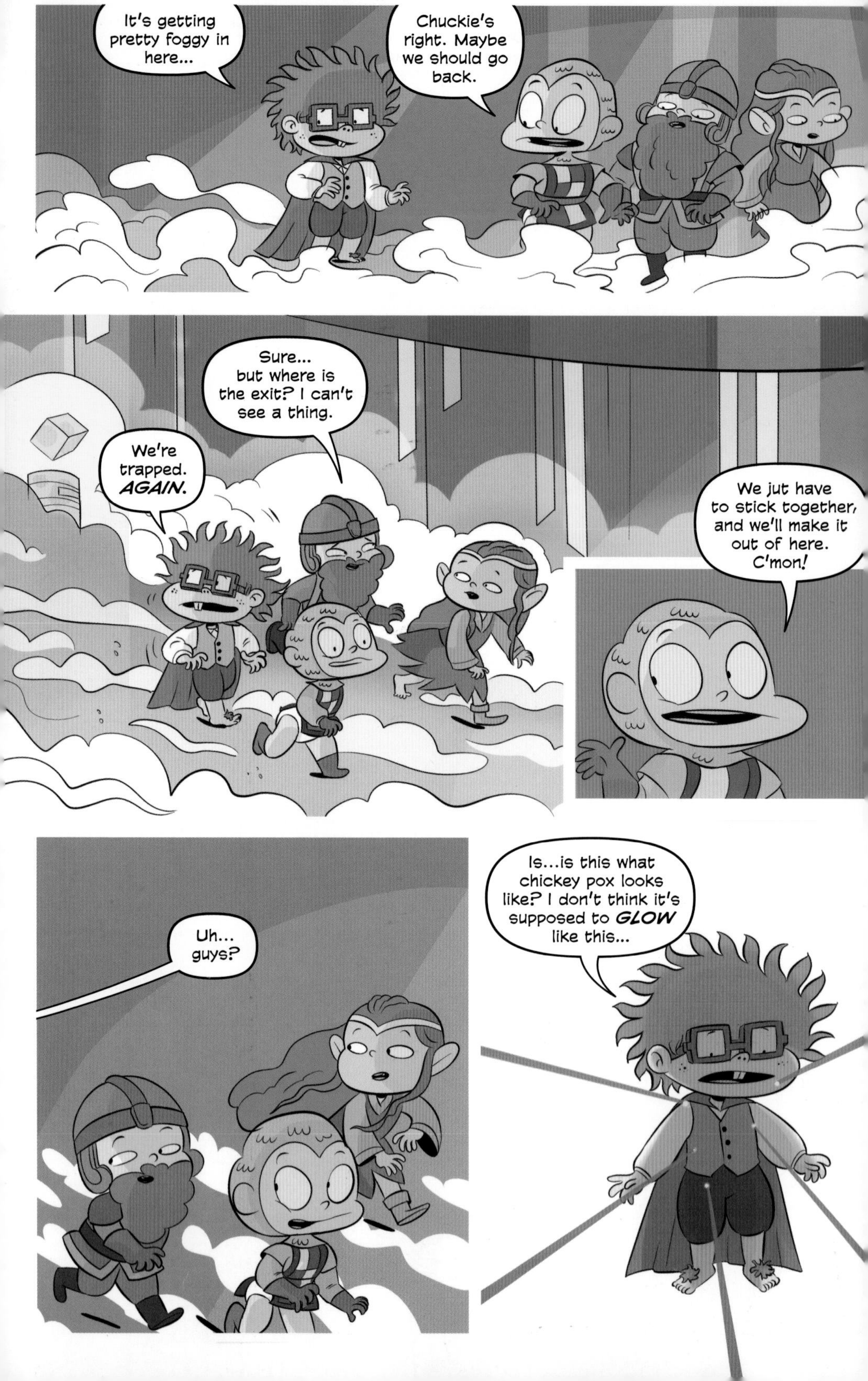
It's getting pretty foggy in here...
Chuckie's right. Maybe we should go back.
Sure... but where is the exit? I can't see a thing.
We're trapped. AGAIN.
We jut have to stick together, and we'll make it out of here. C'mon!
Uh... guys?
Is...is this what chickey pox looks like? I don't think it's supposed to GLOW like this...

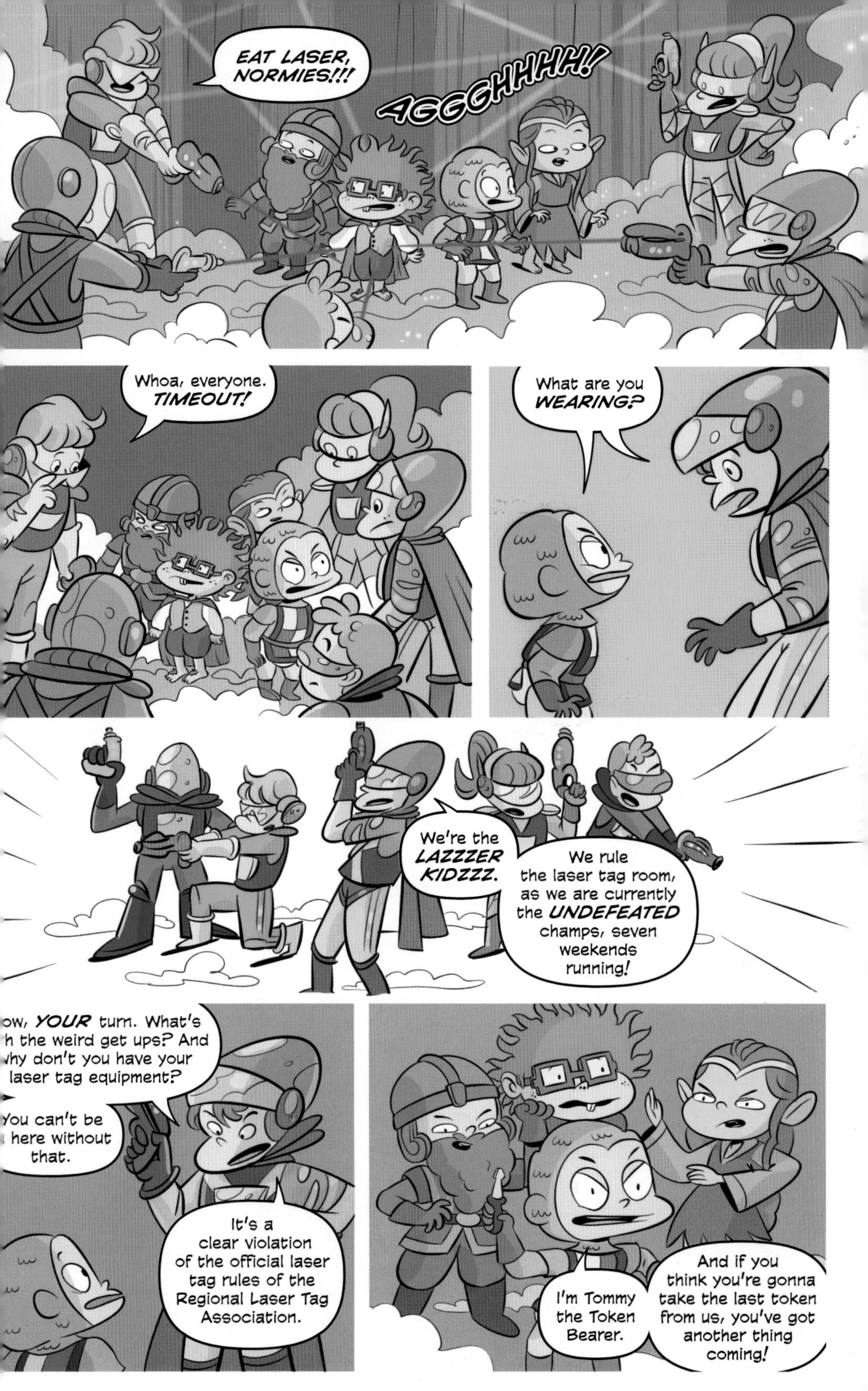
EAT LASER, NORMIES!!!
AGGGHHHH!
Whoa, everyone. TIMEOUT!
What are you WEARING?
We're the LAZZZER KIDZZZ.
We rule the laser tag room, as we are currently the UNDEFEATED champs, seven weekends running!
ow, YOUR turn. What's h the weird get ups? And why don't you have your laser tag equipment?
You can't be here without that.
It's a clear violation of the official laser tag rules of the Regional Laser Tag Association.
I'm Tommy the Token Bearer.
And if you think you're gonna take the last token from us, you've got another thing coming!

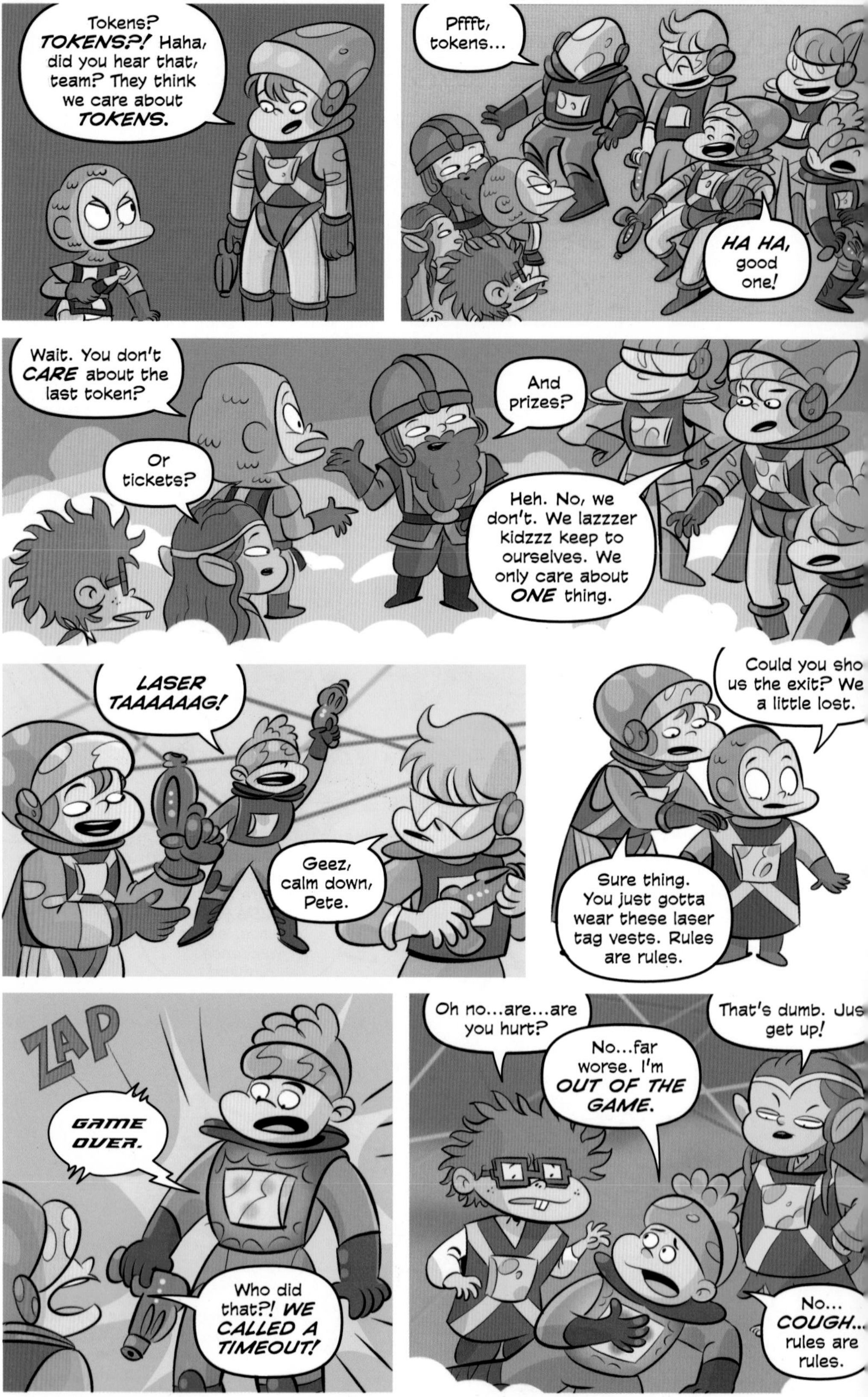
Tokens? TOKENS?! Haha, did you hear that, team? They think we care about TOKENS.
Pffft, tokens...
HA HA, good one!
Wait. You don't CARE about the last token?
Or tickets?
And prizes?
Heh. No, we don't. We lazzzer kidzzz keep to ourselves. We only care about ONE thing.
LASER TAAAAAAG!
Geez, calm down, Pete.
Could you sho us the exit? We a little lost.
Sure thing. You just gotta wear these laser tag vests. Rules are rules.
ZAP
GAME OVER.
Who did that?! WE CALLED A TIMEOUT!
Oh no...are...are you hurt?
No...far worse. I'm OUT OF THE GAME.
That's dumb. Jus get up!
No... COUGH... rules are rules.

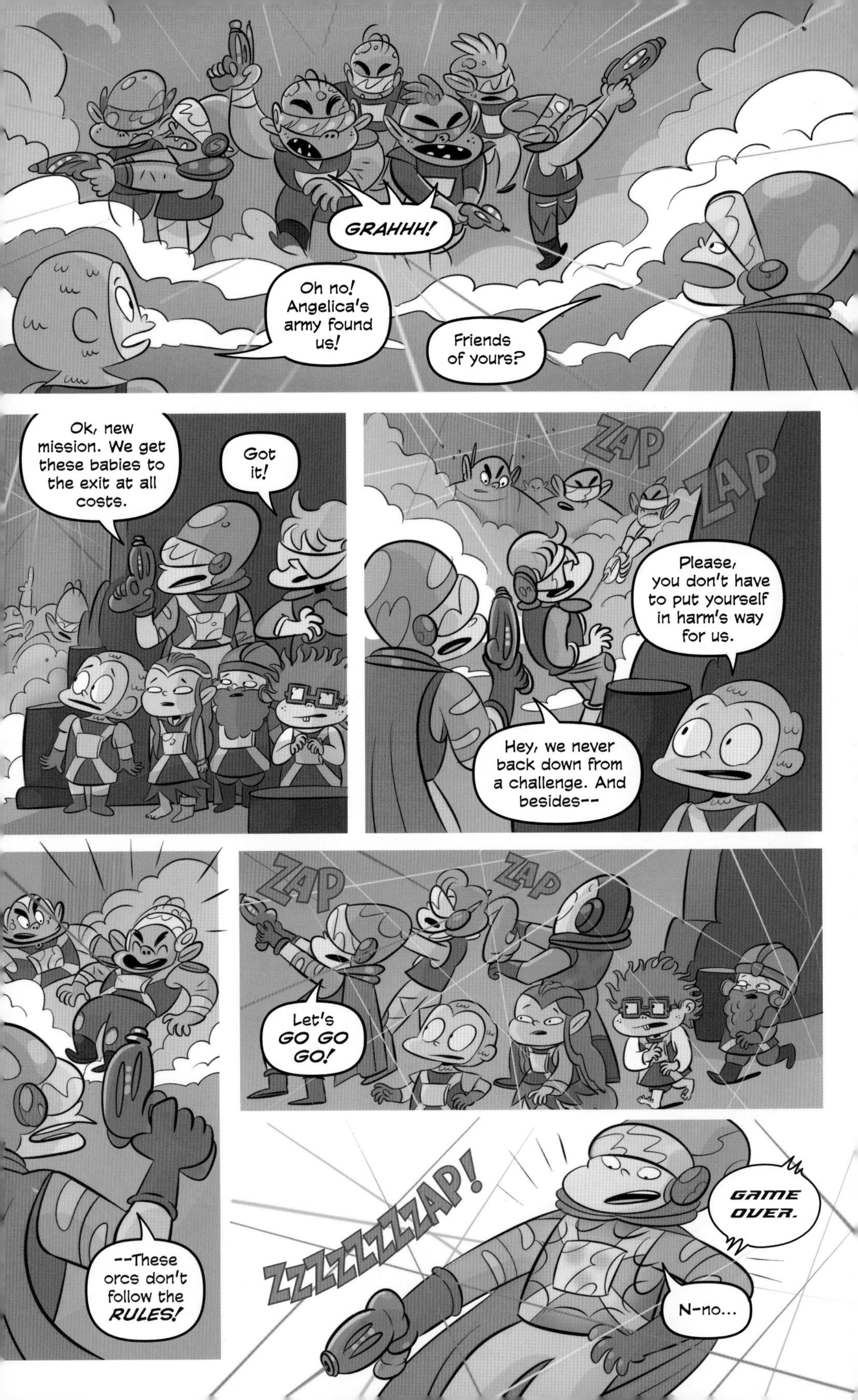
GRAHHH!
Oh no! Angelica's army found us!
Friends of yours?
Ok, new mission. We get these babies to the exit at all costs.
Got it!
ZAP
ZAP
Please, you don't have to put yourself in harm's way for us.
Hey, we never back down from a challenge. And besides--
--These orcs don't follow the RULES!
ZAP
ZAP
Let's GO GO GO!
ZZZZZZZZZAP!
GAME OVER.
N-no...

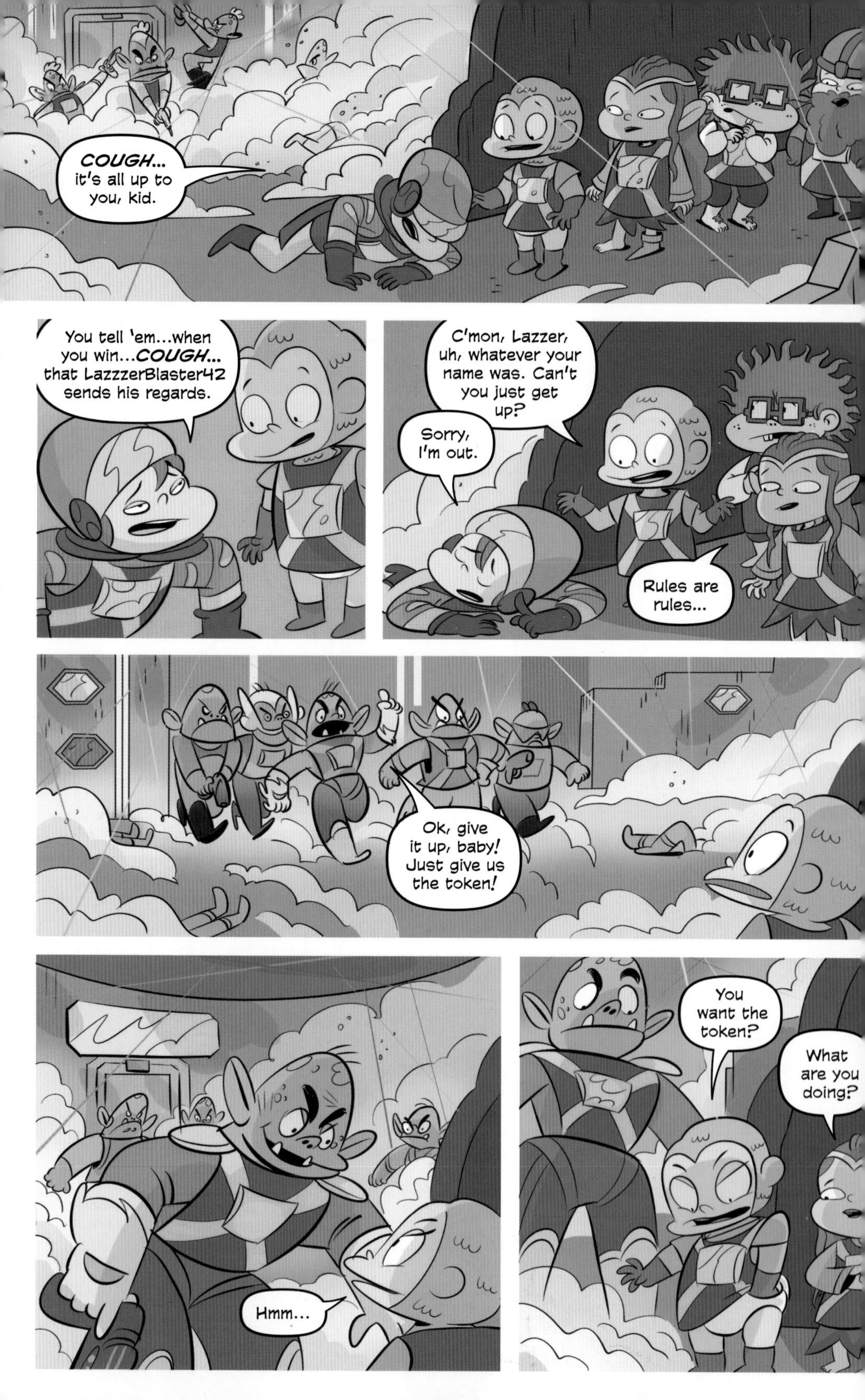
COUGH... it's all up to you, kid.
You tell 'em...when you win...COUGH... that LazzzerBlaster42 sends his regards.
C'mon, Lazzer, uh, whatever your name was. Can't you just get up?
Sorry, I'm out.
Rules are rules...
Ok, give it up, baby! Just give us the token!
Hmm...
You want the token?
What are you doing?

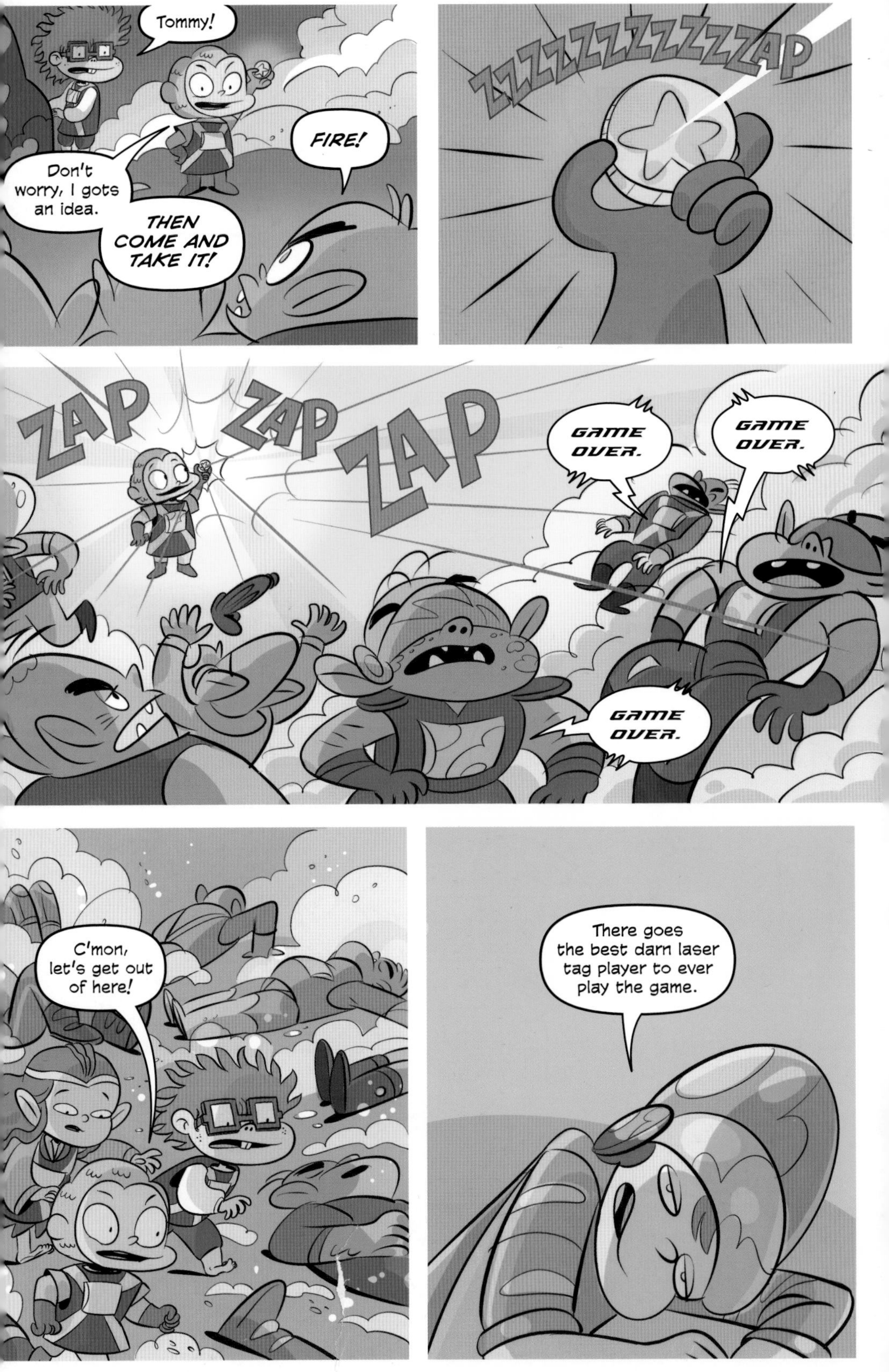
Tommy!
Don't worry, I gots an idea.
FIRE!
THEN COME AND TAKE IT!
ZZZZZZZZZZZZZAP
ZAP
ZAP
ZAP
GAME OVER.
GAME OVER.
GAME OVER.
C'mon, let's get out of here!
There goes the best darn laser tag player to ever play the game.

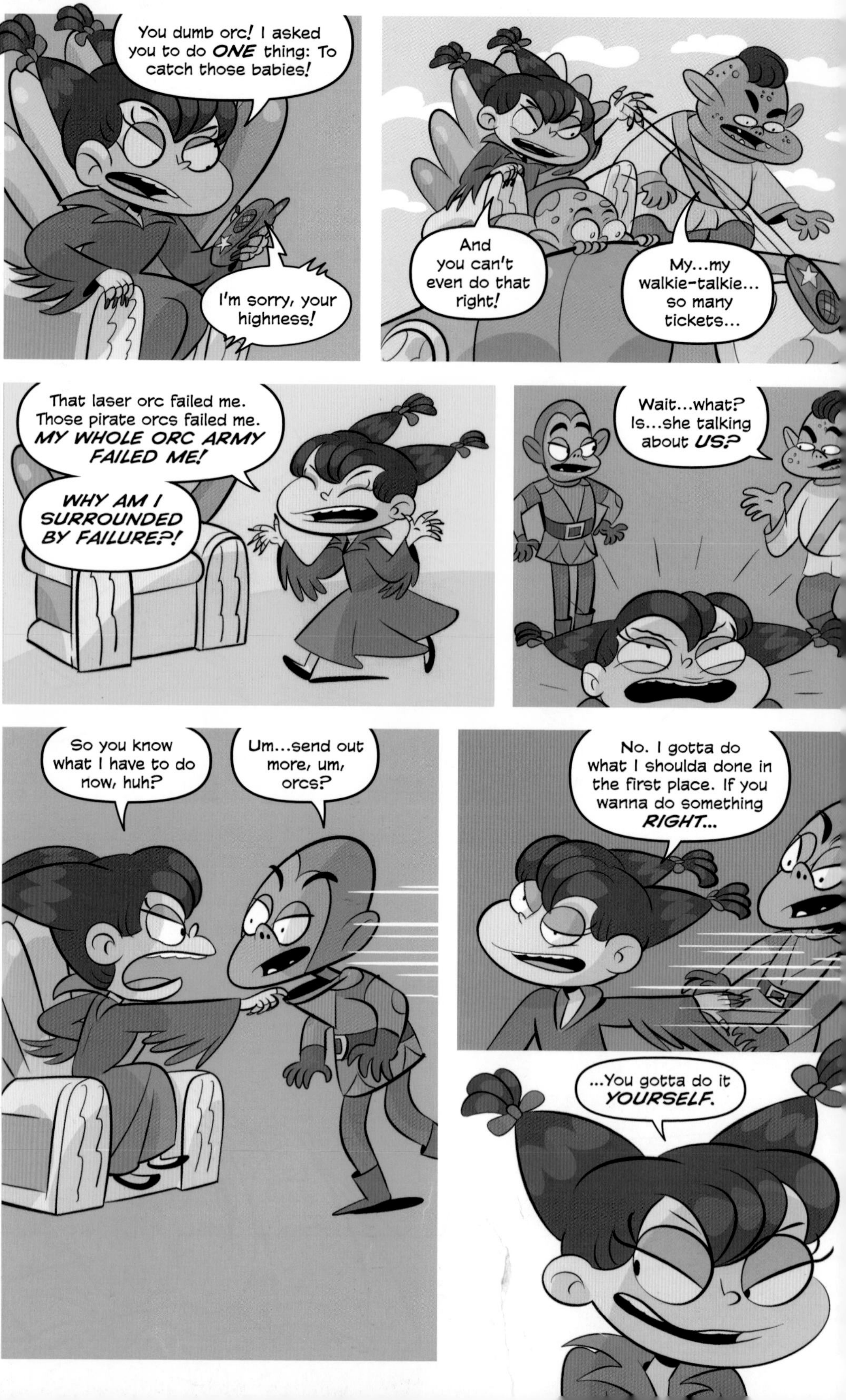
You dumb orc! I asked you to do ***ONE*** thing: To catch those babies!
I'm sorry, your highness!
And you can't even do that right!
My...my walkie-talkie... so many tickets...
That laser orc failed me. Those pirate orcs failed me. ***MY WHOLE ORC ARMY FAILED ME!***
WHY AM I SURROUNDED BY FAILURE?!
Wait...what? Is...she talking about ***US?***
So you know what I have to do now, huh?
Um...send out more, um, orcs?
No. I gotta do what I shoulda done in the first place. If you wanna do something ***RIGHT...***
...You gotta do it ***YOURSELF.***

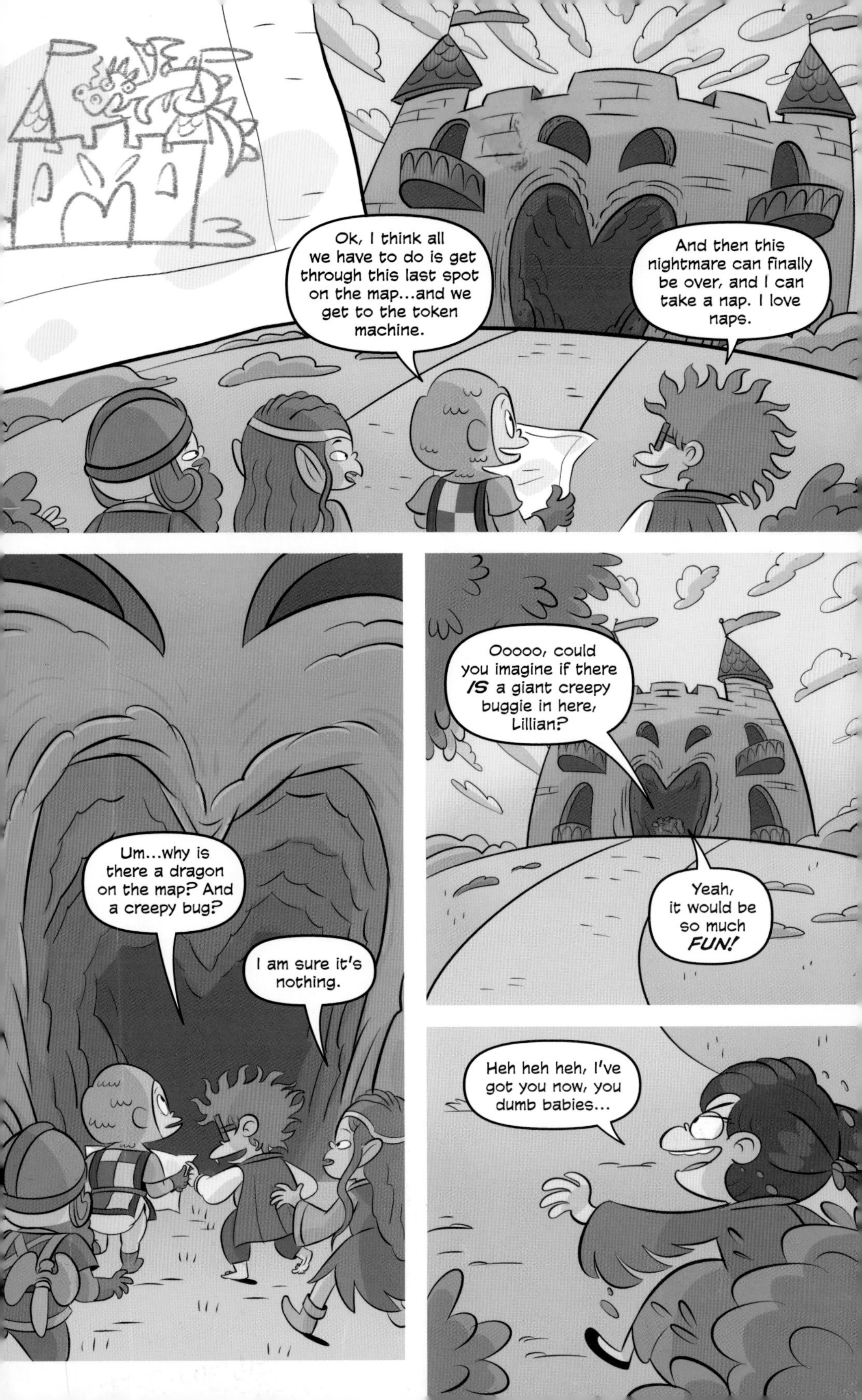
Ok, I think all we have to do is get through this last spot on the map...and we get to the token machine.
And then this nightmare can finally be over, and I can take a nap. I love naps.
Um...why is there a dragon on the map? And a creepy bug?
I am sure it's nothing.
Ooooo, could you imagine if there *IS* a giant creepy buggie in here, Lillian?
Yeah, it would be so much ***FUN!***
Heh heh heh, I've got you now, you dumb babies...

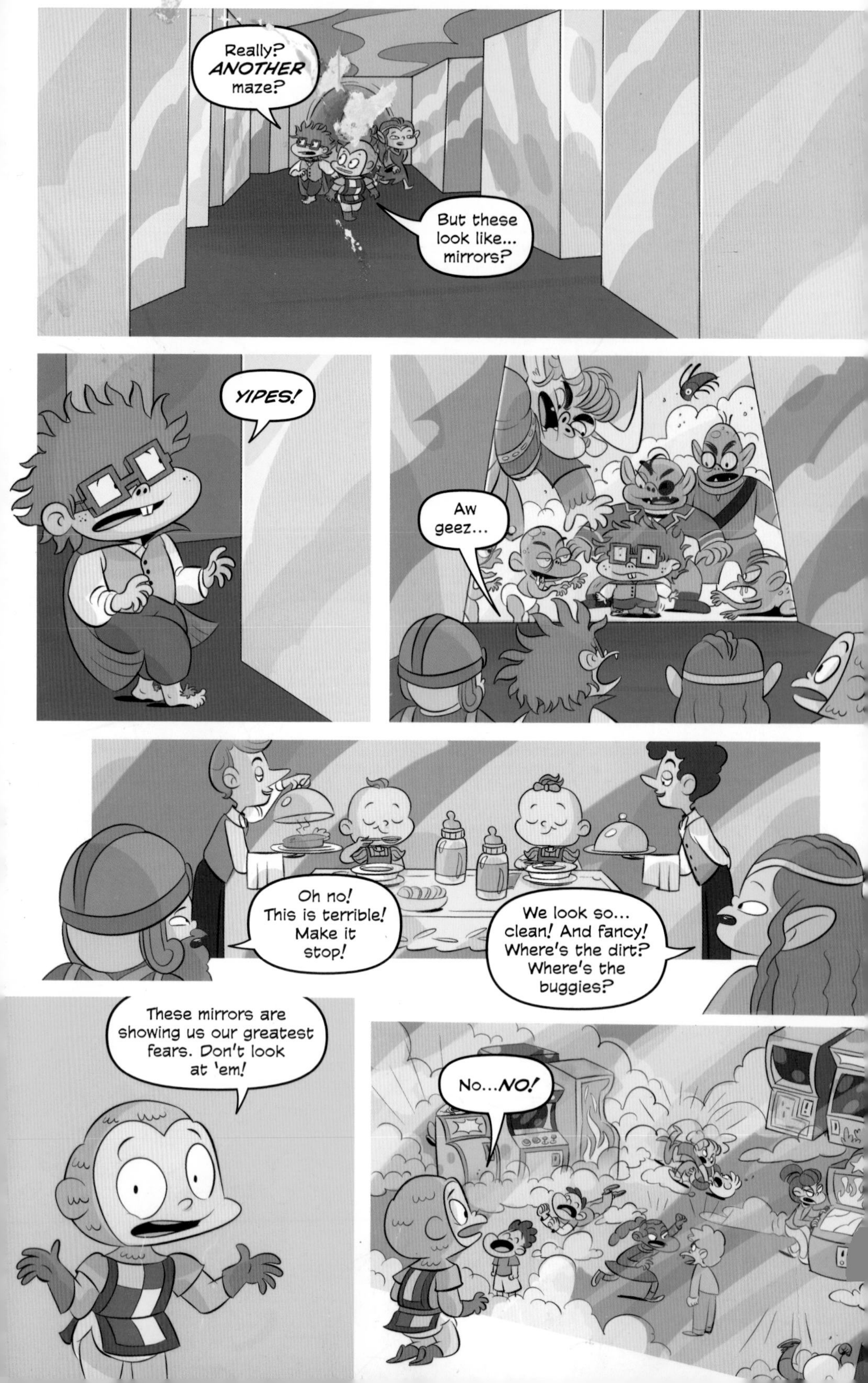
Really? ANOTHER maze?
But these look like... mirrors?
YIPES!
Aw geez...
Oh no! This is terrible! Make it stop!
We look so... clean! And fancy! Where's the dirt? Where's the buggies?
These mirrors are showing us our greatest fears. Don't look at 'em!
No...NO!

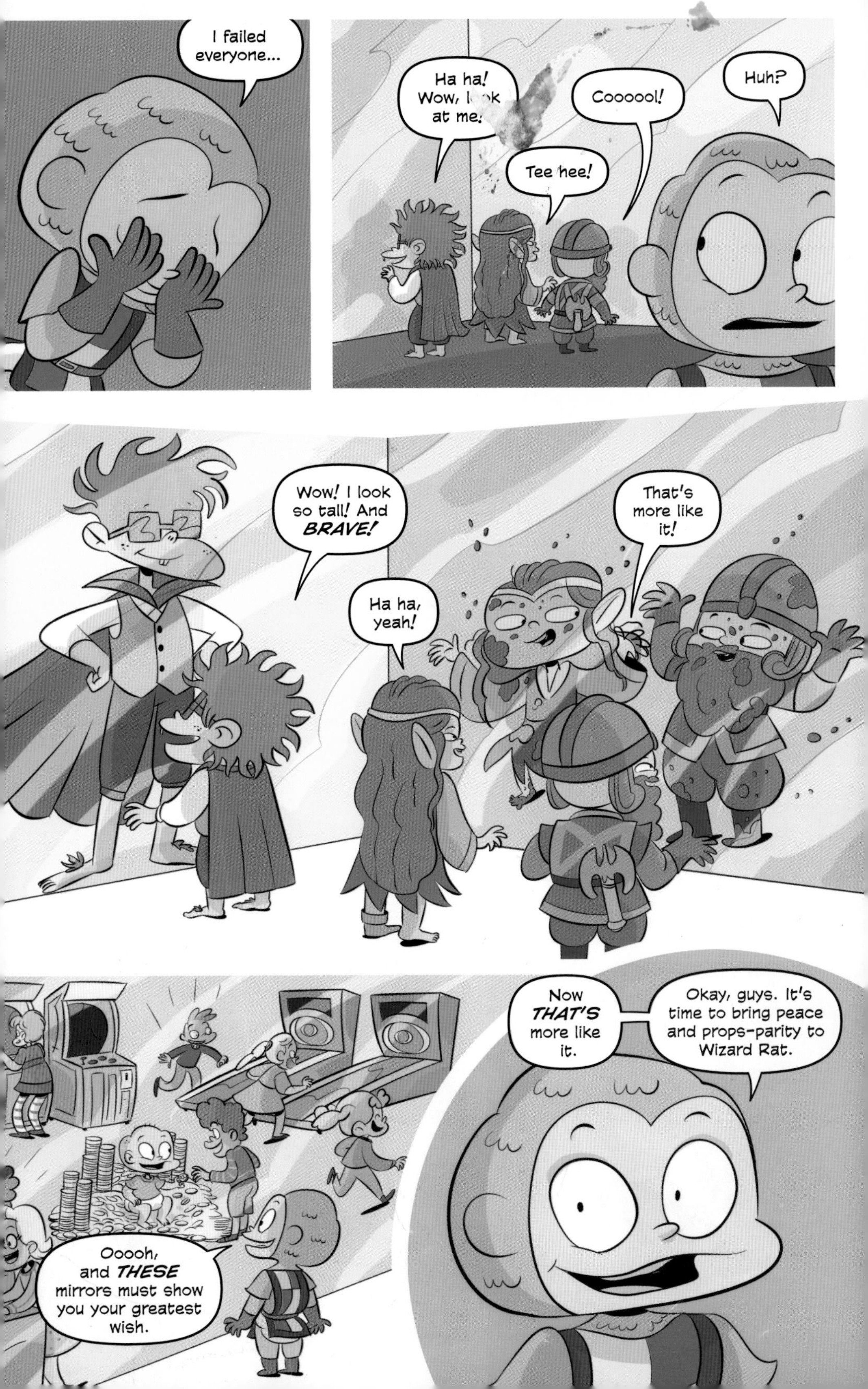
I failed everyone...
Ha ha! Wow, look at me.
Tee hee!
Coooool!
Huh?
Wow! I look so tall! And BRAVE!
Ha ha, yeah!
That's more like it!
Ooooh, and THESE mirrors must show you your greatest wish.
Now THAT'S more like it.
Okay, guys. It's time to bring peace and props-parity to Wizard Rat.

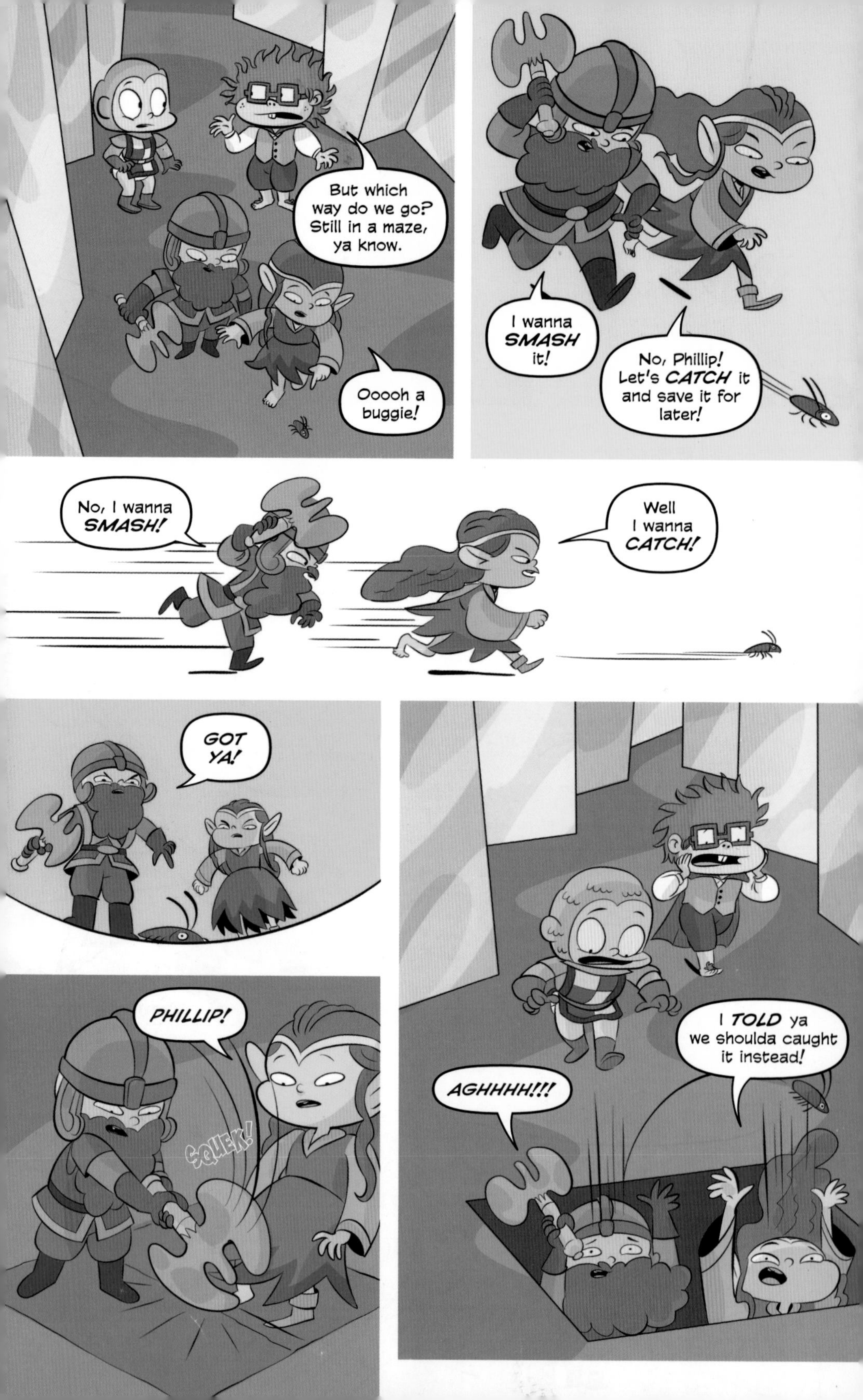
But which way do we go? Still in a maze, ya know.
Ooooh a buggie!
I wanna SMASH it!
No, Phillip! Let's CATCH it and save it for later!
No, I wanna SMASH!
Well I wanna CATCH!
GOT YA!
PHILLIP!
SQUEK!
AGHHHH!!!
I TOLD ya we shoulda caught it instead!

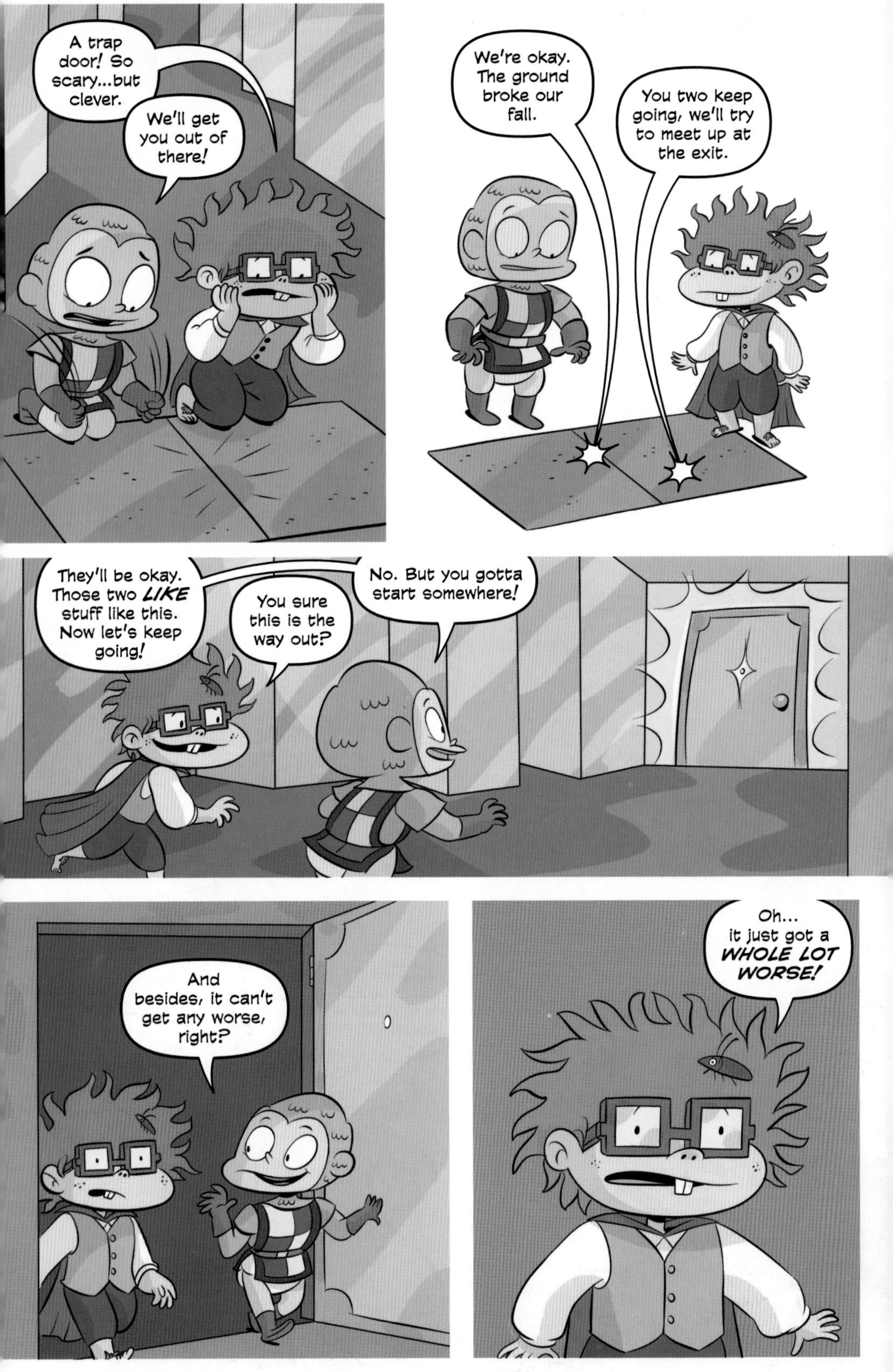
A trap door! So scary...but clever.
We'll get you out of there!
We're okay. The ground broke our fall.
You two keep going, we'll try to meet up at the exit.
They'll be okay. Those two LIKE stuff like this. Now let's keep going!
You sure this is the way out?
No. But you gotta start somewhere!
And besides, it can't get any worse, right?
Oh... it just got a WHOLE LOT WORSE!

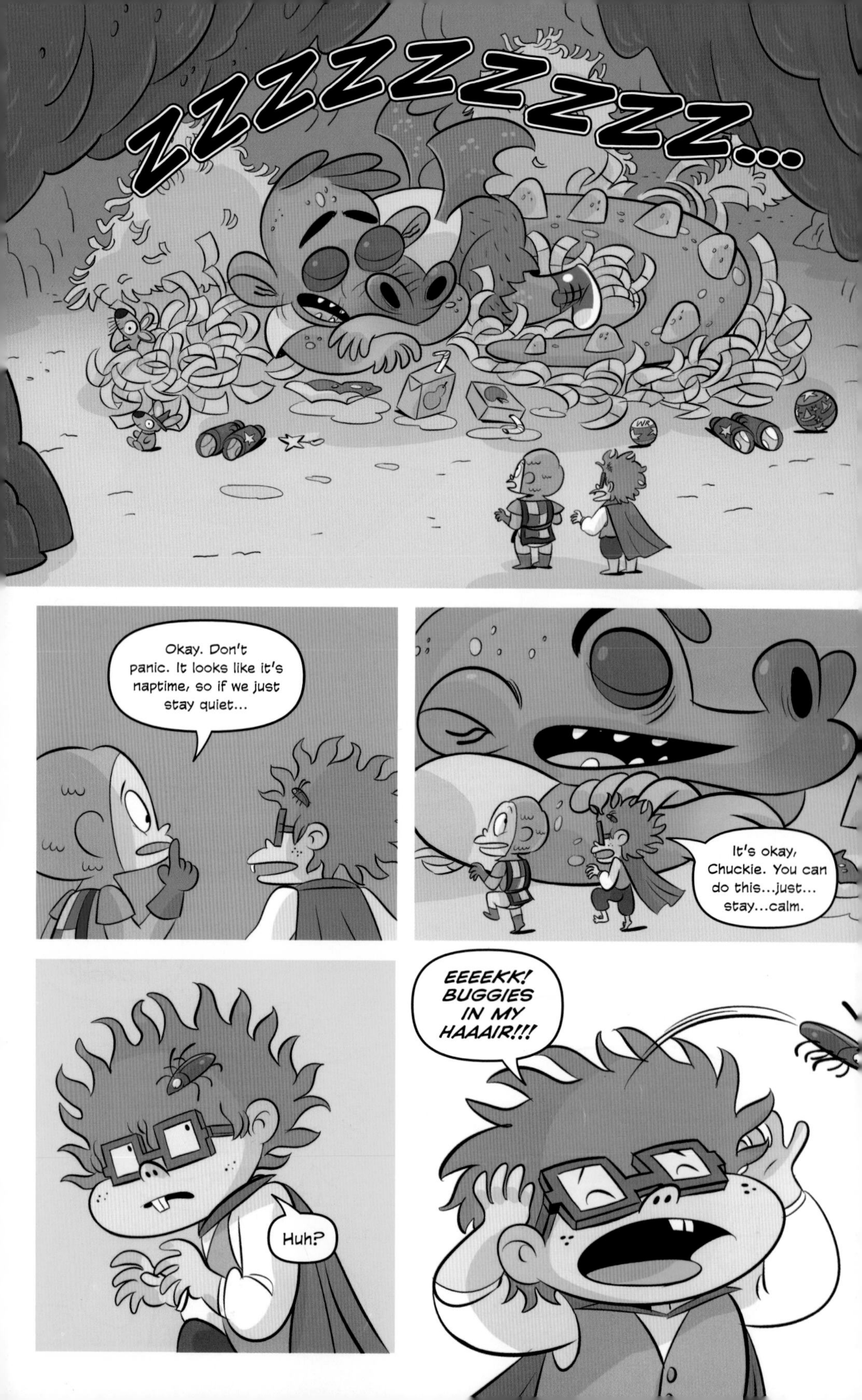
ZZZZZZZZZZZZZ...
Okay. Don't panic. It looks like it's naptime, so if we just stay quiet...
It's okay, Chuckie. You can do this...just... stay...calm.
Huh?
EEEEKK! BUGGIES IN MY HAAAIR!!!

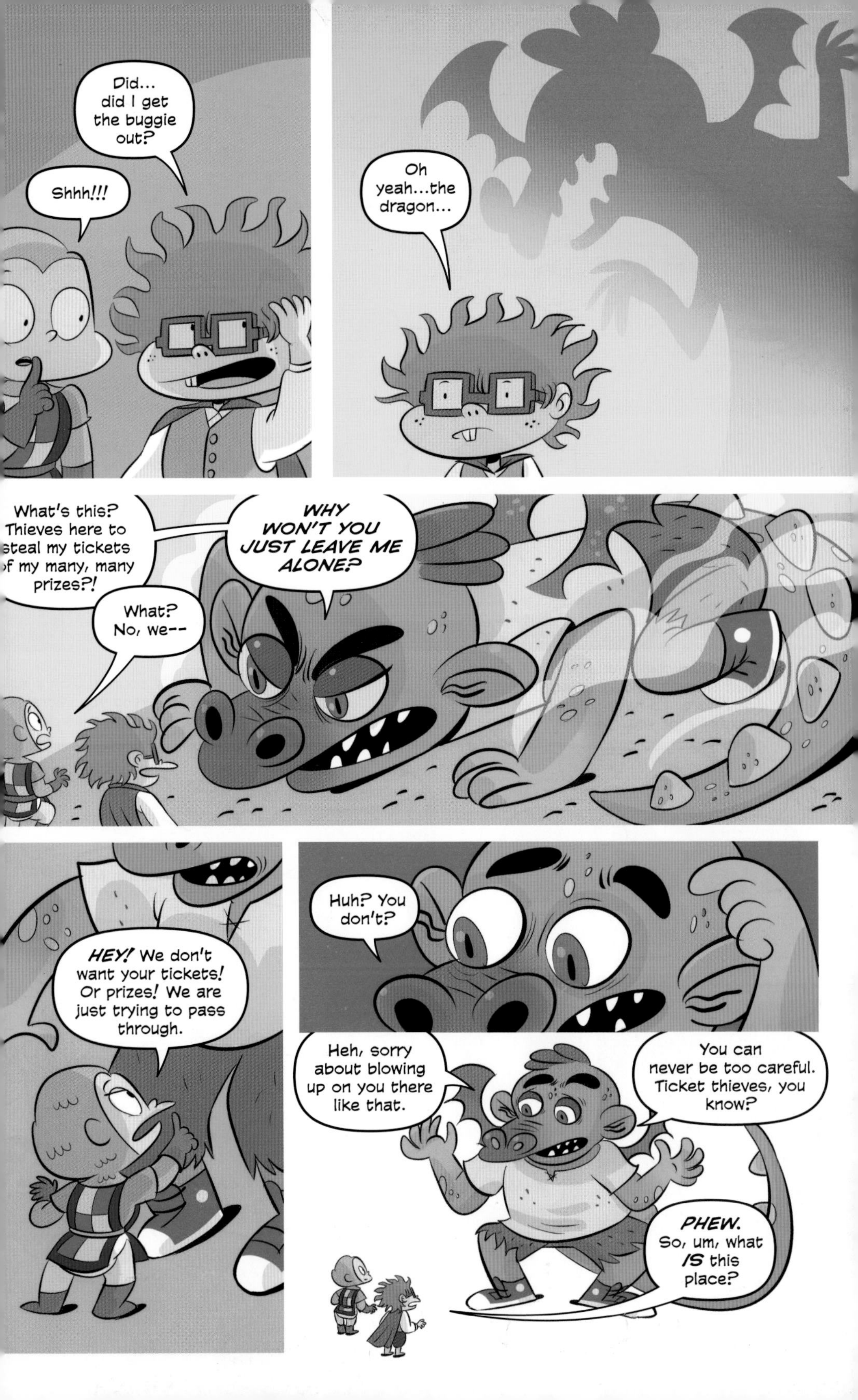
Did... did I get the buggie out?
Shhh!!!
Oh yeah...the dragon...
What's this? Thieves here to steal my tickets of my many, many prizes?!
WHY WON'T YOU JUST LEAVE ME ALONE?
What? No, we--
HEY! We don't want your tickets! Or prizes! We are just trying to pass through.
Huh? You don't?
Heh, sorry about blowing up on you there like that.
You can never be too careful. Ticket thieves, you know?
PHEW. So, um, what IS this place?

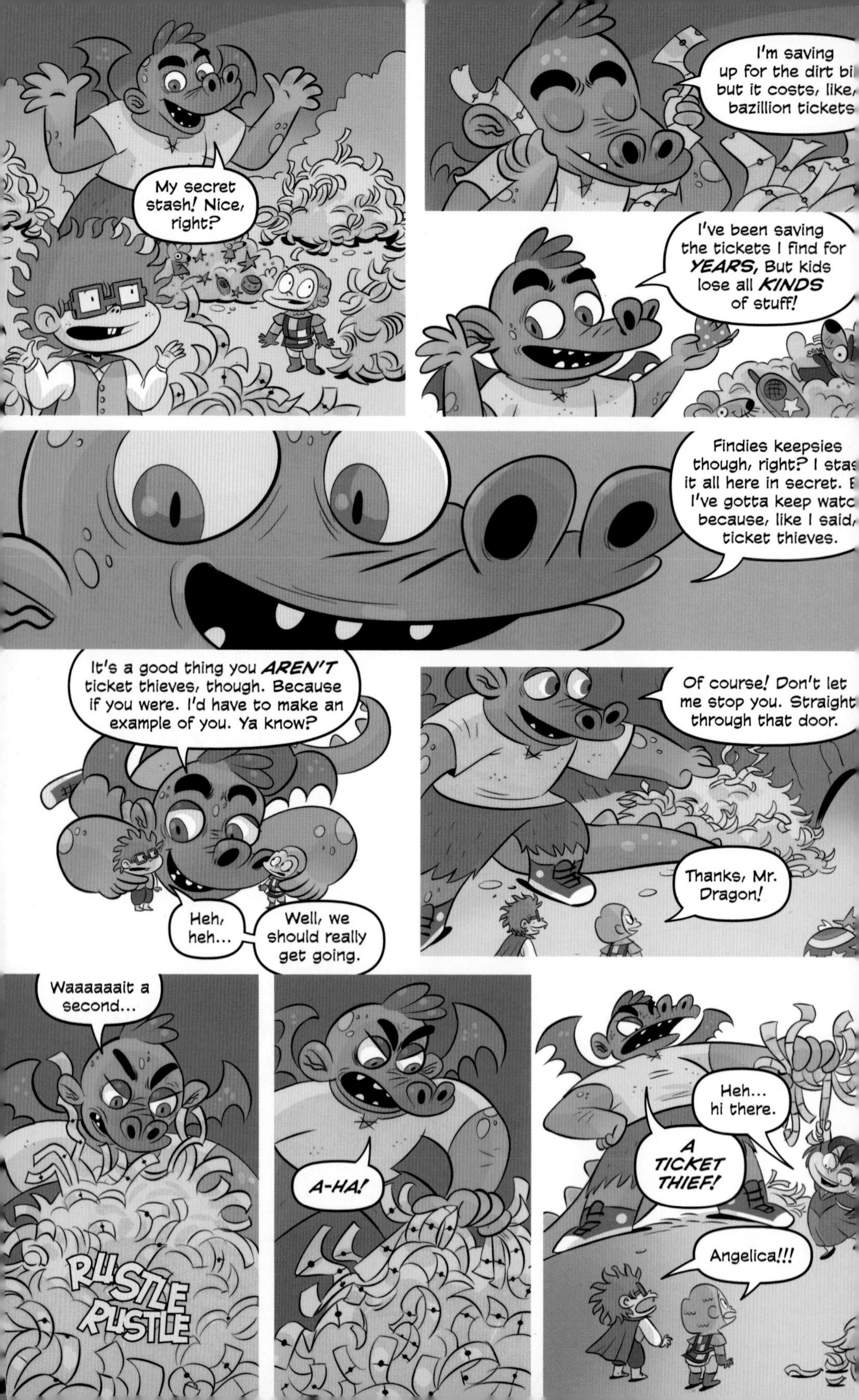
My secret stash! Nice, right?
I'm saving up for the dirt bi but it costs, like, bazillion tickets
I've been saving the tickets I find for YEARS, But kids lose all KINDS of stuff!
Findies keepsies though, right? I stas it all here in secret. I've gotta keep watc because, like I said, ticket thieves.
It's a good thing you AREN'T ticket thieves, though. Because if you were. I'd have to make an example of you. Ya know?
Heh, heh...
Well, we should really get going.
Of course! Don't let me stop you. Straight through that door.
Thanks, Mr. Dragon!
Waaaaaait a second...
RUSTLE RUSTLE
A-HA!
Heh... hi there.
A TICKET THIEF!
Angelica!!!

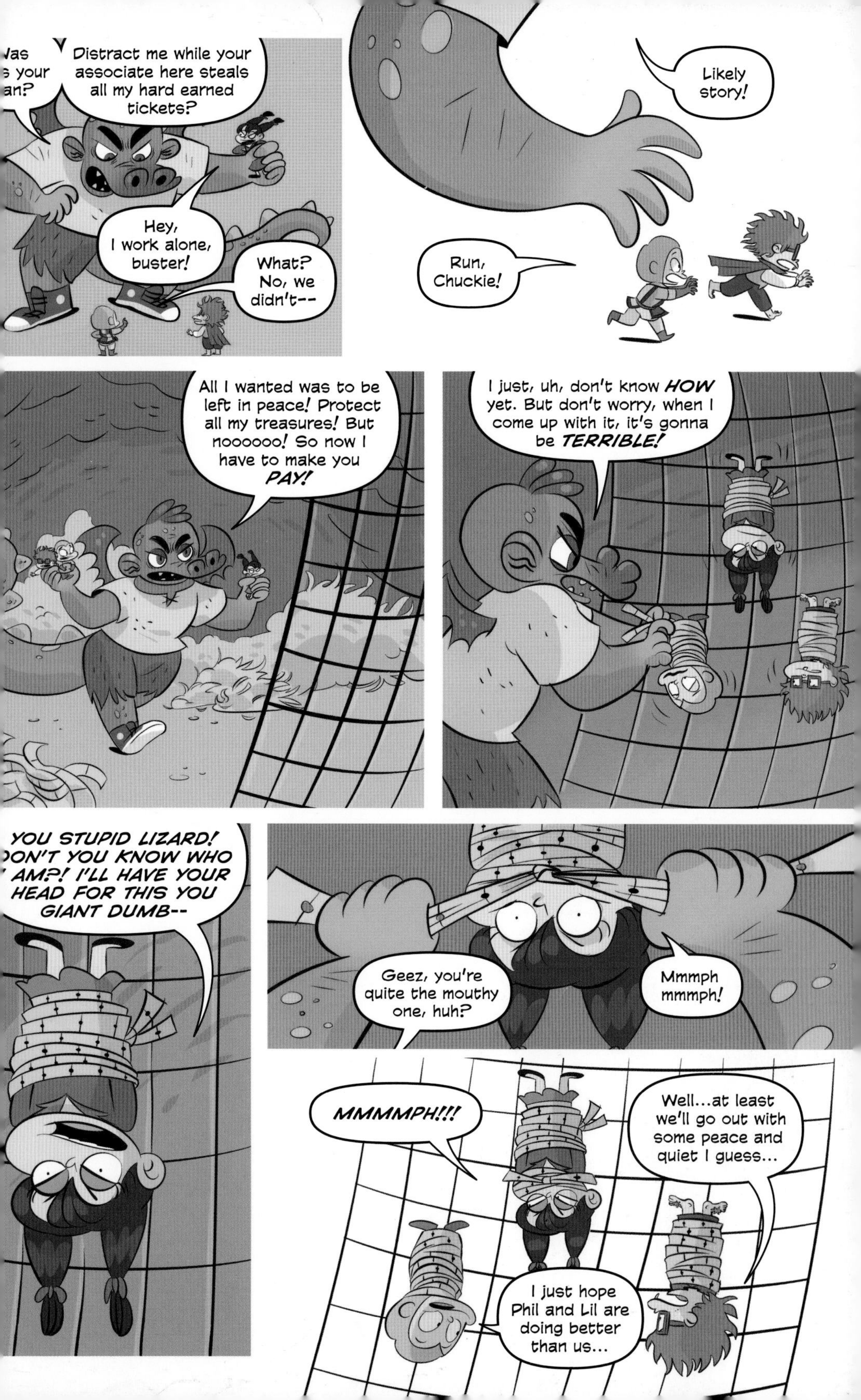

Was
s your
an?
Distract me while your associate here steals all my hard earned tickets?
Hey, I work alone, buster!
What? No, we didn't--
Likely story!
Run, Chuckie!
All I wanted was to be left in peace! Protect all my treasures! But noooooo! So now I have to make you PAY!
I just, uh, don't know HOW yet. But don't worry, when I come up with it, it's gonna be TERRIBLE!
YOU STUPID LIZARD!
ON'T YOU KNOW WHO
AM?! I'LL HAVE YOUR HEAD FOR THIS YOU GIANT DUMB--
Geez, you're quite the mouthy one, huh?
Mmmph mmmph!
MMMMPH!!!
Well...at least we'll go out with some peace and quiet I guess...
I just hope Phil and Lil are doing better than us...

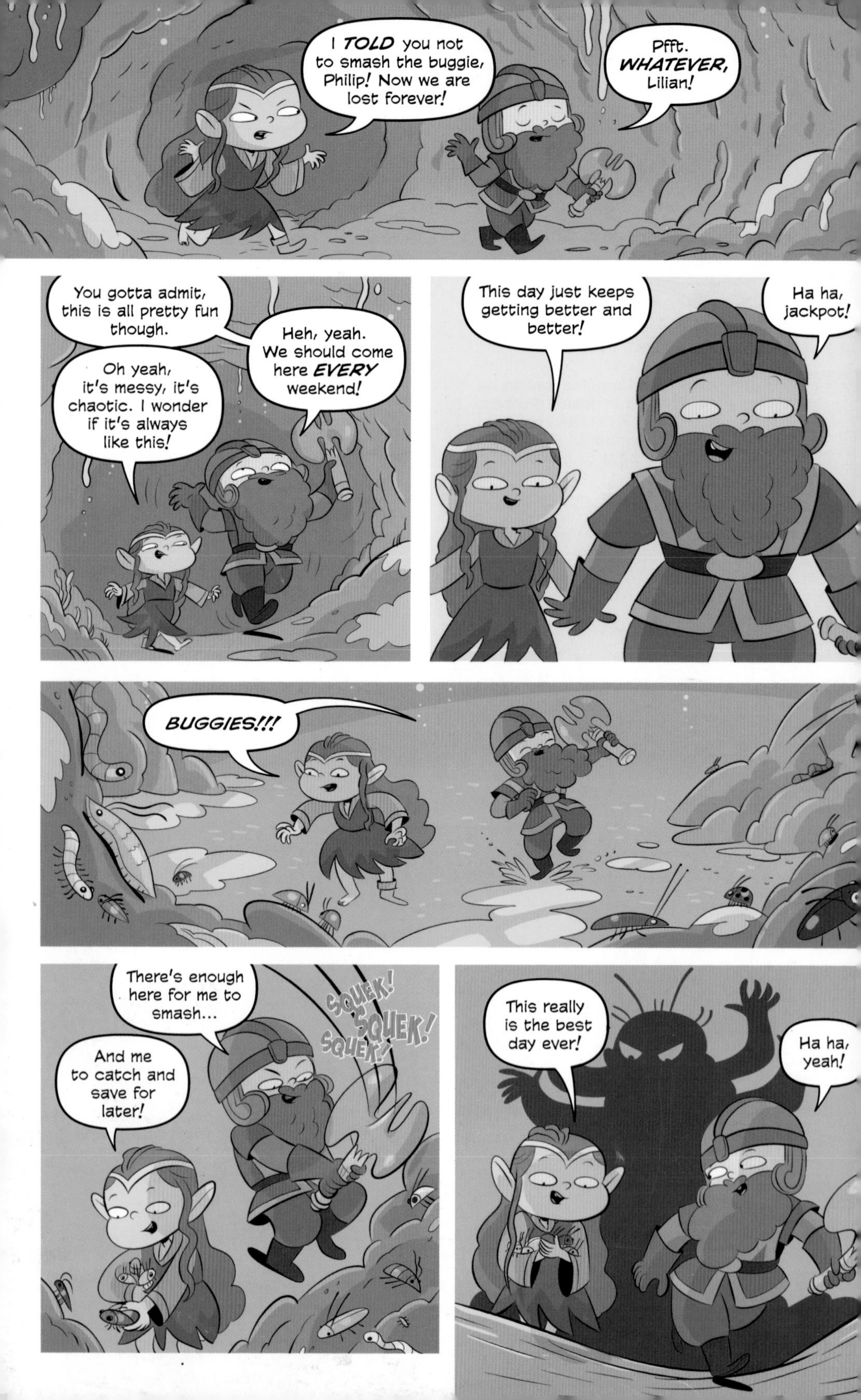
I TOLD you not to smash the buggie, Philip! Now we are lost forever!
Pfft. WHATEVER, Lilian!
You gotta admit, this is all pretty fun though.
Heh, yeah. We should come here EVERY weekend!
Oh yeah, it's messy, it's chaotic. I wonder if it's always like this!
This day just keeps getting better and better!
Ha ha, jackpot!
BUGGIES!!!
There's enough here for me to smash...
SQUEK! SQUEK! SQUEK!
And me to catch and save for later!
This really is the best day ever!
Ha ha, yeah!

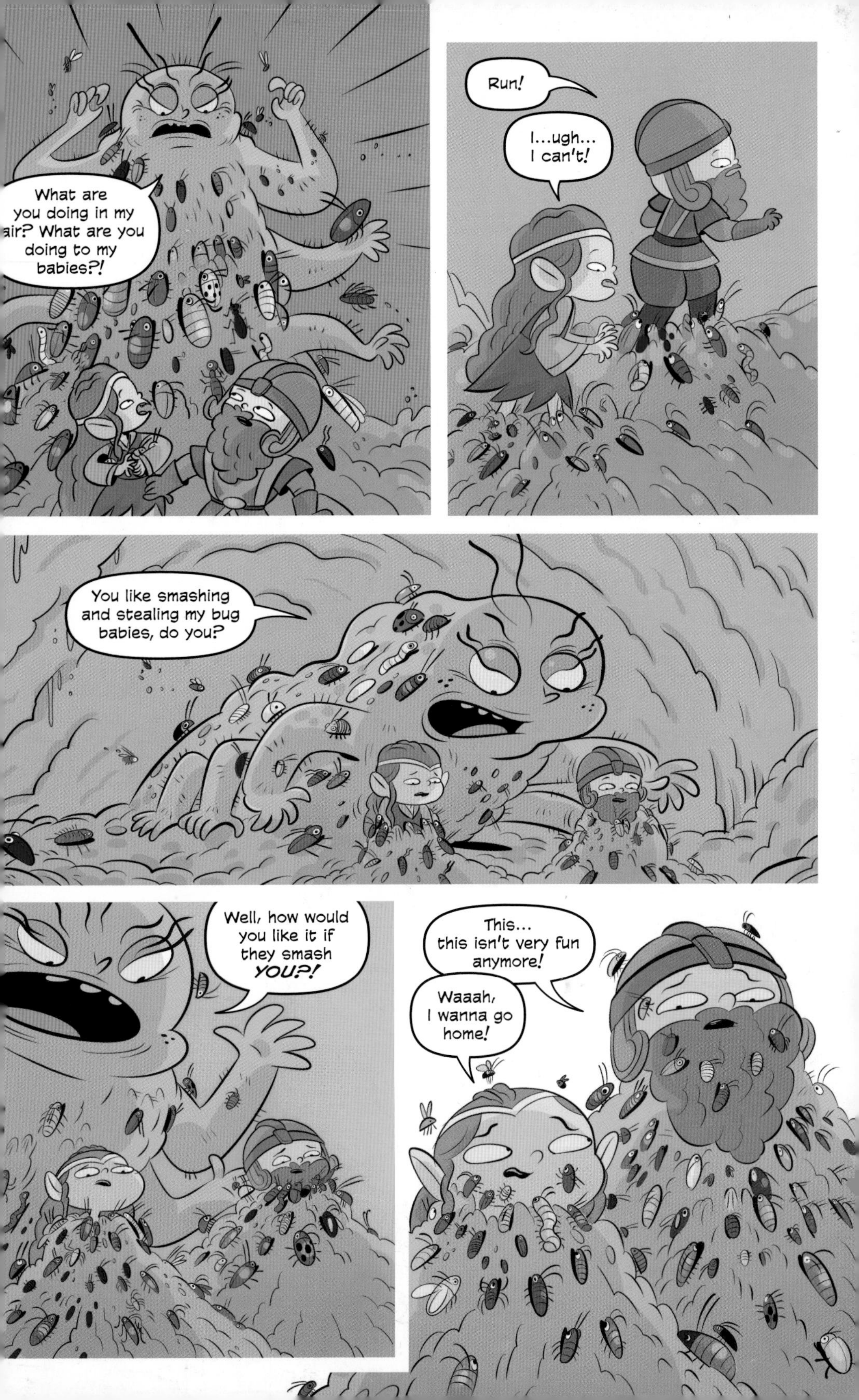
What are you doing in my air? What are you doing to my babies?!
Run!
I...ugh... I can't!
You like smashing and stealing my bug babies, do you?
Well, how would you like it if they smash YOU?!
This... this isn't very fun anymore!
Waaah, I wanna go home!

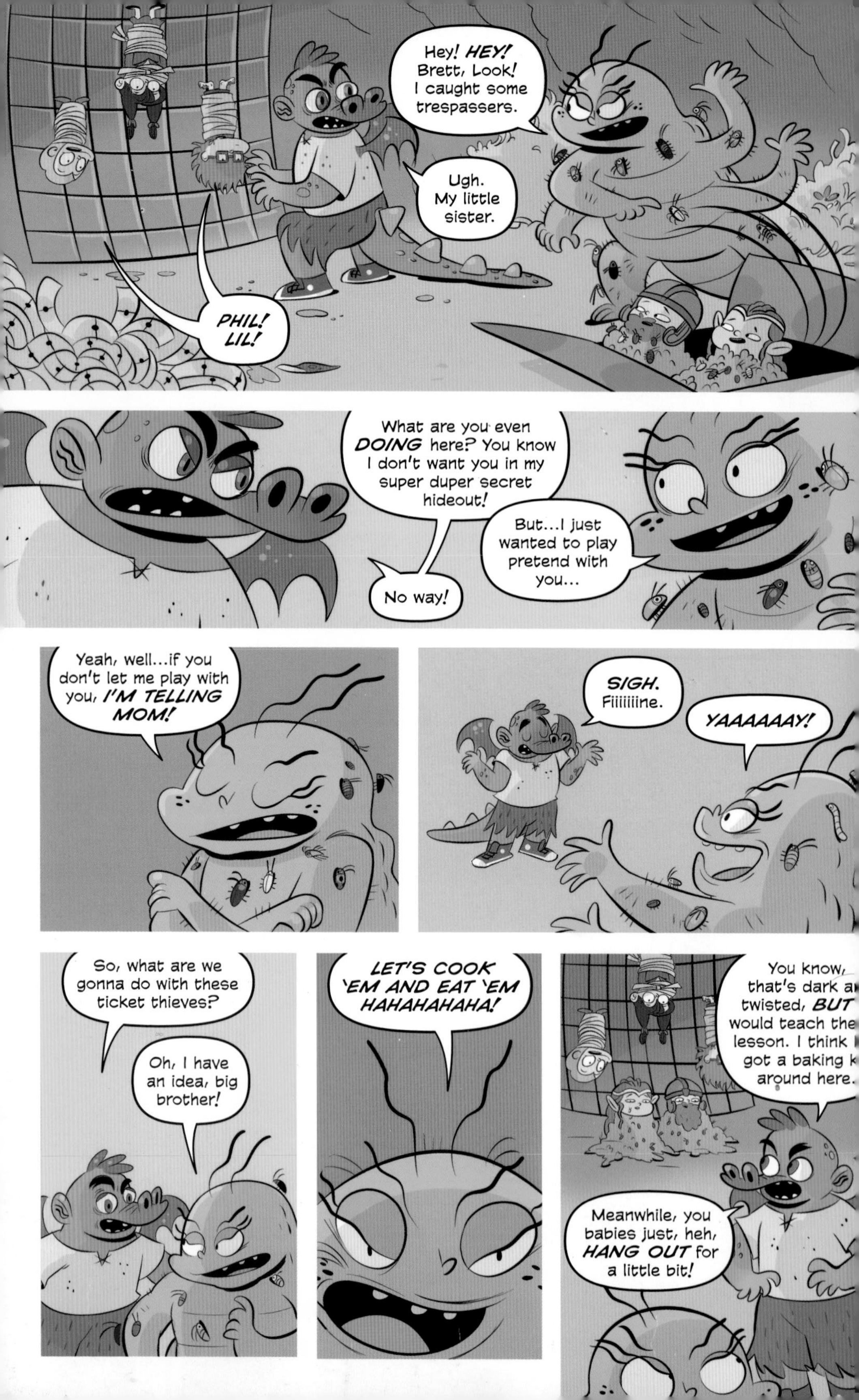
Hey! HEY! Brett, Look! I caught some trespassers.
Ugh. My little sister.
PHIL! LIL!
What are you even DOING here? You know I don't want you in my super duper secret hideout!
But...I just wanted to play pretend with you...
No way!
Yeah, well...if you don't let me play with you, I'M TELLING MOM!
SIGH. Fiiiiiiine.
YAAAAAAY!
So, what are we gonna do with these ticket thieves?
Oh, I have an idea, big brother!
LET'S COOK 'EM AND EAT 'EM HAHAHAHAHA!
Meanwhile, you babies just, heh, HANG OUT for a little bit!

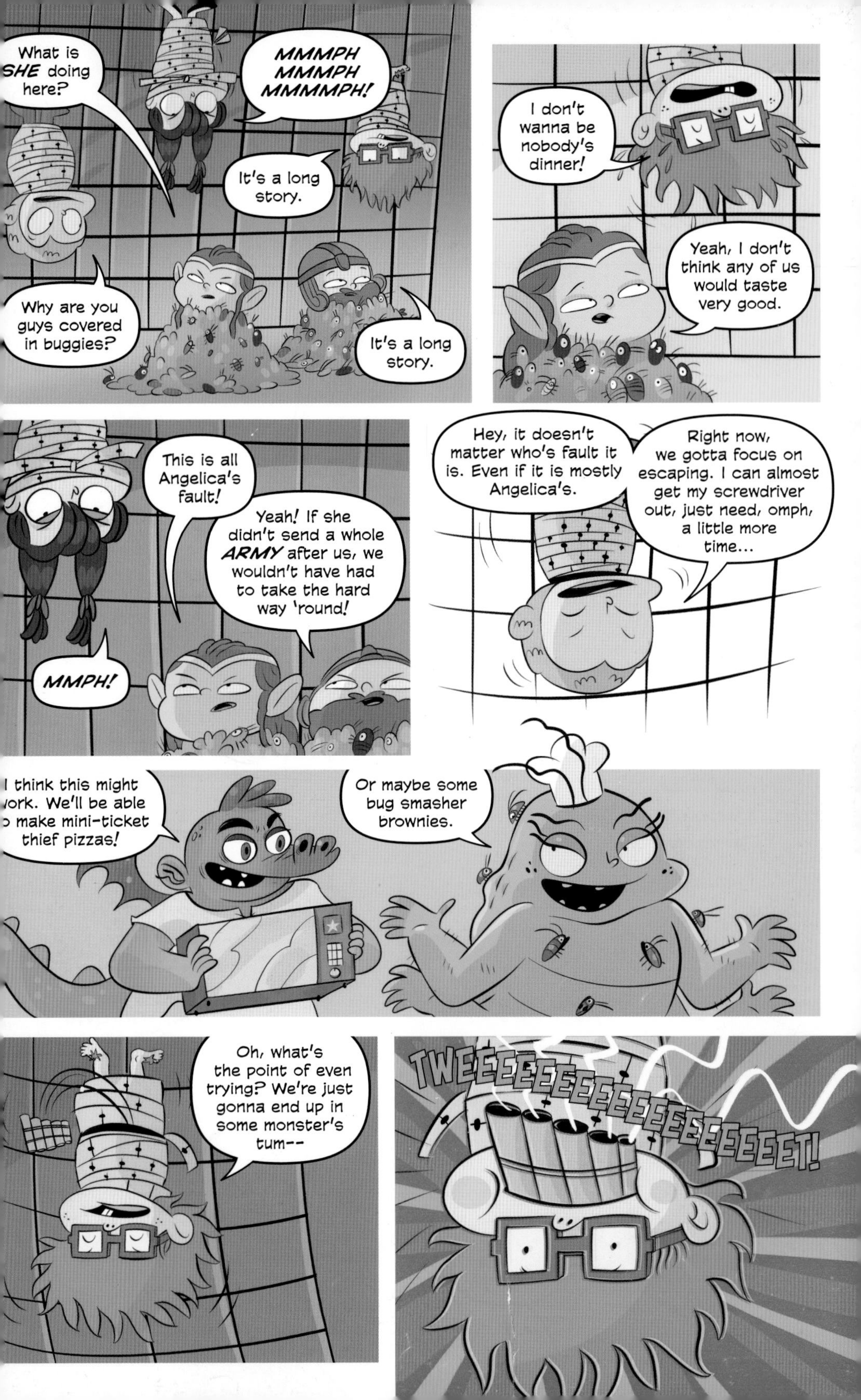
What is SHE doing here?
MMMPH MMMPH MMMMPH!
It's a long story.
Why are you guys covered in buggies?
It's a long story.
I don't wanna be nobody's dinner!
Yeah, I don't think any of us would taste very good.
This is all Angelica's fault!
Yeah! If she didn't send a whole ARMY after us, we wouldn't have had to take the hard way 'round!
MMPH!
Hey, it doesn't matter who's fault it is. Even if it is mostly Angelica's.
Right now, we gotta focus on escaping. I can almost get my screwdriver out, just need, omph, a little more time...
I think this might work. We'll be able to make mini-ticket thief pizzas!
Or maybe some bug smasher brownies.
Oh, what's the point of even trying? We're just gonna end up in some monster's tum--
TWEEEEEEEEEEEEEEEEEEEEEET!

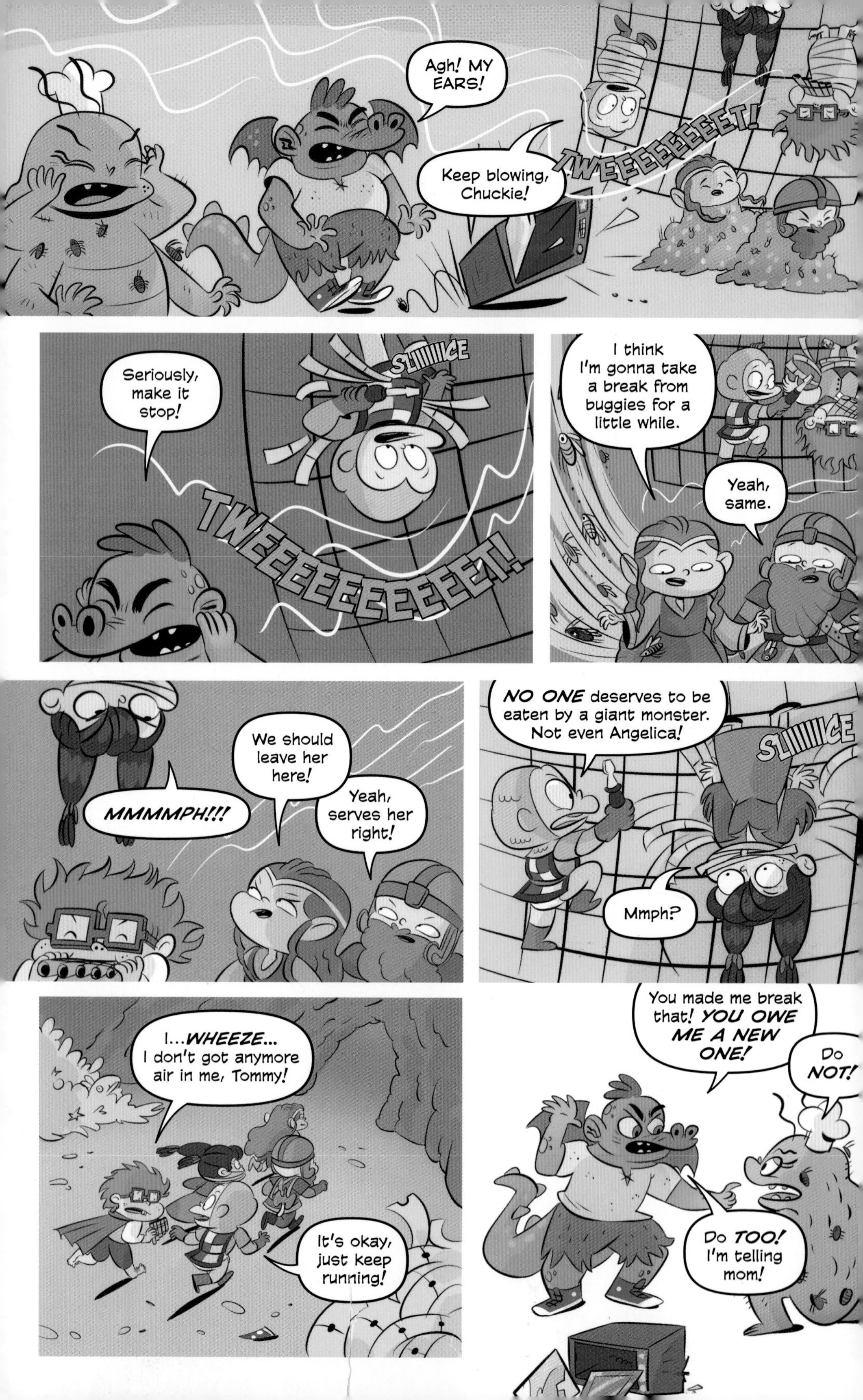
Agh! MY EARS!
Keep blowing, Chuckie!
TWEEEEEEEET!
Seriously, make it stop!
SLIIIIICE
TWEEEEEEEEEEET!
I think I'm gonna take a break from buggies for a little while.
Yeah, same.
MMMMPH!!!
We should leave her here!
Yeah, serves her right!
NO ONE deserves to be eaten by a giant monster. Not even Angelica!
SLIIIIICE
Mmph?
I...WHEEZE... I don't got anymore air in me, Tommy!
It's okay, just keep running!
You made me break that! YOU OWE ME A NEW ONE!
Do NOT!
Do TOO! I'm telling mom!

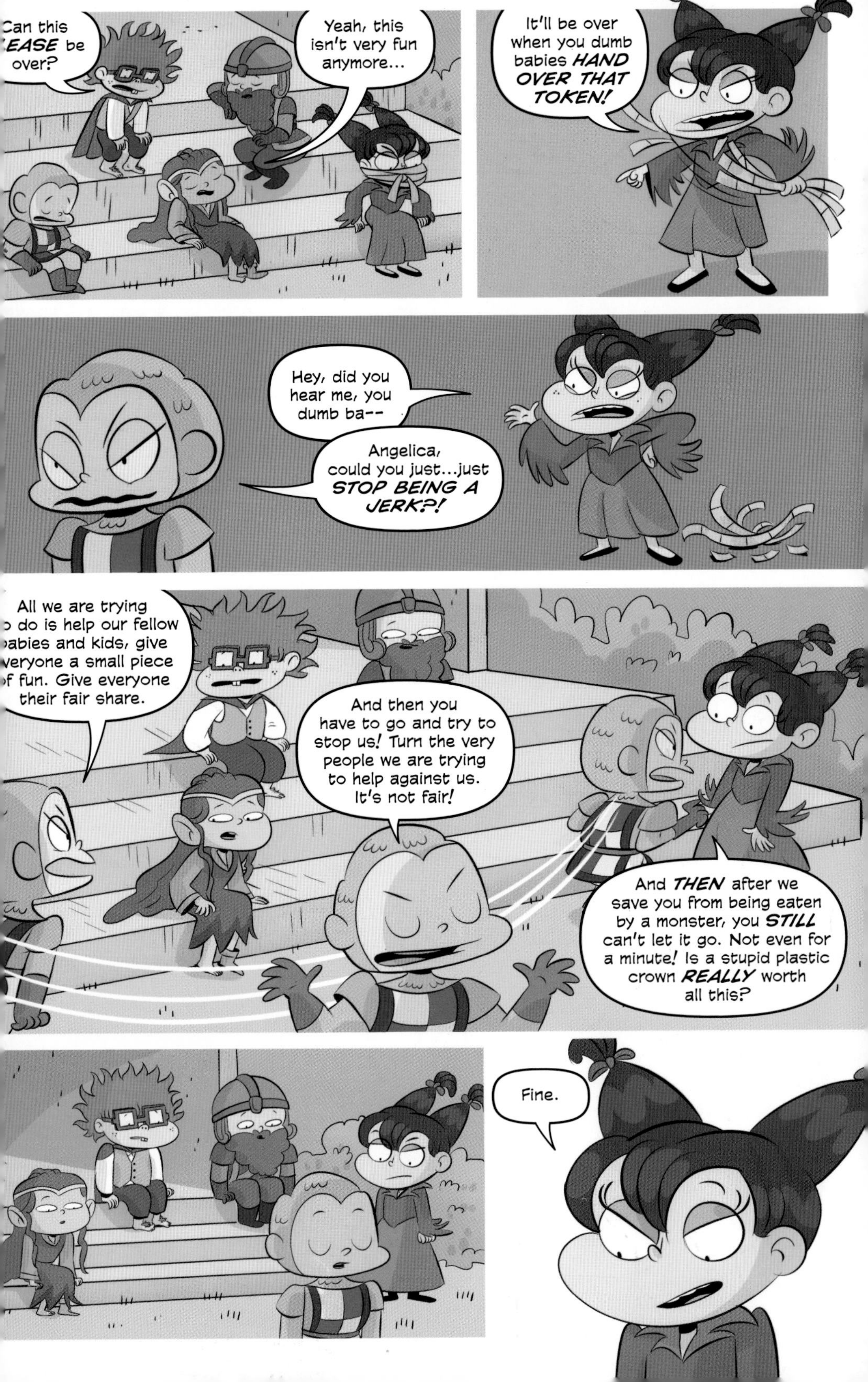
Can this
EASE be
over?
Yeah, this
isn't very fun
anymore...
It'll be over
when you dumb
babies HAND
OVER THAT
TOKEN!
Hey, did you
hear me, you
dumb ba--
Angelica,
could you just...just
STOP BEING A
JERK?!
All we are trying
o do is help our fellow
abies and kids, give
veryone a small piece
f fun. Give everyone
their fair share.
And then you
have to go and try to
stop us! Turn the very
people we are trying
to help against us.
It's not fair!
And THEN after we
save you from being eaten
by a monster, you STILL
can't let it go. Not even for
a minute! Is a stupid plastic
crown REALLY worth
all this?
Fine.

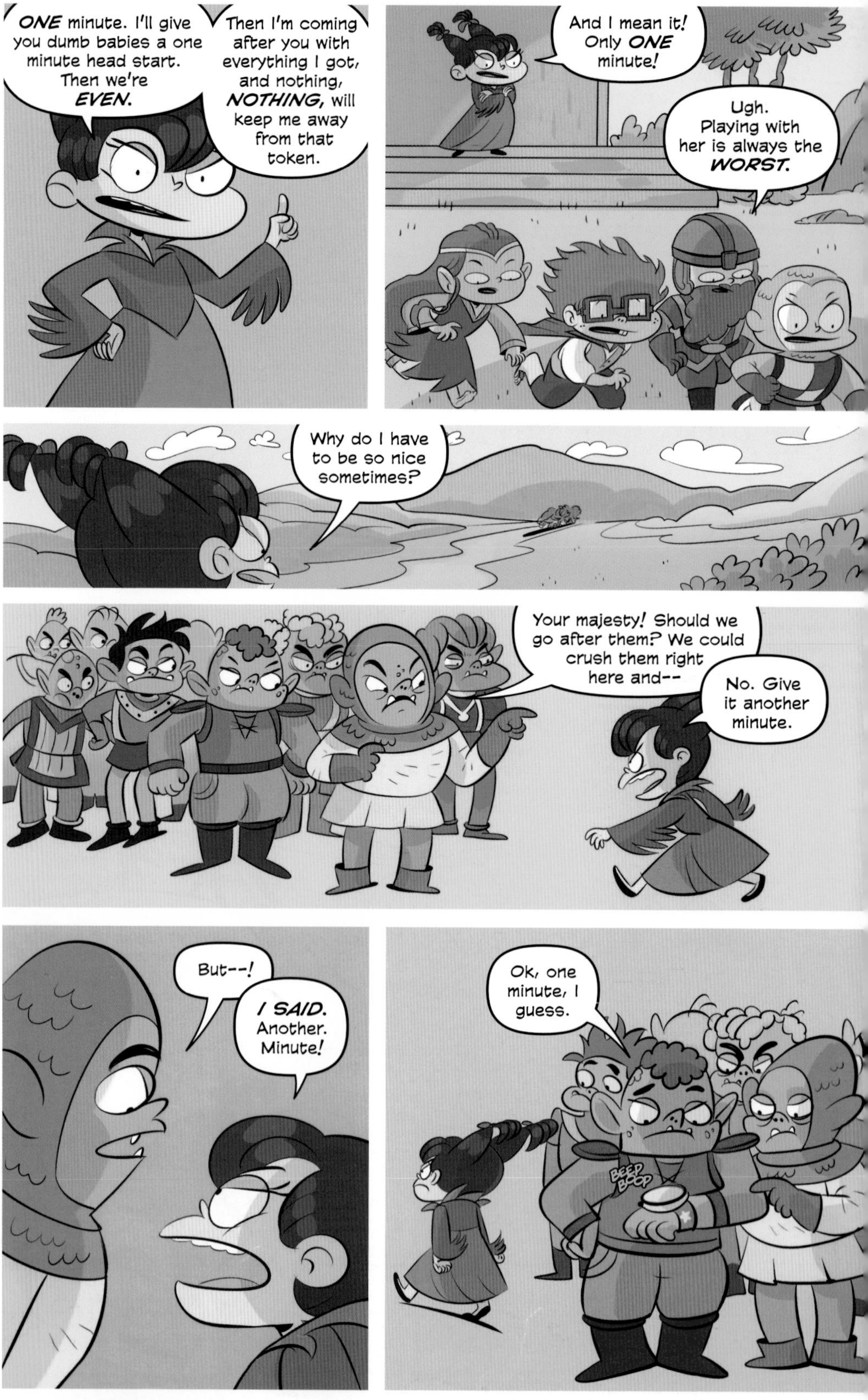
ONE minute. I'll give you dumb babies a one minute head start. Then we're EVEN.
Then I'm coming after you with everything I got, and nothing, NOTHING, will keep me away from that token.
And I mean it! Only ONE minute!
Ugh. Playing with her is always the WORST.
Why do I have to be so nice sometimes?
Your majesty! Should we go after them? We could crush them right here and--
No. Give it another minute.
But--!
I SAID. Another. Minute!
Ok, one minute, I guess.
BEEP BOOP

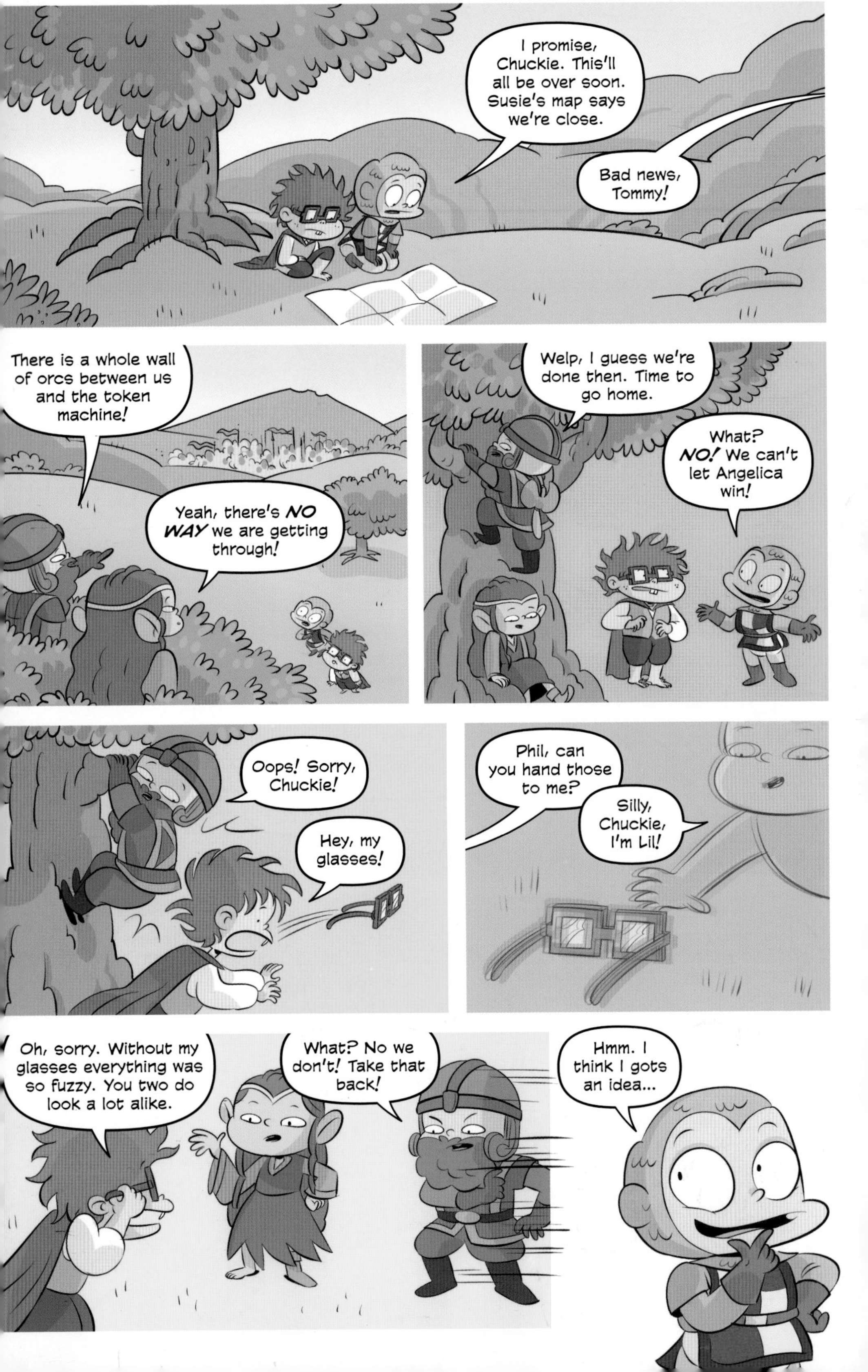
I promise, Chuckie. This'll all be over soon. Susie's map says we're close.
Bad news, Tommy!
There is a whole wall of orcs between us and the token machine!
Yeah, there's *NO WAY* we are getting through!
Welp, I guess we're done then. Time to go home.
What? *NO!* We can't let Angelica win!
Oops! Sorry, Chuckie!
Hey, my glasses!
Phil, can you hand those to me?
Silly, Chuckie, I'm Lil!
Oh, sorry. Without my glasses everything was so fuzzy. You two do look a lot alike.
What? No we don't! Take that back!
Hmm. I think I gots an idea...

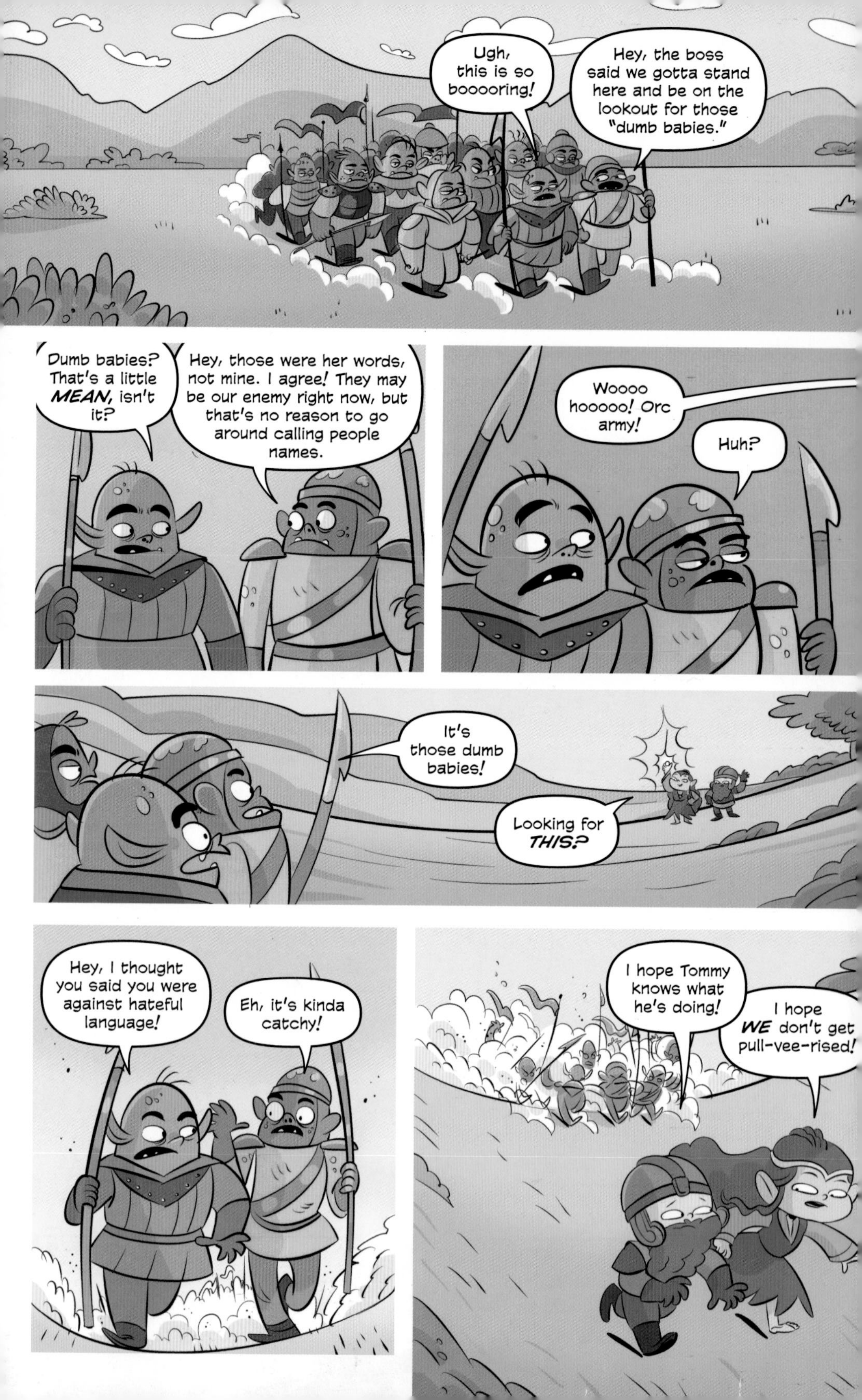

Ugh, this is so booooring!
Hey, the boss said we gotta stand here and be on the lookout for those "dumb babies."
Dumb babies? That's a little MEAN, isn't it?
Hey, those were her words, not mine. I agree! They may be our enemy right now, but that's no reason to go around calling people names.
Woooo hooooo! Orc army!
Huh?
It's those dumb babies!
Looking for THIS?
Hey, I thought you said you were against hateful language!
Eh, it's kinda catchy!
I hope Tommy knows what he's doing!
I hope WE don't get pull-vee-rised!

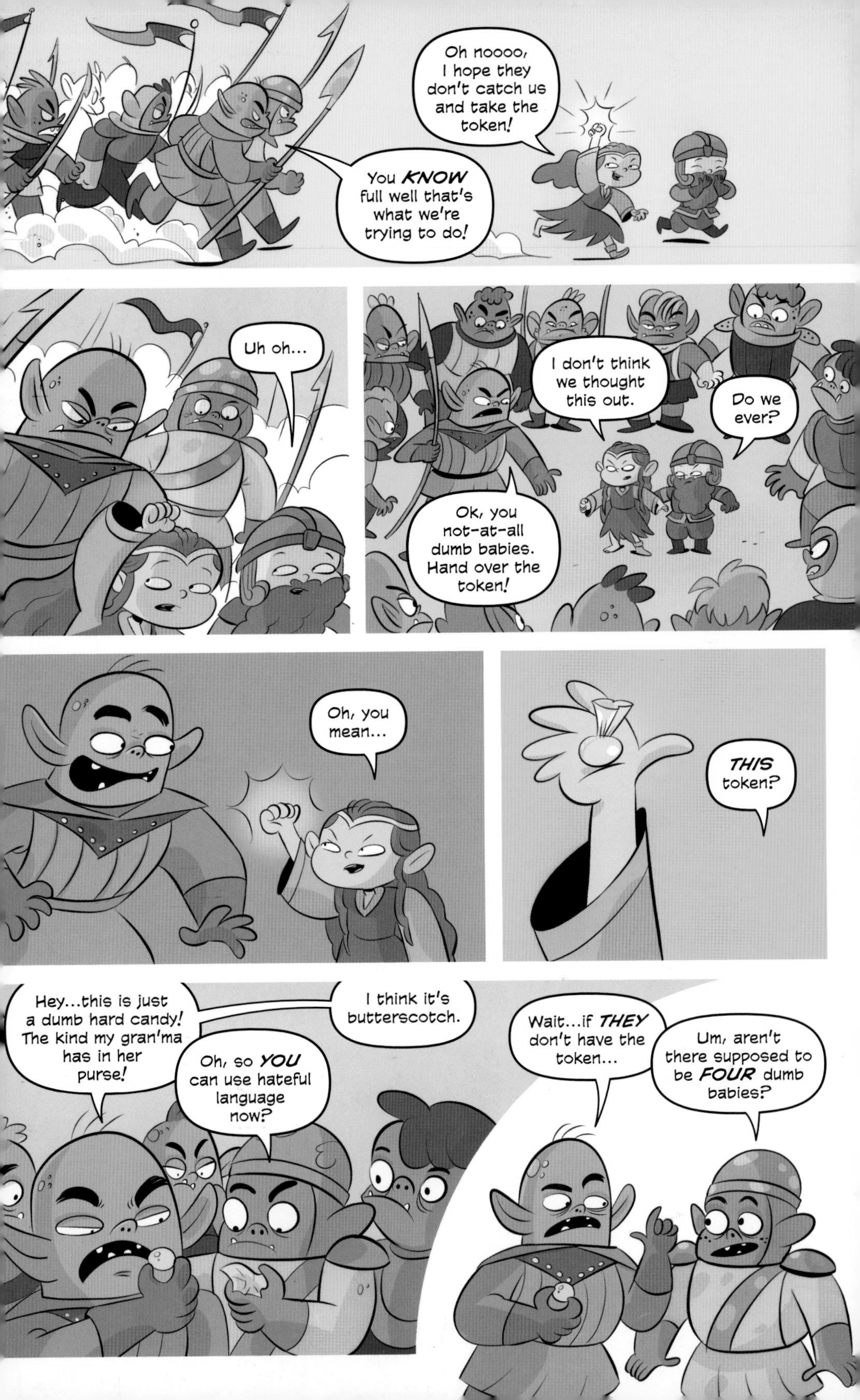
Oh noooo, I hope they don't catch us and take the token!
You KNOW full well that's what we're trying to do!
Uh oh...
I don't think we thought this out.
Do we ever?
Ok, you not-at-all dumb babies. Hand over the token!
Oh, you mean...
THIS token?
Hey...this is just a dumb hard candy! The kind my gran'ma has in her purse!
I think it's butterscotch.
Oh, so YOU can use hateful language now?
Wait...if THEY don't have the token...
Um, aren't there supposed to be FOUR dumb babies?

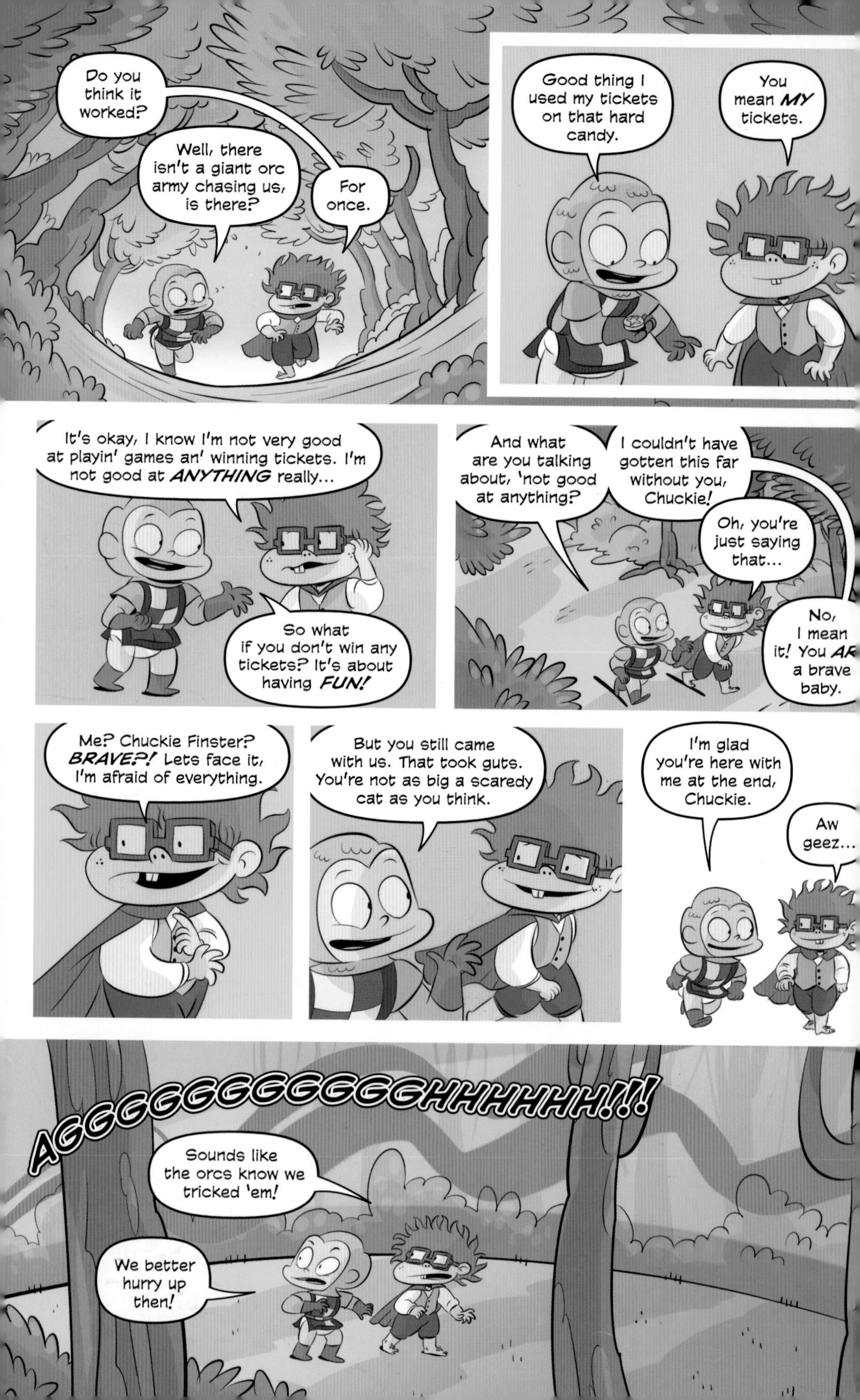
Do you think it worked?
Well, there isn't a giant orc army chasing us, is there?
For once.
Good thing I used my tickets on that hard candy.
You mean MY tickets.
It's okay, I know I'm not very good at playin' games an' winning tickets. I'm not good at ANYTHING really...
So what if you don't win any tickets? It's about having FUN!
And what are you talking about, 'not good at anything?
I couldn't have gotten this far without you, Chuckie!
Oh, you're just saying that...
No, I mean it! You AR a brave baby.
Me? Chuckie Finster? BRAVE?! Lets face it, I'm afraid of everything.
But you still came with us. That took guts. You're not as big a scaredy cat as you think.
I'm glad you're here with me at the end, Chuckie.
Aw geez...
AGGGGGGGGGGGGHHHHHH!!!
Sounds like the orcs know we tricked 'em!
We better hurry up then!

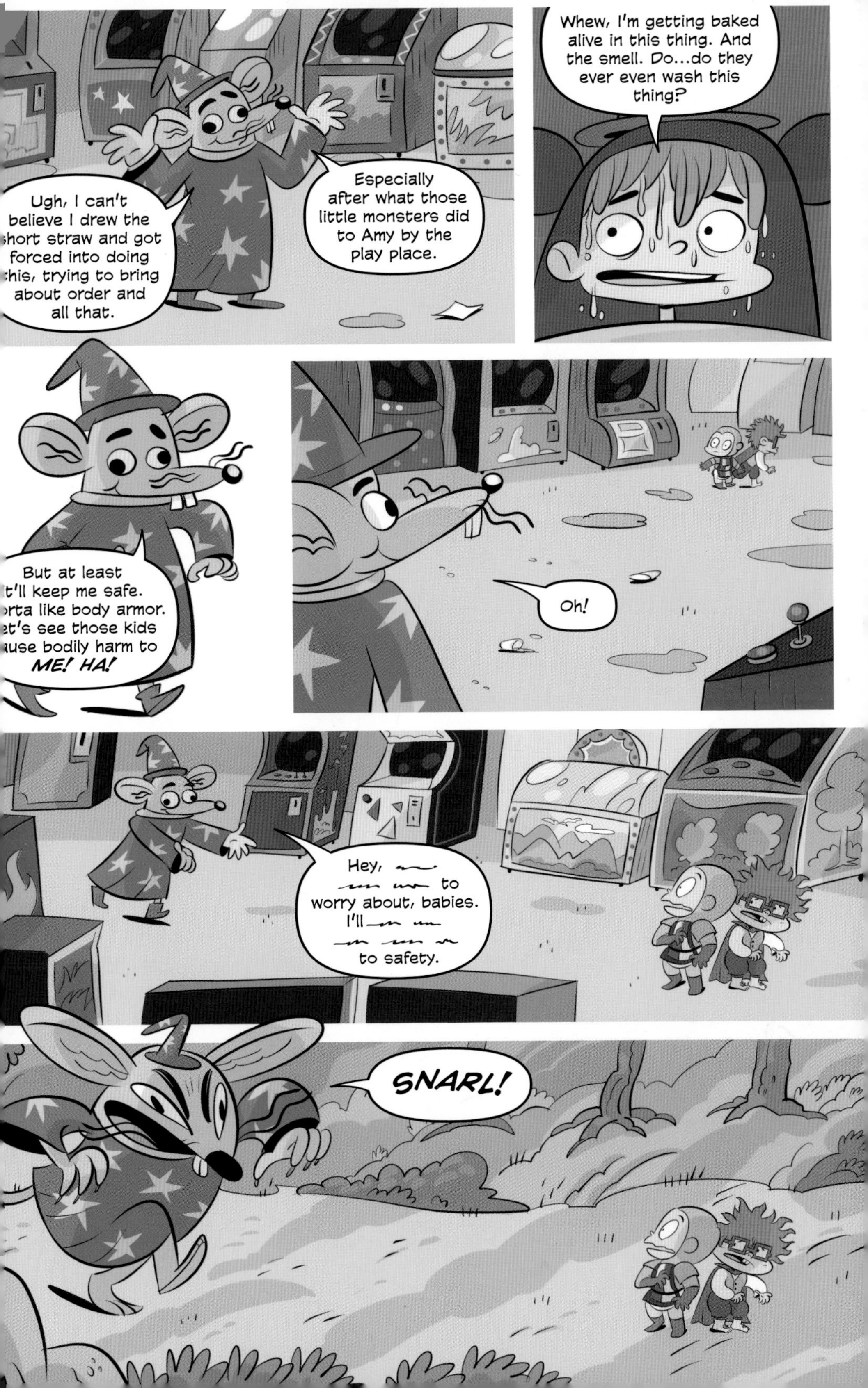
Ugh, I can't believe I drew the hort straw and got forced into doing his, trying to bring about order and all that.
Especially after what those little monsters did to Amy by the play place.
Whew, I'm getting baked alive in this thing. And the smell. Do...do they ever even wash this thing?
But at least t'll keep me safe. orta like body armor. et's see those kids ause bodily harm to *ME! HA!*
Oh!
Hey, to worry about, babies. I'll to safety.
SNARL!

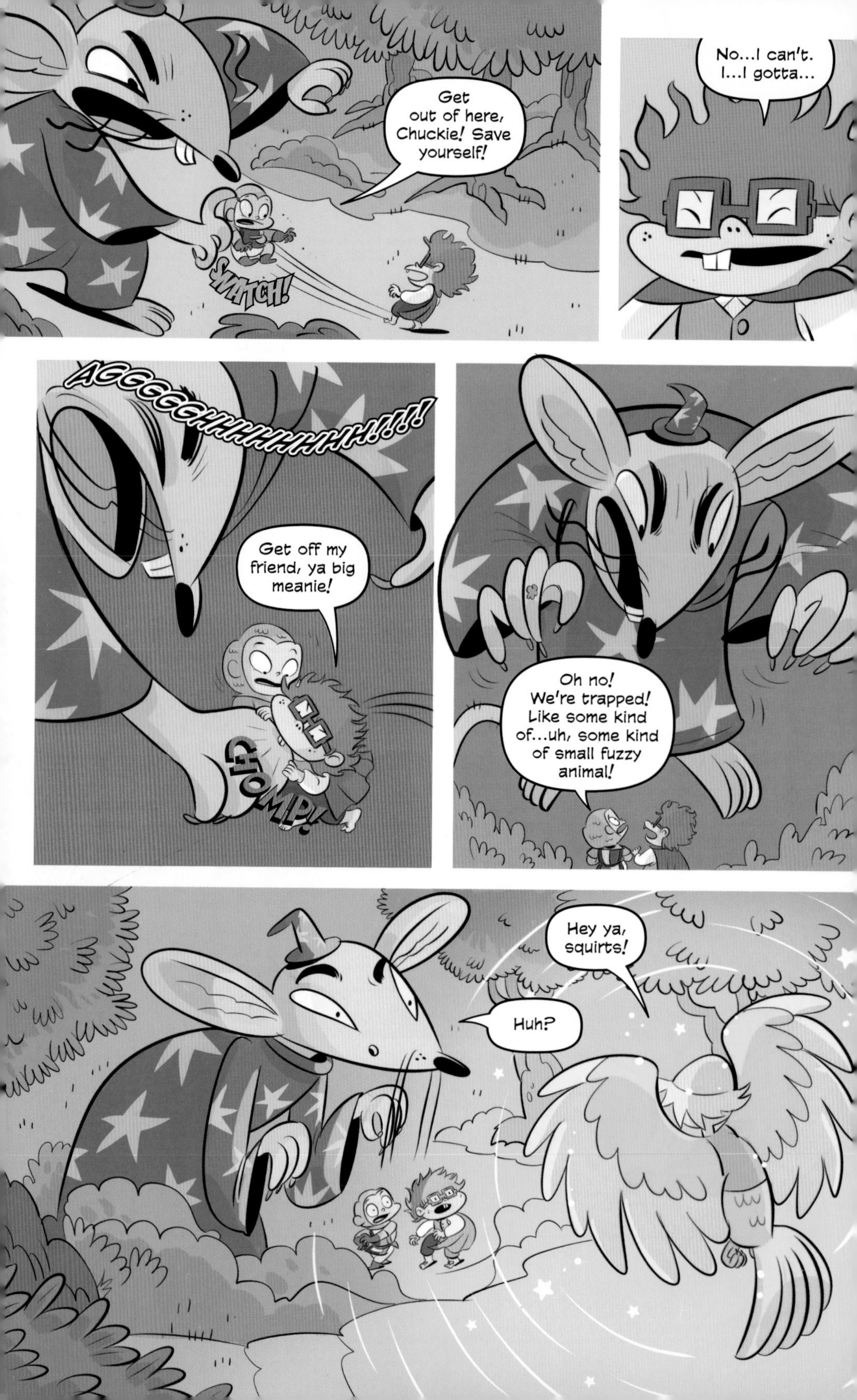

Get out of here, Chuckie! Save yourself!
SWATCH!
No...I can't. I...I gotta...
AGGGGGHHHHHHHHH!!!!
Get off my friend, ya big meanie!
CHOMP!
Oh no! We're trapped! Like some kind of...uh, some kind of small fuzzy animal!
Hey ya, squirts!
Huh?

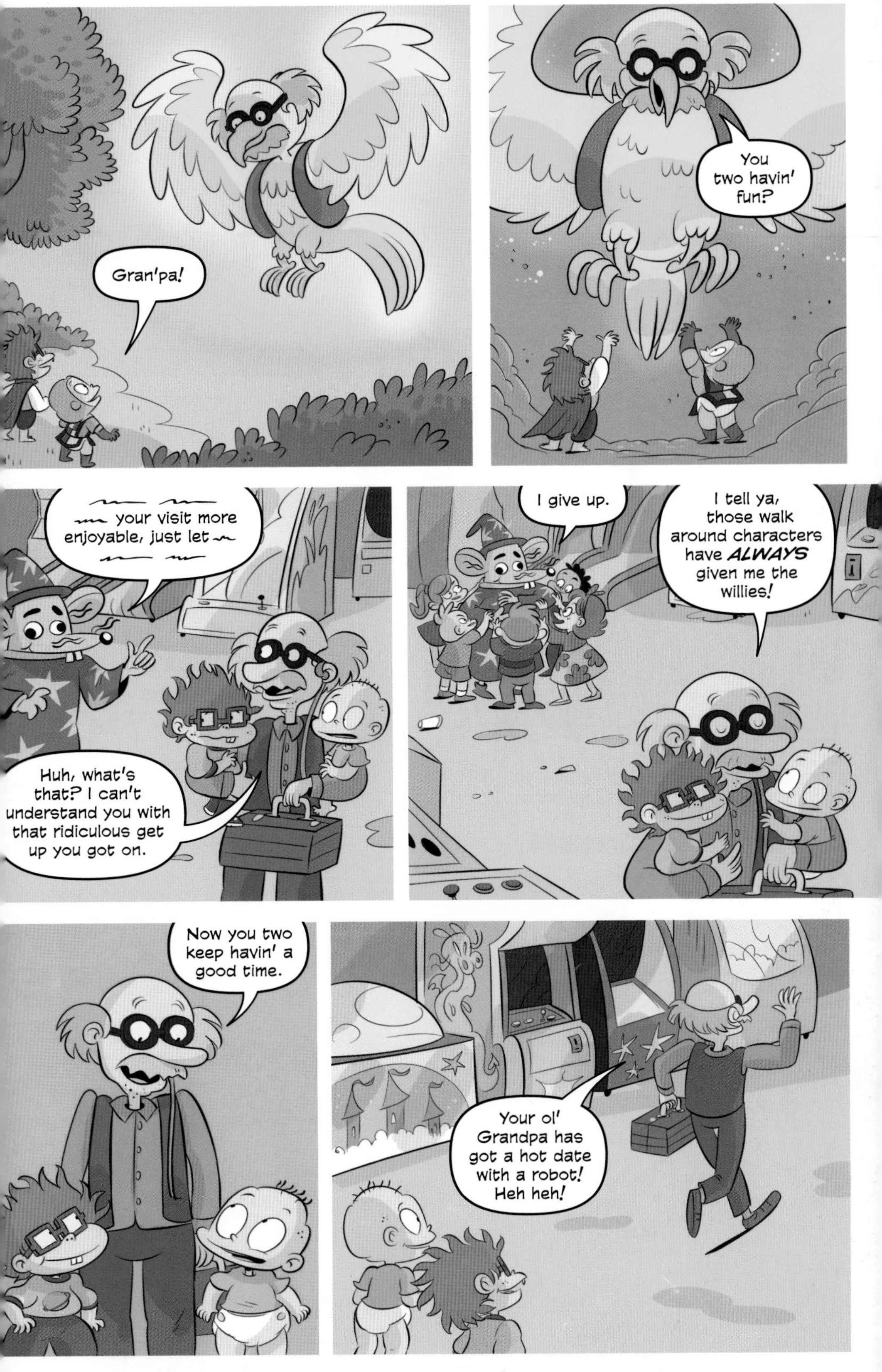

Gran'pa!
You two havin' fun?
your visit more enjoyable, just let
Huh, what's that? I can't understand you with that ridiculous get up you got on.
I give up.
I tell ya, those walk around characters have ALWAYS given me the willies!
Now you two keep havin' a good time.
Your ol' Grandpa has got a hot date with a robot! Heh heh!

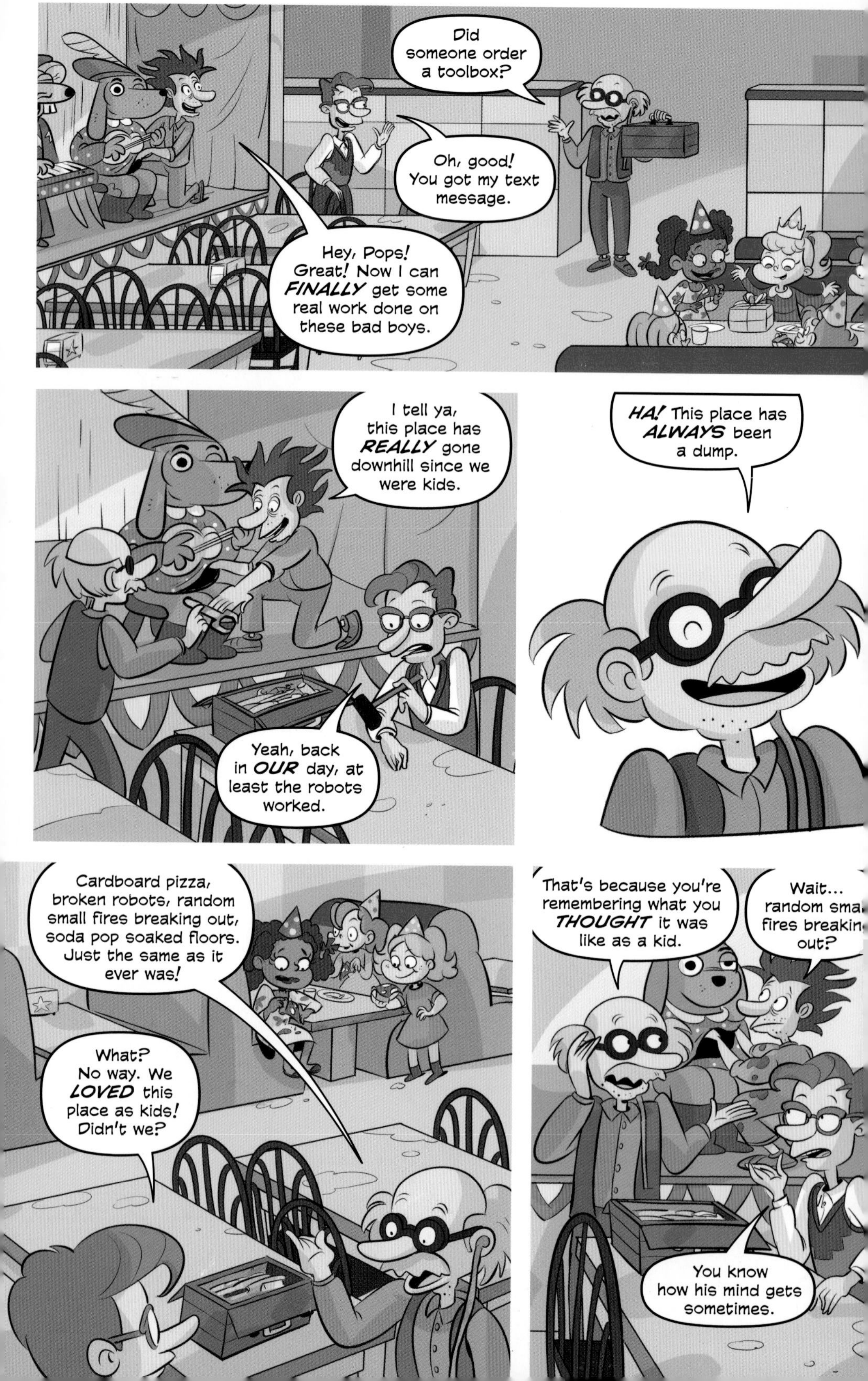
Did someone order a toolbox?
Oh, good! You got my text message.
Hey, Pops! Great! Now I can *FINALLY* get some real work done on these bad boys.
I tell ya, this place has *REALLY* gone downhill since we were kids.
Yeah, back in *OUR* day, at least the robots worked.
HA! This place has *ALWAYS* been a dump.
Cardboard pizza, broken robots, random small fires breaking out, soda pop soaked floors. Just the same as it ever was!
What? No way. We *LOVED* this place as kids! Didn't we?
That's because you're remembering what you *THOUGHT* it was like as a kid.
Wait... random sma fires breakin out?
You know how his mind gets sometimes.

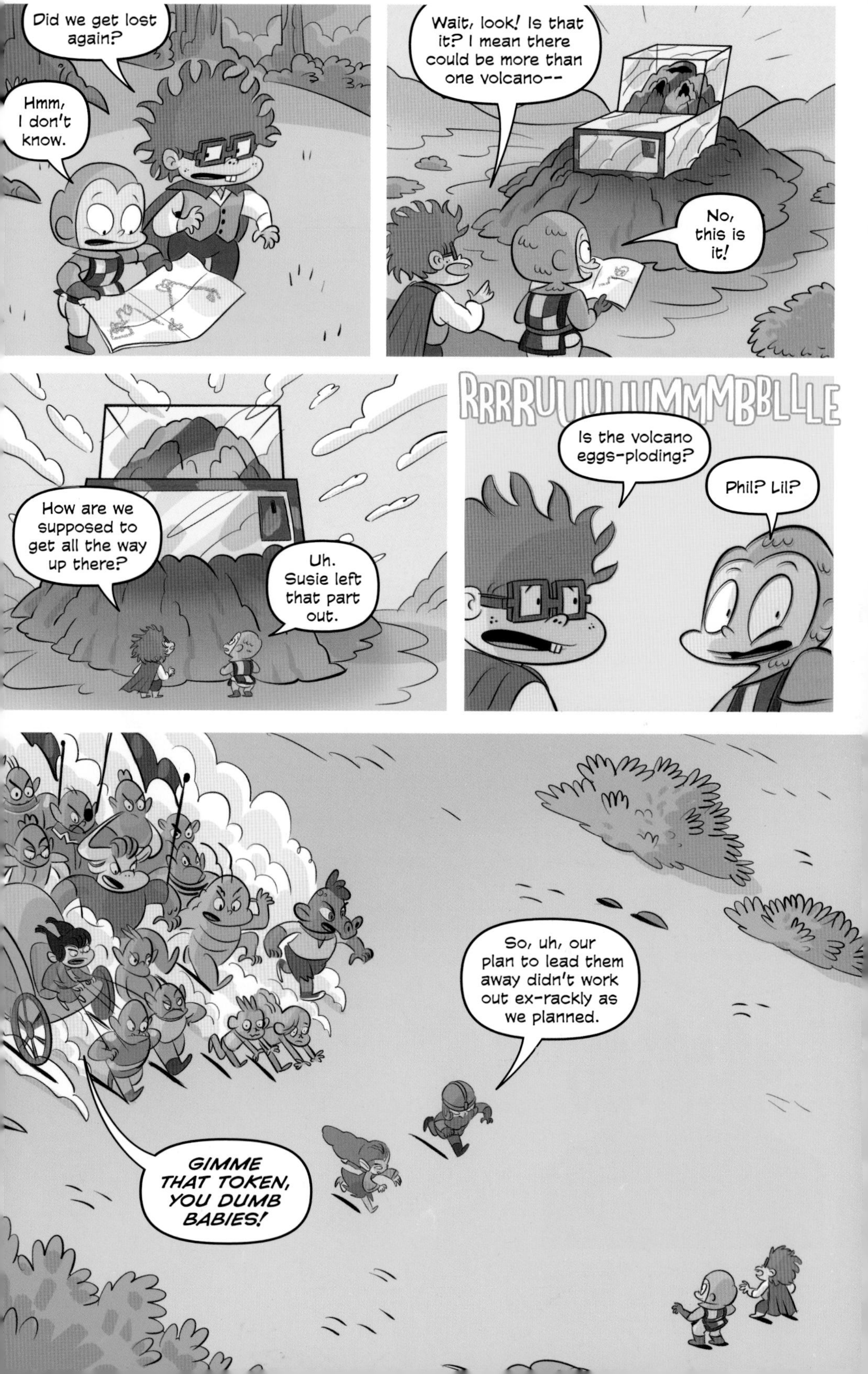
Did we get lost again?
Hmm, I don't know.
Wait, look! Is that it? I mean there could be more than one volcano--
No, this is it!
How are we supposed to get all the way up there?
Uh. Susie left that part out.
RRRRUUUUUMMMBBLLLE
Is the volcano eggs-ploding?
Phil? Lil?
So, uh, our plan to lead them away didn't work out ex-rackly as we planned.
GIMME THAT TOKEN, YOU DUMB BABIES!

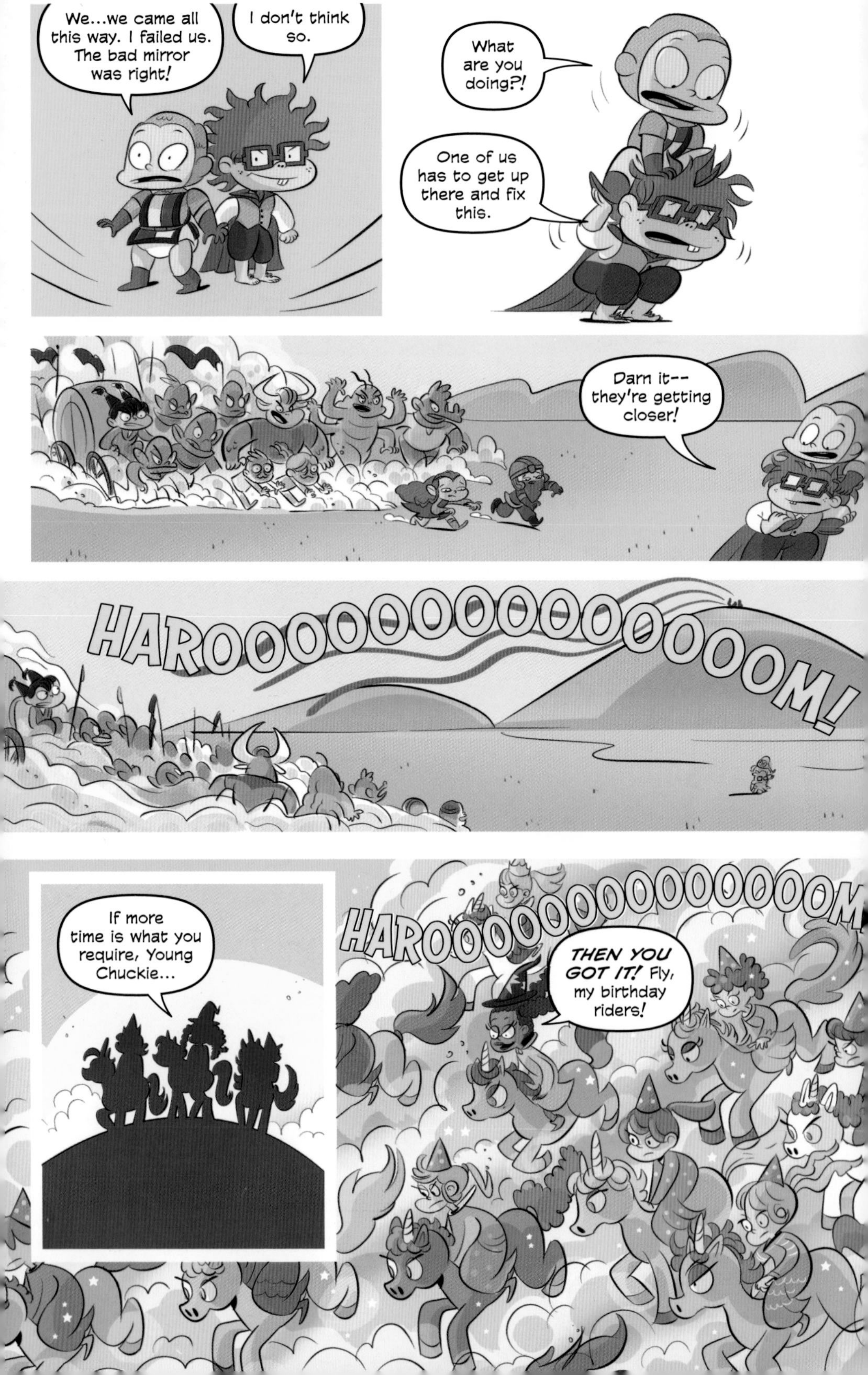
We...we came all this way. I failed us. The bad mirror was right!
I don't think so.
What are you doing?!
One of us has to get up there and fix this.
Darn it-- they're getting closer!
HAROOOOOOOOOOOOOOM!
If more time is what you require, Young Chuckie...
HAROOOOOOOOOOOOOOOM
THEN YOU GOT IT! Fly, my birthday riders!

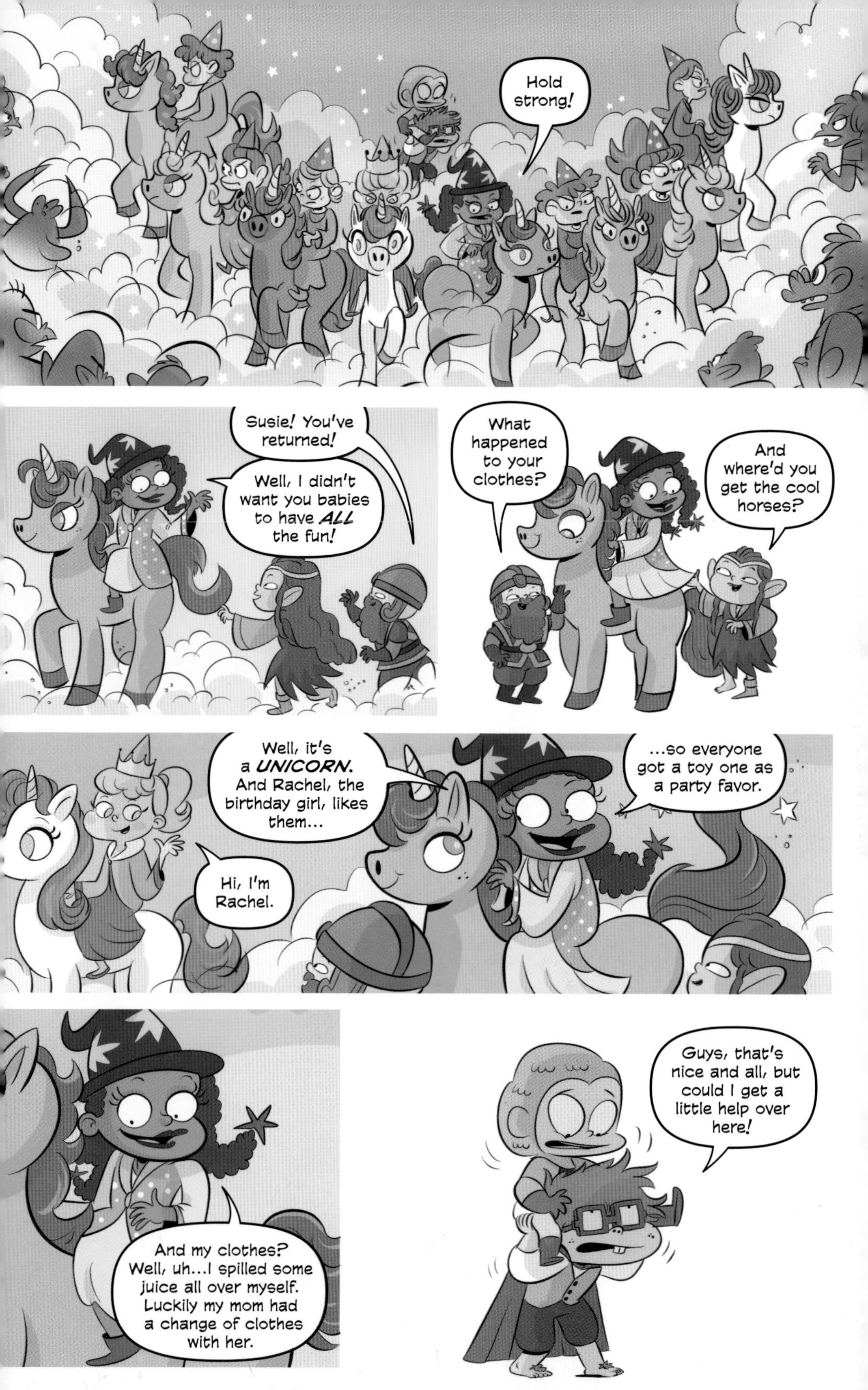
Hold strong!
Susie! You've returned!
Well, I didn't want you babies to have ALL the fun!
What happened to your clothes?
And where'd you get the cool horses?
Well, it's a UNICORN. And Rachel, the birthday girl, likes them...
Hi, I'm Rachel.
...so everyone got a toy one as a party favor.
And my clothes? Well, uh...I spilled some juice all over myself. Luckily my mom had a change of clothes with her.
Guys, that's nice and all, but could I get a little help over here!

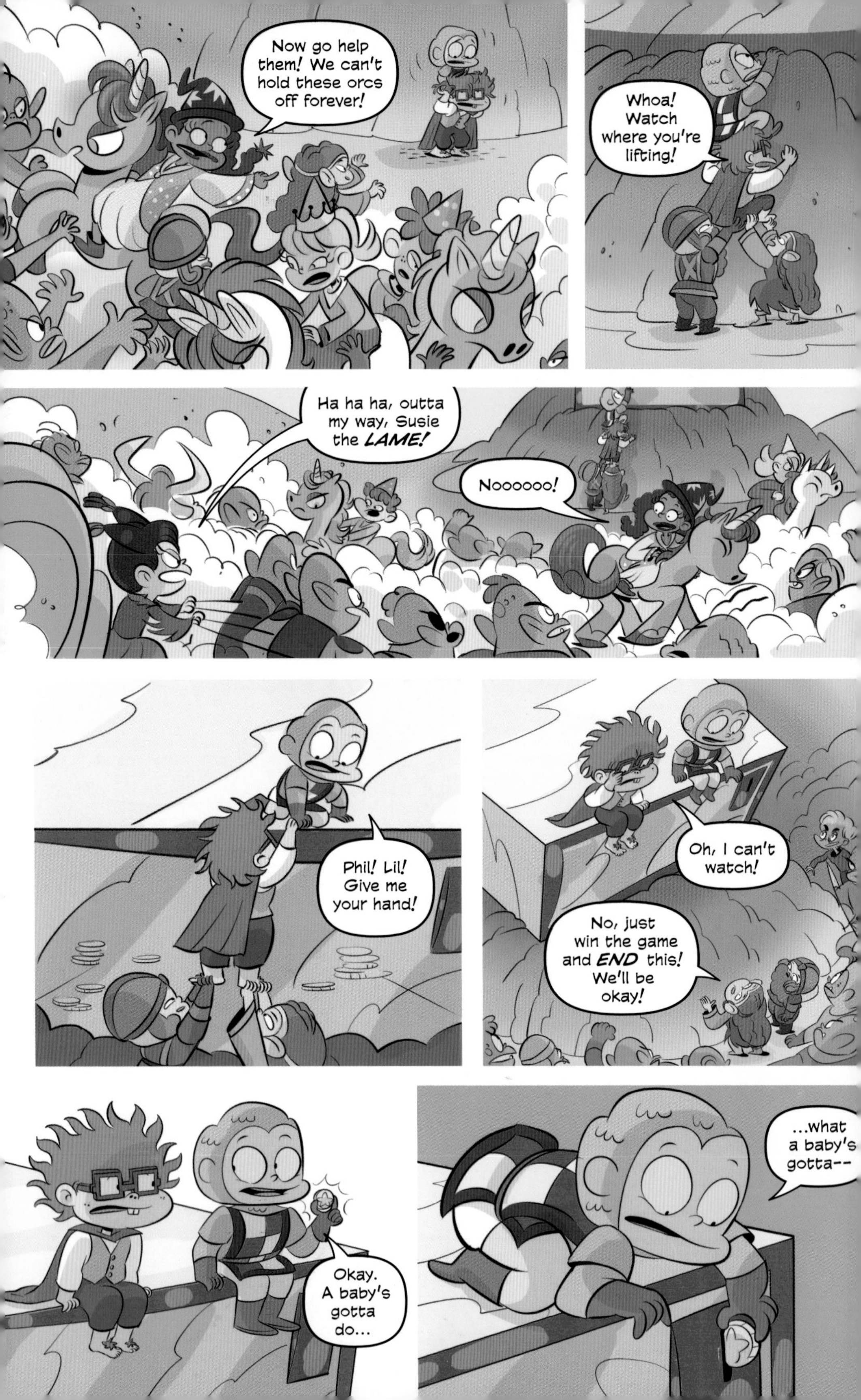
Now go help them! We can't hold these orcs off forever!
Whoa! Watch where you're lifting!
Ha ha ha, outta my way, Susie the LAME!
Noooooo!
Phil! Lil! Give me your hand!
Oh, I can't watch!
No, just win the game and END this! We'll be okay!
Okay. A baby's gotta do...
...what a baby's gotta--

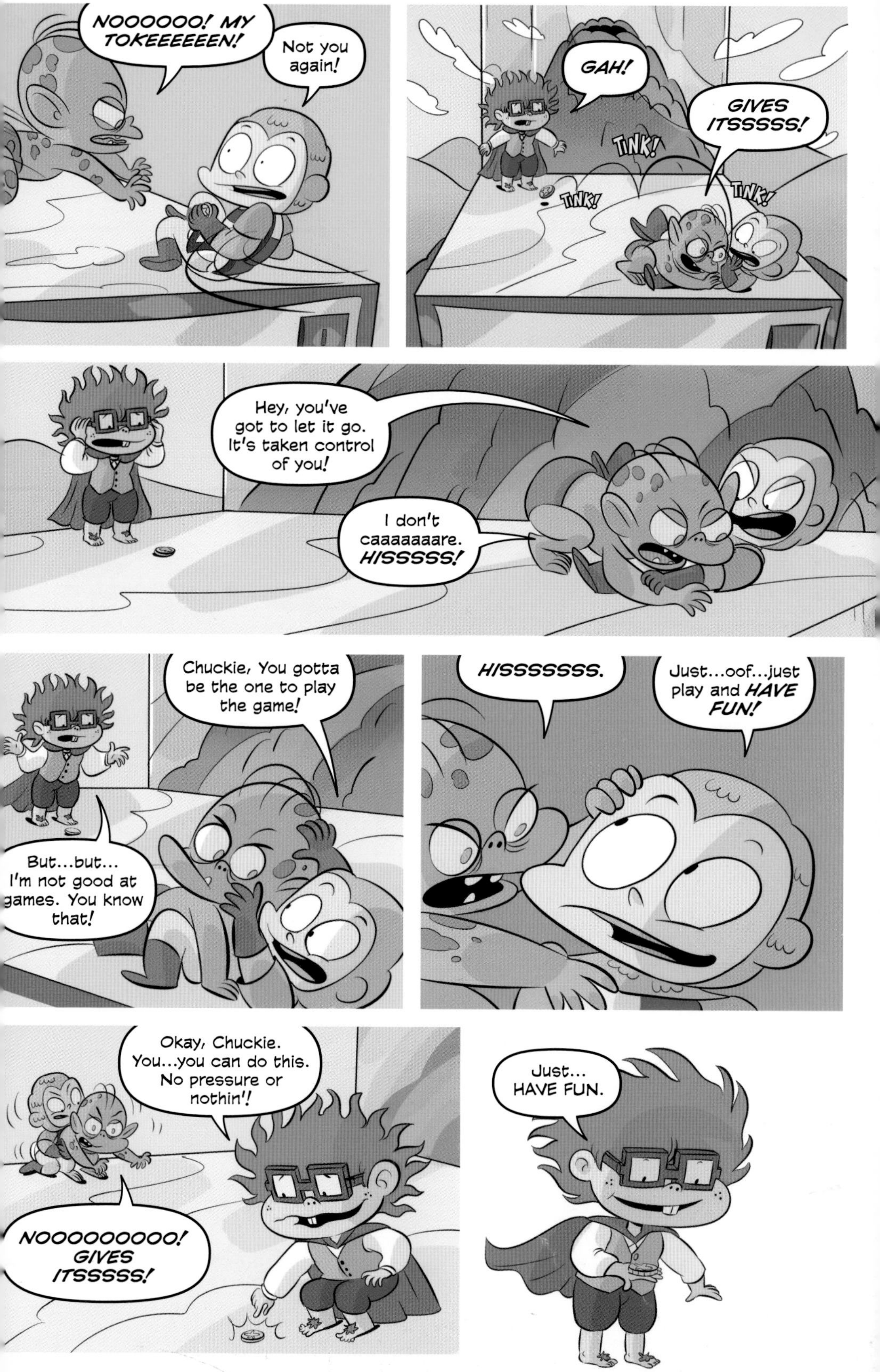
NOOOOOO! MY TOKEEEEEEN!
Not you again!
GAH!
GIVES ITSSSSS!
TINK!
TINK!
TINK!
Hey, you've got to let it go. It's taken control of you!
I don't caaaaaaare. HISSSSS!
Chuckie, You gotta be the one to play the game!
But...but... I'm not good at games. You know that!
HISSSSSSS.
Just...oof...just play and HAVE FUN!
Okay, Chuckie. You...you can do this. No pressure or nothin'!
NOOOOOOOOO! GIVES ITSSSSS!
Just... HAVE FUN.

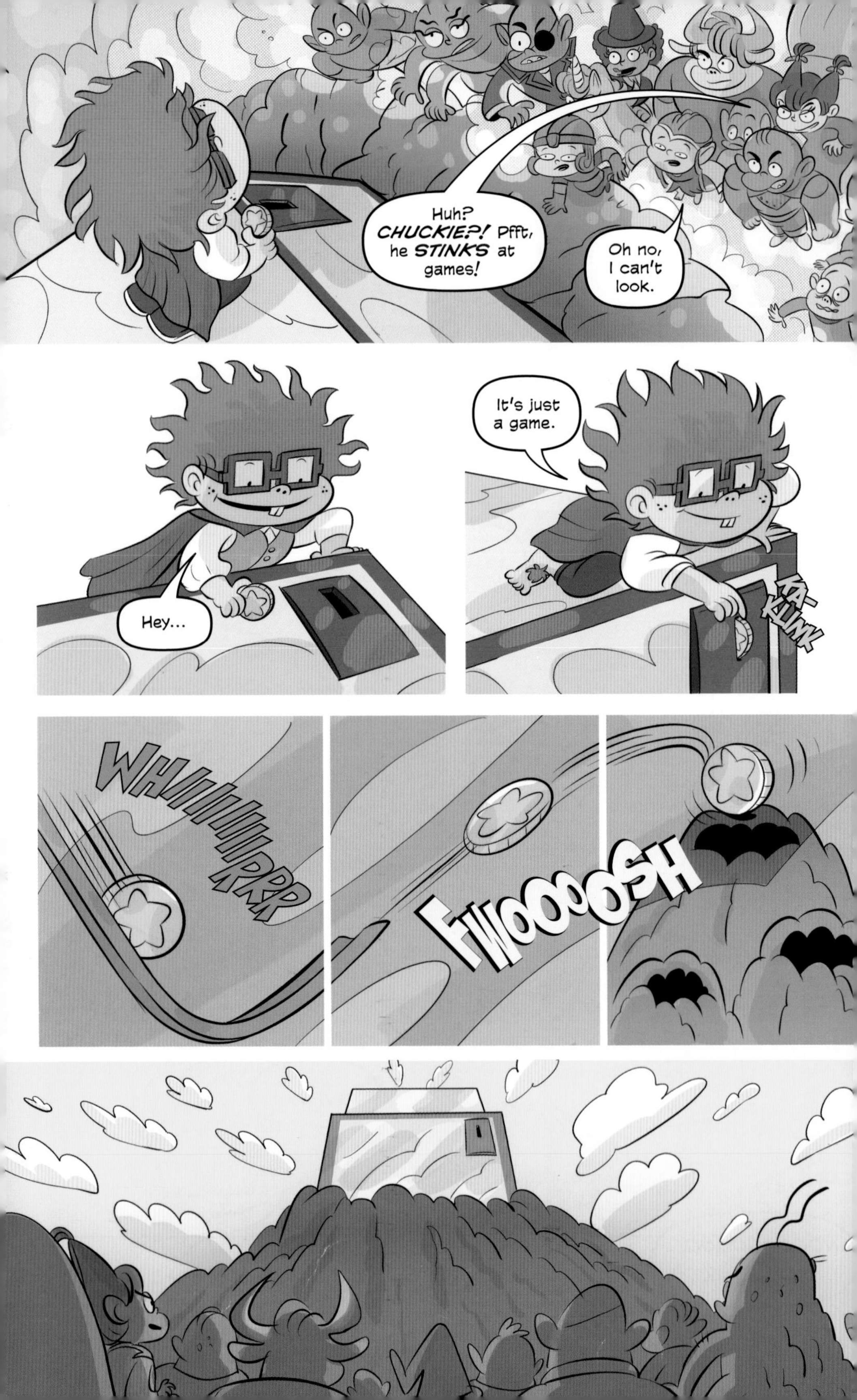
Huh? CHUCKIE?! Pfft, he STINKS at games!
Oh no, I can't look.
Hey...
It's just a game.
KA-KLINK
WHIIIIIIIRRR
FWOOOOSH

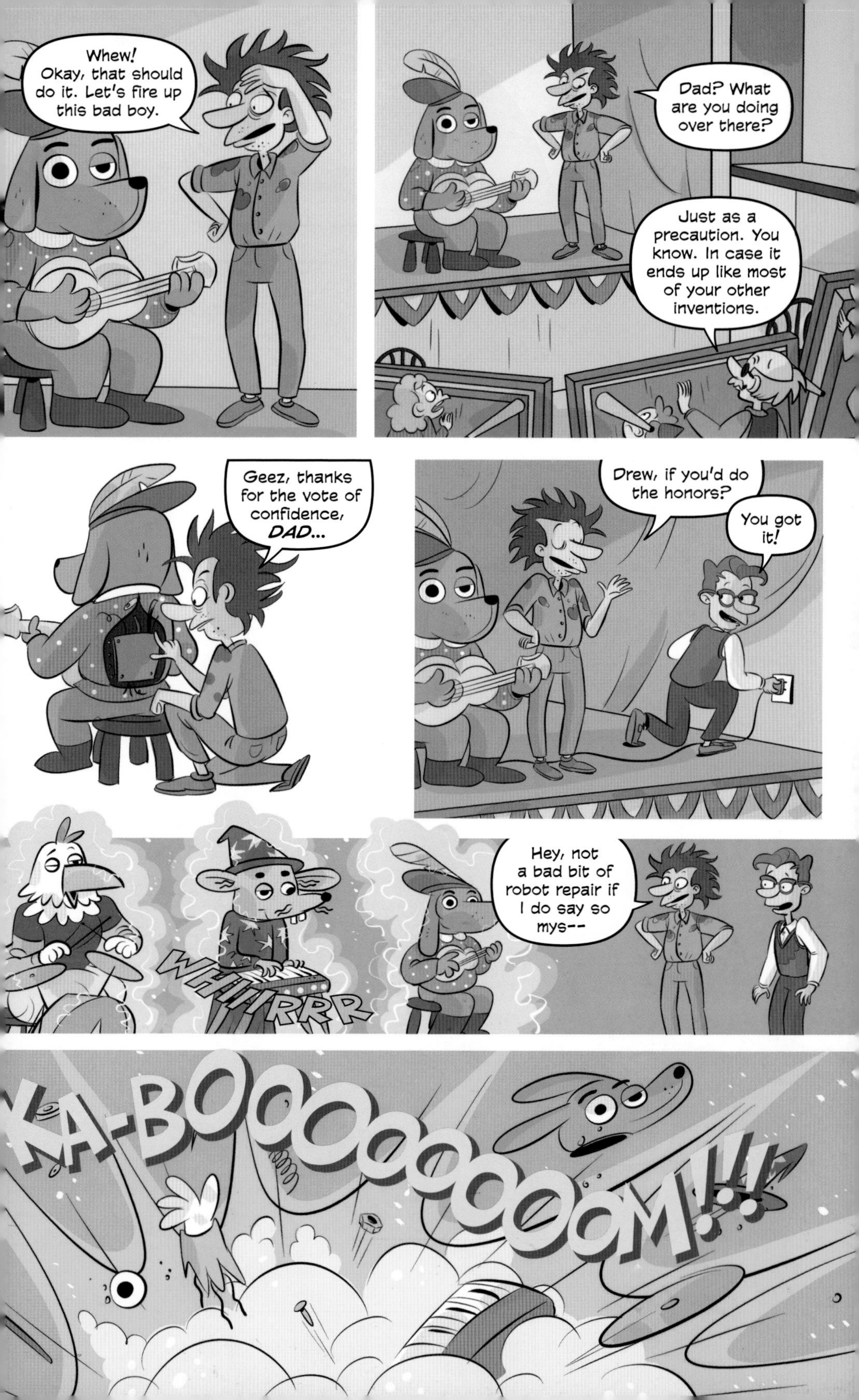
Whew!
Okay, that should do it. Let's fire up this bad boy.
Dad? What are you doing over there?
Just as a precaution. You know. In case it ends up like most of your other inventions.
Geez, thanks for the vote of confidence, ***DAD...***
Drew, if you'd do the honors?
You got it!
Hey, not a bad bit of robot repair if I do say so mys--
WHIIIRRR
KA-BOOOOOOOOOOM!!!

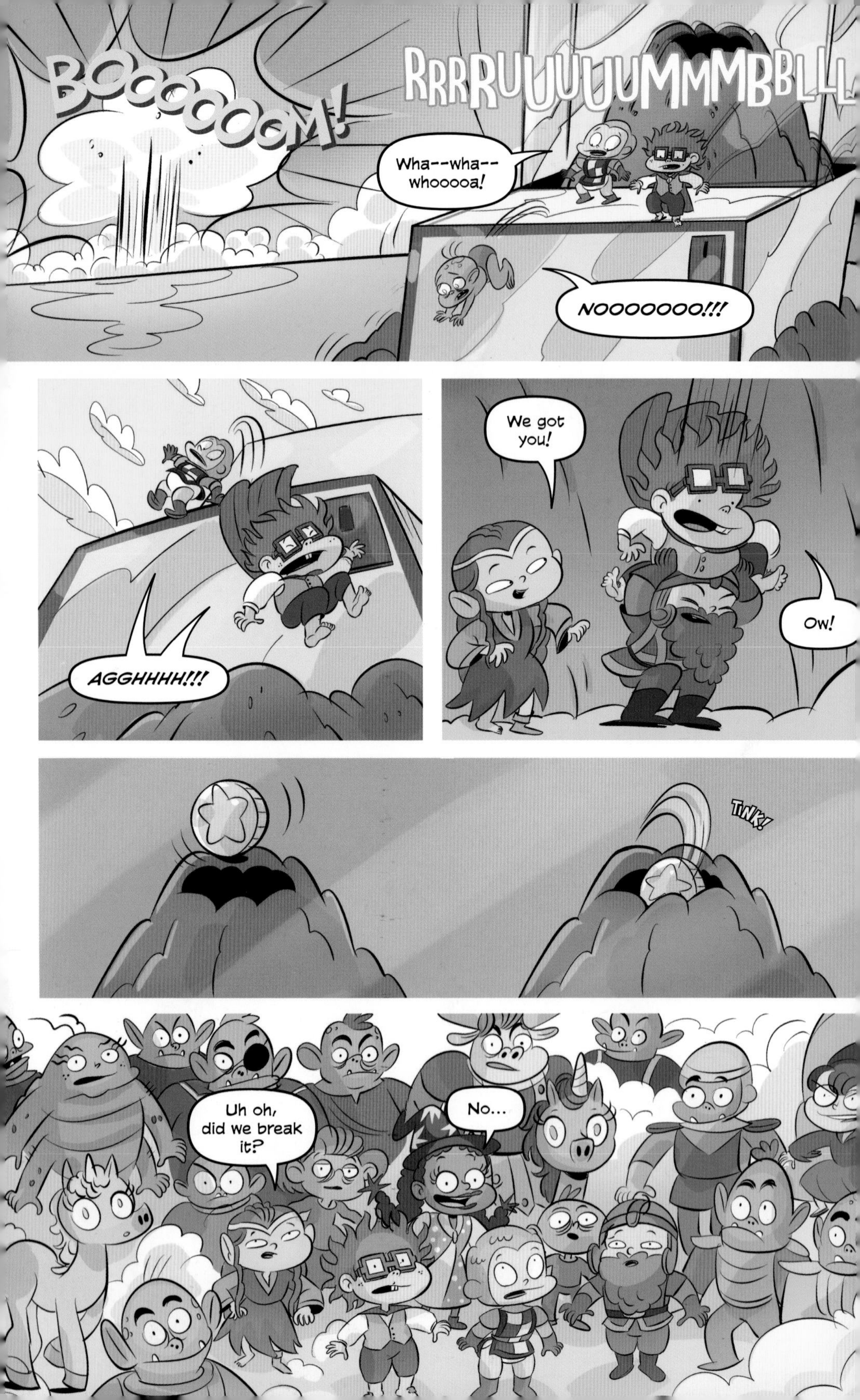
BOOOOOOOM!
RRRRUUUUUUMMMBBLLL
Wha--wha--
whooooa!
NOOOOOOO!!!
AGGHHHH!!!
We got
you!
Ow!
TINK!
Uh oh,
did we break
it?
No...

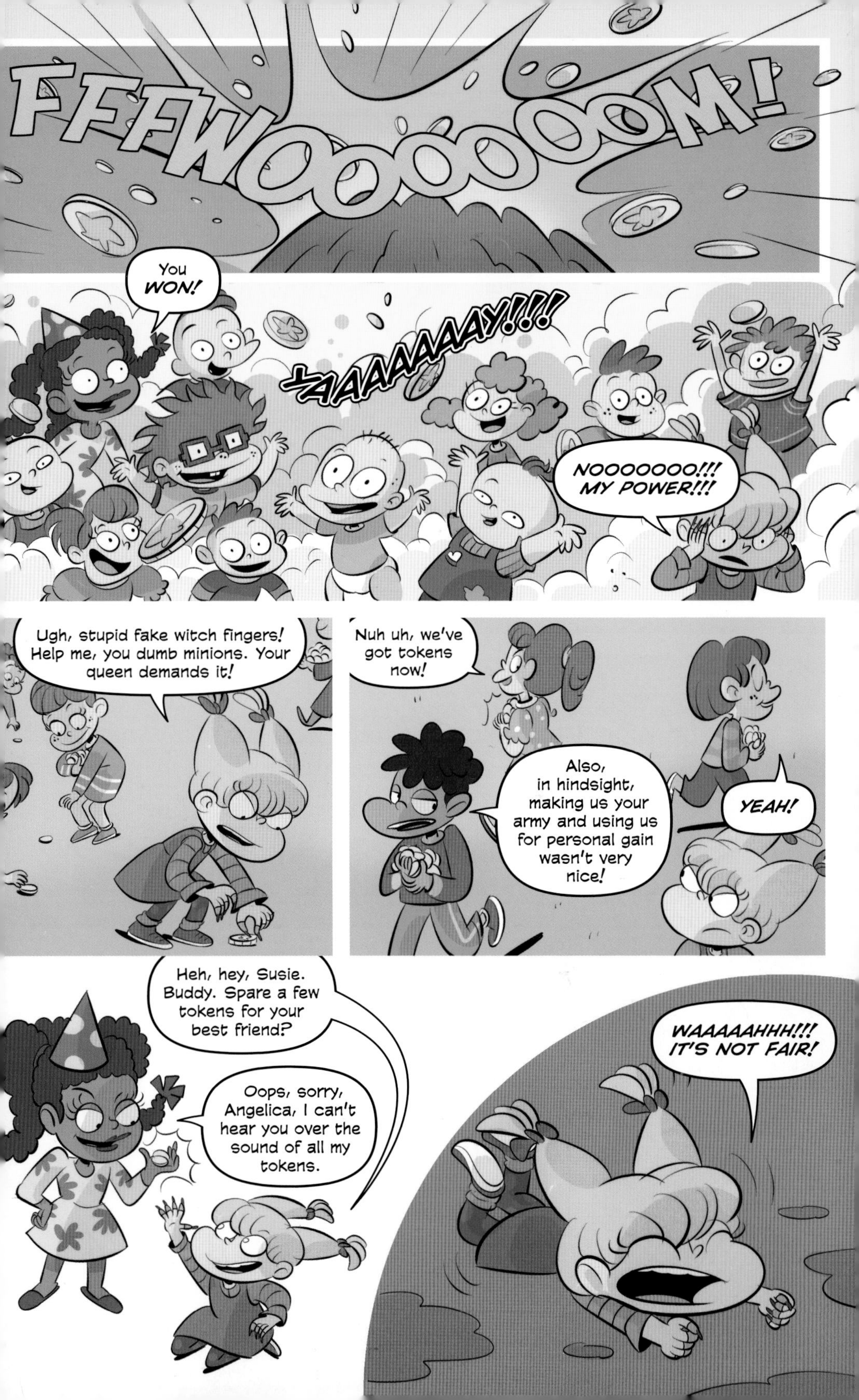
FFFWOOOOOOM!
You WON!
YAAAAAAAY!!!!
NOOOOOOO!!! MY POWER!!!
Ugh, stupid fake witch fingers! Help me, you dumb minions. Your queen demands it!
Nuh uh, we've got tokens now!
Also, in hindsight, making us your army and using us for personal gain wasn't very nice!
YEAH!
Heh, hey, Susie. Buddy. Spare a few tokens for your best friend?
Oops, sorry, Angelica, I can't hear you over the sound of all my tokens.
WAAAAAHHH!!! IT'S NOT FAIR!

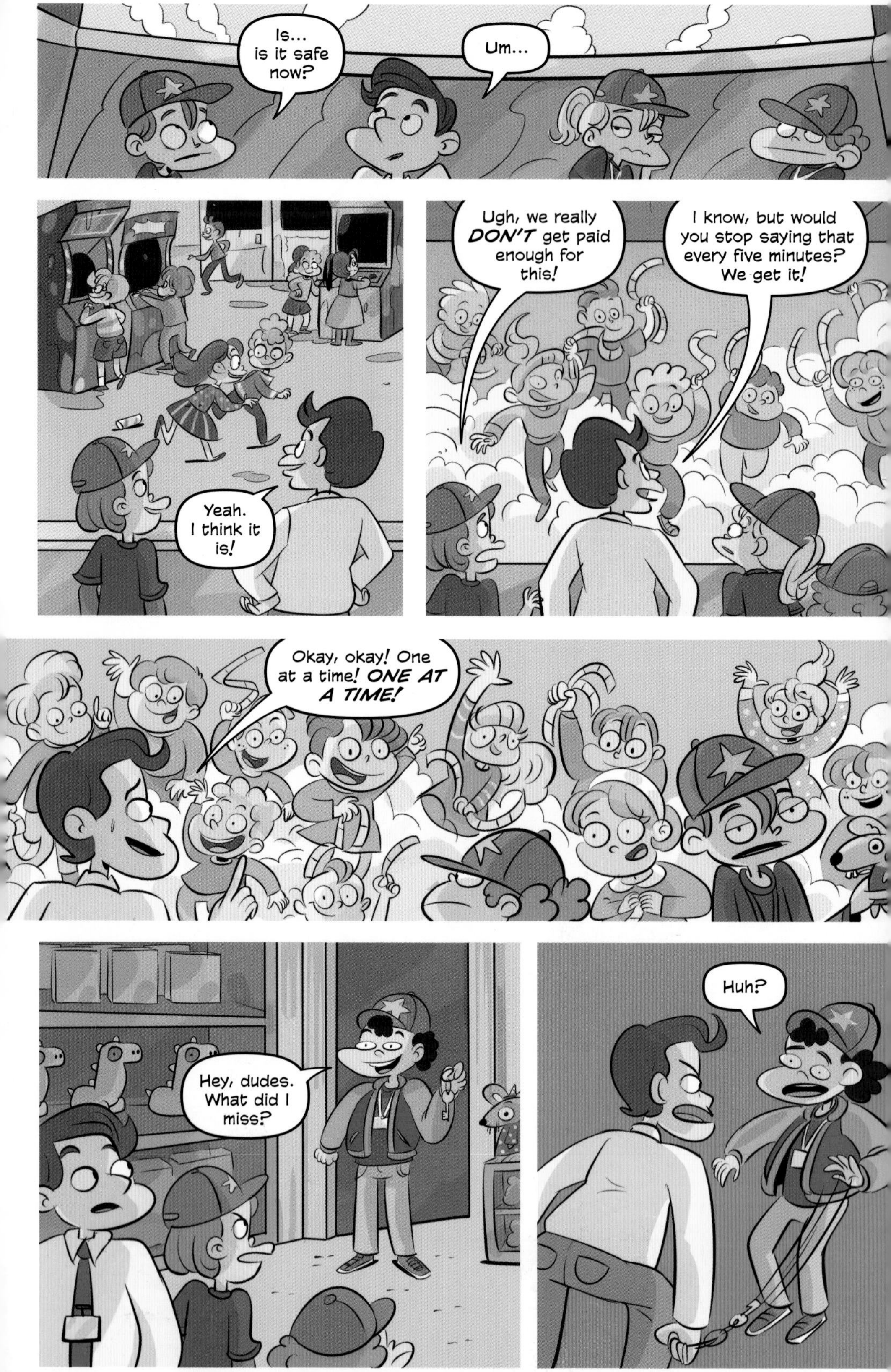
Is... is it safe now?
Um...
Yeah. I think it is!
Ugh, we really DON'T get paid enough for this!
I know, but would you stop saying that every five minutes? We get it!
Okay, okay! One at a time! ONE AT A TIME!
Hey, dudes. What did I miss?
Huh?

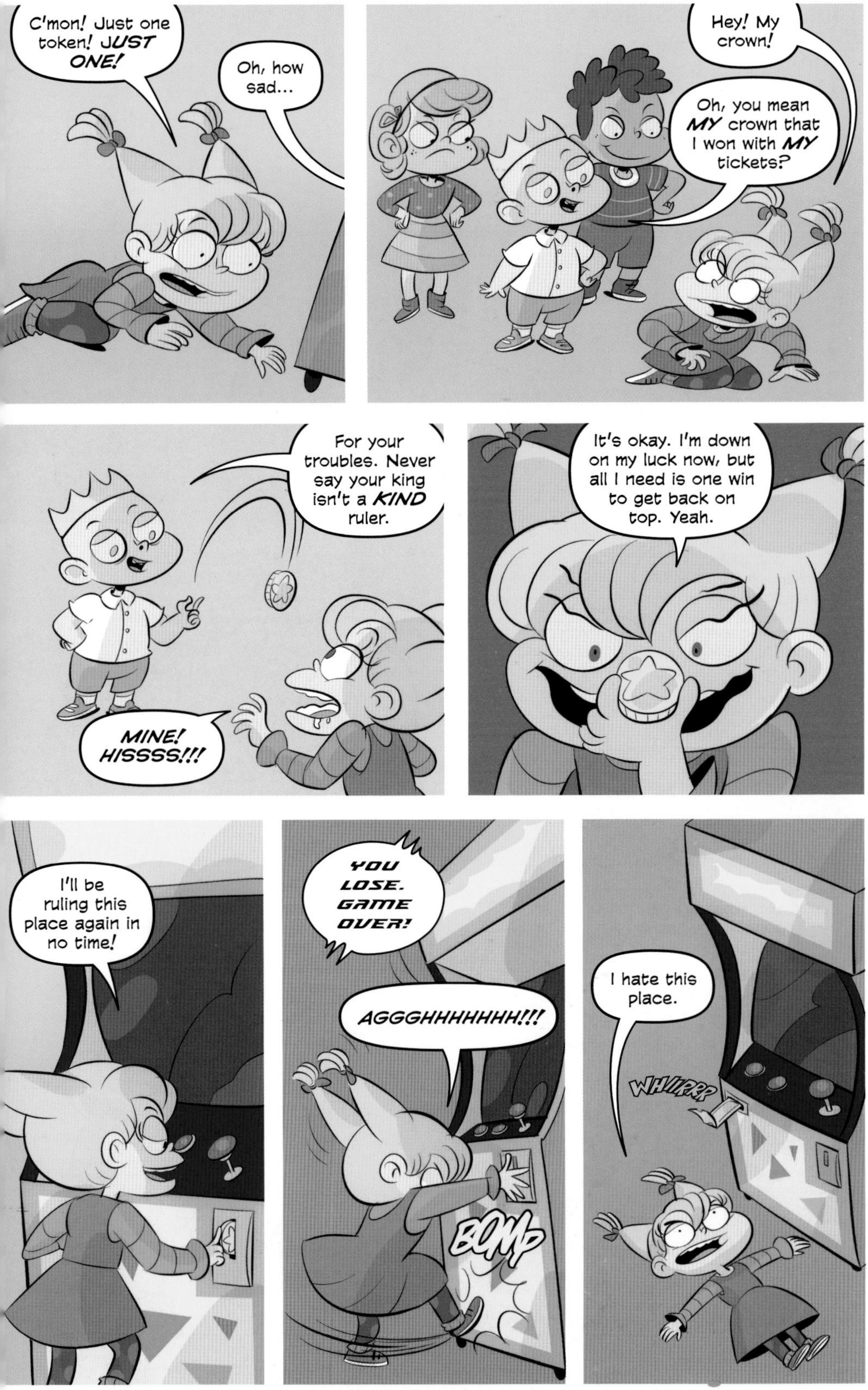
C'mon! Just one token! JUST ONE!
Oh, how sad...
Hey! My crown!
Oh, you mean MY crown that I won with MY tickets?
For your troubles. Never say your king isn't a KIND ruler.
MINE! HISSSS!!!
It's okay. I'm down on my luck now, but all I need is one win to get back on top. Yeah.
I'll be ruling this place again in no time!
YOU LOSE. GAME OVER!
AGGGHHHHHHH!!!
BOMP
I hate this place.
WHIRRR

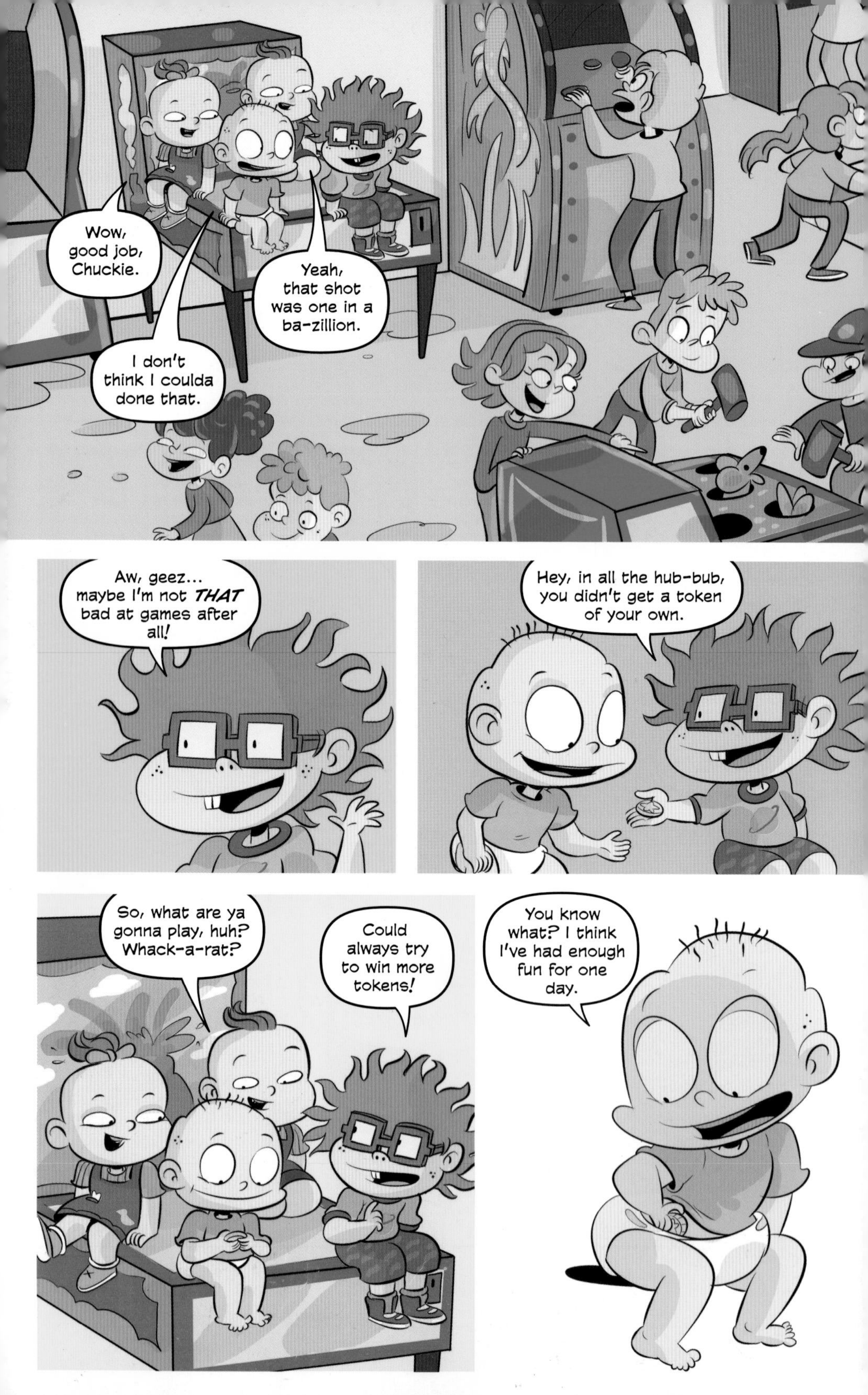
Wow, good job, Chuckie.
I don't think I coulda done that.
Yeah, that shot was one in a ba-zillion.
Aw, geez... maybe I'm not *THAT* bad at games after all!
Hey, in all the hub-bub, you didn't get a token of your own.
So, what are ya gonna play, huh? Whack-a-rat?
Could always try to win more tokens!
You know what? I think I've had enough fun for one day.

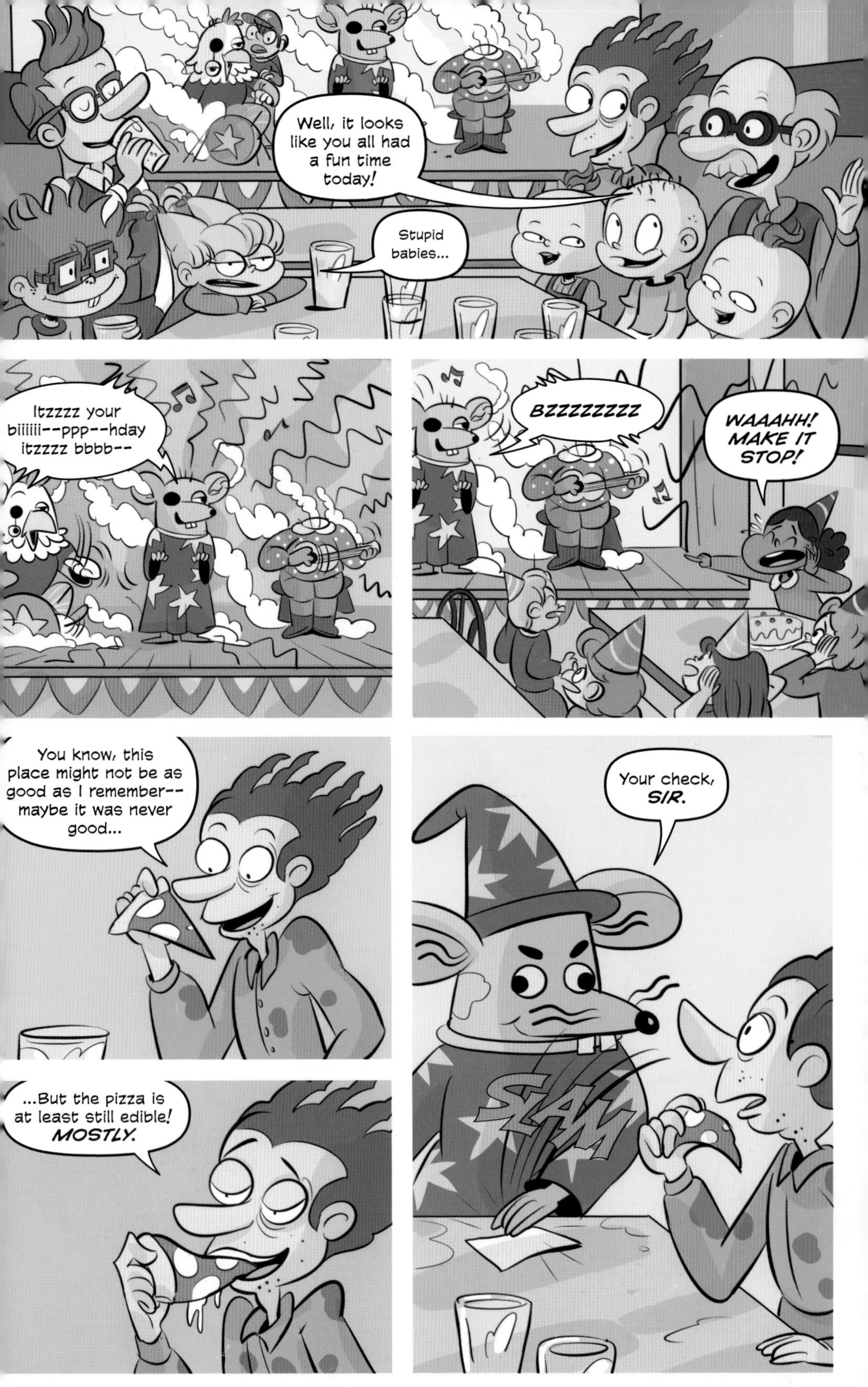
Well, it looks like you all had a fun time today!
Stupid babies...
Itzzzz your biiiiii--ppp--hday itzzzz bbbb--
BZZZZZZZZ
WAAAHH! MAKE IT STOP!
You know, this place might not be as good as I remember--maybe it was never good...
...But the pizza is at least still edible! MOSTLY.
Your check, SIR.
SLAM

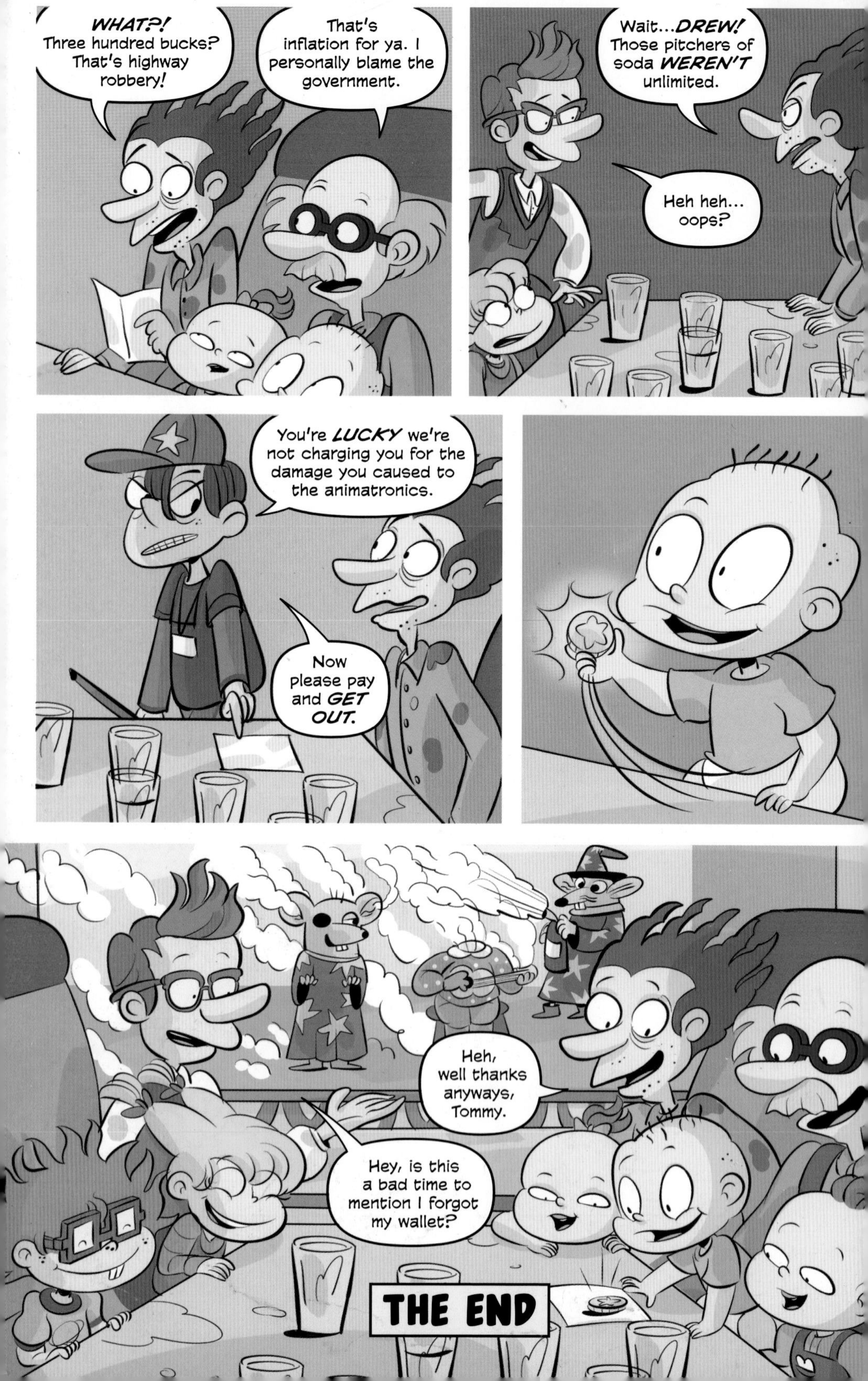
WHAT?! Three hundred bucks? That's highway robbery!
That's inflation for ya. I personally blame the government.
Wait...DREW! Those pitchers of soda WEREN'T unlimited.
Heh heh... oops?
You're LUCKY we're not charging you for the damage you caused to the animatronics.
Now please pay and GET OUT.
Heh, well thanks anyways, Tommy.
Hey, is this a bad time to mention I forgot my wallet?
THE END

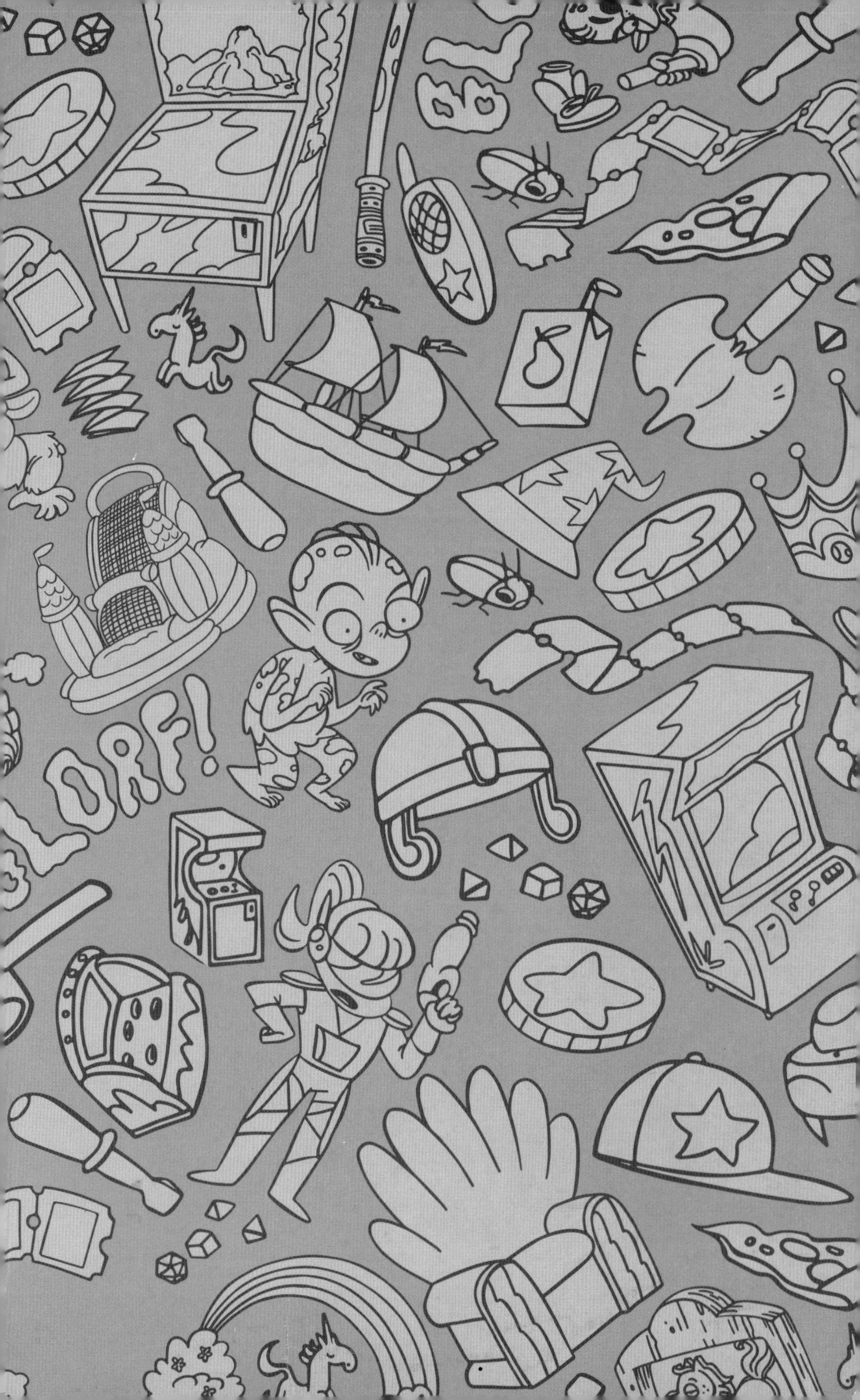
ORF!

DISCOVER
EXPLOSIVE NEW WORLDS

ADVENTURE TIME

sam sykes · selina espiritu · sarah stern
Brave Chef Brianna

KELLY THOMPSON BRIANNE DROUHARD M. VICTORIA ROBADO
MEGA PRINCESS

THE NOT-SO SECRET SOCIETY
DALEY · CRAFTS · CLARK · BRUNI
KEEP OUT
CAUTION

OVER THE GARDEN WALL

STEVEN UNIVERSE
VOLUME ONE

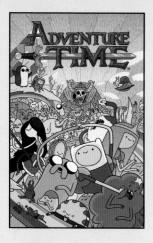

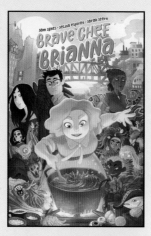

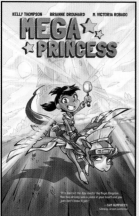

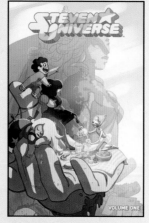

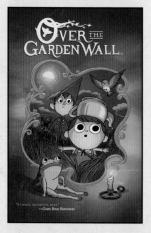

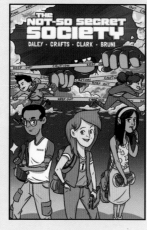

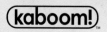

AVAILABLE AT YOUR LOCAL COMICS SHOP AND BOOKSTORE

To find a comics shop in your area, visit www.comicshoplocator.com

WWW.**BOOM-STUDIOS**.COM

Adventure Time
Pendleton Ward and Others
Volume 1
ISBN: 978-1-60886-280-1 | $14.99 US
Volume 2
ISBN: 978-1-60886-323-5 | $14.99 US
Adventure Time: Islands
ISBN: 978-1-60886-972-5 | $9.99 US

The Amazing World of Gumball
Ben Bocquelet and Others
Volume 1
ISBN: 978-1-60886-488-1 | $14.99 US
Volume 2
ISBN: 978-1-60886-793-6 | $14.99 US

Brave Chef Brianna
Sam Sykes, Selina Espiritu
ISBN: 978-1-68415-050-2 | $14.99 US

Mega Princess
Kelly Thompson, Brianne Drouhard
ISBN: 978-1-68415-007-6 | $14.99 US

The Not-So Secret Society
Matthew Daley, Arlene Daley, Wook Jin Clark
ISBN: 978-1-60886-997-8 | $9.99 US

Over the Garden Wall
Patrick McHale, Jim Campbell and Others
Volume 1
ISBN: 978-1-60886-940-4 | $14.99 US
Volume 2
ISBN: 978-1-68415-006-9 | $14.99 US

Steven Universe
Rebecca Sugar and Others
Volume 1
ISBN: 978-1-60886-706-6 | $14.99 US
Volume 2
ISBN: 978-1-60886-796-7 | $14.99 US

Steven Universe & The Crystal Gems
ISBN: 978-1-60886-921-3 | $14.99 US

Steven Universe: Too Cool for School
ISBN: 978-1-60886-771-4 | $14.99 US